THE HOUSE OF SMALL SHADOWS

Also by Adam Nevill

Banquet for the Damned

Apartment 16

The Ritual

Last Days

ADAM NEVILL

THE
HOUSE
OF
SMALL
SHADOWS

ST. MARTIN'S PRESS
NEW YORK

THE HOUSE OF SMALL SHADOWS. Copyright © 2013 by Adam Nevill. All rights reserved. Printed in the United States of America. For information, address St. Martin's Press, 175 Fifth Avenue, New York, N.Y. 10010.

www.stmartins.com

Library of Congress Cataloging-in-Publication Data

Nevill, Adam L. G.
  The house of small shadows / Adam Nevill. — First U.S. Edition.
     p. cm.
  ISBN 978-1-250-04127-2 (hardcover)
  ISBN 978-1-4668-3738-6 (e-book)
  1. Antique dealers—Fiction. I. Title.
  PR6114.E92H68 2014
  823'.92—dc23

                                                      2014003160

St. Martin's Press books may be purchased for educational, business, or promotional use. For information on bulk purchases, please contact Macmillan Corporate and Premium Sales Department at 1-800-221-7945, extension 5442, or write specialmarkets@macmillan.com.

First published in Great Britain by Pan Books, and imprint of Pan Macmillan, a division of Macmillan Publishers Limited

First U.S. Edition: July 2014

10 9 8 7 6 5 4 3 2 1

For James Marriott

1972–2012

The first editor who brought me into print as a novelist, a faithful reader of my first drafts, a fellow devotee of the weird, and a great friend for fifteen years. Who will I rearrange the dark furniture of my mind with now? You are sorely missed, my friend, and always will be.

By a merging and interplay of identities between himself and his beautiful room, he might be preparing a ghost for the future; it had not occurred to him *that there might have been a similar merging and coalescence in the past.*

Oliver Onions
The Beckoning Fair One

ONE

As if by a dream Catherine came to the Red House. She abandoned her car once the lane's dusty surface was choked by the hedgerows, and moved on foot through a tunnel of hawthorn and hazel trees to glimpse the steep pitch of the roof, the ruddy brick chimneys and the finials upon its sharp spine.

Unseasonably warm air for autumn drifted from the surrounding meadows to settle like fragrant gas upon the baked ground beneath her feet. Drowsy and barely aware of the hum emitted from the yellow wildflowers and waist-high summer grasses so hectic in the fields, she felt nostalgic for a time she wasn't even sure was part of her own experience, and imagined she was passing into another age.

When she came across the garden's brick walls of English bond, seized by ivy right along their length to the black gate, a surge of romantic feelings so surprised her, she felt dizzy. Until the house fully revealed itself and demanded all of her attention.

Her first impression was of a building enraged at being disturbed, rearing up at the sight of her between the gate posts. Twin chimney breasts, one per wing, mimicked arms flung upwards to claw the air. Roofs scaled in Welsh slate and spiked with iron crests at their peaks bristled like hackles.

1

All of the lines of the building pointed to the heavens. Two steep gables and the arch of every window beseeched the sky, as though the great house was a small cathedral indignant at its exile in rural Herefordshire. And despite over a century of rustication among uncultivated fields, the colour of its Accrington brick remained an angry red.

But on closer inspection, had the many windows been an assortment of eyes, from the tall rectangular portals of the first three storeys to the narrower dormer windows of the attic, the house's face now issued the impression of looking past her.

Unaware of Catherine, the many eyes beheld something else that only they could see, above and behind her. Around the windows, where the masonry was styled with polychromatic stone lintels, an expression of attentiveness to something in the distance had been created. A thing even more awe-inspiring than the building itself. Something the eyes of the house had gazed upon for a long time and feared too. So maybe what she perceived as wrathful silence in the countenance of the Red House was actually terror.

This was no indigenous building either. Few local materials had been used in its construction. The house had been built by someone very rich, able to import outside materials and a professional architect to create a vision in stone, probably modelled on a place they had once admired on the continent, perhaps in Flemish Belgium. Almost certainly the building was part of the Gothic revival in Queen Victoria's long reign.

Judging by the distance of the Red House to the local village, Magbar Wood, two miles away and separated by hills and a rare spree of meadowland, she guessed the estate once belonged to a major landowner advantaged by the later enclosure acts. A man bent on isolation.

She had driven through Magbar Wood to reach the Red House, and now wondered if the squat terraced houses of the village were once occupied by the tenants of whoever built this unusual house. But the fact that the village had not expanded to the borders of the Red House's grounds, and the surrounding fields remained untended, was unusual. On her travels to valuations and auctions at country residences, she hardly ever saw genuine meadows any more. Magbar Wood boasted at least two square miles of wild land circling itself and the house like a vast moat.

What was more difficult to accept was that she was not already aware of the building. She felt like an experienced walker stumbling across a new mountain in the Lake District. The house was such a unique spectacle there should have been signage to guide sightseers' visits to the house, or at least proper public access.

Catherine considered the surface beneath her feet. Not even a road, just a lane of clay and broken stone. It seemed the Red House and the Mason family had not wanted to be found.

The grounds had also known better days. Beneath the Red House's facade the front garden had once been landscaped, but was now given over to nettles, rye grasses and the spiky flowers of the meadow, thickets trapped half in the shadow of the house and the garden walls.

She hurried to the porch, when a group of plump black flies formed a persistent orbit around her, and tried to settle upon her exposed hands and wrists. But soon stopped and sucked in her breath. When no more than halfway down what was left of the front path, a face appeared at one of the cross windows of the first storey, pressed against the glass in the bottom corner, left of the vertical mullion. A small hand either waved at her or prepared to tap the glass. Either that or the figure was holding the horizontal transom to pull itself higher.

She considered returning the wave but the figure was gone before she managed to move her arm.

Catherine wasn't aware there were any children living here. According to her instructions there was only Edith Mason, M. H. Mason's sole surviving heir, and the house-keeper who would receive Catherine. But the little face, and briefly waving hand, must have belonged to a pale child in some kind of hat.

She couldn't say whether it had been a girl or a boy, but what she had seen of the face in her peripheral vision had been wide with a grin of excitement, as if the child had been pleased to see her wading through the weeds of the front garden.

Half expecting to hear the thud of little feet descending the stairs inside the house, as the child raced to the front door to greet her, Catherine looked harder at the empty window and then at the front doors. But nothing stirred again behind the dark glass and no one came down to meet her.

She continued to the porch, one that should have stood before a church, not a domestic house, until the sombre roof of aged oak arched over her like a large hood.

One of the great front doors crafted from six panels, four hardwood and the top two filled with stained glass, was open, as if daring her to come inside without invitation. And through the gap she saw an unlit reception, a place made of burgundy walls and shadow, like a gullet, that seemed to reach into for ever.

Catherine looked back at the wild lawns and imagined the hawkbit and spotted orchids all turning their little bobbing heads in panic to stare at her, to send out small cries of warning. She pushed her sunglasses up and into her hair and briefly thought of returning to her car.

'That lane you have walked was here long before this house was built.' The brittle voice came from deep inside the building. A woman's voice that softened, as if to speak to itself, and Catherine thought she heard, 'No one knew what would come down it.'

TWO

ONE WEEK EARLIER

All of the small faces were turned to the door of the room. A myriad glass eyes watched her enter.

'Jesus Christ.'

The number of dolls and even their intentional arrangement startled Catherine less than the sense of anticipation she felt in their presence. She briefly imagined they had been waiting in the darkness for her like guests at a surprise party for a child, a century before.

Even if she were the only living thing in the room, she remained as still as the dolls and returned their glassy stares. If anything moved, she would let go of the shriek that had built like a sneeze.

But after a moment of immobility she realized she was staring at the most valuable hoard of antique toys she had seen in her years as a valuer, in her time as a producer of television shows about antiques, and even as trainee curator at a children's museum.

'Hello? Hello, Mr Dore. It's Catherine. Catherine Howard.'

No one answered. She wanted someone to. Having had to let herself into the room was awkward enough.

'Sir? Hello, it's Catherine from Osberne, the auctioneers.' She stepped further inside. 'Hello?' she repeated quietly enough to have given up on anyone being present.

The bathroom door was open, the cramped yellowy space beyond it unoccupied. Unused clothes hangers chimed inside an empty wardrobe. Walnut, but badly scratched. Some yellowing stationery and a poor male attempt at hospitality refreshments crowded one side of the little desk.

The living area of the room appeared unused by anyone besides the dolls. Many of which were arranged on the undisturbed quilt, a handmade eiderdown on a brass-framed bedstead as old as the building. Upon the wall at the head of the bed was a framed woodcut of a small square church set within neat grounds.

The only other item that appeared to belong to the legal guardian of the collection was a trunk. Between the bed and the window a large leather chest had been placed. Upon the lid of the trunk sat another row of dolls. Their little legs hung over the edge of the aged and watermarked leather. A backdrop of fussy, not entirely white, net curtain before the solitary window smothered the afternoon's grey light and formed a fitting background to the little figures, as if they were trapped inside an old photograph.

Even the upholstered chair that partnered the desk was occupied by a doll. And that figure was the most magnificent of them all.

Catherine didn't close the door in case Mr Dore returned, the Mason family's legal representative, and the solicitor instructed to discuss an auction of their 'antique assets' with her. The letter from Edith Mason mentioned nothing else.

She guessed Mr Dore might have popped out and been

delayed getting back to the appointment, though she hadn't seen a pub in Green Willow, nor had she spotted any building in the village offering the prospect of communal activity, let alone food. Even finding Green Willow had been a struggle. Beside the Flintshire Guest House, the village was little more than a line of stone buildings, a closed post office and a weed-filled bus stop. No cars were parked outside any of the cottages.

Catherine checked her watch again. The thin old man downstairs, in the tiny alcove serving as a reception, had definitely said, 'Go right up.' When he handed her keys, he'd not even removed his eyes from whatever he'd been reading behind the counter.

The proprietor issued the impression he was accustomed to, if not worn down by, hordes of visitors to what was a small establishment, barely on the English side of the border between Monmouthshire and Herefordshire. Accustomed to elderly locals being curious about her visits to remote places, Catherine had paused before the tiny counter to say, 'Mr Dore is up there?' The man in reception did not answer, but snuffled with irritation and twitched his threadbare head over his book.

'I'll just go right up then.'

Meeting a prospective client in a hotel room was also a first but, in her brief though rapidly growing experience as the valuer for Leonard Osberne, she'd found that eccentrics and descendants of eccentrics from Shropshire to Herefordshire, the Welsh border, Worcestershire and Gloucestershire, who used the firm to auction the contents of homes and attics long sealed from the modern world, were becoming less unusual. Leonard had a broad range of oddballs on his books. She was beginning to think he didn't have anything else.

The weird seemed attracted to her boss. Or aware of him through some word-of-mouth legacy she had yet to fathom, because Leonard never once advertised their services during her twelve months with the firm. Their office was no more than two rooms on the ground floor of a building in Little Malvern. A place of work that indicated its presence with a solitary brass plate at street level. Office space her boss had occupied since the sixties. Into which she'd introduced a computer and the internet. Another reason why Catherine was never sure how Leonard came by so much trade. The Mason family and their solicitor, Mr Dore, seemed keen on maintaining the enigma.

Sat on the chair before the desk, Catherine carefully held the doll she'd dispossessed of a seat. From its straw hat drifted the feminine scent of a floral perfume or pomander, a rose, jasmine and lavender concoction. From her first cursory examination she believed the doll was an original from the Pierotti family of wax modellers, and in near perfect condition despite being made around 1870. The head and limbs miraculously retained their peach flesh tint. Curled Titian hair and the brows above the sad eyes were of mohair. Inside what she knew was an actual infant's dress, she assiduously checked for other signs of authenticity. The torso was calico stuffed with animal hair, the shoulder plate was sewn to the torso, the hips were seamed. It was original.

Catherine waited another five minutes for Mr Dore to appear. There was no phone to connect her with reception, but she wondered if she should go back down the narrow flight of stairs and enquire about the whereabouts of the solicitor. A legal professional who appeared to have left over three hundred thousand pounds' worth of antique European dolls in an unsecure room, with a stranger.

Catherine placed the doll back upon the chair. There were two collectors and one museum that she knew of who would immediately produce a chequebook after seeing the photograph she had taken of the Pierotti doll.

Her legs felt like they were actually shaking with excitement. Only confusion was spoiling the find.

The prospective client, a woman called Edith Mason, had requested the viewing. Catherine had never heard of her, though apparently Leonard had dealt with her in the past. But Catherine *had* heard about Edith Mason's uncle, M. H. Mason. A man considered to be England's greatest taxidermist. Leonard claimed Mason was also a masterly puppeteer, though Catherine was only aware of his preserved animals in the antique trade. She'd never seen any examples of his legendary work with her own eyes, but had come across photographs of the little of his craft that survived the purges of the sixties, the same decade in which his long life was ended by his own hand. She didn't know much more.

At this viewing, she'd been expecting a few preserved field mice and maybe a stoat mounted in M. H. Mason's signature dioramas, certainly not a Pierotti doll in immaculate condition within the crowd arrayed before her, of what appeared to be equally unspoiled antique dolls. She assumed they must be the property of the niece and heir, who would be close to a hundred years old by now.

On the desk she inspected four Bru dolls with their trademark big glass eyes and babyish faces. The painted bisque heads displayed no scratches, the paperweight glass eyes were in working order and the mohair wigs were perfectly groomed. The pieces had the tiny telltale nipples and gusseted joints that allowed the pudgy stuffed legs to move. All were dressed in period costumes, the bodies beneath made of kid. So definitely bébé Bru. The lower arms and hands were also exquisitely contoured without scuffs or chipped knuckles. Fifty grand without change for the set.

'No way. No bloody way.' On the bed she gently inspected an elegant Gesland 'Manuelita', and five French Jumeau dolls from the 1870s' fashion range. The German porcelain of their elaborately styled heads was in pristine condition. And lined upon the trunk were a group of Gaultier girls with swivel heads, silk gowns, leather boots that actually buttoned up, and luminous glass eyes made by German masters long gone, along with their craft.

To calm herself Catherine gulped at her bottle of water. Leonard was just going to pass out when she showed him the pictures of what had fallen into their laps. And according to Edith Mason's letter, these were 'samples' from 'a larger collection'.

Her camera flash exploded white light into the room as if the miserable guest house had been struck by lightning. Unaware of the time, Catherine photographed each item from a variety of angles.

Mr Dore remained a no-show.

When she finished the viewing she packed away her notes and camera, turned out the lights, closed and locked the door to the room. Downstairs her dinging of the bell failed to summon the old receptionist, who possibly doubled as the owner. She left the keys on the counter of the reception alcove. Unlatched the door and let herself out. As she pulled the door shut she noticed the CLOSED sign faced the street. Forgetting she was upstairs, the unsociable proprietor must have locked up.

Catherine wondered if Edith Mason had insurance to cover what she now estimated to be half a million pounds' worth of antique dolls left unsupervised in a bedroom of a dingy guest house with no online listing.

THREE

Before she headed back to Little Malvern, to tell Leonard about her extraordinary find, Catherine detoured to a place she was once very familiar with, Ellyll Fields, or 'The Hell'. A village between Green Willow and Hereford, where she'd endured the first six years of her life. A place she'd never returned to and had tried to forget. Because the scene of the abduction and probable murder of a child she had known well was a part of the world she'd not felt inclined to revisit in the following thirty-two years of her life. The thought alone of returning had always been enough to make her feel sick. When visiting clients in Herefordshire, she'd even become adept at not seeing that part of the page in her road atlas.

This afternoon would mark a return to a time in her life she'd never shared with anyone besides three therapists and her parents. That morning, for an unpleasant moment, merely driving close to 'The Hell' to get to Green Willow had felt like a trap. And a fate predestined. One she had hitherto suppressed. But as advised by her most recent counselling, returning to the scene would reveal the place to be innocuous and bereft of the poignancy of her lingering childhood dread.

She had been prepared by a cognitive behavioural specialist

to identify and repel outbreaks of paranoia. Which she duly did, because coincidence was rarely conspiracy. She knew her feelings about her birthplace were irrational. And these days, she had to keep in mind, the distant part of her memory that 'The Hell' occupied only really intruded upon her thoughts when she was confronted by compatibly tragic news stories about missing children or bullying.

Despite her own reassurances, and those of others, for the first time since she began working for Leonard Osberne, she wished her boss was able-bodied. Were he not confined to a wheelchair Leonard could have attended to the Mason account in person and she could have maintained her distance from 'The Hell'.

She'd never seen Leonard so excited about the prospect of a new account either. 'This could be big, my girl. If Edith has any of her uncle's work still hanging around out there, we'll probably make the papers. And I'm not talking about the locals. Didn't I promise I'd make you a star! You wouldn't get this kind of work in London.'

Running away was rarely graceful, or even satisfactory, and Catherine's departure from London still harnessed the power to warm her with shame, and occasionally freeze her with panic. Reliving the memory of a particular *incident* that ruined her professionally in the capital still stretched her mental resources beyond a healthy tension. Only once she'd reached her parents' house in Worcester, eighteen months before, did she feel she'd passed beyond the range of her enemies in London, along with the unfortunate reputation she'd fled. But her afternoon in Green Willow and her current journey to Ellyll Fields forced her to acknowledge that by leaving London and coming home, she'd moved back within range of the unhappiest period of her life: the beginning. As if she had been driven back by one of the unconscious compulsions her therapists had been so keen to reveal as a mainstay in her life.

Catherine tried to stayed focussed on the road, but wondered again if her childhood unhappiness had been the reason she'd gone to a university in Scotland, and then to another three distant cities to work after graduation. That she'd spent her entire adult life running from 'The Hell'.

But here you are, girl.

She picked up the A road that would lead her into Ellyll Fields, and her feelings immediately smouldered beneath a messy collage of actual recollections and her memories of photographs from family albums. And in the anxious mix came a force of apprehension that made her breathless.

But she could not deny she was strangely excited to be going back *there* too. Excitement that felt reckless. An unstable desire to revisit a strangeness in her childhood that she considered the only relief in a thoroughly miserable introduction to life.

FOUR

Catherine stood at the edge of a petrol-station forecourt that had not been in her childhood. The only thing she recognized was the humpback bridge over a stream of shallow brown water, referred to as a river when she was a child. Though even the bridge had been lowered and widened to allow freight lorries to shudder through Ellyll Fields in gusts of dusty wind.

The little paper shop where her nan had bought her ten-pence mixtures of sweets in a white paper bag was no more. Gone along with the little plastic boy out front, who'd held a collection box and had a spaniel at his feet. Beside the Wall's ice-cream sign made of tin, covered in faded pictures of ice lollies that once made her mouth water, the plastic boy had stood sentinel in all weathers. She'd often been allowed to put a half-penny coin inside his box.

Catherine wondered what happened to all of the crippled boys and girls with their spaniels, who once stood outside sweet shops. Where the paper shop had been was now a decelerating lane into the petrol station.

There had been a chemist's and a clothes shop beside the newsagent's. Yellow cellophane behind their windows used to remind her of Quality Street chocolates that came out at Christmas. In the chemist's she'd received her first pair of milk-bottle glasses in black NHS frames. Three decades would pass before that particular style of spectacle frame was considered cool. Fashion had not been on her side when she actually had to wear them.

And in the clothes shop she had been bought her first pair of school shoes. Even recalling these shoes made her breath catch. Nor for the first time was she astonished at what remained in her memory.

Few had worn that type of sandal. Even fewer had liked them. They had been brown and made by Clarks. Something else that had since become popular. The certainty of the adults surrounding her in the shop, that the sandals were a satisfactory purchase, nearly gave her the same confidence at the point of sale. Once home with the box and the horrible sandals in their bed of tissue paper, thoughts of the coming school term and what awaited her had created an empty feeling in her stomach, a cold tingling space in which no food would settle.

Her instincts about the sandals had been correct and she came to hate them. She'd cut them with scissors, but ended up going to school in damaged shoes. She'd also worn the sandals at weekends, so news of school shoes being worn in public on a Saturday had whipped round the playground. Everyone thought she did things like that because she was adopted.

Dopted! Dopted! Dopted!

In this dreary place of concrete and tarmac, built over her childhood, a burst of the chant returned to her mind. Followed by another inner refrain of *Pauper! Riffy Pauper! Pauper! Riffy Pauper!* Which of the chants had scalded her with shame and humiliation the most, she couldn't decide. But their echoes still hurt.

In a moment of sympathy, and recognition that her burden might be greater than her own, even little Alice Galloway once asked her, *What's it like to have no real mum and dad? I'd hate it.* And Alice had worn a large brown boot on one foot to correct her strange lurching walk. The boot, and an eye socket packed with gauze, had excused Alice from violence.

During a family holiday in Ilfracombe, Catherine remembered wishing on coins thrown into a fountain, and also after the candles had been blown out on an iced birthday cake, that she could be disabled like Alice. Her adopted mother had actually cried when she told her, in all sincerity, about her birthday wish. Her poor dad had even shut himself in the garage for a day. So Catherine never said anything like that again. The worst Alice ever dealt with was white dog shit packaged in tin foil and a Milky Bar wrapper, and given to her as chocolate by a group of girls from the next grove.

'Jesus.' Catherine shook her head at the side of the dismal road. Its expansion had not come close to burying the rubble of her childhood. 'Jesus Christ.' Who took bullying seriously back then? Maybe her nan, who persuaded her adopted parents to move away from Ellyll Fields for Catherine's sake after Alice Galloway went missing. A relocation to Worcester that also took Catherine away from her nan. A move that broke both their hearts.

'Oh, Nan.' At the side of the traffic-blasted road, Catherine's eyes stung with tears. She sniffed, looked about to see if anyone in the garage shop was looking at her. Then returned to her car on the petrol-station forecourt.

Behind the Shell garage the red bricks of a newish housing

estate stretched away across what she'd once known as the 'Dell'. Scrub really, full of litter and blackberry vines where adults sent rather than walked their dogs. The Dell had been full of dog mess, but local children had still eagerly raced through the narrow tracks on their bikes and sat in the two abandoned vinyl car seats that had been thrown over the fence.

Using the bridge as a landmark she drove through where she remembered the Dell to be, and the small dairy farm that bordered it. Since she'd been away, the farm had also been developed into new housing, and she was soon driving across what she remembered as an eternity of long wet grass only the most foolhardy kids ventured into because of the enormous cows and apocryphal tales of children being speared on bull horns. Once, the field had even been made available for the local populace during the Silver Jubilee. She'd seen photographs of herself as a baby in the field, her pushchair festooned with Union Jack flags.

The new housing estate that covered the Dell and the adjoining field had been created with identical three-bedroom houses arranged in cul-de-sacs. There were no children playing outside of them now. Every house confronted every other house with too many windows. When Catherine pulled over and stood on the empty pavement, the windows on both sides of the road made her feel exposed and small. Curiously, the road surfaces still looked new.

At the western edge of the housing estate she parked in the lay-by of a dual carriageway. The rows of concrete buildings where her nan had lived, set on perpetually windswept grass, all stained with rust about their outflow pipes and speckled with black clouds of soot near the guttering, had been erased from the earth. There was now a Tesco and another petrol station in their place, a DIY centre, a large traffic island, and three new roads leading to places people would rather be.

Her nan's brownish living room with the painting of a green-faced Spanish girl over the gas fire, that looked like the front of an old car, and her ashtray on a metal stand, and the dark velour sofa, and the door with dimpled glass panes, and the smell of Silk Cut and sausage rolls, no longer existed.

Catherine's throat closed on a lump the size of a plum she could not swallow. She decided not to buy petrol at this garage either. She needed fuel to get home to Worcester, but would fill up somewhere else between here and there.

Parked at the northern edge of the housing estate, Catherine discovered the old river had been funnelled into a concrete aqueduct, close to one side of the road. On what was once a riverbank stood a row of identical wooden fences at the rear of private gardens. With the exception of the humpback bridge by the Shell garage, the topography of her early child-hood was non-existent.

She guessed her old den had once been on the other side of these garden fences. Until her sixth year, the den she and Alice Galloway shared, at the furthest edge of the dairy farm's field, had been one of the few enchanting places in her life. Until Alice went missing and Catherine's family moved away, the den was the only sanctuary outdoors that she and Alice ever found in Ellyll Fields. Being so close to its foundations returned tears to her eyes.

She and Alice had discovered a way to circumnavigate the

field of cattle to get to the thin river that once trickled between the shadowy banks, carpeted in dead leaves and sheltered by tree branches that hung over the water. A sanctuary in days when children roamed freely and spent most of their time outdoors.

No one ever found out where poor Alice had been taken in the summer of 1981, but Catherine once believed her friend had found a new sanctuary in some other place. Alice had even suggested the potential of such to her, though only after she'd been gone three months.

How furious they all were at the very idea that she'd seen Alice again. The memory of Alice's mother going hysterical in her parents' kitchen, pulling her own hair out, which made her look like Cat Weasel with a red face, still issued the occasional pang of shame. Something Catherine would never forget, nor forgive herself for being the cause of.

She no longer believed she'd seen Alice after she disappeared either, and hadn't for decades. As a child she had done, and also believed that Alice had come back for her that day. And for most of her childhood Catherine even wished she'd taken the opportunity to go away with her friend too, to follow her to some place better than this ever was.

On the opposite side of the river to their den, a wire fence once protected the *special school*'s grounds. The Magnis Burrow School of Special Education had been derelict when Catherine lived in Ellyll Fields thirty years ago, so it was no surprise to find the school had been demolished, along with everything else.

Landscaped mounds of long grass, dotted with buttercups and dandelions, had once formed an incline topped with a row of red-brick buildings, their windows covered in plywood boards. Now, even the small hillocks had been levelled to make way for the aqueduct and another dual carriageway.

Whenever she'd asked about the empty school next to the farmer's field, she was told all kinds of things by her parents and her nan, who never seemed comfortable when they answered.

'Used to be a home for handicapped children. Mongol children. You know them children that get old, but keep children's faces.'

'Thalidomide children that don't live very long.'

'Children in wheelchairs or invalids with their legs in callipers.'

Like the plastic boy outside the sweetshop who collected her coins? Like Alice? she'd asked. *Like me?* she'd meant.

'Their mothers had them too late.'

'They've gone a bit funny in the head.'

'Some of them went missing, so don't go anywhere near that place. It ain't safe.'

The words of the adults made her sensibilities cringe now. But along with Alice's unexpected return to the den, three months after her disappearance, Catherine had once believed that some of the special children had also been left behind.

Until her early teens, when therapists and doctors persuaded her to accept the idea that her hallucinations were just another example of an unhappy, if not 'disturbed' childhood, she'd been convinced the children she'd seen in those abandoned school buildings were real, while also seeming a bit unreal, like so much of her childhood had been.

Years later she accepted the children were hallucinations,

inserted into her world as imaginary friends or guardians. And in hindsight, for the derided and lonely, no one knew better than Catherine how important an imagination was when you were small. If the only real friend you ever had went missing, you just made up the rest.

She must have been six when she tried to tell her nan and parents about the special schoolchildren who had been left behind.

'It's them tearaways from the Fylde Grove you've seen,' her dad had said. 'They've already smashed the windows. You shouldn't be going over there. Keep away from it.'

The children from the Fylde Grove never went anywhere on foot. They rode around on bicycles they threw down with a clatter as they dismounted, and had loud voices and untucked shirts and florid faces and hard eyes. And you could only reach the special school by creeping around the perimeter of the field, or by going up a long drive to the gates covered in barbed wire, which were never open. The main entrance of the derelict school was also on the main road, where no child was permitted to go by bicycle.

Catherine never once saw children from the Fylde Grove anywhere near the special school, nor anyone else for that matter. The special school and its children had always belonged to her and Alice. And the children she had seen in those derelict buildings were very different to the 'tearaways' from Fylde Grove. Where the children inside the derelict special school came from had been one of the great mysteries of her childhood, but they were among the few children she could remember being kind to her and Alice.

Sat in her car, a recollection of *that* section of the school's fence, fixed between concrete posts, returned to her mind so vividly that she could practically feel the wire again, clutched between her fingers, as she watched Alice hobble up the grass bank to the old buildings, during the afternoon of the day she went missing.

Catherine changed position in her seat and opened a window to try and ease away the discomfort that was nine parts psychological and one part heartbreak, an old crack that would never heal.

Only when she was alone in her den on the riverbank did she ever imagine she'd seen the children, on the opposite side of the wire fence she'd peered through, while she sat on the slippery tree stump with the three old paint tins around her like drums, a scatter of dried flowers upon the leaves she had collected to make a carpet, and the plastic tea set that had gone green from being left outside for too long. And only when she was so heavy with anguish that her misery had felt like the mumps, had they appeared. Children in strange clothes allowed to play outside when it was going dark.

She'd usually felt like that on a Sunday afternoon, when the sky was grey and the air drizzly and even her bones were damp. Right before she walked home for a tea of beans on toast that she could barely swallow at the prospect of school the next day.

After the police interviews, she never spoke about the children again outside of a therapist's house.

But the longer she looked out through her windscreen at the dual carriageway, and the garden fences along the border of the estate, and the concrete ditch that diverted her little river, and considered all of her memories and the way they'd haunted her, the more foolish and insignificant they all seemed to be now. She wondered if coming here had finally allowed her to let go of all that. And in a curious way being here again after all of these years did feel necessary.

Her thoughts drifted to the evening ahead, and to her boyfriend, Mike, and she held precious an image of his smile. Even though he'd not been his usual self for a few weeks, she believed he genuinely looked forward to being with her. And she thought of dear old Leonard behind his vast desk and how he had come to rely upon her and think of her as a favourite niece. A month ago he'd even become tearful over a lunch that involved a lot of wine, and had explained to her how important she was to his business, and that he wanted her to 'keep it' once he'd 'been wheeled off to that great auction in the sky'.

Catherine thought of her own flat in Worcester with its whites and creams and quiet interior. A place she always felt safe. There was no more London to endure now. She even had a great haircut, which could never be underestimated. She was happy. Finally. This is what happiness felt like and this was her life now. Career, boyfriend, her own home, her health. As good as it gets. What happened all of those years ago was over. Let go of it. The past had even been physically removed and its ground covered with tarmac, bricks and concrete. It was gone and it wasn't coming back.

Catherine dabbed at her eyes and checked her make-up in the rear-view mirror. She sniffed and started to smile. Turned the ignition key.

FIVE

'Well, they seem pretty keen to work with you, my girl, because you have been cordially invited to the Masons' home, the Red House, no less. To discuss an evaluation this Friday. It's out Magbar Wood way. Can you make it?'

Leonard's unfolding of the letter, fussing with the desk lamp, and the removal of his *other* glasses from their case was slow and methodical, as was every administrative chore he performed behind his desk. Part of Catherine still operated on deeply ingrained London time and something inside her chest, that she would never be able to extract, turned and tightened as these lengthy preparation rites preceded the most simple of tasks.

But his fastidious rituals were also a source of reassurance. Because at Leonard Osberne's in Little Malvern, life was never frantic or tense with power struggles. No one undermined you and there was no favouritism. She never felt sick before meetings, or stayed awake an entire night transfixed with rage after one. By the time she left London, she'd come to believe that human nature forbade places like Leonard Osberne's from existing. The closest Leonard ever came to a reprimand took the form of requests for her to 'please don't worry' and to 'slow down'. He always tempered his most judgemental remarks about the oddballs they dealt with into something warm.

Leonard was genuinely kind, a quality she would never take for granted. And some days, she and Leonard did little besides eat biscuits, drink tea and chat.

Catherine hung her coat over the back of her chair. 'Of course I can. My gut is telling me this is going to be the equivalent of a lottery win, Len.'

Leonard grinned across his desk. 'This is the type of auction that happens once in a career, Kitten. When you're my age you'll still be boring your assistant by recounting the story.' He smoothed a hand over his fringe and Catherine tried not to stare at the futile gesture at tidying an unruly strand of hair. Because the only thing she would change about her boss was the terrible grey hairpiece. Though even that she was getting used to. It may have taken her six months, but it was the one facet of the meticulously dressed man that didn't fit. The wig was ghastly and left a small space between his thin face and the false hair. Today, he hadn't fitted it properly again, as if he were deliberately trying to provoke derision from anyone who saw him. When she met Leonard for the job interview, a few minutes were required to discipline herself to not stare at his wig while they talked.

'You know it. I haven't seen dolls even close to being in that condition since my days at the Museum of Childhood. Which reminds me, I need to call them. Put some feelers out. I still have a few contacts down in Bethnal Green. They might take a few. And there were so many in that room. The Masons even have a perfect Pierotti!'

'All in good time.' Leonard peered over his glasses. His watery eyes were framed between tortoiseshell spectacle frames and a thicket of ungroomed eyebrow that looked as rigid as steel wire, and didn't quite match his hairpiece. 'We haven't signed a contract yet. I sold some of her uncle's pieces in the seventies, and Edith Mason led me a merry dance, I can tell you. This was before I even laid eyes on what she wanted to sell. One of M. H. Mason's dioramas, some voles in their whites playing cricket. I'd never seen anything like it. The umpires were field mice and the groundsman was a weasel. You should have seen the pavilion. Absolutely marvellous. Though from what I understood from Edith Mason, her uncle never recovered from the Great War. You know he killed himself?'

Catherine nodded. 'I read that somewhere.'

'Cut his own throat with a straight razor.'

'God, no.'

Leonard sighed and shook his head. 'Terrible. Hardly anything of his work has ever come up for auction, so beyond the dolls, I am very intrigued by what else Edith might have hidden in that heap she lives in. Though after Mr Dore's bizarre absence at the viewing, I'd hazard a guess that Edith Mason hasn't changed her tactics one jot since our brief business. I'm staggered she even remembers me.'

'There was a lot of loot in that room.'

'You think she should go bigger?'

'What I saw will get on TV, Leonard. There's enough for an exhibition. And if there are Mason pieces available too, well . . . Potter's estate went for a million.'

'And Potter wasn't fit to tie M. H. Mason's bootlaces. But we can handle it, Kitten. This firm once auctioned the contents of a castle.'

Catherine laughed. Leonard began to smile, too, and chuckle. 'Oh, will you make the tea? Can't you see I'm comfortable sitting down?' Leonard slapped the armrests of his wheelchair.

'Stop it!' She never wanted to laugh when he made jokes about his incapacity, and always felt guilty afterwards if she did.

'Here,' Leonard offered the letter from Edith Mason.

'Nice paper.'

'I know. She really shouldn't be using stationery that valuable. She should let us sell it. That's Crane paper with a high linen rag content. At least eighty years old. I know a collector in Austria who'd have it off us like that.' Leonard snapped two long fingers in the air beside his awful hairpiece. 'But her handwriting's not what it was. She must be close to a letter from Her Majesty. And she'll be madder than a mongoose by now, too. But I know you can handle her. You've got form, girl.'

'I think I love my job.'

Leonard snorted in appreciation, then frowned. 'Curious part of the world, though, Magbar Wood. I've been down there once or twice.' He looked around the walls of the office. 'Before I had this place. Even then it was the land that time forgot. Ever been? Didn't you spend some time down that way?'

'The Hell. Ellyll Fields. Yes. Part of my so-called childhood.' Catherine thought of the service station and empty grey dual carriageways. 'I went there, where I used to live. After the viewing in Green Willow. It's changed a lot. What I remember is gone. All of it. How did you know I was from there?'

'You mentioned it once.'

'Did I?'

'Must have done. And the place has an unfortunate history. Kids went missing from a school there, before you were born I think.'

Not all of them. Catherine busied herself with the tea things so Leonard wouldn't see her face. Margaret Reid, Angela Prescott and Helen Teme: she could even remember their names. Everyone in Ellyll Fields in the seventies was familiar with those small smiling faces, photographed in black and white. To an older generation they were close to icons in Ellyll Fields. Though when Catherine was the same age the girls were when they went missing, they were icons fading on the newsprint that bore their remembered images. When her nan told her the story of the missing girls who were never found, probably as a warning about strangers, she had shown Catherine her own yellowing cuttings that she kept in an old shortbread biscuit tin. Back in the day, only the local nans still kept the horror alive in Ellyll Fields. No one else seemed keen on remembering the abductions. And once Catherine brought her curiosity about the three missing girls to her home, along with the awful black danger she attributed as existing beyond their grainy likenesses, her father lost his temper with her nan for 'filling her head with horrible things like that'. When Alice Galloway went missing, not for the first time did Catherine attribute a great wisdom to her nan.

'I hardly remember all that. We moved away when I was six. I had no idea Green Willow was close to Ellyll Fields. I only found out by looking on a map to find that guest house. I've never been to Magbar Wood either. With the exception of a family holiday to the seaside I doubt I ever went further than a mile from our house. We were skint. My mum and dad never talk about that time in their lives. Pretty sure they've never been back either.'

'Ellyll Fields is between the two places. They're still all aligned on a Roman road, despite town planners meddling with that whole area, in all kinds of ways. And they have been doing so since before you came into this world, my girl. You know, I took you for a border girl the first time I laid eyes on you.'

'Get away.'

'It's the fiery hair and green eyes with those astounding freckles. Even after Monmouth was shoved on the map, the valleys have always been full of beautiful girls with your colouring. Like it or not, you are a classic example of a Dobunni maiden.'

'A what?'

'The tribe that was down there before the Romans. Raised merry hell.'

'You're old enough to know that? I never took you for a day over seventy-five.'

'Steady. Don't make me come over there. I could still reach you by lunchtime, and don't you forget it, my girl.'

Laughing, Catherine came out of the kitchen with the tea things, but felt a couple of inches taller as she moved. Leonard had an eye for a strange beauty in the artefacts they valued and sold, in the same way he noticed things about her. Little things she couldn't possibly identify through the opaque fog that worrying about her weight often enshrouded her within. He made her feel better about herself than she ever could, and more than any boyfriend had done too. It wasn't that Leonard was incorrigible – he wasn't. She always understood that he genuinely admired her and was proud of her. Even protective. After her debacle in London, his gentle mentoring and grace had done far more for her than a course of antidepressants and a new therapist.

'Well, I look forward to meeting the frightful Edith Mason on Friday.'

'If you get past the housekeeper. It says in that letter that there is one of those too.' Leonard grinned. 'Never underestimate a housekeeper, Kitten.'

SIX

Uncomfortable with what she intuited as a scrutiny, by whomever had spoken from inside the Red House, Catherine pushed her voice inside like a shy child. 'Hello?'

She peered around the door without touching it and blinked at the gloom to adjust her sight. Saw a narrow space with tall ceilings. A vestibule with walls papered in claret and patterned with a geometric design that looked medieval. 'Hello?'

All of the interior doors she could see were closed, one on her left, another one on the right-hand side of the passage. Probably cloak- and boot-rooms. The top panels of the closest doors were made of red stained glass, as was the light shade above her head. It truly was a red house.

Framed pictures hung upon the walls near the doors, but she couldn't see beyond the glimmers of protective glass. And she had no time to admire the red and black encaustic tiles of the floor, all original and uncracked, because something squeaked like an old wheel that needed oil, somewhere higher up inside the building.

Squinting, Catherine realized that the end of the narrow reception opened into a wider area. With a clatter of heels against the tiles, she entered the Red House reception and crossed the vestibule to peer into, but not enter, the hall. Her eyes found and followed four walls of an aged hardwood panelling, until her groping sight found a carved newel post at the foot of a steep staircase on the left-hand side of the hall, with balustrades moving upwards like ribs.

Bones inside a crimson body.

'I . . . It's Catherine. Catherine Howard. From Osberne's.' Inside the hall her voice was flat, small, strengthless.

Dim reddish light fell from a distant skylight out of sight, and within the crimson haze Catherine made out a dark silhouette on the next floor. Seated in something lumpen. The top half of a thin body and what resembled a long neck was leaning forward to see her, but remained half concealed behind a row of wooden balusters.

'Had you used the house's bell for its intended purpose, Maude would have greeted you. She is somewhere below.' The voice may have been dried out by age, but the tone was sharp enough to make her feel immediately diffident.

Catherine flinched at the rapid ring of a small handbell from where the voice had originated. 'Shit.' She hoped her own voice hadn't carried through the thick air of the hallway. Air that smelled of something chemical and pierced the odours of floor wax, varnished timber and mustiness that tried to smother it. The concealing odours reminded her of the barely functioning antique shops and provincial museums she visited, but the sharp underlying scent was unfamiliar.

Her confusion and the dregs of drowsiness from the heat and pollen outside intensified in the stifling, almost lightless interior, enough to disorient her. She reached out and touched a wall.

The indistinct figure upstairs regarded her in a silence that grew tense and heavy, like a strange gravity, one that oppressed Catherine so much she thought of herself as a nervous child before a stern teacher in an ancient boarding school.

'Maude will show you to the drawing room.' At the same time the woman spoke, she drew back from the railings. Catherine made out a smudge too white to be a face, atop what must have been some sort of chair. And what did she have on her head? *A hat?*

The figure was wheeled backwards with an alarming suddenness. The squeak of the wheels and creak of the floorboards that the chair rolled across, carried off and away, above Catherine's head and out of sight.

And she was left alone, standing in the mouth of the hallway, not sure whether she was suffering from her usual social bafflement, or whether fear made her reluctant to take another step inside the Red House. Which glowered all around her, sullen but observant, staring directly at her with a barely restrained hostility.

The sharp peal of the handbell had provoked a reaction from deep inside the crimson tunnel that began at the front door, crossed the square wood-panelled hall, and continued to what must have been the back of the large building. Muffled footsteps approached from out of the distant darkness. A shuffle that drew closer, suggesting someone old with restricted mobility was feeling their way towards her.

Despite her existing discomfort, she felt a fresh aversion to greeting whoever was on their way to meet her, from *somewhere below*. This Maude, she presumed.

The natural light available had either followed Catherine through the front door, or fell blood-misty from the skylight above the stairwell. And this hem of vague luminance soon revealed a white shape approaching through the lower passageway. A form seemingly suspended above the ground, with no limbs, jerking itself towards the hall.

Before her confusion could become fear, a portly figure materialized wearing a brilliant-white apron, which in the half-light she'd momentarily taken for a ghost. It was a woman, with a curved bonnet of hair bobbing from side to side atop a squat body that moved with difficulty. As the housekeeper struggled into the hall and was better lit, Catherine's scrutiny of her turned into gaping.

Every trace of the feminine had been worn from the lined skin of the round face confronting her. And Catherine couldn't recall ever seeing a face so grim, the kind of face that appeared behind wire during wars that were photographed in black and white. The woman's hair, as white as a lamb's fleece, looked as if she had cut it herself around the rim of a bowl with a knife and fork. The apron was pressed out by her hips, belly and bosom, all of which were large. Mannish lace-up boots peeked beneath the stiff hem of a gown. At the other end a high collar disappeared under the woman's jowls.

Faded eyes beneath unkempt eyebrows fixed upon Catherine, though the woman did not speak. Her expression was utterly humourless, alive with irritation and what looked like disapproval.

Catherine smiled and cleared her throat. 'I'm Catherine. Catherine Howard.' She walked into the hall and extended her hand.

The curious figure turned and waddled to the foot of the stairs and began to climb without a word or backward glance.

She watched the woman's wheezy ascent. The back of

what she thought was a gown was actually a high-waisted skirt that dropped to a pair of thick ankles. An undecorated blouse, criss-crossed with apron strings, was separated from the skirt by a thick leather belt. Both the skirt and blouse were tailored from an unappealing grey material as coarse as sailcloth, and the cuffs of the puffy sleeves were stained. The clothes resembled those worn by nineteenth-century factory workers, which made Catherine wonder if an eccentricity, long cultivated in rural isolation, because the Red House was as remote as any house could be on the Welsh border, had now become something less charming. She'd seen plenty of decline before, but never like this. Trailing from the mute housekeeper came the acrid scent she noticed in the reception.

Halfway to the first floor the housekeeper paused, turned her pale face to Catherine and watched her in silence, waiting for her to follow. Which Catherine hesitatingly did, climbing into the vaulted wooden interior as though she was inside a strange church tower, its walls ancient and oaken. There were two storeys above her and she could see balusters around their edges. A great skylight of stained glass angrily watched over the stairwell.

'Maude?' she asked. The woman said nothing and continued up, into the Red House.

They arrived at the bottom corner of an L-shaped corridor on the first floor, also poorly lit. All of the interior doors were closed, which kept the light out, and the house upstairs remained silent and rigid with a tension that registered as a pressure against Catherine's thoughts.

Amidst the fragrance of polished wood and the inescapable staleness of old furnishings, a blend of jasmine, rose and lavender endured as a trace of the house's owner, who Catherine must have just seen wheeled along this passage. Perhaps returned to one of these rooms by the child she had seen from outside, looking through the window. Catherine thought of the doll sat in her lap at the Flintshire Guest House. Same perfume.

The first-floor walls were wooden like the hall below, which increased the dimness, and all of the doors she could see were six-panelled, the top two fitted with red stained glass.

Maude moved to a door at the heel of the L-section and listened for a moment before she knocked.

'Enter,' said a distant voice.

With an expression of morose disapproval on her crumpled face, the servant held the door open for Catherine. Around the housekeeper's bulky shape, she caught glimpses of a room better lit than the communal areas. A room intense with distractions about its walls, and one she didn't make it far inside before coming to a shocked standstill.

Catherine thought she'd walked into another world. An enchanted but nightmarish glade of an artificial Victorian forest. One in which scores of small bright eyes watched her from every surface they had clambered upon.

SEVEN

Speechless, Catherine turned about. And saw red squirrels in frock coats paused in the eating of nuts upon the piano. She looked away and a fox grinned at her from the low table it stalked across. A company of rats in khaki uniforms all stood on their hind legs on parade on the mantel.

She turned again and came face to face with a crowd of pretty kittens in colourful dresses, jostling to get a look at her from inside a tall cabinet. Some of them were taking tea. Others curtsied.

Animals cluttered the room, all silent and still with what felt like caution at her intrusion. Or perhaps they were poised in anticipation of their next moves. Not a square foot of any surface was free of them.

Beside a vast ornamental fireplace of marble, Edith Mason sat alone within the confines of a black antique wheelchair and seemed pleased with her guest's reaction. Beside the chair, a long red setter had stretched itself around one wheel. A dog that watched Catherine with a single wet brown eye under a raised brow. In the sunlight that fell through the arched windows the dog's ruby fur shimmered. The dog, at least, must be real.

'Even now my uncle's marvels can still affect me, and I see them every day. But for you, I think the cat will have your tongue a while yet.' The woman smiled and her thin teeth looked yellow within the small mouth. 'Please take a seat. Maude will bring tea,' Edith Mason spoke without acknowledging the presence of the housekeeper, whose removal from the room was announced by the angry thud of the door pulled shut.

But even a perfectly conserved Victorian drawing room filled with preserved animals could not upstage the visage of Edith Mason in the flesh. So much powder clung to the woman's ancient face that the skin papered to the bony features looked bleached, and her tiny eyes were made ghastly by their red rims. The lips about the teeth were non-existent and the nose was a blade, the light seemed to pass through the side as if it were pure cartilage. It was a difficult face to look at and Catherine struggled to do so.

Her scrutiny moved to the elaborate hair, styled about the shrunken head in a cottage-loaf fashion. A mass of silver hairpieces threaded with the woman's own grey wisps. There must have been a kilo of padding inside the arrangement. Catherine had only seen the style in costume dramas, or photos of women in the early 1900s. She was tempted to believe the outfit was for her benefit, some bizarre display of fancy dress prepared and laid on for the valuation. She didn't know how to react, what to say, or do. She just stared.

'I'm ninety-three, my dear. And I have not once been tempted to paint that hideous rouge upon my mouth.' Edith Mason stared hard at Catherine's lips. 'Once upon a time it was considered offensive. The mark of a whore.' *Whore* came across the room with sufficient force to make Catherine blink. The word was delivered with spite, a riposte to her horrified leering at the elderly woman's head.

She should leave. Despite the evident riches a single room promised her bewildered eyes, her most trusted instincts warned that if she were to stay, she would be made to suffer. In her professional experience, the greatest treasures were most often guarded by the slyest and cruellest dragons.

'But what do you girls know? You are slaves to so much. And we girls have never had much say in the way of things.' The old woman smiled, but this time with her eyes too.

Catherine was compelled to return the smile, though her body felt ready to shatter like the porcelains at an end of the mantel that two stoats in convict uniforms were entwined about.

'Please.' Edith Mason wafted one bony hand in the air. So pallid were the fingers before the black silk of the woman's high-necked dress, Catherine's eyes followed the hand's trajectory as if mesmerized. And she was glad to see the hand was, in fact, gloved. 'Take a look. I know you must be dying to mooch among our things. I bet you can't wait to get your hands on them. To put prices on them.'

'There's no hurry.'

'Don't be coy with me. I have no patience with all that. So let's be clear about one thing: we did not invite just anyone here to dismember our estate. Things that no soul in this world has the skill to craft now. Let alone appreciate their true value and meaning. We want someone who will understand what was once created here. We may have dealt with your firm in a satisfactory manner before, but only when we have found a person with the necessary insight and sensitivity will we allow an auction. So consider this an interview.' The word 'auction' seemed to cause the old woman great pain and she grimaced. If Catherine were not mistaken, her eyes also shone with tears before she looked away to the windows.

'Your home . . .' Catherine didn't know what to say, but felt she had to say something. 'Is incredible.'

The woman's expression changed swiftly and Catherine struggled not to recoil in distaste. Edith Mason's smile had broadened to reveal more of her teeth and what gums were left to hold them in place. 'If only you knew how unique. But perhaps you will come to.' The smile turned into a glare. 'If we decide to employ your firm.'

'We're so excited about this opportunity. To be invited here and to—'

'Yes, yes. All right, dear. I was starting to like you. From the moment I saw you in that lane I knew you had humility. That it was genuine. And we like good manners here, Miss Howard. We like silence. We like to be left alone with our endeavours . . . But we don't like . . .' Her train of thought drifted and she stared out across the room again, as if listening to an earpiece. A trickle of soot struck the grate inside the fireplace. They both flinched.

Edith looked to that side of her chair, warily, then returned her terrible stare to Catherine. 'What do you know of my uncle?'

Catherine glanced at the floor to evade a scrutiny she found awful, and saw hand-woven carpets with oriental rugs arranged over them. She tried to organize her thoughts that reared and fell over themselves. The medieval geometric design of burgundy and green in the carpet weave bombarded her mind. Small lifelike eyes watched her from every angle, gleeful at her awkwardness. Only the dog appeared to feel sorry for her.

She doubted she would be given much space here to talk in, and that nothing she said would be of interest to the elderly woman. If she did speak, she assumed what she said would only serve as ammunition, that she would be rebuffed and contradicted. An attitude she'd never become accustomed to, even after a lifetime of practice.

She forced herself to concentrate. 'We know . . .'

'Not we, *you*.'

'I . . . I am, of course, aware of his skill. As a taxidermist.' She thought of the catalogue copy she'd mentally drafted the previous week. 'From what little of his work has ever been shown, perhaps he was the greatest of them all. And my colleague tells me your uncle was also a legendary puppeteer—'

Edith was not to be flattered. '*They* are not for sale. They were like children to him and they are not for strangers.'

'Of course. But just in this room, from what I can see, we'd have enough for an exhibition.'

The old woman glanced about herself. 'These are mine. He made them for me when I was a child. And they will accompany me to the grave, my dear. So you'd do well to keep your hands off them.'

Then why am I here? she wanted to ask.

'They keep me company in my room here. They help me pass the time. And there has been much time spent here. More than you can imagine.' She sounded sad now. 'Don't you, darling?' Edith Mason reached one spidery hand down to touch the dog's head. But the red setter seemed more interested in their guest and continued to stare at Catherine with what looked like sympathy for her predicament. She offered the dog a weak smile in acknowledgement.

Edith issued a sudden unpleasant laugh that rang off the

china and glass. 'Still fooling people, brave Horatio. He was my uncle's favourite hound. His champion rat catcher. But poor Horatio caught his last rat in 1928. My uncle left him to me, to look after. And he's still waiting for his master to return. Day and night. Aren't we all, my brave darling?'

Catherine stared at the dog. It wasn't possible the animal was preserved. The expression and the posture, the glossy lustre of its fur, a wet nose, moist eyes . . . how? She stood up and approached the squirrels who watched her from the piano. Looked at them quickly, but with an expert's eye, and wouldn't have been surprised if one of their noses twitched, or if one of their red-coated bodies leapt up the curtains to hang from the pelmet.

These weren't the tatty and patched horrors of junk shops, nor what sat in the darkness of attics, only to be brought back to light in house clearances. And Mason had crafted at least fifty gifts for his little niece in one drawing room. As a child, Edith must have slept in a room full of dead kittens wearing party dresses made of taffeta, chiffon and delaine. No wonder she was mad.

But what else pounced, sat up, stalked and pranced out there in the many rooms of this vast building, perfectly preserved by a grand master? It was a big house and the last original Mason diorama sold for eighty thousand pounds at Bonhams in 2007. An individual piece, of the quality displayed about her, could fetch up to ten today. Mason had been the best of them all and the market had been starved of new pieces since the 1970s, when there were few takers for taxidermy. She knew only too well that less than five per cent of Victorian taxidermy had survived until the next century, the rest had fallen apart or been destroyed. But not here. Not inside the Red House.

What was she even doing here? If this room was an indication of the treasures within the building, one of the big London firms should have been notified. This was a job for Sotheby's, not small fry like Catherine Howard of Leonard Osberne, Valuer and Auctioneer. She fought to conceal her excitement; revealing it might be a mistake.

The American museums paid a lot for birds too, the ones the Victorians had stuffed into extinction after enclosing their habitats. 'No birds?'

Edith's head trembled in a brief palsy of rage. 'Birds! My uncle was no plumassier. He had no time for feathers! These,' she wafted a thin white hand in the air, 'are trifles. He mostly composed with rats. Animals like us. He had his Damascene moment during the war. At the front. I recall him once telling my mother, his dear sister, that we were all just "vermin under the stars and nothing more".'

'I see.' Catherine gazed around herself again. 'He did so much. I never knew.'

'My uncle only considered commissions when the house required it of him. Some of those pieces you may have seen in your grubby trade. It was all that ever got out. He had no interest in fame, competing, or exhibiting, like the others. When the demand for his work dried up, he sold land so the Red House would survive. We have been prudent, but we need to be maintained, dear.'

'He did all this . . . for its own sake?'

Edith smiled. 'I think you begin to understand a little. He only began his great works when interest in his craft had gone. It was out of vogue, dear, for most of his working life. My uncle was no scientist, and no worshipper of nature. He was an artist. A magician! And now . . . now we get letters coming to the house. People want to know if there are any more animals? Are they valuable, dear?'

Catherine suppressed a smile. 'Could be. To collectors. That is what I'd like to find out.' The door clicked open and Maude shuffled in, burdened with a tray laden with what looked like one grand's worth of original Wemyss ware.

'And you might, Miss Howard. In good time. I've decided I like you enough to show you a little more. You have respect for his work. I can see it in your lovely eyes. But we must take tea first. The cakes are home-made. Will you pour? My hands are not so good.'

'Of course.' Suddenly glad she never fled, Catherine smiled at the dog and thinking nothing of it, she said, 'I must say old Horatio is very well trained. He never even sniffed at the cakes.'

What little warmth existed in Edith's face slipped away, and her bloodless features stiffened into a grimace. 'If you are trying to make a joke, please don't. You are not to make fun of my uncle's things. Not ever. Am I understood?'

EIGHT

'Go *in*, go on, go inside.'

'But . . .'

'*In. In.*' Edith's insistence carried the threat of anger.

'Lights?'

'We keep them in the dark. We don't want them damaged.'

'Then how do you see them?'

'Oh, will you *get* inside, you silly girl!'

Catherine stood inside the doorway and stared into total darkness. Behind her, in the narrow passage where she had been instructed to wheel and position Edith Mason, the footplates of the wheelchair touched her heels, as if the elderly woman had managed to roll her chair forward a few inches by herself to add emphasis to her demand. 'The ceiling light has not been replaced in years. You will have to open the curtains. Would you have me draw the curtains with these hands? Are you afraid, dear. Afraid of the dark?' Edith tittered.

Catherine took a step inside as though the floor was ice, her hands outstretched, her eyes so wide they stung in their sockets. The air was close, humid, thick with the scent of polished wood and the chemical taint. Which was stronger, more pungent the further she moved through the darkness.

'Stay on the left. The left!' Edith warned, though a stern tone did not disguise her mirth, if not glee, at Catherine's discomfort.

The low heels of Catherine's sandals clattered and scraped across the floorboards, the sound rang hollow in what she sensed was a large room. There was nothing soft inside the space to cushion the noise or to protect her.

Catherine looked back at the grotesque but featureless silhouette of Edith Mason, framed by the faint ruddy light of the ground-floor passage. The figure was motionless, propped upright, the outline of the head ungainly and vast upon wizened shoulders.

Groping through oblivion in the unfamiliar room of a sinister house suddenly felt like a test combined with a childish dare and a horrible prank designed by a cruel mind. She was doing this for the contract and she loathed herself for it, her actions were suddenly unacceptable to her. She was allowing herself to be goaded, to be manipulated, to be bullied for some illusory promise of advancement. Was that not part of the reason she left London? She'd not even been here an hour and she was frightened in the dark and Edith Mason was inside her head. She grimaced at the elderly woman's silhouette and despised it.

'Don't pout, dear.'

Catherine flinched. *How could she see?*

'You wanted to see them. That's why you came here. You must work for your supper.'

Part of her also wanted to shriek with laughter at the absurdity of the situation. How was this possible? She had not long been in her car driving through a recognizable world. No one would believe her about this. It was surreal. It was mad. But there was nothing entertaining about the experience, not in the smelly darkness. *And what was that?*

'You . . . lied.' Catherine turned and looked into the nothingness opposite the door she had just crept through. She'd heard it once, to her right on what she guessed was the far side of the room. A shifting of fabric across wood. Against the floor. Or had someone just slid off a chair? *The child.*

'What did you say?' Edith said from the doorway, the outrage in her tone barely contained.

'There is somebody in here. You tricked me. I don't find this funny.'

'You are alone in there.' Now her voice seemed cruelly playful. 'Nothing else is living, though it may appear so.' If this was intended as reassurance it had no effect. If the old woman closed and locked the door, she would be trapped.

Quickly, Catherine decided to go for the window she had been promised. But why had she stayed? What had she been thinking? The face at the window, the dog arranged to startle her, the horrid outfits, Maude's unpleasant silence, and she had been called a whore, there was definitely an inference. She was the victim of an elaborate joke, played on a commoner who had come here to finger the family silver.

She raked her hands through the void, fingers scrabbling for purchase while anger got her to the curtains. Of which there were many layers. Her fingernails scraped down what felt like heavy velvet, but it would not part, so she edged sideways, breathless with anxiety.

'That's it. You're nearly there. I can hear your progress.'

Catherine glanced again at the doorway. And realized Edith's silhouette was no longer looking in her direction, but to the side of the unlit room, opposite the door. From which direction there now issued a scraping. Sharp metal against masonry, but faint. And then a flap of cloth. She would have screamed if her air wasn't sealed inside her petrified lungs.

She turned back to claw at the curtains until her hands found where they parted in the middle. When she tugged the drapes apart there was no light. She was still sealed in darkness. Her fingers found more fabric; it was thinner. She tugged at it.

'Be careful with my curtains!'

Slowing herself with the last shred of her composure, Catherine found her hands and wrists to be tangled in what felt like lace, swathes of it. Beyond that layer of fabric her fingernails scraped at wood. And for a horrible second in which she felt true paralysis, she realized it really was a trap. She had been sent to a false window. The door to the room would now slam shut, a key would turn in the large brass mortise lock that she had admired like a fool. It was as if she was stuck fast inside the dream that began when she left her car. She blinked her sightless eyes and wanted to dig her nails into her wrists until they bled. Opening her mouth wide she swallowed the darkness, then clenched her teeth shut.

'The shutters are retractable,' Edith called from the doorway, her voice now flat and merely imparting instructions. 'There is a latch in the middle. Unlock it. But be careful! Those shutters have protected that window since 1863. Push them back to the sides. Oh, do hurry, you're wasting time, dear.'

Catherine found the little lock and unlatched the wooden shutters. Creaking like an old sailing boat, they moved to the sides with little resistance. And she stood, dazed and empty, with her face seared by a white light that came directly from salvation, from heaven.

She turned to face the harmless old woman in the wheel-chair. Tension softened from her shoulders and her pulse eased. Until she saw what was kept inside the dark room under lock and key.

NINE

Under an overhead light, suspended from a black chain that dropped from a plaster ceiling rose, the great display case was raised from the ground to the height of an average table. It must have been six metres long, four wide and one deep.

About the tableau, the walls were papered with the medieval design she had seen elsewhere on the unpanelled walls of the Red House, in a rich burgundy colour that sucked at the natural light. There was a high wooden skirting board and a long cornice around the room's edges, a simple iron fire-place, and one plain wooden stool at the head of the case, but nothing else. No other furniture or decoration was allowed to impede or distract the viewer's horrified fascination of what M. H. Mason had created and displayed in his home.

Catherine remained speechless long enough for Edith to visibly enjoy her mute gawping. Perhaps that was why Maude never spoke, and why Edith spent her life surrounded by a silent and captive audience of rodents and woodland animals. Other personalities just interfered.

'It often took my uncle years to finish a tableau. This one took ten, and one year of planning before he skinned the first rat.'

Catherine was still unable to respond.

'There are six hundred and twenty-three individual figures

inside the case. The dogs caught them all. Dogs taught not to mutilate their prey. And there haven't been rats at the Red House in decades. Perhaps they still remember.' Edith grinned at her own jest. 'My uncle became so proficient, he could set up a rat in sixteen hours. But he planned the pose of each one to the minutest detail before he made the first incision. The legs of rats are terribly thin and they were the most difficult parts of the animals to position, but he became expert. And they were all individually measured for their uniforms by my mother.'

Catherine wheeled Edith before her along one side of the great wooden case. After a series of darting glances that made her dizzy, she still failed to comprehend the complexity of the diorama.

The viewing pane offered a window into hell. 'I don't understand . . . why has no one seen this?' The wheels of the chair squeaked, the floor groaned, the sound felt as unwelcome as her voice inside the space, as if the room had been asleep.

Edith smiled. 'Oh they did, once. But you are privileged, Miss Howard. You are the first person, outside of this family, to see *Glory* in seventy years. Though many wished to, once they'd heard of its existence from the few that actually did see it. That was before my uncle realized the futility of the piece as a warning. It was once displayed in Worcester before the Second World War, but only briefly. He hoped it might act as a deterrent to another grand slaughter. But he wasn't happy with the reactions to his work. The papers called him unpatriotic and cruel. Someone wrote that he was deranged, dear. Schoolboys loved it for the wrong reasons. So my uncle brought it home. It divides into ten cases. I declined every request to see it once it came into my care, on my uncle's instructions, until people forgot about it. Now, I have little choice. But my uncle understands.'

'He . . .' But Catherine soon lost her train of thought, and also failed to ask Edith what might have caused the disturbance in the room she had just floundered through in the dark. It had been paramount in her mind after she'd opened the blinds. But before *Glory* one could think of nothing else.

'You must understand, my uncle came home from the front a changed man. His experiences in the Great War devastated him. He may have enlisted as a non-combatant, but he went to the front line to be with his men. And to give them what little comfort was available in horrors we cannot imagine. He saw such sights . . . things. He lost his faith. Not just in God. But in men. In society. In humanity. His loss of faith was colossal. You could say it was total. A terrible burden to endure for a chaplain.'

'Chaplain? He was . . . '

'A man of God, yes. The village was once his parish. He became a chaplain in the thirty-eighth Welsh Division. A private project. There were lots of them at the time. But he volunteered in 1915, not long after his two younger brothers. They were beloved to him and he hoped to take care of them.'

Edith sighed, and raised eyebrows neatly drawn upon her alabaster forehead. 'Harold, the youngest, fell at Mametz Wood. In 1916. Not long after they arrived. It was one of the battles of the Somme. Their division was then engaged in the third battle of Ypres and Lewis fell at Pilkem one year after Harold. Poor Lewis was gassed.'

And all of the rats in the mud were Mason's recovery, or a meticulous continuation of the nightmare. Catherine gazed again at what she had, at first, thought were little men, because so lifelike were their postures upon their hind legs, so animate and human were their expressions of terror and pain and despair and shock, and so convincing were their little uniforms and weapons, as was their suffering in the soil, that for a few seconds she was sure she had been looking at a crowd of tiny men mired in one of hell's inner circles.

The black landscape itself was so convincing, wet and churned and colourless, she imagined she could smell it through the glass. The sides of the case were painted with photographic precision to continue the vision of trenches, torn wire, shell blasts, mine craters, thick smoke and splintered trees, as if to infinity in every direction.

It was the most animate she had seen Edith too. The spiky and hostile persona she'd endured unto the threshold of this room appeared to have retreated at this chance to hold forth about her uncle, a man cherished in her long memory. 'After Lewis was killed, my uncle was invalided out with enteric fever and dysentery. He'd been suffering from both for some time. My mother said it wasn't the fever, but heartbreak that brought him home that first time. And he could have sat out the war, but he returned to his company and to action as soon as he was well enough. To continue his duty. My mother told me, when I was old enough to understand, that he was determined to die at the front. So that he could be with his brothers.

'But he was chosen to live, my dear. He came home again in 1918, wounded this time. At the Battle of Cambrai. When his division captured Villers-Outreaux my uncle suffered a terrible head wound from shrapnel. It disfigured him. But may have saved his life.'

'I didn't know.' Catherine swallowed the emotion that had come into her throat. 'It's . . .' she didn't know what to say. 'It's a terrible and sad story.' And it was odd, because in the Red House, it felt like she had just heard recent news. 'I'm so sorry.'

'Should such things be forgotten? My uncle didn't think so. He wouldn't allow himself to. After the war he lived here in seclusion with his sister. My mother, Violet. She brought him back to the world. Because they had work to do. They did everything together. I suppose you will have to itemize them all?'

'Yes.'

'It cannot be dismantled. That is our only stipulation. It must remain intact.'

'Of course. Who would even think of it?' But many would, as well she knew. If there was not a sole buyer at the right price, each of the ten sections, or worse, would need to be sold off piecemeal. The diorama was magnificent, but it was also dreadful, and she struggled to imagine anyone who would want to look at it for long. A museum might be interested, though their best hope would be an art gallery. Because that's what it was, it was art. Edith was right, M. H. Mason had been an artist. And a very great one to have affected her so profoundly. She thought she could have stood in the room for one entire day and still not have seen half the detail inside the case.

'Time for one more. And that will be sufficient for one afternoon.'

'There's another?'

'There are four.'

TEN

You can't sell them, she wanted to shout. *They must be exhibited, in a place where everyone can see them.* Otherwise the auction catalogue would be the only record of M. H. Mason's intact collection, and his work could be scattered throughout the world to never come back together, after over half a century undisturbed inside the Red House.

'I . . . I just can't believe it.' The next room featured a gas attack. And it seemed all of the creator's wrath, grief and anguish at young Lewis's death had been invested into the one hundred rats, dressed in muddied khaki, that rolled and choked and kicked and bled in the communication trench, while all around their position the air sparked with shell bursts and was strewn with fetid vapours.

The landscape replicated the last one, a thing murky and dreary and endless, stirred and roiled by great spraying impacts, still and marshy in dismal pockets, but appearing agitated in others as mud fell in waves from the black heavens. And as the dying rats sank, were engulfed and submerged in the mire, their eyes ran red. Catherine had to look away from the two blind and wretched creatures that clawed at each other and wrenched their matted throats upwards as if to snatch at clean air amongst a copse of devastated, skeletal trees. Their expressions were impossibly, but entirely, human.

'Difficult to believe that it is not a portion of the Western Front brought home in a box. Though in one way it was. Inside my uncle's mind. But my mother made the stage sets. The filth and the dirt of the land are plaster and burlap. It's built over a wire frame and painted to create an illusion.'

'They've been here. All this time.' *In the darkness*, she wanted to add.

'Nothing in this house has changed since my uncle passed. Even his shaving brush, his comb and glasses are still in the very same place and position they were in on his last day.'

Catherine turned her horrified face to Edith, who nodded with satisfaction. 'Even his razor still lies where it fell.'

'But you—'

'Followed his instructions? To the letter, my dear. It surprises you. I doubt you've encountered the same sense of duty and loyalty out there.' Edith raised one hand as if to dismiss the remainder of the entire world. 'But in the Red House such qualities are cherished. I am his curator, dear. It was the last task he set me. Attending to his genius for all of my life has been a great privilege. But I doubt you could understand. Though I can't blame you for that.

'And the tableaux were to remain in the everyday rooms of the ground floor upon his instructions. Besides the service rooms, each of the rooms down here contains his earliest works. There is so much to see. To itemize. I hope you have the time, Miss Howard.'

'Earliest works?'

'He moved on to other things, dear. He came to look upon these as trifles. I believe only my mother's powers of persuasion prevented him from destroying them all when England declared war on Germany in 1939.'

Catherine stared up at the ceiling and again imagined the volumes of fragrant, preserved air, the near priceless treasures within each and every room. 'Unchanged,' she murmured. 'The whole house has not changed.'

'Why would we change it? And anyway it is forbidden.'

'Forbidden?'

Edith never answered her. 'Please take me back to the lift. I need to rest. Maude will show you out.'

'Of course. Can I . . . Please, can I come back?'

'I don't know.' Then as a teasing afterthought she said, 'Maybe someone will contact you.'

'Right. I'll wait to hear. And thank you. I mean, for showing me.' She could hardly organize her thoughts. They came in flashes, then derailed or vanished and she was again looking down at a rat's face in the mud, its jaws pulled apart in a scream. But if Edith was telling the truth, the entire building was a perfectly preserved Gothic Revival house from the middle of Queen Victoria's reign with all fittings intact. Perhaps the best example of such in all of England. And one filled with immaculate antiques and a million pounds' worth of Mason's own work.

She couldn't imagine *Glory* selling for less than two hundred thousand pounds at auction. *Gas Attack* would fetch half of that. And there were another two Great War dioramas locked away on the ground floor of the house. There were the dolls too. His notorious puppets weren't for sale, but she should at least see them and persuade Edith to exhibit if her uncle's skill in their creation was anything like his preservation of rats.

Again, she wondered why she was here, as if there had been a mistake and she had someone else's identity and she should confess her status as imposter before it was all too late. She was giddy and weightless from excitement or shock, but wasn't sure which. Her clothes clung thin and cheap, everything about herself was inappropriate here. She was out of her depth. She wasn't a quick girl, she didn't pounce on opportunities. She bit her lip. Stopped herself.

'Ms Mason?' she suddenly thought to ask, as she pushed the wheelchair through the dark passage to the reddish hue of the distant hall. 'Who is the child?'

Edith stayed quiet for a while as if she hadn't heard. 'Child?'

'Yes. At the window. I saw someone before I came inside.'

'What?' Beneath her in the heavy chair, the great powdered head turned to one side. 'There is no child,' she added as if Catherine had said something idiotic to someone elderly and irritable, which she surmised she may have done. Particularly if it had been Edith at the window. *But it couldn't have been*.

'Climbing, I think—'

'Climbing? What do you mean? There is only me here. And Maude. And as you can see . . .' She opened the palms of her frail gloved hands as if to indicate the existence of the wheelchair.

'And in the room . . .'

'What are you talking about? What room?'

They reached the hall. 'The room with *Glory*. There was a noise. A sound. I thought—'

'The bird? There are birds in all of our chimneys. We

cannot get them out.' Edith raised her little bell and began to shake it feebly.

Catherine reached down to help her.

'Leave it!'

From deep inside the Red House a door opened and Catherine recognized the shuffle of Maude's old, tired feet.

After Edith and her chair had been fitted into the stairlift by Maude, amidst protestations and much supervision that Catherine thought unnecessary, and once Edith and her chair had begun a steady though noisy climb upwards, the ancient woman regarded Catherine one final time with her small red-rimmed eyes. 'I will remind you not to mention what you have seen inside this house. It is private. They are still our things. We do not want callers.'

Catherine couldn't wait to get home and tell Mike. 'Of course. The visit is confidential.'

Edith continued to stare at her with an unpleasant intensity. Catherine dropped her eyes to Maude who looked through Catherine. The housekeeper's gaze was directed at the vestibule before the front door.

'Goodbye,' Catherine called out to the diminutive figure of Edith Mason, trembling on its rattling ascent. There was no answer. 'And thank you again.'

In silence, Maude showed Catherine to the front of the house. She'd wanted to flee for most of the time she had been inside the building, but now identified a frustrated desire to stay and see more. She had been spoiled, but also teased.

At the threshold of the Red House, the housekeeper looked over her shoulder quickly, back towards the hall and the strained sounds of the stairlift. And without looking at Catherine, Maude clutched one of her hands and pressed her mannish fingers into Catherine's palm, to leave a piece of paper behind.

'Oh no, you don't have to . . .' Catherine said to a closing, and then a shut door, thinking the housekeeper had tipped her like a tradesman. It wouldn't have surprised her if these two isolated and out-of-touch figures still observed such a custom, but when she bent over to chase the paper that had fluttered from her hand and come to rest on the tiles of the porch, she could see that it wasn't money. It was a crumpled piece of brown paper.

Beyond the thick door came the muted yet frantic peal of the handbell.

Catherine picked the paper up and straightened it out. It was spattered with what looked like grease. She turned it over. Written in pencil in stubby capitals were four words. DON'T NEVER COME BACK.

ELEVEN

Twice her wheels bumped across catseyes as if she had fallen asleep at the wheel. Late afternoon, but her journey home resembled a familiar route retraced in darkness. The fugue of the great house's interior remained thick inside her mind. Her place in the world felt odd too, as though she was returning to an old neighbourhood where she was no longer remembered.

Beyond the meadows of the Red House the world suggested only the bland and temporary to her imagination. The city she returned to seemed predictable and disappointing. The British Museum had a similar effect upon her heart, during all of those Sunday afternoons she spent there to escape the dismal rooms she'd rented in London.

Adjusting to the sight of dual carriageways, and their service stations, and garden centres near Worcester, required a conscious effort, that seemed more about regaining familiarity with the terrain than her experience of the Red House should warrant.

The impact of the house's strangeness and the incongruity of her place inside it combined uncomfortably with her memories of alienation as a child in Ellyll Fields. Feelings she didn't want stirred tugged at her heart again. Near Hereford, she even entertained the idea of never returning to Magbar

Wood and the neighbouring Red House. She tried to think of excuses she could make to Leonard. In a spurt of sickly panic that surged from a defensive instinct she'd been trained in therapy to repel, she briefly considered running somewhere new and not coming back. But where was left?

Parked outside her flat in Worcester, getting out of the car was like waking from a deep sleep only to leave part of herself inside a dream. A physical reassembly of herself seemed necessary before she could climb out of the car. Inside her flat, finding affection for her furniture and belongings was a struggle.

She had been uncomfortable and struck dumb in either shock or wonderment for the entire duration of her visit to the Mason house, but had left eager to return and see more. Until Maude gave her the note. The note was the trigger.

She left the note inside her bag. She didn't want to see the handwriting again. It was bully writing. Blunt, direct, designed to upset, unnerve, and linger long after the perpetrators had fled the scene. She'd show it to Edith. Or should she not?

The note could be nothing more than territorial spite directed at an imposter. Maybe she had been a glaring and awful reminder of *out there*, a thing creeping inside to cheat an old lady. Or was the note a warning? But of what? A ninety-three-year-old woman?

You don't have time for this now.

Catherine identified the cognitive root of where the imagined persecution bled. Some days everything was a trip-wire to set off paranoia. She derailed the irrational train of thought before it left the platform to shriek though her mind at InterCity speed.

An auction fraught with pressure, expectation, and a high profile she might be unequal to awaited, as well as her having to manage a difficult character. There was no escaping that. The note from Maude didn't help matters, and visiting the Red House was hardly a common experience. So it was natural to feel strange, disorientated. *That's all it is. Relax. See things as they actually are.*

Mike didn't like her in this mood either. He found her 'exhausting'. The last therapist's exercises worked if she made an effort. But only the excitement involved in getting ready to meet Mike succeeded in finally acclimatizing her to the world she'd stepped entirely away from, on the lane before the great house of M. H. Mason.

Joan Baez on the stereo, a glass of chilled chardonnay on the dressing table. The pencil skirt and satin blouse from Karen Millen, new stockings with seams from Agent Provocateur that Mike had given her for her birthday, all made her feel a bit vintage. And she realized that through her outfit she might even be trying to catch a tendril of what had curled out of the Red House behind her.

The place wasn't even remotely sexy, though it possessed mystery and elegance in abundance. But the professional opportunity the auction offered was sexy. Very sexy. If she could keep that at the forefront of her mind, she'd get through this job. And she gleefully imagined the outraged faces of her ex-colleagues, the bitches back at Handle With Care in Soho. If Edith hired her, the auction would make a few Sunday broadsheets, lifestyle magazines, and the national broadcast news channels. Handle With Care would crawl to her on their knees to produce a documentary about Mason's treasures. Catherine Howard, the misfit the quick girls hounded out of her job, and the city, would smile at them from a wreath of glossy pages, and as a talking head from local television studios. *Lost Treasures of M. H. Mason: War Hero, Taxidermist Extraordinaire, Puppeteer. Represented by Valuer and Auctioneer, Catherine Howard of Osbernes. The Red House. The Treasures of . . .*

She'd have the rooms of the Red House lit properly for the catalogue. Best to capture them in that setting. Mike could do the photos. God knew he needed the work, as well as cheering up. She also had catalogue copy to consider; the press release was even more of a priority. She'd get up early on Saturday and make a start. No, she'd start on a draft of a contract first. If she could pull this off, there would be a new car in her future, and she could buy her own flat in the development for young professionals, overlooking the river, or maybe take a house in Hallow.

Don't get ahead of yourself.

She checked her outfit in the full-length mirror at the end of her bed. She looked good. *Was the beauty spot too much?* Edith would be aghast at the sight of her scarlet *Kiss me* lipstick, and Maude would probably grimace at the intensity of the colour against the pale skin of her face. *Jam tarts*, that's what girls were called who wore make-up at her secondary school in Worcester. At least the lipstick was red. She let her hair flop down and was reminded of a doll.

TWELVE

'You wouldn't believe it. If she'll give us permission to photograph it, room by room, you could have an exhibition. It could be the book you've always wanted to do. And the kittens! Did I tell you about the kittens?'

Is he even listening?

Mike's face was pale and he hadn't made an effort with his hair, but she told herself she wouldn't mention that. He didn't like being criticized, even in good humour. Maybe he was thinking about what they'd *lost*. Maybe it was his turn to be sullen and withdrawn. Totally flat, so not a flicker of enthusiasm could be coaxed into life about anything. Now that she had come back to life, maybe it was his turn to retreat.

'You OK, babe?'

His eyes found her, then flicked away, back to the surface of his pint which looked inelegant on the table opposite her outfit, which he'd noticed with a sudden intensity when she arrived. But he had withdrawn his attention just as quickly.

Mike had been waiting for her, uncharacteristically early and smelling of beer. Had started drinking without her. 'Tired,' he said, his voice almost a whisper. He breathed out and his fingers writhed and knotted until he tucked them beneath the table. He'd been 'tired' for at least a month now.

She interrogated his face with her eyes. He wouldn't look

at her. Something was up. This was the first time she'd seen him in a week, too. He'd been 'busy', but with what? He didn't work. She'd only noticed his expression now she'd finished her breathless monologue about the Red House, a narration only interrupted by her frantic mouthfuls of wine. She was getting giddy and needed to slow down.

His expression was also unfamiliar. Furtive. He kept biting at his bottom lip and it looked red. His eyelids seemed half closed as if to protect her from an unstable intensity behind them. A realization that she'd not seen Mike like this for a while gave her a little shock. He might have been smoking cannabis all day in his dismal room again, but hadn't he promised her he'd stopped to make himself more fertile?

A waitress brought the main courses. Mike didn't look at his. Catherine was ravenous, but held back. 'What? What is it?' She reached over the table to touch his hand that reappeared to hold his pint glass. He'd been fingering his mobile phone in his lap. He had been sending a text when she arrived, too. *To who?*

'Not easy,' he said, then swallowed.

'What?'

'Nothing.'

'Black pepper?' the waitress asked, through an uncomfortable half-smile inspired by her suspicion of a lover's tiff at the table she served.

But there was no trouble between her and Mike. They were stronger than ever, even after what happened last winter. And they had found each other again after seventeen years apart, as if their reunion had been destiny. They'd once been a couple of hesitant sixth formers who only managed to speak to each other three months before school ended, and who then loved each other with a consuming and volatile passion for the following two years as geographic undesirables at their respective universities. Until, way back then, he'd broken up with her and broken her. But they had been reunited through Facebook two summers back, because a connection like theirs not even time could dim.

I often think about you. He'd left her a message after finding her, after he came looking for her. They'd exchanged fifty-three messages during that first evening of reconnecting. She'd fallen in love with him all over again after reading the first message. It was the *often* that did it. Mike had quickly become another reason to leave London, the clincher.

Catherine shook her head at the offer of the pepper grinder. The smile on her face was tight enough to ache. The waitress withdrew silently on black ballet pumps.

'There's something wrong. Is it . . . ?'

He looked at her. Shook his head. 'No. Not that. Not everything is about that.' Then Mike looked about himself as if he saw the pub's restaurant for the first time and was puzzled as to how he had come to be sitting inside it.

She smarted at his defensive response. They'd both been upset about the miscarriage, though she suspected he'd never been able to articulate his own disappointment so as not to hurt her feelings. But it had to come out eventually, *because things like that just do*. She was thirty-eight and he wanted to be a dad. Her irritation must have shown on her face.

'Sorry. That was unkind.' His tone didn't convince her the apology was genuine. 'Look, this is not a good idea. Let's take off.'

'But—'

'Sorry.' He shook his head. 'I can't eat this now. No appetite.'

She wondered whether she would be able to eat ever again, *once he's said what he has to*, and banished the thought as soon as it flared red inside her head. *Once you refuse to deal with an enquiry, it becomes a habit. It's easy really.*

'Then . . .' But she couldn't say any more, her throat had constricted. She suddenly felt sick.

'I haven't slept all night.' He smiled without any warmth. 'I've even been bloody crying. I didn't want . . .'

'Mmm?

'Look, can we go? To my place so we can be alone.'

She was following every word out of his mouth as if she could see them in the air. The blood stopped moving inside her body.

But this wasn't what she thought *it* was. They would go back to his place and he would smoke a joint and then they would end up in bed. He'd go mad for her in the hold-ups and heels. In the morning he'd be as excited as she was about the Red House.

'This isn't the right place.'

'For what?' The question was out of her mouth before she could snatch it back. Her declaration was spring-loaded with provocation. *That will just make it easy for him.*

And it did. 'I've been thinking. About this. Us. Fuck, this is hard.' He started to smile as if he needed encouragement and sympathy from her to do what he was about to do. 'You look gorgeous tonight, but . . . I have to go through with this. Sorry. I'm so, so sorry. The last thing I wanted to do was upset you after . . . you know. But I can't keep it up any more. I'm just so fucking miserable. I can't do it. Us. I'm sorry.'

And then he stood up and quickly walked across the dining room with his head lowered. Briefly, he paused to let someone enter the pub, and then almost fell out of the door in his haste to get away from her.

THIRTEEN

While Mike spoke, Catherine was sure the room had fallen silent. But now cutlery chimed and the PA system played something she once recognized but couldn't identify now. In the distance someone said, 'a new till roll', but their voice seemed too loud around her head.

Catherine sucked in her breath and tried not to be sick into her lap.

'You'll be lucky,' someone else said, but their face was fuzzy and indistinct.

The room lurched like a ship in a gale, then righted, was solid and stable again. But it looked different. It was really bright now, clinically lit. She couldn't lift her hands, she was paralysed. And momentarily she thought she was sitting really close to the opposite wall and staring into its white painted surface. Then her vision seemed to retract across the room to her chair. She could not swallow. Her jaw was so heavy. Her mouth was open.

There was nothing but panic recognizable in the maelstrom inside her, faint but coming fast from the distance towards her conscious mind. Thin white hands were slapping around the walls of her skull. She heard herself make the sound of a sob and thought she was sliding off her chair.

She held onto the table and into her mind came a memory

of her inability to breathe when Mike called her after so many years of silence. And she recalled the ever-expanding light and joy from her heart that smothered and concealed everything else because the rest of the world no longer mattered when he came down to London to meet her. She saw snapshots of their weekend in Barcelona, being drunk on the beach in Minehead, dressing up as a pony girl and jockey for a New Year's Eve party, sex in a borrowed tent in the Lake District, a Latitude festival, the pregnancy test, them sitting side by side on top of the Worcester Beacon and deciding *to go for it*. All of this flashed through her, life with him as it ended. And she knew that she was more in love with him at the very instant he left her than she had ever been before. The critical point. He'd walked out at the very peak of her intensity. The damage he had just done could not have been more severe if they had been together for another ten years before this scene occurred.

Permanent damage.

The waitress was whispering to the youth behind the bar. They were looking at her. Everybody was. She fumbled with fingers made from wood. Tears came off her chin and splashed against the back of her hands. *Never coming here again*. Idiot thoughts came and went. She still couldn't swallow. She was stoppered and stuck inside, nothing was moving. There was a cold pain inside her stomach too now, like a cramp. Incongruously, self-pity filled her with what felt like helium and a brief euphoria.

She ruffled two twenties on to the table. *Thank fuck you've got cash*. The thought of a card transaction nearly made her scream with horrible laughter. *You'd have me operate a machine with these hands?*

She knew she wouldn't get across the room and to the door on her heels. Her humiliation at the table wasn't sufficient, the universe wanted her down on her hands and knees, sobbing as strangers grinned.

Why?

Because he's found someone else.

You are too intense, you are exhausting, you are pessimistic, you are depressing, you are strange, no one actually wants you around once they get to know you.

He's met someone else. He's been withdrawn for weeks. Should have trusted your instincts. You suppressed them as an unhealthy paranoia, just like you've been shown how to.

He's met someone else to have children with.

Because you miscarried.

She walked home, pressed into the cold brick walls of the town that seemed to be a thousand miles long, and she looked at a blurred and watery world but didn't see much of it at all.

FOURTEEN

Catherine got to her bedroom with a bottle of lemon vodka and yanked the curtains closed. Outside, a group of laughing men walked under her window.

She freed herself from the skirt that had been a hobble the moment she put it on, a fool's tapered manacle. She tugged both stockings down her legs and fell upon the bed. Rolled on to her side and choked as much as cried.

A sudden thought made her snatch at her BlackBerry and she scrolled through menus to delete the folder that contained all of *his* messages. Get them out now so there would be no time spent trawling through them and imagining clues in the coming months, or even years. But her hands were shaking too much to operate the ridiculous keypad. She let it drop to the floor.

How could he? Why? Is there someone else? Who? It's not possible, because of . . . started until her head hurt and she ran out of conspiracies and clues.

She stayed on the bed until it was dark, sipped the vodka. When her phone chimed the arrival of a text message, she scrambled undignified amongst the detritus of her outfit, shoes and underwear on the floor. It was a message from a company asking her to claim compensation for being mis-sold insurance. She sent the word CUNTS back to them. Then felt the urge to send messages to Mike.

Tell him you're pregnant again.

Silence and indifference are the greatest weapons.

She deleted the three lines of text she'd composed. Even in her grief, their churlish and pathetic sentiment shocked her into the first assault of self-loathing. And that's when it really went wrong. She felt her own gears changing and the engine of her heart revving to reach despair as quickly as possible. Nought to sixty in three seconds.

Put me in a case with the kittens. So I can be safe from the pain. I can wear a pretty dress and have big open eyes and never have to go out again. Because there's not enough of me left to take any more pain. I'm done.

She stood up and tried to run for the kitchen and the scissors with the orange plastic handles. But weaved. Her legs felt useless. 'Fat bitch,' she said at herself. She'd been brought back down to size, so it was time to cut herself down to an appropriate stature. At least *he'd* know why she did it.

And in no time at all, she found herself standing on the kitchen lino in bare feet and holding the scissors that had almost leapt out of the rattling utensils drawer beside the sink. She held the points of the scissors before her belly. Stared at them with horror. She knew she wouldn't do it again. But at the same time a reckless hateful desire to punish herself made the closed blades twitch.

Each hand around the handles fought with the other. She imagined the metal going in, deep, and then she would turn it around inside and sever all the relevant tubes and she would put an end to her useless body. The desire to do this was getting hot and urgent. But the other hand went white-knuckled to keep the scissors out of her flesh. Some curious instinct for survival had made an unexpected appearance and she was almost impressed with herself.

Some of you is normal.

She threw the scissors and they struck the microwave and bounced back within reach. *That evil force you always knew was there wants you cut.*

Patsy Cline. Get Patsy on the stereo. Top yourself to Patsy.

No one's getting topped, you melodramatic twat. You can't go yet. The suffering isn't over and you have to take it, and take it, and keep on taking it, because that's what life is, bitch.

She laughed horribly. Then sank to the lino and sobbed so hard she couldn't breathe.

The clock on the DVD player said 6:49. Saturday morning. She moved from the floor to the sofa and stayed there until Sunday night.

Eventually, slowly, the shock retreated like a briny tide and left mudflats behind. Above them was a grey horizon. The activity in her mind was no longer frenzied, it was dispassionate. It was as slow and dreary and monotone as sleep-deprived acceptance usually is. It was acknowledgement through exhaustion. And in acknowledgement there was some relief. It got you to the bottom faster. On the bottom you suddenly saw everything clearly and as it was.

On Sunday morning, she opened the filing cabinet inside herself and got out every folder for a thorough scrutiny. By Monday morning she'd reached the last file. It took that long to re-examine the evidence.

With a remarkable clarity and in forensic detail, her memories were all waiting in Technicolor with an audio track. She drew the inevitable conclusions from them and unravelled the six months of psychotherapy her parents had recently paid for.

First, she revisited the London years and the swivel chair in the ticket office of the children's museum, and the boredom that became a physical pain before she made assistant curator. The flat in Walthamstow appeared next, with the determinedly upbeat girls who were prancing at 5:30 in the morning with their blonde ponytails swinging (shoulder-length blonde highlights at the weekend), to do Pilates and body pump, but with whom she never made it past small talk.

She watched herself undermined by a bitch in the specialist antique publishing company who stole her ideas for two books. She saw again the bulbous features of the fat male colleague, who made two rebuffed passes before she left that job for a junior position at an auction house, while renting a room for five hundred pounds a month in Kilburn and trying to live on the remaining three hundred of her salary.

Then there was an auction house for two miserable years and a bad break-up from a long relationship with an older man she could not love, who tried to throttle her when she finished with him.

Two years at an independent television production company followed, Handle With Care, and a year full of exclusion and spite from a consensual coven of *quick* girls with wannabe Kate Moss wardrobes, who she still wanted dead.

When her recall arrived at *the incident* with one of them,

their leader in effect, she put her memories on fast forward through the resulting crisis that made her parents come and fetch her, although they were on holiday in Portugal, before she began six months on antidepressants in her teenage bedroom at her parents' house, right here in dear old Worcester. *You couldn't cut it so you had to be brought home by your parents at the age of thirty-six.*

But there was Mike. Mike had been there for her when she came home to Worcester. He limited her slide and shortened the downward spiral.

She meandered ahead to the job as an estate agent, before a chance meeting with Leonard, a specialist in toys, which led to her dream job as a valuer in Little Malvern. Thirty-seven by then and things were looking up. She found her own flat and was strong enough to inhabit it. She'd never been happier. Not ever.

Miscarriage. *Fast forward for God's sake.*

She clutched her hands to her face and began a slow rhythmic moaning, wretched in a towelling robe with two-day-old make-up blackening her cheeks.

Single again. Childless.

A moan of anguish came out of the pit of her stomach. The sound terrified her, so she cut it short and stared at the wall instead, until the fabric of the cushions started to burn her legs and bum.

She moved back to her bedroom and stayed there until Wednesday morning. Sometimes she slept but always hated waking up. At noon she had wanted to die again, but only briefly.

Leonard had left eight messages since she'd called in sick. The sound of his kind voice only made her cry more. An old man in a wheelchair with a bad wig was the closest thing she had to comfort.

On Wednesday afternoon she suffered an 'episode' of the kind she had not experienced since her first year at university. A trance. One of her old episodes that began the day Alice Galloway went missing.

When she broke from the trance she lay on her sofa in the same position she remembered herself to be in when conscious. Her mouth and chin were sticky with blood.

The television screen and V&A poster of Renaissance Marionettes came into focus on the wall on the other side of the living room. The sun was no longer pouring through the net curtains. Outside, dusk had fallen and turned her unlit flat blue-grey. A car reversed and a distant chime of an ice-cream van faded to silence.

Against the sofa fabric her skin was hot, her jogging bottoms were damp and creased under her buttocks and thighs. Catherine stayed still for a while until the swoops of nausea subsided. If she tried to walk she would fall.

Black sky over a meadow. Plastic boy outside the sweet shop. Row of children standing on a hill, clouds moving over them swiftly. Boy with a painted wooden face. Bright-red roses in shimmering golden air.

Some of the images faded when she chased the final fragments of the trance. Other parts stayed as if the past was yesterday, pieces that had returned from a far distance inside her; the part of herself where what she thought were memories were dreams, and what she thought were dreams were memories.

The last time she'd suffered an episode was on a Sunday

afternoon in her parents' conservatory. That day she came out of a trance and back to the world with her head hanging between her shoulders and a chin wet with blood and saliva. It had been the summer holiday before her second year at university. She must have been nineteen. So this was the first trance in nineteen years.

Sat in shock, the idea that she had not just drifted away in a daydream, but had been engulfed, was paralysing. *It* had come back, all over again.

FIFTEEN

Wire covered in dark-green plastic, municipal green. Too high to climb over. Wire formed into diamond shapes she slipped her fingers through. She could squeeze her entire hand into a gap, even if it felt like she would dislocate a thumb. She'd got her hand stuck once and tugged and twisted her wrist and made her thumb go all red where it was squashed between the wires. Once the panic subsided, and she was as exhausted as a fish caught on a line, her ringing hand was released by the fence.

She'd never seen the children move into view. They would just be up there in the derelict school, above the den, when the back of her neck prickled and she knew she was being watched. And she would look to the place between two of the buildings where the grass and weeds were as high as her knees.

Some of the children were smaller and younger than her, others were eight or nine. Older children. All stood in a group with the raggedy boy out front and the girl in the old hat beside him. 'A bonnet' her nan had called the same kind of hat on one of her dolls, Gemima. It had been like a tunnel around Gemima's cloth face.

The air would go a bit wavy around the children of the special school, and above the grassy slope, like it did when it was so hot in the summer she'd sit in the shade all day.

She didn't know what most of the children looked like. Only remembered bits of the boy with messy hair, in the ragged suit and callipers on his legs, and the girl in the dress and bonnet.

The special schoolchildren would stare at her and she would stare back at their dark and uneven silhouettes, each wary of the other. Had they been children from the Fylde Grove, even with the fence protecting her, she would have run for home before the stones whipped past her head. But the other children never threw stones.

Only the raggedy boy came near the fence. To the section where the green wire sagged, and where the wire had been unravelled beside one concrete post. Where she had unwoven the wire with her small hands, one link at a time from the frayed bottom upwards.

Alice had sat and watched her unthread the wire. 'Better not, Caff. We'll get in trouble. We's not allowed to.' But Alice had also asked when the children of the special school were going to reappear.

As soon as Alice was told about the children of the special school, she believed Catherine's stories. Alice hadn't needed proof because she yearned for the same thing. Escape. In Ellyll Fields there was only so much comfort two little misfits could give each other.

Once Catherine started picking at the wire, she could not stop until the unthreading created a space large enough for a child to fit through.

She only went to the den once more after Alice went missing. At the very end of the summer holidays, before her family moved. Their sanctuary had been wrecked, and the fence by the river repaired. And that was the day she ran home in tears and said she'd seen Alice and made her mum cry and had her legs slapped.

I did. I did, Mum. Alice was up on the hill and she said, 'You's comin' up the big 'ouse, Caff. Wiv us, Caff? They's callin'.'

She never knew what upset her mum so much, the story about Alice, or because she'd been back to the den. The police and Alice's mum came round and Catherine recounted her story again, which upset Alice's mum even more than her own mother. The kitchen was full of crying women, one who couldn't even stand up.

She never saw the children leave the plastic bag either. The bag of coins was just there when she went to her den alone, one afternoon right before Alice went missing, when she was buoyant with relief the school day was over, but also pale and weakened by the day's torments.

She'd kept the fifty pences and the ten pences, but the other coins were either very old or from other countries. These her father took when he found them in his shed where she'd stored them. She'd lied about them when questioned. But the coins she'd found were real because her dad had seen them too.

'Not seen one of these since I was your age.' Her dad had inspected the coins she knew she couldn't spend at the paper shop.

In her trance, she'd even smelled the shed scents of cut grass, oily metal, fresh timber and creosote while he talked to her all over again like she was really back there. 1981.

And then she'd left biscuits on the plastic serving tray of her tea set, for the children of the special school, on their side of the fence. They took the tray and the biscuits, but left metal spoons that looked older than the ones that her nan kept in the sideboard with the sherry decanter. Catherine buried the old spoons in a handkerchief.

Smelly Cathy Howard, Smelly Cathy Howard. Dopted, dopted, dopted.

She'd heard that again in her trance too. And also seen the three girls from the year above her in junior school, waiting outside the school gates for her every afternoon for three weeks, until her mother went up to the school to speak to her teacher about the chunk of hair that had been ripped from her scalp.

The raggedy boy only came closer to the fence the day after her mother and father had a talk that she'd overheard, about moving her to a new school. Because of the bullying. She'd watched her adopted parents' blurry shapes through the dimpled glass of the hall door. Her mum had been crying.

The next day she sat in the den for an entire Sunday afternoon and was so cold she stopped feeling it. And she shivered and stared through the fence at the empty brick bungalows and prayed for the children to come back. She was alone that day because Alice was recovering from an operation on her leg.

She gave up on the children and took to staring between her shoes, wondering how to avoid ever going to any school. She only looked up when she suspected she was no longer alone.

There was no sound of their approach through the long wet grass on the other side of the fence, nor did she catch a flicker of movement from the corner of her eye. But she looked up to see the raggedy boy stood in the grass, closer to the fence than to the buildings of the special school. In the distance, the other children had formed an uneven line and watched.

She'd never seen one of the children so close before. The raggedy boy's face was round and was either painted or he wore a mask. His small thin body was covered in a dark and grubby suit like the ones she had seen in her nursery rhyme book. His face was one big grin and he waved a small white hand that poked from a tight sleeve too small for his arm.

White hand, white teeth, white hand, white teeth, white eyes . . . she'd felt dizzy with him so close. His hair was a thick black mop, a wig made for a girl.

She stood up. In the distance, the girl in the strange hat put both of her thin arms into the wavy air.

Then Catherine was pretending to pour tea from her greenish plastic teapot into the paint tins, while a crowd of children who smelled funny stood around her inside the den.

The memories had come back for her, and swept through her. She'd even been able to smell the rivery stagnant dell. How was that possible?

In the first half of her life she had been told she always came back to the world from a trance with her mouth open. When 'out of it', her expression was reported to be vague, and her eyes distant. Her parents told doctors all of this while she sat in silence on plastic chairs in surgeries and hospitals and offices. These were the first times she'd heard her 'episodes' described.

Teachers at the new school added to her awareness of what she looked like when she was entirely withdrawn from the world. Children at the new school crept up to form circles around her beneath the tree at the bottom of the school field to wait for her to wake up. She would come to covered in leaves, twigs and litter they had placed on her head and body. Once, she woke with a dead snail in one hand.

Flatmates and friends in shared accommodation at university had not been so cruel. They thought she was epileptic and resisted the urge to tease her, a temptation she read behind their half-smiles. She burned with shame when they told her how she looked during her time away.

She would pass through school assemblies, entire films and train journeys in the same state with no recollection of the time elapsed while 'she was away with the fairies'.

Sometimes her nose bled and people tried to shake her awake. Once an ambulance was called and she woke up beside a bus on a stretcher, wrapped in a red blanket. Her secondary-school teachers kept sending her home.

Doctors had tried to medicalize her 'condition'. The doctors, to whom she had been taken as a girl, claimed it was all kinds of things, as did the two specialists the doctors referred her to. At one time she was a narcoleptic, a catatonic, and suffered from hypnotic states. She was scanned and doctors with soapy hands and coffee breath kept looking into her eyes from close range.

No one ever asked what she saw when she was 'out of it'. What she looked like seemed to be the most important thing to other people.

She could not slip away on command, though as a girl had wanted to. After a bad day at school, if she'd had a choice, she would have eagerly returned to wherever she went in a trance. In trances she experienced a joy so intense it made her nose bleed and left her body drained.

The trances occurred when she was tired, and it was like going to sleep with her eyes open. Sometimes it occurred when in deep thought, but only when relaxed. It was the most at peace she'd ever felt, being transported deep inside herself and far away from the world.

By her late teens the episodes almost never occurred. Then she was caught up in the ways of the world, and there was little sanctuary there. Anxiety, tension, despair aplenty, but little calm. She was partly relieved the trances had either gone into remission, or that she had grown out of them. It was difficult enough to fit in wherever she found herself, without passing out and dribbling through a gaping mouth. But part of her had come to secretly miss the condition too. It was the last thing that connected her to Alice. In the perpetual white noise of London anxiety, the episodes never came to save her. Only being drunk enough to stop caring about anything had helped her there.

But now they had come back.

Catherine wiped the blood off her top lip with the back of her hand. The nausea soon vanished with the dizziness. Memory had briefly dulled the jabs of pain in her stomach that Mike had left behind. Mike must have caused the relapse, so close to the place where it all began.

On Thursday someone delivered a letter to her flat by hand. They had gone by the time she scraped the latch off the front door and peered into the street she had not walked upon since the previous Friday night. It was addressed to her, care of the Osberne office. Leonard must have sent it on to her.

The heavy linen envelope was sealed with red wax like a court summons from the nineteenth century.

Feeling leaden and sore, as if she'd pulled every muscle in her abdomen while crying intermittently for a week, she opened the envelope on the breakfast bar.

The letter was from Edith Mason. Written untidily by hand on antique stationery, it was more of a curt request than an invitation to begin the valuation of the contents of the Red House the following day, Friday.

She'd only been away from the Red House for one week and her life had fallen apart. But she doubted even M. H. Mason and his rats could stitch it back together again.

SIXTEEN

Leonard sat beside her and held her hands. His touch was light, the palms of his hands dry. She didn't know hands could be so dry. Maybe it was age. When she finally stopped crying and looked up, she noticed her boss's small grey eyes were moist.

'This scoundrel. This, this . . . bastard. I'd like to give him a piece of my mind. And more.'

The notion of the thin old man in the wheelchair enacting some kind of chivalrous revenge on her behalf was ludicrous. Sniffing, she began to giggle, but laughing made her feel as if she were also being unkind. 'Look at me. What a mess. And bothering you with this. I'm sorry, Len.' Outside the office, it was going dark. She'd only gone to work in the late afternoon to explain to Leonard the real reason why she had been missing for a week.

'Nonsense. Nothing to apologize for. I'm flattered, and very glad that you have confided in me. Though I don't understand it. Is he blind? A congenital idiot? I mean, to let you go? He's a first-rate fool and I'd like to see him get his comeuppance. It would give me a great deal of pleasure to have a hand in it! Where does he live, Worcester you say?'

'Please, Leonard. Don't even think it. I can't tell you how

much it means to me that you're even willing to listen. I'm being pathetic. But please don't get involved.'

'You are not pathetic. And we cannot account for the idiocy of others. My God, he's looking a gift horse in the mouth. The way he has gone about this. It's appalling. And not a word since to ask after you?'

As she recounted the whole sorry tale from the previous week, Leonard had not said a word, just winced and sucked in his breath. But she could tell he was genuinely upset, as if his own daughter had been jilted in a horrible fashion.

'He doesn't know what he wants. Thinks he does. Or did. He's so directionless, listless, but then so angry. Like he's still a teenager. But I couldn't help being in love with him.'

'Then you're better off out of it. And it sounds to me like you can count on his downfall, if it'll make you feel any better. And so will she, I'm sure, whoever this hussy is. Rest assured, my dear, justice has a peculiar way of making unexpected appearances. Any ideas who it might be?'

'No idea.'

'Best not to know. It won't do you any good. And she'll never be your equal. He'll realize it too late. This is on him, not you.'

Catherine nodded. 'I seem to bring it out in people—' She stopped. Hearing her own paranoia out loud made her feel pitiful, even ashamed. 'I don't know why I am ever surprised.'

'Now stop that. You are a beautiful and gifted young woman. Special. Unique. I don't deal in anything else, my girl, and wouldn't with a partner in this firm. Not everyone can see how exceptional you are. But there are plenty who can.'

Catherine looked at Leonard. His eyes had clouded and he looked past her, into the distance. 'We've both seen enough of it. Exclusion. Mockery. Hurtful things. I know. I know.' Leonard cleared his throat.

Now Catherine felt selfish and foolish, and even more childish, if that were possible. Here was a man in a wheelchair, disabled for all of a life he'd turned into a success. But nothing would have been easy for him. Perhaps that is why he still traded on the fringes, amongst the misfits and outcasts, where he'd also been manoeuvred. And had he ever known love?

'The only defence,' he no more than whispered, 'is finding others. Like minds. And belonging.' He turned to her and smiled. 'Like us, kitten. Like it or not you're stuck with me. We're cut from the same cloth.'

'A pair of nutters.'

'That's one word for it. Now, let's get that dinner I owe you.'

'You don't. My treat. It's the least I can do for putting you through this.'

'Nonsense. And maybe we should postpone your trip to the Red House. I'm not sure Edith is a fitting antidote to what you've just been put through.'

'No. I want this. For us. For the business. It's too good. I won't let *him* wreck it.'

SEVENTEEN

'You look pale, dear. And long in the face. Anything the matter?' Edith said as Catherine wheeled her through the utility corridor. For today's visit, Edith wore a tweed skirt and jacket, trimmed with leather, that looked to have been designed for outdoors as well as having the canny ability to pass as contemporary, and of quality. But so wizened was the elderly woman the clothes might have been handed out by a charity in the Blitz. Her skeletal hands were concealed again, this time inside a fur muff.

'No. I'd rather not—'

'Because you left here quite elated with what you discovered under our roof. You wished to return and I granted your wish. We have enough of our own troubles here without you bringing more to us.'

What could she say to that? What could be said to anyone so determined and self-involved? She'd never felt more insubstantial in her life. She was merely to be picked up and dropped, invited and then insulted. She was bobbing flotsam and it was dangerous to consider herself anything else.

Merely crossing the threshold of her flat that morning had required a mighty exertion. And she now wondered if she had come here as an attempt to start rebuilding herself and to show Mike what he had lost, or whether she had nowhere else to go and she could do nothing but follow instructions and mimic her former self.

Why not just sit still upon a mantel in peaceful repose like a preserved rat?

Catherine stopped her thoughts because they were giving her *that* expression in a white face already aching with misery. She intuited that it would not be beneficial to let Edith see her face like that. At least she'd remembered not to wear make-up.

'Stop here.' Edith turned inside the wheelchair and looked up at the wall of the hall. 'That was taken in the garden.'

Squinting in the faint rouged light, reaching up and onto her toes, Catherine followed Edith's gaze to a dim brownish photograph of a woman in a long dress. 'Family, Miss Howard. Family are everything. Why go into the world and try and prove otherwise? I bet you wish you hadn't.'

'Pardon?'

'My mother, Violet Mason. A genius in her own right. You know why? I will tell you. She had the foresight to sublimate her own talent to assist her brother's vision. She was the background and foreground painter of his tableaux, dear. She was also his seamstress, costumer and set builder. For the entire duration of his vocation. There is no shame in serving something greater than you ever will be yourself.'

Even in the dimness and against the dark panels of the wall, Violet Mason was an unappealing sight. A thin, severe face that looked to have never smiled, glared from behind a patterned veil and from underneath the wide brim of a Watteau hat. The full crown was piled high with black roses, and the hat's size and the cottage-loaf hairstyle both dwarfed and accentuated the narrow face grimacing below. The thin mouth and small eyes suggested a suppressed rage that was unnerving to look at, even in the thinnest light. A high-necked blouse, reinforced by bone, functioned like a pedestal to mount the horrible head, to support it. In the background of the picture, dark foliage blurred into sepia and shadow as if the very world was fading and disintegrating around the formidable woman.

'I can see the family resemblance, Ms Mason.'

'And here. You can see her with my uncle.'

Catherine pushed the wheelchair forward. The misted effect used in the picture's development, and the dour tones of what was a staged formal portrait, did not detract from the catastrophic head injury the man must have suffered at the front. The silhouette of the side of Mason's face, partially turned away from the camera, was uneven. A fraction of the forehead was missing. No wonder he'd shunned the world. The other half of his face was perfect, proud, handsome, generously moustached, but sad.

Beside the vast wooden chair he sat upon, that looked to have been carved decoratively on the high back and along one visible arm, his sister stood beside him. From behind a spotted net, that was triangular from the wide brim of the elaborate hat to her pointed chin, her black eyes were stern with either disapproval or malice. Catherine was tempted to believe the veil was a form of protection for the viewer, and she had never seen such a tiny waist, probably pinched by an S-bend corset. Folds of white satin formed the corsage of her blouse, ending at her belted waist. A long skirt, and the lower embroidered corsage, fell to a tiny foot inside a pointed boot. Curiously, the Masons both wore white kid-skin gloves.

The painted background behind the two figures broiled like storm clouds and suggested a seething absence of solid matter. She'd never seen anything like that in a photograph from the same period, which must have been the 1920s or even 1930s, though here were the stylings of the late Victorian era. Typically, the family portraits she had seen from that time were set before painted depictions of English gardens or Italian vistas. But this background had been chosen for a reason she didn't understand, and one she found herself unwilling to dwell upon. But she did notice that the backdrop also featured what looked like tiny bright stars. Or maybe they were blemishes in the photographic paper.

Before passing into the unlit passageway of the ground floor that led to the rooms displaying Mason's dioramas, they passed a selection of other photographs that Edith did not draw Catherine's attention to. But she looked up at them as they passed by and she caught glimpses of two tall figures dressed in black against lighter backgrounds, but surrounded by a group of what she thought were children.

'Stop here!' Edith commanded from her chair in the barely lit passage. 'This one, I think. This is the right one, yes, I'm quite sure. Now, if you would be so kind . . . The door is unlocked.'

EIGHTEEN

The thin teacup rattled against the saucer Catherine had perched upon her lap. From her chair in the drawing room, Edith watched Catherine's nervous fingers with either pride or pleasure.

'What is the point of art, Miss Howard, if it does not move us?' Edith said with a sly smile.

As before, Horatio the dog stared at Catherine with a wet sympathetic eye. The other animals of the silent, stuffed menagerie waited patiently upon their perches for her response to what she had just seen.

'It's . . . extraordinary.'

Edith nodded her head slowly. 'The very word.'

And it certainly was a word for accurately describing what she had just seen in two of the ground-floor rooms set aside to display M. H. Mason's early works. Catherine believed she'd just seen at least one thousand dead rats, imbued with human characteristics and apparel down to the minute detail of their uniforms and facial expressions and postures. One diorama depicted nothing as living. No-man's-land, strewn with shell craters, demolished trenches, blackened tree stumps and rats. Dead rats. Rats that had looked so similar to small lifeless men in filthy khaki, she had been forced to lean over the glass display case to make sure they were, in fact, rats. They had no tails. Some of them were only bones inside hairless grey skin.

The second piece had affected her so much she even thought, for a moment, that she could hear the crackle of rifle retorts, the far-off thunder of artillery and the muffled thumps of exploding ordnance in wet mud. That case had featured a long weary line of men – *no, they were rats* – walking abreast of each other from a trench and into a pitted horizon wreathed in white smoke. It was called 'Ten Men Standing at Reveille'. Edith commented only once, to say her uncle had watched three hundred men reduced to ten left standing, in less than six minutes, at the Battle of Bapaume.

Catherine lapped at her tea and wondered if she could endure hours alone in those dim rooms, cataloguing the entire contents of every square inch, of each case, without going mad. No wonder they hid them in the dark.

That morning, the doors to the relevant ground-floor rooms were unlocked and the windows unshuttered in advance of her visit. Maude must have been busy. And Maude had not done more than glance at her since she arrived, and within the solitary glance there was not even a flicker of dismay or surprise at seeing the unwanted guest return. Despite the note, the housekeeper had remained as indifferent and unfriendly as ever. *Because she is mad. Edith is mad. Mason and his horrid sister were mad. They are all mad. They live with thousands of dead rats.*

Maude was unconcerned by the injury her foot or ankle had sustained since Catherine's previous visit. She only wore one boot and her hobble was more pronounced as the other foot was entirely encased in a bandage. She should have been resting. Asking Maude about the injury seemed like a useless gesture, and Catherine's pity would make a weak show of appearing for anyone but herself. Edith seemed entirely unaware that Maude had even suffered an injury and issued orders as if the housekeeper were a slave.

'You must understand, dear, that my mother and uncle were Victorians. They believed animals had souls. That they were good and evil. The Victorians were fascinated by an animal's true nature. So they depicted it.' Edith looked to the red squirrels prancing upon the piano forte and smiled.

And rats are most like us. Pests. Vermin. Scurrying. Frenzied. Determined to survive in any landscape and in any conditions.

'I think you understand, Miss Howard. Understand perfectly.' Edith smiled as if acknowledging Catherine's thoughts that she had heard as loud as the handbell the old woman began to ring. 'I'm afraid I must rest now. It's time for you to go. But before you leave your home on Monday, do not pack too much. We don't like our home cluttered with things that don't belong here. Just prepare your toilet. We have everything else you will need.'

'Sorry?'

'While you work to prepare the world for our treasures, you shall live upstairs with me.'

Catherine nearly choked as she smothered the gasp of horror that tried to slip out. Then felt paralysed by a sense of social awkwardness she imagined growing to unbearable proportions if she ever spent one night beneath the roof of the Red House. 'No, I really couldn't impose like—'

'Nonsense!'

Catherine flinched. Her watery, perfumed tea slopped over the saucer's edge and on to her skirt.

'Time is wasted with all this toing and froing in your motor car. The matter has been decided. Maude has prepared your room.'

Catherine coughed to clear her throat. 'She has?'

'But you must be patient with us. We are unaccustomed to guests.'

From shock at the very prospect of staying at the Red House, her head felt empty, her mind a void. No thoughts echoed inside her. She felt like a doll; something to be positioned by the insistent and capricious will of a nasty little girl.

NINETEEN

Catherine had been waiting in her dad's car for three hours when she saw them together.

Mike opened the little iron gate at the front of the short path that led to the terraced house he shared with two trainee teachers in Worcester, and he paused to look out at the street. Surreptitiously, so the woman beside him wouldn't notice he had done so. So *she*, the woman he had left her for, would be untroubled by the gesture. It was like Mike expected Catherine to be there, watching. Because she had form. She was a nutcase.

Catherine had parked tight to the curb, positioned some distance from the house so Mike wouldn't see her when he left or entered the building. He always walked up the street and away from the shops in St John's Wood. She'd never known him approach the house from any other direction, so was sure he would not see her position when he came home, *if he came home*. To make herself harder to identify while she conducted surveillance, she'd even borrowed her father's car. Her red Mini would have revealed her pitiful behaviour even in Mike's peripheral vision.

She was there because what had given her no peace since he dumped her at the dinner table in public was the fact that he still had not attempted contact, in any medium. Not even an apologetic text message, or a letter including reasons, explanations, an insincere desire to remain friends, or any other insulting platitude designed to make her feel better. Nothing.

Catherine could think too easily of reasons why he'd rejected her. He'd probably known her at her best, each time they had been together, so even at her best she'd been made to remember she was intolerable. But before she went away for a few days to work in residence at the Red House, she urgently needed to know the exact reason why he had broken her heart. And now she did.

Mike had offered no opportunity for discourse because communication would have forced his hand. Explanations would have been required. Disclosure of motive for what he had done. Who he had met and replaced her with.

Mike's flight from her had been frantic, trousers-in-hand. She understood this now. Because he had been desirous of immediate availability to see *her*, this other, such was his need for *her*.

Her.

For Mike, Catherine had thought such cruelty was not possible. Until proven otherwise.

When Catherine thought of the *incident* at Handle With Care, she realized the *incident* was one of the few things that had given her real satisfaction in her professional life. Though what she had done was contrary to her nature, because she always directed harm inwards and not at external targets. But everyone has a limit.

The events and feelings and thoughts that led to the *incident* she had discussed endlessly in therapy for six months following the first act of violence she had inflicted upon another human being. And she admitted that directly after the *incident* she experienced a profound calm. The endless loop of anxiety, fear and loathing had stopped for a few hours. Because she'd no longer cared about anything. The future, the past, repercussions, how she looked to everyone else was irrelevant. And the only emotion that she could identify in the period of tranquillity following an occurrence in which she'd drawn blood was relief. She was thankful there was no going back. She had done something so definitive and shocking, the entire period of her life in London, and even the city itself, was closed to her for ever. She'd freed herself.

She never wanted to repeat what she did to *her*. It wasn't a case of her having learned a new strategy to deal with her tormentors, nothing like that. But as someone who had been brought up to believe that fairness should be a universally observed value, she did feel that justice had been done, albeit briefly. As well as feeling relief, she'd also felt satisfaction.

The only person she ever admitted this to was her last therapist, whom she had asked, 'How often do any of us feel satisfied in a lasting way, in this life?'

She still had no regrets and felt no guilt about the *incident*. The only thing that still alarmed Catherine was that she often wished she had gone all the way and killed *her*. And that, surely, was wrong.

Her. *She* had a name. A name Catherine had avoided speaking out loud, though often screamed the name through her imagination. So she and her therapist had settled for pronouns in therapy. But *her* and *she* was actually a woman called Tara Woodward.

And Catherine had gravely underestimated Tara.

Catherine had always believed that Tara never pressed charges because she did not want to be associated with the tawdry process of police statements and court appearances, and of victimhood, because it was bad PR for her status, self-image, and her professional and social reputation. It was counterproductive to the entire idea of Tara.

If Tara had dragged her through a criminal court, then in Catherine's defence of her actions as a last resort against a bully, Tara's behaviour at work would have been recounted under oath, in greater detail than Tara would have wished, before Tara's employers, her family and the press. And the *incident* would have made headlines: a female subordinate with no history of misconduct resorting to violence against an office bully, an Executive Producer no less.

Had it gone to court and had Catherine been found guilty, which she almost certainly would have been, as well as being regarded as unstable, Tara's card would still have been marked indelibly. There would always have been doubts about *her* thereafter. Suspicions that would have followed Tara up the tiers of corporate television. Rumours would have been whispered in offices and stairwells and media pubs every time she did something unethical. And Tara excelled at the unscrupulous behaviour that people like Tara needed to repeat, everywhere they worked.

Tara probably didn't have any choice. Urges to undermine and destroy others defined Tara as much as the skinny-fit jeans with high heels, the asymmetrical cut of her designer wardrobe, the Marlboro Light and *Charlie* huskiness of her upper-class voice, and the long fringe through which her small eyes peered out. And those cold blue eyes were forever searching for weaknesses and diffidence and hesitation and victims. These urges had been in place long before Catherine met Tara. They may have been forged in private school, or before. Tara would always need a perfect victim and she had found one in Catherine.

Within minutes of the *incident*, Catherine had been sacked and removed physically from the premises of Handle With Care, and Tara had taken stewardship of Catherine's production, and her contacts and ideas. Those, that is, not already in Tara's possession. So Tara's strategy did ultimately pay the intended dividends, but never in the way the woman envisaged.

After the confrontation in the ladies' toilet, Tara had also deployed damage limitation more quickly than most major cities drowned by floods. Tara had calmly pulled her wet fringe out of her eyes, and wiped the blood off her forehead to only briefly inspect it on her manicured fingertips. And Catherine should have guessed, in those tremulous bright moments of sparkling adrenaline and heavy breaths, that Tara's reptilian mind had probably made a decision about how to react, or rather how to manage the *incident*.

Sitting on the floor of the toilet stall, with only a solitary Jimmy Choo remaining on one of her long feet, Tara had called their boss on her iPhone. A man who sat no more than twenty feet from the office toilets. And when Tara said with a familiarity that verged on intimacy, that 'Jeremy. You need to come to the toilets. *Now.* There has been an incident.', Catherine should have known she had not heard the last of Tara. Even after the woman who functioned as human resources in the company, promptly cleared Catherine's desk into a plastic bag and shoved it into her bruised hand on the mews street outside the Handle With Care offices, the lack of police interest and an arrest should have been adequate forewarning that she had merely taken *things* with Tara to a whole new level. One that was being *actioned* now.

Because Tara had come back into her life. Tara had waited nearly two years for an opportunity. Such patience was monumental. Now Catherine was back in the antiques business, Tara must have tracked her down.

But how did *she* know about Mike? *How? How? How? Facebook! Catherine is in a relationship with Mike Turner.* Tara must have befriended her under an alias, or befriended Mike, or Facebook had changed privacy settings like they always do, and Tara had then discovered Mike. Or Tara knew people down here and had put her feelers out. However she had done it, Tara had devised a way of meeting Mike and seducing him. The tall, confident, posho from West London had gone straight for the heart. Mike would have been a pushover.

Catherine went cold all over, but was also in awe. *You thought you were mad, but you have nothing on this bitch.*

And Tara wasn't afraid of Catherine. She strode up that tiny path and virtually sprang into Mike's hallway. She was prepared to slum it in the provinces with a no-hoper, a wannabe photographer, for a considerable pay-off. Couple of weekends in Worcester and Putney Bridge and then Mike would never hear from Tara again. Or Catherine, because of the nature of his deception. Mike wasn't important, no more than a pawn that gets knocked off the board by a marauding queen.

It was Catherine's turn to sit on the floor of a toilet cubicle with blood on her face, at least metaphorically.

With his arms full of takeaway, wine and a DVD, Mike followed *her* into the house like a rat smelling carrion. A night in.

TWENTY

Smelly Cathy Howard. Smelly Cathy Howard. Dopted. Dopted.

The children at the new school could read her mind. That's how they knew the chant from her previous school.

That day in the upper playground the hot pressure of humiliation had blurred her vision. She tried to hide her face from the crowd, but the children would keep appearing wherever her vision settled. The eyes of the children were wild and red. All of their mouths were open. She'd never seen them so excited.

Until something else caught her eye, in the distance. A raggedy boy stood behind the painted metal fence that bordered the top playground. When she noticed him, he raised one small hand into the wavy air above his head.

A skipping rope lashed the back of Catherine's thighs and the burning sting brought her close to fainting. The rope wound between her legs and bit the back of one knee. She cried out and fell down to the gritty tarmac. The forced laughter of the children in the playground seemed to thin the air so she couldn't breathe.

Through hot, watery eyes she saw the blurred shapes of the girls attacking her. One of their arms was raised as if to crack a whip upon a horse. She suddenly feared the wooden handle of the skipping rope and clamped her hands across her skull and shut her eyes tight, expelling a stream of salty tears down her cheeks and into her mouth as she did so. But the rope never fell.

Instead, silence came to the playground. Not a voice or slap of foot upon the tarmac could be heard outside of her personal darkness. Even the birds stopped their incessant twittering in the treeline behind the concrete domes she had once been forced inside to nearly suffocate from panic.

When she opened her eyes she found herself looking at the backs of the children closest to her, and saw creased blue cardigans and checked pinafores. Beyond them, the others in the playground faced forward, all stood still as if the headmistress had just walked into assembly. And she saw that all of their noses were bleeding in two bright rivulets that reached their chins.

In the distance, close to the staffroom windows, Miss Quan was the only thing moving in a scene of perfect stillness, and in such a strange way Catherine wondered why none of the children were looking at the teacher as she jerked her white face up and down, and gulped at the air like a fish, while raking her hair out at the sides of her head, tugging it loose from the hair clips with her bony fingers. The iron bell that called an end to dinnertime rolled back and forth close to her feet.

Around the scuffed shoes of the children, leaves began to blow in dusty circles, caught in the current made by the sound of the ice-cream van playing 'Greensleeves', but like it was playing the music too quickly through a big metal trumpet.

None of the children were looking at the playground

fence beside the main gates either, where the van played the discordant summons. And when Catherine looked up there she saw no van, nor the raggedy boy looking through the fence. That was because the boy wasn't up there any more. He was now stood between the faded white lines that formed the old hopscotch grid on the top playground.

It was the raggedy boy that all of the children were staring at, because they could also see him now, as he showed them the tiny rounded teeth of ivory in his black mouth, and his wide white eyes in what looked like a painted wooden face.

And in the sudden stampede of white socks and grey shorts and blue cardigans and pleated skirts and school shoes, that followed the arrival of the boy, and in the terrible screams that forced Catherine to clamp her dirty hands against her ears, the raggedy boy with the lopsided black wig upon his round head vanished as the rout of hysterical children formed a din in the air filled with leaves and stinging grit.

The chaos stopped as soon as it started. Stopped when Catherine stood up. And when she was standing, she realized her pants were wet through and her bottom was going cold. The back of her thighs still burned from the lash of the skipping rope.

But of more interest was the flock of children in the distance that ran towards the lower playground, even though the ice-cream van had stopped playing its tune and even though the raggedy boy had gone. The children sounded like a flock of hungry seagulls, little screeching voices bouncing off brick and concrete. Perhaps he was amongst the fleeing children, pumping his thin legs in the woollen trousers, up and down, trousers that were too short with frayed hems on legs supported by black iron callipers that were screwed into his lace-up boots. Maybe he was down there with them, still showing those white eyes that looked excited, but in the wrong way, in the stampede of dishevelled shirts and pullovers, and wild faces and wet red mouths that the other children had collectively become in their haste to escape him.

A group of teachers came out of the staffroom with their cigarettes and coffee mugs. Two women knelt beside Miss Quan who lay on her side. The other teachers stared across the playground at Catherine, until one of them picked up the handbell and began ringing it hard and fast while she strode towards her.

Catherine awoke from the trance on the floor of her living room beside a bottle of lemon vodka. What was left of it had run out of the bottle and soaked the rug. Blood from her nose had stuck her face to the laminate floor. She thought she might be sick, but didn't move because she knew she would be if she tried to get to the bathroom.

Her eyes were swollen, dry and sore, like she'd been swimming in the sea. Saliva was drying on her cheeks and her mouth and throat were hot. Her underwear was sopping and had gone cold.

On her hands and knees she waited for her vision to settle. She remembered seeing Mike with Tara during the afternoon before she'd been consumed by the trance. She also thought of her impending residency at the Red House. And she felt more miserable than she could ever remember feeling.

It was dark outside and the curtains were open. There was no traffic. Somewhere a metal roller door on a truck was pulled down. A dog's claws skittered past her street-facing window accompanied by the clink of the chain the dog was attached to. A far off ice-cream van's tune passed out of her hearing.

TWENTY-ONE

It had been twenty minutes since Maude closed the bedroom door. Catherine was still unable to do anything but stare around herself in astonishment. Nothing inside the room had changed since the early twentieth century.

Upon the single brass-framed bed the lace bedspread and scatter cushions were hand-made, and probably crafted a hundred years ago. In an alcove, beside the window and the dressing table, stood a vast ornamental washstand. One equipped with a patterned bowl, soap dish and water jug. She'd only seen them in the line drawings of ironwork catalogues stored in museum archives.

There was a single wardrobe, mahogany, with decorative mother-of-pearl wings either side of a long vertical mirror. An elegant table and chair for writing letters was positioned to the right side of the dressing table. The grate in the fireplace was clean and the room appeared free of dust or any noticeable wear. Varnished to resemble a hardwood, the floor was pine and mostly concealed by hand-woven rugs of red and green. Under the hem of the eiderdown was a chamber pot, which made her wonder if a bathroom had ever been added to the property. She wanted to laugh. The Red House was a goldmine.

She took pictures on her phone and desperately wanted to

send them to her boss, but there was still no signal, and hadn't been since she reached Magbar Wood. Which would mean no Wi-Fi either. The continuing absence of phone reception contributed to the unease she had failed to quell since her return; this was a time in her life when she needed to speak to the people who cared about her. She felt as if she had gone out over deep water inside a flimsy craft, without a life jacket.

Her room was on the second floor, at the rear of the property. Following the pattern of what she knew of well-to-do Victorian households, it appeared that family and guests slept on the second floor at the Red House, while the first floor was for entertaining and the ground floor functioned as a utility area. Such a tradition being maintained wasn't charming either. It suggested a system was in place with strict rules she might not be able to second-guess. An extensive and complex network of codes of conduct might be strung across every doorway and point of contact with her hosts, like a vast web. Transgressions and humiliating oversights awaited like traps. Failure to observe the merest nuances of what was expected of a guest could cause outbursts or silences. And somewhere out there on the same floor as her bedroom, in the long, dark corridors of panelled walls, burgundy drapes and closed hardwood doors, was Edith Mason's room. The idea of her being so close already felt like a permanent scrutiny. Now Catherine was inside the room, she didn't want to leave it.

To keep her mind preoccupied, she unpacked her travel case, and set up her digital camera and laptop on the table, on which to record the inventory and write the catalogue copy while saturated by the building's ambience. At some point she would need to call a professional photographer to do the house justice. People would marvel at what they saw inside the auction brochure. Rooms untouched since M. H. Mason's death, their furnishings and furniture, the exquisite period details, the exhibits. It would look like a programme for a great international exhibition. The house didn't need a valuer, it required a curator. How was this house possible?

And there were M. H. Mason's marionettes Edith wanted to show her that afternoon, or as she had described it, 'To introduce you to'. If Mason had been able to fool her with a preserved dog, she could only imagine the masterly crafts-manship of his marionettes. Edith had said they were the final part of his vision, cultivated behind closed doors and, it seemed, also starved of public scrutiny. More dolls awaited her too, of which she had only seen a portion.

Edith was broke. That's why Catherine was here. Perhaps Maude hadn't been paid in a while, and the presence of a valuer was an unpleasant reminder of their parlous fiscal state. It would explain why they were being difficult, so she must take into account the discomfort the situation was inflicting upon her hosts. Allowances needed to be made. Nerve had to be held.

With her unpacking complete, Catherine examined the intricate woodcuts on the walls of her room. Five framed originals placed about the dark-red paper. She didn't recog-nize the artist's signature, but they looked mid-eighteenth century.

Even with the overhead bulb on, the light was thin and winey, so she had to get close. The two pictures above the head of the bed featured a scene from vintage village life. Perhaps a satire, as the faces of the characters in the parade were grotesque, their features exaggerated into great noses and protruding chins, their expressions cynical, if not cruel. They milled around what looked like a cart with a platform or stage mounted upon it.

A third picture featured a stage again with curtained wings and a backdrop, upon which a motley assortment of small, tatty figures pranced. Their dress was Tudor period, but she could not tell whether the figures were travelling players wearing masks, or marionettes. The indistinct faces of the actors only defined themselves with sharp white eyes and unappealing grins. The audience was depicted crudely as uncouth, ribald, even feral, with great open mouths and wild eyes.

The other two scenes featured a market square filled with children. Ragged children. Urchins. Skeletal creatures with huge eyes. Some supported themselves on crutches. One was pulled along the rutted earth in a wooden cart by an older girl in a tatty dress. The theatre the children were drawn to was in the background, and at a distance, the action upon the stage indistinct.

Catherine moved to open the window to allow more light into the room, and to see the rear garden. The window was another Gothic tripartite, hinged inside the casement.

Against the outside of the leaded panes of glass, a number of flies bumped and nudged with their plump bodies. She had encountered the flies again on her way into the house that morning. It was nearly winter. The summer had been late, but the number of flies was as unseasonal as the warm weather. They had the building surrounded.

At the window she studied the flies' antics more closely until a flash of white motion from below distracted her. She leant against the casement and peered out.

In the distance, at the far end of the overgrown garden, between a row of untended apple trees, she located the movement. A figure in white, moving back and forth across a short area, as if busy with some task.

She wondered if it was Maude, but then realized the figure was too thin and tall. Maybe a gardener. No, because the grounds had seen no attention in years. The wooden arbour was mostly collapsed and the garden walls were concealed by brambles and ivy. Mounds of vegetation covered several objects she assumed were lawn ornaments or furniture. The edge of a stone sundial, or perhaps a bird table, could be glimpsed through a motionless torrent of tree branches.

The figure that paced back and forth wore brilliant-white clothes. It disappeared for moments and then partially reappeared amongst the dark greenery engulfing the garden, until it seemed to be trapped and tugging at something to free itself. Adjusting her position and screwing up her eyes, she became more sure that the person was male, a tall man.

Momentarily he appeared at a break in the choking foliage and turned in the direction of the house. He'd spotted her at the window. But Catherine could not see the raised face, or even a head, because it was covered.

Once she understood the mask to be the gauzy protective headgear of a bee-keeper, she relaxed. Slowly, the figure raised both arms into the air. The large hands concealed by protective gloves wavered, or possibly even beckoned to her. *To come down*. No, because the man then pointed at the meadow, and repeated the gesture vigorously, as if indicating that she should go. *Leave*.

As if caught spying, she withdrew from the window and

returned to the gloom. Then felt a sign of recognition should be returned, a friendly wave. Somewhere below in the house, a door slammed shut. And when she looked out again the figure in white had gone, along with the flies.

Ten minutes later, an abrupt knock at the door gave Catherine a start. She turned, touched her hair and patted her skirt down. It must be Maude, sent to collect her. But she really didn't want to be alone with the housekeeper, who had yet to speak to her or explain the note.

The warning.

'Yes?' Her voice was frail. She cleared her throat. 'Come in.'

A second quick knock. Followed by silence.

Maude wasn't coming inside, but she had been summoned.

Outside her room, the only light in the passageway dwindled the further it seeped from the pointed arch of the dark stained-glass window at the far end. Further down the corridor the squat and cumbersome silhouette of Maude was some way from her door, but Catherine could not tell which way Maude was facing, or whether the housekeeper was looking at her.

When she established that Maude was in retreat from her door, Catherine followed the woman, accompanied by the clack of her shoes against the bare wooden floorboards, a commotion that rebounded noisily from the panels of the walls. Her sounds were unwanted and intrusive. The rest of the Red House remained silent, as if commemorating the passing of some great personage while she disturbed the mourning like a feckless and unwelcome guest. Maude's movements issued nothing but a distinctive shuffle. Catherine reminded herself to wear shoes with softer soles.

Below, from the landing that circled the hallway, Edith's bell pealed.

TWENTY-TWO

As with her second visit, Edith's tweed outfit was practical and less of a period costume, so perhaps the black silk dress had been worn for effect that first day. One of the games Leonard warned her about. But Edith's hairstyle was again concocted from hairpieces and fashioned into a cottage loaf that appeared too heavy for the tiny head the arrangement engulfed. The face under the vast wig was more haggard than ever, if that were possible. The pointy tension of her glare had slipped as if the woman were medicated. Her eyes were unclear and her mouth open, making her look dopey. And if those were false teeth they were in a poor state of repair.

Edith recovered and summoned a glare to cut short her scrutiny. 'I trust your room is satisfactory?'

'Yes. Very nice.' *A museum piece.*

'Good. It was once popular with guests, when the grounds were at their best. But that was some time gone. I wonder who used it last?' She gazed at Catherine with rheumy eyes as if expecting her guest to supply the answer. Edith turned to Maude. 'Is it time, dear?'

The housekeeper looked ahead, through Catherine, as if she weren't of any consequence or even present. And pushed Edith's chair into the adjoining passage on the second floor.

Catherine assumed the puppet theatre would be on the ground floor with the exhibits. 'You were going to show me your uncle's marionettes.'

No one answered her.

Between the two second-storey corridors, there must have been a dozen rooms. All were closed and locked away in darkness, doors barely lit by the red skylight above the hall and the one arched window at the far end of each communal passage. Catherine resisted the urge to ask for the lights to be turned on while marvelling how their old eyes could even see in such poor light.

Maude halted the wheelchair outside the second door in the dim corridor, the one beside Edith's room. Without waiting to be dismissed, Maude shambled off and never once looked at the door she'd parked Edith in front of. Her departure seemed born of anger.

'Are all your rooms furnished?' Catherine asked, unable to stop herself estimating the value of the Red House's contents.

'Of course. Everything still has its place.'

'I think you might be surprised at the value . . . of your things. The furniture and the ornaments.'

'Is it not enough that we must part with my uncle's masterpieces? Yet you want to sell every stick of furniture out from under us?'

'No, I just meant . . . I was trying to say—'

'Well don't. The more time I spend in your company, the more I am certain you have very little to say that will be of any use here.'

At first Catherine stiffened with shock at the outburst, then warmed with anger and squeezed her hands together.

Why must it be like this? There was never a good time to speak, to venture an opinion. And being in the house had already begun to feel horribly prescribed, like a script was being followed and she didn't know her lines.

She wondered how much she would be able to stand. Knew she wasn't up to the visit after the break-up with Mike, and the return of the trances. The quick reminder of Mike and her episodes made her feel weak and sick. The distractions she'd hoped to find here were almost certainly unreachable. 'I'm sorry. Look, I don't think I—'

'Quiet! The door. There. There, girl.'

Catherine reached for the brass handle set within an escutcheon of metal in an oval shape.

'Don't touch it! How will they make sense to you if I don't guide you?'

'I don't understand what you want.'

'They are no longer accustomed to audiences. To strangers. One must be careful. Respectful. Always. My uncle taught me their nature.'

Who or what Edith was referring to was lost on Catherine. She was stuck inside a nonsensical dream. The world within the building never settled into familiarity, it perpetually became unreal, even surreal.

Edith lowered her voice to a reverential whisper. 'They are shy and gentle creatures. Once they performed freely. But they have not done so in a long time. They are fragile like people, as innocent as children. And can be as cruel. They are blameless and they may seem impassive while they dream. But they are not inert. They wait. Like they waited for my uncle. But like all children, dear, they grow up and they go their own way.'

Catherine closed her eyes and wished she could also close her ears to the nonsense coming out of Edith's ghastly mouth. The visit wasn't going to work out. No genuine inventory could be recorded. No auction would take place. Because Edith Mason was insane. Nothing would be possible here, beside her bafflement and torment, before what age and isolation had done to these pitiful old creatures.

The conspiratorial look in Edith's eyes intensified. 'They enchanted us once, but they are not toys. They are too powerful to be played with. As my uncle used to say, to truly know them is to know suffering. And dread. For they are a tragic people. One does well to tread carefully, fearfully and respectfully among them.' The mad utterance was said as a rebuke, or even a warning.

Catherine's response was silence.

After such an introduction she was not sure she wanted to even see them. Nor was she keen to regard what she assumed were marionettes as living beings, to maintain a pretence which seemed mandatory in Edith's company around the preserved animals, and most probably the dolls too. But the charade would need to be maintained throughout her dealings with the estate. Others at the auction would also be expected to adopt such a ludicrous attitude towards stuffed squirrels and antique German dolls. The situation was absurd.

Perhaps all of this was an elaborate joke being played upon her by the elderly woman. A prank the mute servant may have tried to warn her about.

Edith looked at the door with a respect born of wonder and fear, and nodded her head, sagely, as if satisfied she had been understood. 'Now, if you feel able to treat them as you would wish to be treated, we may go inside,' she said, as if hearing a response from the other side of the door to an entreaty neither of them had made.

Catherine opened the door upon darkness. Within she heard the faintest creak issue from an item of furniture. Then came silence.

'The light. There. On the wall. There,' Edith whispered with an urgency that panicked Catherine.

She found the light switch and clunked it down. A thin yellow glow spread from a dim bulb in a heavy glass shade suspended from the ceiling on a chain.

It was a large room, and unlike the other rooms of the Red House, the walls were painted white and decorated by hand under the picture rail. Frescoes of animals dressed as people encircled the long rectangular space. But before Catherine could properly assess the decor, her attention was stolen by the array of small white beds with metal frames. Children's beds in a room for children. It was a nursery.

She wanted to throw her head back and shriek with laughter, and also scream, though she didn't know why.

'Come, we may go further inside,' Edith said. And they did, but as they entered Catherine became aware that within each of the ten little beds a small head lay at rest upon each small pillow. She was glad that the heads she could see were turned away from the door.

'Stop. Here is far enough,' Edith said and raised one gloved hand when they had moved no more than one full rotation of the chair's wheels inside the room.

But Catherine needed little encouragement to stop. She didn't like puppets and never had done. As a child she was always nervous when a puppet first moved, that lazy uncoordinated wobble when a marionette rose from being seated to standing, or the sway before a puppet leapt about a stage. The thin legs had always made her afraid they might step off a set and venture beyond the illusion of reality they commanded on television or a stage, that a step of a small wooden foot through a proscenium arch, and into the audience, was possible.

A ventriloquist's dummy on television once made her duck behind the sofa of her nan's house. The waver of an animal's thin furred legs in a children's television programme that she vaguely remembered as an infant, even though the long-eared creature's strings were visible, had endured in her imagination as a thing of a most sinister nature.

And even on occasion in her professional life, she could still feel uneasy when left alone with a lifelike antique doll in a shop. It often struck her as odd that her aversion had become part of her profession. This was not the first time she'd wondered if some terrible and intangible internal magnetism had pulled her towards what she'd feared as a child.

Her unease at the threshold of the nursery room also grew to a suspicion that she wasn't at the Red House to perform a valuation at all. That her presence was an unwitting invitation to mix in the old woman's delusions, cruel fantasies and dementia. To participate. She was a novelty and her purpose was still being defined. She was being taken advantage of by an elderly woman who might turn on her, banish her, and end the opportunity of her lifetime. Because there would never, in all of the world, be another like this one.

Edith touched the back of one of Catherine's hands. The fingertips were hard as if she wore thimbles inside the white satin gloves. 'Do not touch them. They do not wish it.'

Catherine was happy to comply, and relieved she could see no more than their heads in the thin light. Judging by the pointy lumps of the small bodies under the neat bedclothes, they appeared to be about as large as ten-year-old children, but with some exaggeration to the size of the partially visible heads. Their dimensions were unappealing. She'd hoped for fragile figures hung on a plethora of tiny threads, and crafted exquisitely down to the minute details of their costumes by Edith's talented mother. But not this.

The fact that most of the heads were covered, or near-covered with a sheet, and turned to face the shuttered windows at the head of the room, gave her the unwelcome impression of the figures mimicking naughty children, who feigned sleep and stoppered their giggles by stuffing bed-clothes into their little mouths. The nursery also resembled a room crowded with small dead people whose winding sheets improperly covered their faces.

Protruding from the bedclothes on the bed closest to her, from what little she could see, the puppet was a depiction of an animal more than a recreation of a human character. The tatty brown head of the hare had its black mouth open too, which was heavily whiskered and jagged with ivory teeth.

What may have once been a fox or a badger, wearing a bonnet, lay in the bed beside the hare. And she realized with distaste that the puppets were probably an extension of Mason's taxidermy, constructed or adapted from preserved animal remains.

But the idea that Mason had built the small beds and ded-icated a room to them was the most disturbing thing of all.

'Puppets have long been messengers. You do know that dear?' Edith whispered her madness from the chair and

Catherine wished she would stop speaking. 'My uncle told me they were first created as depictions of gods by ancient peoples. And spirits. Maybe even angels. That possessed sacred knowledge. The puppeteer communicated their wishes to the world. He was a priest, a shaman, a wise man. His troupe is 'other'. It is why there is a special tension whenever the lights come on in a theatre and they appear. We don't admit it. We tremble in secret. Nothing in all of the performing arts can match such drama. Don't you agree, dear?'

Edith turned her thin head, her eyes alight with an intensity and enthusiasm Catherine found unpleasant when so near the small beds. 'What accounts for that? That is the question you would ask if you saw my uncle's troupe perform. But who is the director? The master or the actors? In the end my poor uncle and mother could never decide.'

I bet they couldn't, but neither can you.

'You may ridicule what I tell you, but your doubts are the doubts of a blind and unfeeling world. One that has lost touch, that is unseeing. Sightless before enchantment and mystery. Much of this died before my uncle's time. But he sought it out in a world determined to destroy its innocence and magic. And he kept it alive. He made the unknown known and the unseen seen. There is no greater skill. And you must relearn the fidelity and openness of a child, or all of this will be lost on you, for ever.'

Catherine's eyes darted from what looked like the rear of a crudely carven wooden head, mercifully concealed by the pillow that the weight of its head indented, to what appeared to be a shock of unruly black wig that splayed across the white pillowcase like a long-haired animal.

She glanced from this to what looked like the muzzle of a preserved dog's head on the far side of the room, and felt her gut tighten at the sight of a pale-blue sun bonnet that was water-stained, but spilled luxurious chestnut curls, suggesting the presence of a real girl asleep beneath the patchwork quilt. That figure also seemed uncomfortably familiar.

And what little she saw of the troupe had nothing to do with innocence and magic. It was a testament to a man deranged by war and loss and isolation.

At the foot of each bed stood a pair of tiny boots or slippers. Beneath the closed scarlet curtains was a large leather trunk, studded with rivets at the joints and down each side. She was sure it was the very same case she had seen at the guest house in Green Willow. If the light had been better, and under a closer inspection, she was certain the initials M.H.M would be stencilled below the iron lock.

'Let me tell you their names.'

Please don't.

'Why, here's Little Mad Moll. Beside her is John Swabber. There's Leatherhead, Rhymer Warble, Knavish Fiddle and Riffraff Tattle, always the villains of my uncle's plays. Grizell-Killigrew, Trusty Baiter and Fair Rosamund on the other side. And that's Nobody on the far end beneath the window. There were once twelve, but poor Jack Pudding and Popelote Tumbler were lost a long time ago and never recovered.' Edith dropped her voice to a fainter whisper. 'It was a tragedy for such a group of close friends. I shouldn't even mention *their* names in here. The others won't like it. Now, we mustn't disturb their rest any longer.'

Catherine swallowed. 'Quite.'

'The light. Quick.'

Catherine's hand was on the light switch before Edith finished speaking.

'Take me out. We have intruded for long enough.'

Glancing back to make certain no small head turned to watch her go, she couldn't pull the wheelchair out the room fast enough. But a curious sensation engulfed her as she hauled Edith away. One she had only experienced in moments of panic before an adversary in her professional life, but she now endured the notion that the occupants of the room were listening to her thoughts. That somehow her feelings were amplified within the space of the room. Even more alarming was the idea that she would be sleeping on the very same floor that housed the nursery.

She tried to keep her anxiety out of her voice. 'The lock. I mean, the door. Key. Shouldn't it be locked?'

Edith looked pleased. 'No, dear. This door is never locked. Would you lock a child in a room?'

TWENTY-THREE

And here she was again in a room she would not believe existed unless sat inside it.

Ten small wooden chairs had been arranged in two neat rows. Children's chairs. White chairs with upright animals in human clothes hand-painted upon them, a familiar motif.

Catherine sat on one of two upholstered seats made for adults, placed either side of a projector that belonged in a museum of cinema. And this is where Edith's mother and uncle must once have sat together, presumably with their inanimate cast gathered around them, to watch recorded performances of what Edith had called the 'cruelty plays'. Maude had been waiting to start the show after Catherine was done in the nursery.

A white sheet served as a screen, replacing the backcloth of Mason's intact puppet theatre, a large structure that filled the width of the room, created from detachable parts to allow transportation between the house and rear lawn. The visible larger framework, bridge and proscenium, were constructed of wood and carefully painted in a regal gold and red. A rich purple drapery in the wings allowed for scene changes.

In itself, the theatre was a work of art that deserved display, and was much bigger than the German and Italian marionette theatres Catherine had seen daily while working at the Museum of Childhood in Bethnal Green.

Edith wasn't going to last for ever, which made her wonder if any provision had been made for the care of this side of M. H. Mason's work. Heirs had not been mentioned and the theatre troupe was not for sale. So what would become of this final evolution of her uncle's weird vision?

Before leaving her alone in the 'theatre' Edith told her of the BBC's visit to the Red House after the war. Which produced a great deal of excitement for her uncle, followed by an equal share of disappointment. According to Edith, during M. H. Mason's visits to a cinema, in Hereford, during the Second World War, he identified a new medium for communicating his obscure work to a wider audience. The rats' gruesome pleas for world peace had backfired, but he'd subsequently moved on to bigger things. Or so he'd thought at the time. A message his niece and curator didn't appear wholly cognisant of either. But the film crew from the BBC, who were invited to film his marionette dramas, never returned after the first visit, or broadcast whatever footage they left the Red House with.

Edith may not have pitched it to her on those terms, but Catherine's interpretation of the facts suggested one visit to the Red House had been enough for the BBC. And she now sympathized with the film crew's decision as an unpleasant tension mounted inside her while sat before the screen, an apprehension of impending discomfort.

When Edith was wheeled out of the room by Maude, in cynical preparation for what she called 'a masterpiece', she'd added, 'This is the only copy we have. It was deemed too upsetting for children.' A reminder of which inspired rage in the invalid. 'My uncle never said it was for children! They assumed, as all fools do, that his theatre was a simple entertainment for infants. They were as imbecilic as the audience they believed it intended for!'

The outburst left Catherine wondering if the master version of the film still existed in the BBC archive. But one copy had survived here and such was the excitement created by the reel's arrival in '1950-something', a projector had been purchased by Mason when funds were more plentiful. A projector that still worked.

This was to be a private performance that Edith and the projectionist did not wish to see. Their departure from the room had been swift. Maybe they were bored of it. The film appeared to be one of few entertainments in the Red House, so the household may already have watched it to death. But as Catherine wondered whether Edith had ever known television, or radio, or music in her life, her attention was seized by the activity on-screen.

If the opening shot was a statement of intent, Catherine would have been happy to miss all of what followed the first image, filling the length and breadth of the screen. A smiling face of painted plaster, in black and white.

Dropout, flickers and degeneration of the film suggested it had been made much earlier than the fifties, as did the absence of sound. The eyes in the face on-screen must once have been intended to convey delight, or a cheeky joy, but their expression had faded. Rounded babyish features, including rouged cheeks, were networked with black cracks. The nose was gone. In its place was an ugly hole. The dim, immobile grin suggested a cruel delight at the viewer's shock.

The hair resembled a clumsy toupee, a modern clownish

addition, lacquered or greased either side of a central part-
ing. It was an old head and probably manufactured before
Mason's time, but Catherine had dreamed of something similar before. In her memory, it jerked awake a sense of
something from her trances about the children of the special
school. And had this marionette been concealed beneath
bedclothes in the nursery that morning too? When she
recalled the mop of curly black hair upon a pillow, she
winced. The comparisons made her flutter with panic, then
frown with incredulity, before considering the absurd possi-
bility of a connection between the film and her hallucinations and trances. A connection she quickly dismissed.
At one time ventriloquist dummies and male puppets all
had that kind of head, nor was the hairstyle uncommon.
She'd seen a bonnet in the nursery, too, but female dolls from
the 1880s also wore bonnets. Though what had first put
such figures and images into her imagination as a child still
baffled her.

The camera withdrew and the remainder of the figure was
revealed. Catherine shifted upon her seat. The neck ruffle
and tatty velvet jacket signified Tudor stylings, but the legs
were pure M. H. Mason. The hind legs of a large dog supported the upper body of the figure, which began to
soundlessly clap its chipped wooden hands as it withdrew to
the side of the stage.

Unsteady, tottering, but with a rotation of the hips that
was uncomfortable to watch, the movements of the figure
were reminiscent of a circus dog trained to walk upon its
hind legs. Catherine thought she saw strings, but then the
bright flickers may also have been flashes of dropout on
damaged film stock.

A curtain was drawn back to the wings of what she realized was the very same stage at the head of the room she faced. But in the film the stage backcloth depicted a dungeon in great detail, replete with wet stones and a solitary barred window. Pieces of wooden scenery had rolled down from above.

Hung in chains, a bedraggled, limp figure struggled to raise its wooden head and look at the camera. The face was stained with a dark fluid and the features were partially obscured. But what she could see of the carven face was neatly bearded, like an Elizabethan man. The figure's countenance was sad but noble, if not regal, and made her think of both Christ and King Charles I.

About the sombre refined face, dark and luxuriant curls fell across a soiled linen blouse. A pair of tattered leggings completed the outfit. The carven feet were large, exaggerated, hoary.

The head tilted and moved as if it spoke. If there had been sound on the film perhaps the prisoner would have been imparting its woes, though Catherine found herself relieved the audio track was absent.

The curtains closed. Then reopened.

In the second scene, the imprisoned figure appeared even more wretched and mournful in appearance as it stood in the wooden dock of a court or aged public building. There was a second character onstage for this scene. A monstrous hare which gesticulated aggressively with its thin forelegs. Large and entirely white eyes dominated the hare's head. Remnants of whiskers bristled around an open black mouth that boasted small teeth. She must have just seen its foul head in a nursery bed too.

Its sagging body stretched out of a small wooden box that doubled as a pulpit. The fur of the chest was patchy and worn and revealed two lines of pale teats. The hare wore a black cloth or silken headdress, and must have been presiding in judgement over the man who remained the only distinctly human figure in the scenes that followed.

Once the curtains reopened after the trial scene, the action of the play had moved to a murky refuse-strewn street scene, with churned mud and slouching wooden houses artfully suggested upon the backcloth. The prisoner was now mounted upon a cartwheel, over the rim of which his tired but proud wooden face hung.

The scenery may have changed, and though well painted, the new backcloth added the only reassuringly artificial aspect to the jerky, but unnervingly lifelike motion of the marionettes on stage. So authentic was their propulsion about the space, Catherine became convinced the film had been created with still-frame animation, not puppetry. After all, Edith's memory could hardly be counted upon.

A motley crowd of figures dressed in rags paraded onto the stage from the wings and circled the cartwheel menacingly. Catherine caught glimpses of sackcloth and ceramic faces, wooden teeth, and animal ears. Several of the crowd had canine legs. Others moved on wooden limbs, their feet shod in pointed leather shoes.

Small white hands and the occasional bristled paw were thrown into the air to shake clubs. The crowd was stoked into an animal frenzy by the hare, which pranced and frolicked at one side of the stage. It was presiding over a second scene and appeared gleeful to do so.

With their scruffy backs to the audience, the rabble

crowded about and obscured the man upon the cartwheel. Their thin arms rose and fell repeatedly as they assaulted the prisoner.

Catherine covered her eyes and only peered back intermittently through her fingers until the slaughter had concluded. The exhausted crowd of ruffians staggered away after an awful minute of eager violence.

The thin wooden limbs of the victim had been smashed. Splinters protruded through its scant garments and were dark and moist.

Catherine assumed that it was at this point in the performance of Mason's cruelty play that the BBC director must have finally, perhaps reluctantly, realized the drama was not only unsuitable for children, but for anyone.

Despite the wear on the print, which now lightened and darkened as if the film was about to catch fire on the projector, Catherine struggled to watch as the broken figure was raised into the air by the mob. An evil crowd that struggled under the weight of the cumbersome pole upon which the wheel had been fixed.

The curtains fell. But didn't remain drawn for long.

The lifeless, misshapen and wet figure reappeared still strapped to the cartwheel upon the upright stave. But high up, on centre stage, the pole was set against a backcloth that was either entirely black or craftily designed to reflect a cold nothingness. And she wondered again if that forlorn wooden face now issued a soliloquy to camera on the missing audio track, because although his body was terribly broken, the glass eyes of the long face were open.

Catherine longed for the end, but worse was in store.

In the next scene, against a return of the town's backcloth, the anthropomorphic horde in rags returned to attend to the remains of their victim, who it seemed had been left to reflect overnight, beneath the featureless sky, on its tortured state. But this time the crowd approached the cartwheel in a representation of awe and reverence. They began to prod and study the broken man.

The first figure to distinguish itself from the shabby peasants was hooded and reached out a long pair of furred arms to seize and snatch away the head of the executed prisoner. The thief then crept to the front of the stage and caressed the long tresses of the stolen head with its black hands. But what was more appalling than the careful stroking of the leathery fingers through the feminine curls was the dark ape-like face that leered out of its hood to bare teeth at the audience. At some point it appeared Mason had come into possession of a primate.

Behind the monkey beggar clutching the disembodied head, the rest of the cast began pulling at, shaking, and tugging the remains of the executed man until he came apart in their mostly wooden hands. At one point the plucking of his parts became a frenzy.

Once a substantial item had been secured, and often from the ground it had fallen to, the piece would be snatched up and coveted against the chest of a peasant and carried off by the scuttling, hunched-over figure, seemingly in rapture with its booty. One by one, the marionettes departed the stage until nothing remained on the cartwheel or the horrible ground below.

The Master of Revels who opened the performance returned for the final scene, and took quick steps on its hind legs to centre stage. Once in place, it directed the audience's attention to the collection of ornaments and cases mounted upon little Doric pedestals across the rear of the stage. The receptacles had been painted and designed to resemble ornate jewellery boxes or elaborate urns. One object resembled a book, opened to reveal a tiny skeletal hand where there should have been pages. A gilded box fitted with a glass screen contained a foot. A small trunk lined with a silken material stored a jaw bone. She understood this to be a reliquary of the condemned man's constituent parts.

Catherine's curiosity about the identity of the condemned, executed, dismembered, and now martyred man was overshadowed by her deep concern for the damaged mind behind this portrayal of the character's hideous end in the filthy street. Mason may have changed his medium from rats to marionettes, but the themes appeared to be the same.

The film flickered to an end and Catherine groped her way to the light switch. Behind her, the loose end of the film slapped in a still-turning reel. The screen glared white.

TWENTY-FOUR

For a while Catherine was left alone. While she waited she studied the little white chairs, and wondered if Mason and his sister arranged screenings for their hideous creations, or whether children had once been here to watch the actual cruelty plays. Neither option made her feel any better and an urge to flee the house nearly overwhelmed her into actual flight.

Rats she understood. The war tableau expressed a sensitive man's trauma at the loss of his young brothers and at what he had experienced in war. But this slide into the grotesque and primitivism suggested a bloody and inhuman version of justice from the medieval era, within a Tudor and Stuart aesthetic. A regression into even darker times. But quite how he arrived there from the Great War mystified her.

The narrative of the play had been simple and sensational. A lurid tale for the unsophisticated with a crude and ugly cast, grubby animalistic presentations of the semi-human, the mob as animal. Mason's insanity must have been full-blown by the fifties. But the film had been affecting. That she could not deny, even from a bad print without sound projected onto a white cloth.

There was none of the rapid jerking of early films or any sense of a miniaturized world. Onstage the figures had not glided like rod puppets, or bobbed in the telltale style of string puppetry, and she could not be certain she had seen any silvery threads against the background, even when it was black.

The stage was large enough to host child actors, but the figures could not have been children in costume because of the animal legs of some of the characters. All had moved according to what they had been constructed from. Animal limbs moved naturally, articulated wooden limbs moved as one would have expected them to move. So the play must have either been filmed slowly with cameras, frame by frame, or Edith's uncle had employed several masterly puppeteers.

And the cast must have been comprised of the marionettes she had seen in the nursery. The heads were too similar to be anything else. Mason had indeed taken his bizarre and unpleasant art to a whole new level of artistry. And she'd been the first person to see it in decades.

The cinema screen was made from a rough weave of plain cloth. Multiple layers of fabric backdrops were tucked away in the wings, ready to be drawn by a flyman, when the stage was used for drama. The back of the theatre was pressed against the wall, but looking up from the front of the stage, Catherine could see no portable bridge, or platform behind the proscenium arches on which Mason or his sister would have knelt and concealed themselves from the audience without making a sound. If they were the puppeteers, they would have needed to crouch behind the stage, or stand behind the backcloth.

On closer inspection she found the joinery of the theatre to be masterful. A series of detachable wooden pegs allowed dismantling prior to transit and reassembly piecemeal. And the curtains were handmade by a highly skilled seamstress; Edith's mother, Violet.

The ground-floor room must have become the theatre's final resting place once public performance had been exhausted or found unfit for purpose, and perhaps once Mason was too old to continue the shows. But who was their intended audience, or what was the purpose of any of this?

Outside the room, the sound of Edith's wheelchair prompted Catherine to step away from the stage. Being caught conducting an uninvited inspection would not go over well. Or, at least, she had a feeling that it would not.

By the time the door to the room had clicked open, Catherine had resumed her seat beside the antique projector.

'Won't you stop it!'

'Sorry, what?'

'It overheats!'

'I don't know how. I didn't want to touch it.'

Maude bustled behind her chair and brought the whipping tail of the film to a clanking halt. To escape the glare from Edith's red-rimmed eyes, Catherine went to the window, drew back the layered curtains and retracted the shutters quickly, as if she was desperate for clean air.

'Well?'

'It was . . .'

'What? Speak, girl.'

'Very clever. For its time. The movement of the pieces . . . Was it still-frame?'

'What are you talking about?'

'The animation. It must have taken hours.'

'Nonsense. They were artists. They rehearsed. The performance was second nature. Shows in my uncle's day were performed in one take. Once my uncle was satisfied with rehearsals he was never required to interfere with a performance.'

Catherine's thoughts stumbled in an attempt to follow the conversation. She felt she was being given misleading information before a crowd of strangers who all stared at her. 'Your uncle didn't work alone?'

'He trusted no one but my mother who was wardrobe and set designer.'

The self-serious tone Edith adopted about her uncle's work suddenly made Catherine want to laugh madly again. Did the woman believe that what she had just watched was real? Edith was not going to be much help in understanding her uncle's marionettes.

'One can only admire how such small actors could issue such power, don't you think?'

'Quite.'

'It is the greatest testament to my uncle's art that he can still captivate an audience, even with this poor facsimile of the original, more colourful, work.'

Perhaps it was time to play along with the woman's enthusiasm and delusions. This was no place for logic. Maybe her visit could only be survived by collusion with fantasy.

'This is the only film we have left. It was the first of the cruelty plays that my uncle learned. A very old play. I often think it fitting this tribute survived. The other films are damaged and will no longer play. *The Face at the Window* and *The Dead Witness* were the last to go.'

'Learned?'

'Yes! Do you know nothing of our great dramatic history?

Barnaby Pettigrew and Wesley Spettyl toured this play for
years. At Stourbridge Fair, Worcester Theatre, Coventry.
Even Covent Garden and Bartholomew Fair. It was always a
sensation. It was their duty that Henry Strader was not forgotten.'

'Who?'

'You know, my uncle even believed the Master of Revels'
head was carved by the great Billy Purvis, head-carver and
puppet-maker. And the Master of Revels was ready when my
dear uncle reminded him of his calling!'

'Sorry, who was Henry Strader?'

Edith sucked in her breath as if scandalized. 'The greatest
of them all. The first known Martyr. Did you learn nothing
at school? Were you even now paying attention? You have
just watched the account of his terrible end. The very title of
this play is *'Tis Pity Henry Strader was Broken Upon the
Wheel*. Murdered for his art in Smithfield. The Smooth Field,
my dear. In London, in . . . in sixteen-something. I forget.
Executed for sedition, for witchcraft. He was then torn apart
in the street by a mob. It was the first history lesson my
mother taught me in this very room.'

'Afraid I'm unaware of him.'

'What an appalling education you must have received. Are
you telling me you know nothing of Strader's great march on
London?'

'Sorry, I—'

'The lame flocked to Strader, dear. And followed his
troupe from Stourbridge Fair to London. Some even called it
the second Children's Crusade, but it was perceived to be a
rebellion. Strader's following became so great, so unruly, he
was murdered for his vision by the authorities. His killers

made his troupe watch. Can you imagine it? He was the first of the known Martyrs of Rod and String. A local hero no less! Born near here. Parts of his remains were said to be holy, and were even returned to this part of the world after his execution. I was schooled in this black history right here.'

Again Catherine was confused and mystified by what Edith was referring to, or the timescale involved in what she appeared to be suggesting was a theatrical legacy continued by her uncle. And not one she had ever heard of.

Edith was wasting her time and Catherine felt another flare of annoyance. The puppets were unsellable. They were an unpleasant curiosity that she could dine out on for years, if she could bear to remember them, but they were nothing else. Edith's history lesson was almost certainly pure fantasy. This and the nursery had nothing to do with her valuation and the first day of her visit was nearly over.

'My uncle saved an entire English tradition, my dear. Outlawed for being in league with one devil or another, by fools. Ha! Did you know that Tiberius suppressed them, and that Claudius banished them too? This troupe have known dangerous times. Their entire history has been one of persecution. I mean,' she lowered her voice as if in fear, 'you saw what happened to poor Henry Strader at the Smooth Field for resurrecting the tradition. For daring to contradict the Church and government. He was the first martyr my uncle could even find a name for, my dear. But there were others. After him, for certain. And before him, too, you can be sure of that, though he never traced them.'

Edith sat back in her chair, smiled, and showed her yellow teeth, as if delighted at the opportunity to correct her guest's woeful ignorance. 'You know, in the summer when I was a girl, we had theatre on the lawn. My uncle staged those plays of Henry Strader that were remembered. The Martyr wrote nothing down. It was too dangerous. And much was lost. But in his own time he was more popular than Shakespeare. I saw *The Magician's Fate* and *The Beauteous Sacrifice* before I was ten. Now, how many little girls do you know who can say that?'

TWENTY-FIVE

Unhindered by a voice from behind her back, or the peal of Edith's little bell, Catherine passed through the garden gate. She tried to walk casually, though an attempt to move soundlessly made her movements furtive. She experienced a deep discomfort at leaving the building without asking, but then was aghast at herself for assuming that she needed permission to leave to make a phone call.

After the screening of the film, Edith had been wheeled to her room to sleep before dinner, and Maude had retreated to her fiefdom on the ground floor to prepare the evening meal. Both rooms were situated at the rear of the property, and she realized this was her best chance to leave the building unobserved. Her request to begin work on the inventory had been treated to an embarrassing silence before Maude escorted her to her bedroom without a word. Was she then to wait there all afternoon until dinner?

She needed a phone signal and urgently wanted to share her experiences with Leonard, and get his advice on what to make of it all, and what to do. But she now worried that as soon as she got behind the wheel of her car, leaving the Red House even for half an hour would make a return to the building difficult. *Unbearable* would be an exaggeration, but not a great one.

As she walked away, she desperately tried not to look back at the house. If someone was watching from a window, her glance might be an admission of wrongdoing, of not keeping her hosts abreast of her movements.

The nape of her neck cooled as if a cloud had passed across the sun, or the shadow of the house had lengthened to keep pace with her scurrying down the lane. The house's scrutiny began to feel like a tangible pressure, as if there was now a disapproving face at every window behind her. She was struck with an instinct to cringe, and could not prevent a surreptitious peek at the house just to make sure that no one was, in fact, observing her. But the peek became a double-take, in which she was forced to stop and face the building.

In a solitary glance, she had been shocked by a mistaken impression of a sudden change in the Red House's character. For a moment, in her moving vision, the overgrown garden had climbed even higher up the dark walls of the house's front. The bricks of the building had appeared unkempt, blackened with age or even dereliction.

The illusion was caused by the way the nearby trees cast their shadows over the first storey, abetted by her sight briefly dimming under the canopy of a small fir tree crowding the garden wall. The house was now restored to its former hideous magnificence.

Catherine reached her car and got inside quickly. Turned the engine over and put the car into first gear. As she drove away as slowly and as stealthily as she could manage she hoped the occupants of the Red House wouldn't hear the sound of the engine.

She slipped her car through the tunnel of hawthorn, but

struggled to see the lane as shadows rolled over the bonnet and across the windscreen in a strobe effect. Emerging from the natural tunnel, strong sunlight blinded her and she was forced to brake. She fumbled with sunglasses and the sun visor.

In the rear-view mirror the black claws of the roof finials were skeletal against the sky.

Once she was moving again, the idea of escaping Edith's unpredictable moods, at least for a while, allowed the tension of the day to seep from her shoulders and neck. There would be no friendship or even familiarity between them. Hoping for such was tiring and destined for repeat disappointments. Just an evening meal to get through and then she could sleep. If she could photograph every item for sale the following day, she wondered if she might even complete the valuation offsite, at home.

But finishing the valuation begged the question, what next? In the months ahead the catalogue would need approval, contracts would require signatures, and arrangements would have to be made for an auction. Her visits to the Red House would be endless, her exposure to this madness limitless.

She also suffered a persistent anxiety that Edith wouldn't let her go. That her firm's contract would be dependent on her staying at the Red House for weeks, even months. Her role had already fallen into being led to curious rooms, introduced to their interiors and inhabitants, before being whisked away. Boundaries upon her freedom to roam and work independently had been set in stone that morning. The idea of enduring even one more day of the obsessive supervision and tormenting felt like it would break what little spirit she'd summoned to get herself out here in the first place.

But the prospect of the Red House experience continuing was also unhealthily intriguing. She couldn't fully suppress her fascination. Part of her was recklessly and guiltily eager to stretch and reach for the enigmatic here, for all that was undisclosed about this weird family. She wanted to throw open doors and see everything at once, while being desperate to flee every other minute of the day.

Catherine swapped her hands on the steering wheel and bit her nails until the fingertips on each hand were sore. Inside her mouth the chips of polish tasted like pear drops.

Two miles beyond Magbar Wood, her phone revealed two blue bars of a reception signal. There was nowhere to pull over on the narrow road, so she stopped the car in the middle of the lane to call Leonard. She tried his desk phone; she'd never known him leave the office before eight.

'Hello, Leonard Osberne. Hello. Hello?'

Such was her relief to hear Leonard's voice, she had to clear her throat of emotion before she could speak. 'Leonard, it's me.'

'Kitten! How lovely to hear from you. Are you OK? How was your first day?'

'Insane.'

'How is the charming Edith?'

'Well, like most sticklers for good manners, she's as rude as they come. But it's not just Edith, it's . . .'

'Go on.'

'I just need a second pair of ears, Boss. Because . . . well, today has been . . . They're crazy, Boss.'

149

'Mad as snakes. We know that. It won't make it any easier to start with, I understand. And you've gone out there after a truly ghastly experience. To be frank, I'm glad you called because I've been worried sick.'

'I would have called earlier, but there's no signal at the house.'

'Well I'm all ears now, Kitten. So what's on your mind? Or is it your heart?'

How could she even begin to explain her day? Or more precisely, how it made her feel? 'I'm genuinely not sure about this, Leonard.'

'Oh?'

'Edith and Maude. I really do not know what to make of them. It's like they're only interested in trying to conjure all of this mystery and reverence around Mason.'

'Has anything been said about the contract?'

'Nothing. I'd say any mention has been deliberately avoided. I've escaped for a bit, but it's only convinced me that other motives are at work out here, disingenuous motives. I think she might just be playing with us.'

'Edith will dance about like a spider and keep changing her mind. I know that much. And sometimes we must suffer in our trade. But unless she's thrown you out, she'll come round eventually. I'm sure of it.'

'Even if we get to that stage, it's going to take a lot of stamina to endure her, Len. You really should come out. I could do with some backup.'

'Of course. I plan to.'

'Glad to hear it. There's a stairlift here too, so you can get round easily.'

'Tomorrow's full. Maybe I'll come the day after. But what has upset you? Can you be specific?'

'Something . . . is just not right. Edith won't get to the point at all about what's available for auction. Which is why I'm just not convinced there's ever going to be one. I haven't even started the inventory. Haven't seen a single bloody item. Instead, I've seen the most awful film and had this big history lesson about a puppet tradition that I've never even heard of. Henry Strader? Ring any bells? And Mason's old puppets. She talks about them like they are children, you know, living. They sleep in a room next to her. She just seems intent on disturbing me. She's such a bully. And this man, this Strader, who her uncle was obsessed with, they have this film of him being broken on the wheel. A cruelty play, that's what she called it. Edith claims the play is hundreds of years old. It's worse than a horror film. I'm supposed to be here for the tableau, the dolls. But it's like they're already out of the picture. Irrelevant. So I'm not even sure we'll ever get to a contract, and if we do, it could be cancelled on a whim.

'But where does she think it will all go, I mean is there a will? Any surviving family?'

Leonard was silent for a while, save for the little sucks on his pipe stem that she could hear through the phone. She could visualize his frown while he considered what she'd said. 'Perhaps she can't help herself. It's in her nature, after so much time alone out there. Maybe she can't resist you. Who can? And she's making the most of you. Testing you with a load of nonsense. Though I have heard about Strader. He was supposed to have been executed for witchcraft, I think. Or maybe it was treason. Or both. He was put to death while touring London. But the authorities let a mob do the dirty work. His plays were supposedly highly seditious, and mystical. Apparently, a huge unwashed mob of peasants used to follow Strader around, if my memory serves. Orphans mainly, lepers, cripples. They thought he was a healer, a saint, the second coming or something, a saviour.'

'That seemed to be the gist of it.'

'And he was a local lad too, from out your way, so maybe that's why it took Mason's fancy once he'd killed everything on four legs and dressed it up. I'll look Strader up for you but I also wouldn't be surprised if Edith has also become attached to you, my dear. It's why she wants to share all of this with you. She won't show her hand, yet, but I am sure it will come. Dependency on new company is a hard thing to acknowledge when you've prided yourself on isolation. I mean, Kitten, you might just be the first guest they've had in that house in decades. You're like the sole friend who came over for a sleepover and she wants to show you all of her toys. And she wants a passive audience too, for all of her jumbled-up stories. But she'll keep the upper hand by playing hard. I've seen it all before, my dear. Maybe in not such a colourful way, but it goes with the territory.'

'Maybe.' She did feel as if she was an unwitting player in a performance, one born from decades of routine, tradition, and the stifling hierarchy of a servant and mistress, now gone from the world beyond Edith's isolation within those red walls. But the more she considered the woman, now she was out of her grasp, the more the whole idea of Edith troubled her. 'No woman still dresses like that, Leonard. The hair, the bleached face. It's impossible. A costume? Is Edith playing a role? And Maude's total silence, is that a performance too? She still hasn't said a word, nothing. No explanation about the note. The two women function, but it's like they've gone completely mad. It's like some crazy prank.'

Her instincts suggested she was being prepared for a greater revelation. Now she was free of the building, the idea was hard to suppress. Or maybe, like Leonard claimed, they were merely apportioning out their helpless strangeness because they had nothing else to offer. She wanted to believe that.

'In these situations, Kitten, I always extend my imagination into their perspective. Use your imagination and it'll take the sting out of Edith's bite. Edith is very old, lonely, surrounded by relics of a world and of people she loved who are long gone. She's clearly always revered what her uncle left behind. It's what she's protected and curated, on his bizarre instructions, I might add. That is clear from what you have told me. And we can safely assume that old Mason was pretty disturbed by the time he took his own life. She would have been in that house during the great patriarch's end. God knows what kind of shock and trauma his suicide inflicted upon her. But she stuck it out. No wonder she's half crazed. Maybe even frozen in time, from that period.'

'Then she needs a doctor, help. A social worker. Not a valuer.'

'We both know none of those types would even make it through the gate.'

'Then me being here feels wrong.'

'Then look at it another way. From what you have told me, she's also endured a long imprisonment. Mason pretty much confined his niece to that house. And still does, even though he's dead. Imagine what Mason's treasures have deprived Edith of. The freedoms, liberties, opportunities we've taken for granted, as our right. Edith won't have known any of it. But you can bet she's spent most of her life thinking about the wider world, resenting it while desiring it. And it would be reasonable for Edith to now despise her uncle's work, even while she covets it. She's broke and needs to sell it all. So what has her life been for? I've seen this happen, Kitten. At their end, some people experience a terrible revelation. But we must hold her hand while she goes through this. I think that is what she is asking you for. She wants to share all of this with you before she says goodbye to it, for ever.'

Catherine was no analyst, though she'd known a few, but now Leonard put it like this, she wondered if the Red House was smouldering with a resentment that had become something much worse. Futility was a powerful force, as well she knew.

'Maybe. This helps, Boss. Thanks. But I still have to go back and sleep over. It's like willingly going to bed to have an awful nightmare.'

'If it's too much, just say the word and pull out. I won't think any less of you. We can try and persuade her to let me in, even if she has her heart set on you. Your well-being must come first. I'm a businessman, but I fear you might not be ready for this job. And I feel wretched for talking you into it. I got carried away when you told me about the Mason pieces. It would be a glorious end to my career. I've been selfish.'

'Don't feel bad. I can't . . . The last thing I want is for my dysfunctional private life to interfere with my work. You know that, Boss.'

'Yes, but we all have our limits.'

'I'm not there yet. I had a wobble last week. A big one. But I also know this is too good to let go of. Let me try another day. See if I can at least photograph everything and then I'll pull out. Maybe tomorrow night.'

'You sure?'

'I think so, Boss.'

'But the next time we go together.'

'OK. I better get back. There'll be hell to pay if I'm late for dinner.'

TWENTY-SIX

Catherine's expectations about formal dining at the Red House were confirmed.

Feeling awkward and as breakable as the crystal she sipped from, she sat tense and uncomfortable on her chair, determined to make this the last meal she ate in the oppressive dining room. Because this was a feast to be endured within a thick, uncomfortable silence that made looking at each other across the table unbearable. Neither of her hosts appeared to have the strength to endure the meal, and she wished they hadn't bothered with staging the performance.

The wall lights were not turned on. Four candles in holders, around which silver serpents were entwined, lit the table but only partially illumined the surrounding room. Catherine wanted to be enchanted, but the mournful silence and wretched faces of her companions made her feel so self-conscious she began to feel irrational and worried she might say something foolish.

From the little she could see there was something masculine about the dining room, a touch of its former master, with ruby-red and river-green wallpaper, designed with a miniature version of the geometric design she had seen elsewhere in the house. Dado rails remained along all of the walls. Oil paintings hung high from horizontal rods of polished brass, each picture depicting an age-darkened still life of rustic breads, grapes, game, fish, and birds with limp necks beside thin knives laid upon metal plates. A frieze around the top third of the walls featured a vine heavy with fruit.

But at least she'd had the foresight to change into the only dress she had packed. A decision she congratulated herself on as Edith had also dressed to eat. Her host's ivory gown of embroidered silk concealed her entire body save her gloved hands and colourless face.

'Ms Mason. It's extraordinary to see such a fine gown still in existence, let alone being worn.' This was the first time anyone had spoken since Catherine had been shown into the room, and her voice sounded phony and irritating within the grand space.

'It belonged to my mother.' Edith just about smiled, and what little of a smile appeared on her lipless mouth was an effort to maintain before she quickly returned to a preoccupation with a matter unshared. Her eyes were cloudy and her arms limp. If she leant any closer to the table, she'd be face down in her soup.

At least the food provided a temporary distraction from Edith. There was a delicious home-made vegetable soup, two small pheasants with new potatoes, a cheese soufflé, a plum pudding with fresh cream, a sweet white wine, and a burgundy.

The meal must have been prepared for Catherine, because Edith did no more than blow on a spoonful of soup and push at her pheasant with a heavy silver fork. Though at one point, Catherine suspected she had seen Edith pressing the side of a piece of bread with her tongue. But she never took a bite. Edith's thin hands could barely support the weight of the cutlery, and it looked like she'd forgotten how to hold it. Perhaps Maude spooned food into her mouth when they were alone.

After her pretence of eating, and then an exaggerated dabbing at her mouth with a napkin, Edith finally closed her eyes and seemed to just switch herself off. She slept soundlessly with her head bowed, while Catherine nervously slipped tiny pieces of the food into her own mouth, trying not to clink the plate. She swallowed some of the food unchewed.

The coils of artificial hair on top of Edith's head spoiled Catherine's appetite before she reached the dessert. She suspected she could smell the piles of grey hair: a sickly floral perfume and the camphor of aged fabric kept from moths. She also wondered if a window was open because she detected an odour of damp in the room, like moist vegetation or cold, wet earth. Surreptitiously, she peered around her chair to trace the odour. The windows were all closed.

But she discovered that the mantelpiece above the great black marble fireplace displayed the source of the loud iron ticking. And she knew at a glance the clock was early eighteenth century. A timepiece set between four marble statues with a Greco-Roman theme. There was a bust of a man with a mean, arrogant face, perhaps a Roman emperor. This was set beside a sculpture of a muscular man being throttled by a serpent. Two willowy female figures, supine upon stone couches, faced each end of the room.

Mason and his sister, Violet, had probably eaten every meal here, year after year during their long occupancy of the Red House, sat at either end of the table like her and Edith were now. But had they been so silent, perhaps running out of things to say to each other?

Maude watched the charade in silence beside the serving trolley. Once she was satisfied Catherine had finished eating she cleared the table. But not a word was exchanged. The permanent expression of suppressed rage on Maude's crumpled face was sufficient indication that any private discussion about the note from Catherine's first visit would be unwelcome.

Could Edith's behaviour truly be an elaborate ploy for attention, as Leonard had suggested? Tonight the woman seemed barely able to tolerate her presence. Or perhaps the compulsion to be judgemental and controlling was a role the woman barely had the strength for at this hour.

Coming back had been a dreadful error. She should have kept on driving. She needed familiarity, warmth, support, and suffered a sudden fear that a last chance had been missed and now it would be too late to leave. She had to say something. Speaking might force a resolution she was desperate for, because tomorrow and the day after were at risk of being whittled away just like today.

'Ms Mason?'

It took a few seconds for Edith to look up. 'My uncle never tolerated chatter at the dinner table.' She almost spat the word 'chatter' at Catherine and her dark gums and thin teeth were briefly exposed in a grimace.

'Sorry.'

'But as you have begun, you may finish. What is it?'

Catherine cleared her throat. 'The dolls I viewed in Green Willow.'

'Yes?'

'Well . . . they . . . I don't think I have seen a finer private collection. Ever.'

Some warmth returned to Edith's little reddish eyes. 'Thank you. They were gifts from my mother and uncle. They spoiled me.'

'You were loved. Cherished. I can see that.'

'The dolls were not for playing with.' Edith added this refrain with such sadness that Catherine instantly forgave her for being unpleasant. In a heartbeat she saw how lonely and afraid Edith was. She had been left behind. And how could she estimate the damage inflicted upon Edith as a child, by a mad uncle and mother, as Leonard suspected? The force of her recrimination and shame for thinking badly of her host surprised her.

'You have a kind heart, Miss Howard.'

'Catherine, please.'

'I will address you as I see fit. But you are quite right to assume that I wait here alone.'

'I . . .' Had she spoken out loud? Or had her expression communicated more than she would wish to a woman un-accustomed to conversation?

'But not for much longer.' Edith spoke to the table's surface.

Catherine's courage to continue the conversation deserted her.

'You must make allowances for those who live so long. Whose role is unexceptional. My time is almost done. My use was what it was, I fear, and no more. So take them. It won't matter much, I suspect, if I am no longer here for their safe keeping. They must now watch over other children as they sleep. Only innocence can give them life. Please make sure they are well looked after.'

Flushing with embarrassment before more evidence of the woman's decline, Catherine decided she'd be better off if she just gave up trying to understand anything Edith said to her. It was hopeless. 'The dolls. I think a private collector, or even a museum, would be—'

Edith waved her napkin with irritation. 'I have no interest in these other places.'

'But if I may begin the inventory with them. They are a speciality of mine.'

'Because to you they also live. I knew it immediately. Your presence here is not ideal, but at least the vulgarity and coarseness we have encountered in others is mostly absent in you.'

She wanted to be flattered, but it was the 'mostly' that spoiled the moment.

'So take it all. I don't know why I cling. The house seems to wish it all comes to you.'

All. The word boomed inside her.

'But before you begin, you must see where my uncle worked. I've decided to let you in there tomorrow.' The smile disappeared from a face that looked dead in a moment of unwavering candlelight. 'I know you wish it. I am too old, and have been here too long, for you to hide things from me.'

Catherine tried to change the subject. 'If it is all right with you, ma'am, if you can tell me what it is you want included in the inventory, I'll restrict my work to those areas of the house. I don't want to trouble you any more than I have already.'

'Don't be impatient. Nothing infuriates me more than impetuousness. We won't be rushed, Miss Howard. All that is here, all who are here, are part of the Red House. This is a curious house that has known many times and lives. But nothing of it is indivisible. All must be understood in its proper and rightful context, and to begin with, in the places my uncle worked and brought such strange life to this house. Nothing has value unless it is considered properly. By degrees. And in the correct sequence. Don't you agree?'

'Yes,' Catherine said automatically, but had no idea what Edith had actually asked her. She glanced at Maude, but looked away just as quickly from the housekeeper's face because it stared with a barely contained malice at Edith. Catherine suspected the couple had been chastened by something she was not privy to. There was no warmth between them. They were as indifferent to each other as strangers. What bound them together, and motivated Maude to continue with the fatiguing care required by an elderly invalid, was mystifying.

But if she was not permitted to begin the inventory the following morning, and was manoeuvred into another digression involving M. H. Mason's grotesque hobbies, she would force the issue. She was prepared to leave empty-handed, save clutching a handful of stories no one would ever believe. And then Leonard could try his hand here. And she would prepare her excuses to avoid any more meals before tomorrow too. Regardless of Edith's decline, she knew her own mental state made it unhealthy for her to remain in this environment.

'You have time, dear. And there is much to understand.' Edith's voice had softened, was almost wheedling. She also grinned in what looked like triumph as if the woman had won some war of wills Catherine would only understand later. 'Now you are with us, there is less to distract you from this exceptional opportunity. There is more for you right here, than you ever found *out there*. I sense you are a young woman accustomed to disappointment.' Edith slowly moved her head in the direction of the window behind her chair. 'Out there.'

Was Edith now, impossibly, referring to her break-up with Mike? Had Leonard said something to Edith before she arrived? No, he'd only written Edith one letter, and that was before she split with Mike. Besides Leonard, she'd only told her parents about the break-up. The news worried them, but also wearied them. Or was Edith even hinting something of her flight from London, the *incident*, maybe her childhood, everything. The idea stunned her, baffled her into silence.

No, she was being paranoid. Edith could not possibly know about Mike, or anything of her life *out there*. 'Oh really. Why do you say that?'

'We keep to ourselves, but we are not blind, dear. Your eyes are full of a broken heart.'

We? Leonard must have said—

'I never went in for all that. My mother did once. Must have done, though she never discussed it with me. I never knew my father. But I had my uncle. He introduced me to other things. More rewarding pursuits.' Edith grinned her yellow grin. 'There are other things one can love. A different kind of love maybe, but love all the same. A more enduring love. One perhaps that is everlasting.'

'Today,' Catherine said to deflect Edith's uncomfortable taunts, or her investigation, or whatever it was. 'This afternoon . . .'

Maude removed the serving platters as if the meeting was

adjourned and nothing Catherine could say would be of any consequence.

'Thank you, Maude. The food was wonderful.' Maude didn't look at her to acknowledge the compliment. Edith's eyes closed again.

'Earlier, I saw someone in the garden.'

Maude dropped a steel serving spoon upon the trolley. The sound electrified the darkness.

Edith raised her head. 'Perhaps you were mistaken.'

Their attention felt like an exciting luxury. 'No. There was a man in white. He was definitely in the garden.'

What followed between the two women was quick, but not quick enough to evade her notice. Despite the void and coldness between them, Edith and Maude exchanged a glance. One of fearful acknowledgement rather than surprise.

'I think he was a bee-keeper. He was trying to get my attention.'

Maude turned and continued to busy herself with the dishes, her back to her employer. And it was Edith's turn to stare at the back of Maude's head with loathing. 'A friend of Maude's who used to tend the honeybees. But who is forbidden to enter the garden.' The housekeeper retreated across the dining room, the serving trolley rattling before her.

Edith cramped her face into an expression of disgust. 'I don't feel at all well. Her soup never agrees with me. She puts something in it. Will you take me to my room? I wish to retire. Maude will undress me.'

'Of course.' Catherine stood up, buoyant with guilty relief that she had diverted the hostility away from herself and on to Maude. 'If I may, I'd like to start early tomorrow, with the dolls if that's OK.'

Edith ignored her and had already dipped her head to rest.

Only once Edith was propped up amongst the pillows, still fully dressed, did Catherine relax her shoulders and straighten her spine. Moving the unresponsive figure up to the second floor and through the house had taken all of her concentration and strength.

Once she had mastered the stairlift, she found the building so poorly lit she felt she was in danger of wheeling the woman into crevasses of darkness. And only as Catherine turned to leave, giving the wall of dolls at the foot of Edith's bed a look of longing, did Edith speak.

She circled Catherine's wrist with her hard fingers which felt terribly cold through the silk of her gloves. The sudden contact made Catherine start, and turn in time to glimpse the hand retreat like a crab to Edith's lap. 'I would offer you the library, or the games room. But I am poor company this evening. It would be better to go to your room.'

'Yes. Of course. I have a good—'

'And to stay there.' Edith closed her old eyes, as if she had turned herself off again. And fell soundlessly asleep.

TWENTY-SEVEN

Night engulfed the Red House.

There was no light emitting from the shuttered house, no street lamps or light pollution from neighbouring buildings. The absence beyond the open window in her room was vast, total. Even with the overhead light switched off, the surrounding garden walls and trees and far-off meadows had disappeared. And there appeared to be too many stars in the sky, an incalculable scatter of iridescent debris. She'd thought her feelings of unfamiliarity and vulnerability could not get any worse, but they did. They now stretched into the kind of cosmic perspective she'd forgotten was possible.

Looking up at the sky, a force stronger than gravity enclosed her in a claustrophobic acknowledgement that she stood as a speck upon a speck, in a never-ending cold space she could not understand. A sudden terror fused with awe gripped her mind, until she could not tell fear apart from wonder.

Where did fear end and wonder begin?

If she had not been inside the house she suspected she would be swept upwards, or extinguished by a brief awareness that she was trapped on a planet that didn't matter to anything up there. Extinction seemed to be a better option than awareness.

She felt like a child again. An inexplicable regression. Would other people feel the same way here? Would they cope and handle themselves and know what to do and say, or would they wait fretting and alone in a forgotten corner?

Her first day had done nothing to distract her from the agitation and misery of Mike either, that kept rearing up in sudden waves of memory and pain. And she'd needed a great deal more than an unproductive day that had left her confused, anxious and unsettled, to keep her mind occupied. She also found herself increasingly desperate for a respite from bearing witness to any more of M. H. Mason's grotesque dementia. She didn't think she could stand it a moment longer. The Master of Revels' face, and the ten white occupied beds of the nursery, had stubbornly superimposed themselves over any other recollection she had of the Red House's immaculate treasures.

Catherine retreated from the window to the glow of the bedside lamp.

Midnight. She had been sent to her room before nine. The last three hours without a phone signal, Wi-Fi and her inability to concentrate her skittish thoughts on a book, had felt like three times that length of time trapped by the darkness. She was an exhibit in a museum no longer visited because nothing existed outside of the museum.

Her host's presence lingered around her as a kind of impending disapproval. The arrested time, the deranged artefacts, the expectant silence, and the tragic history, had all insinuated themselves inside her. She could feel their presence as though a dull brownish light had been introduced into her mind.

Funereal scents of rose water, lavender, wood polish, and

chemicals might be all she would ever smell again. All investing her with uncertainties and fears and a reticence she had not known since the emotional landscape of her childhood. And she did not welcome a return to that time.

The dangerous turning of her mind against itself was almost tangible. Some instinct tried again to convince her that she was no longer here to work. Her hosts had already forgotten the true purpose of her visit. She was here because of an unfortunate set of circumstances that had compelled Edith to take her in, like an evacuee or unwanted child during the school holidays. And now her presence had left everybody clueless as to how to amuse her or tolerate her outbursts. She transmitted tension like static. She could go crazy.

Go crazier.

Catherine clutched her face and wished she had something to drink. Why hadn't she brought vodka with her? *Because it's not allowed.*

She closed her eyes and engaged in the old breathing exercises. Cleared her mind. Focussed on one point in the reddy flickering darkness behind her eyelids.

Today was a write-off. But no more ghastly films or beds filled with bestial puppets tomorrow. Exactly what was intended for auction had to be established, catalogued and photographed. She would have to be firm.

The quick regrouping of her wits derailed at the sight of the camera on the writing table. Like an ex-smoker near a casually discarded packet of cigarettes, she was scared to be alone with it. There were pictures of Mike on there. A trip to Hay-on-Wye and the Worcester Beacon in Malvern taken within the last few weeks. Her throat thickened, her jaw felt too heavy. She remembered so vividly his expression of delight when he opened his door to find her on the other side of it, and she began blinking back tears.

How? How?

How had this happened so quickly?

And now she was here.

But what makes sense when you have no control?

Catherine reclined against the pillows on the bed and thumbed her way through the album on the memory card she had yet to transfer to her PC. Maybe she wanted to be in pain.

When the little camera felt too heavy to hold, and when she needed both hands to cover her eyes, she dropped the camera onto the bedclothes.

She checked the sheets. Clean. Slipped off her clothes and put on a cotton nightie. Against the dark rug her pale feet and painted toenails looked incongruous. She was a plastic bangle amongst fine heavy jewellery encrusted with precious stones. She was cheap, insubstantial and unacceptable. In here, almost anything in the modern world would feel the same way. And how could she even lie upon a bed at the Red House? She missed her flat and her own things so much it hurt.

With the bedside lamp doused, she could see nothing around herself, not even the bed. She squeezed her eyes shut and longed for sleep to take away her mind and deliver her straight into the morning. But across the screen of her mind played a montage of the day's sights and events to keep her just above sleep. A replay of the leering hare's threadbare face, and the vile scrabble of tatty heads and quick limbs about Henry Strader upon the wheel, pulled her eyes wide open and she held her breath until the images subsided.

The absence of light offered no comfort. She reached for the bedside lamp and decided to try and sleep with it switched on.

Far beyond her room, inside the great house, a door opened. Then closed. It must be Maude. The idea of other life in the building gave her a brief childlike comfort.

With her back to the dusty light of the lamp, she forced herself to run through what she hoped to achieve the following day. She seemed to run through the cycle of tasks for hours, and eventually fell asleep with a mind full of rats dying in the soil of Flanders.

Only to awaken when the house came alive.

TWENTY-EIGHT

She struggled to remember where she was. For a moment she believed herself to be underground because she could smell cold earth and wet timber. And she continued to mumble to the white-eyed hare of her dream as it pranced back and forth within a dark space, like a tunnel, that she had been trying to escape from. The wild hare had swung its large head about with a fierce and nonsensical joy.

Squirrels in red hunting coats had promised to show her a way out of the earthen tunnel, but that only led to a tea party of saucer-eyed kittens who spoke in tiny voices and said that she should stay inside because of what was up in the sky. She didn't remember anything else.

Now she was awake, she lay rigid, too frightened to move. Her hair was damp upon the pillow. Distant bumps filled her ears, and then her head with desperate ideas about what caused them. Stupidly, she thought of Maude moving furniture in the middle of the night. Maybe it was morning and the curtains were so thick they had shut out the light. She checked her phone: 3 a.m.

Sounds of an old house and its shifting timbers, it could be nothing more. Unfamiliar sounds in unfamiliar places, and there was always a rational explanation for what caused them. But now came a rhythm, like a small, hard hand striking a door. Not her door, but one in the distance. And also a suggestion of movement in the corridor outside her room, somewhere between her room and the knocking. Further along the corridor, nearer the staircase, came a swish and bump, swish and bump, like a crowd of children jostling within a school corridor. Yes, and now there were feet going up and down distant stairs. *Maude?*

The noises separated and coalesced into one, then distinguished themselves again in separate origins at different distances.

There are no children here.

Outside in the corridor came a sudden shuffle that moved across the face of her door and then paused. Catherine said, 'Maude,' but hardly heard herself. She noisily cleared her throat in warning and moved within the bed to make it creak.

A faint scuffle across a floorboard.

She received the impression that someone, or an animal, now waited beyond the door of her room to listen to her movements.

Catherine sat up, wondered what she should do. She pushed the heavy covers off her lap and stared at the door. There was a key in the lock. She hadn't thought it her place to lock herself inside a room in someone else's house. A consideration she now regretted.

She swung her legs out of the bedclothes and placed her feet on the floor as quietly as she could manage. She tiptoed to the door and placed her ear against the wooden panel to listen.

In the distance the bumps and jostle – and were there voices now, low voices? – passed beyond the range of her hearing as if the sounds were descending the stairs. Outside her door someone passed quickly again but in the opposite direction, back towards the staircase. It sounded as if they were low to the floor like a dog. Into her imagination came an impression of Edith Mason with her bleached face, red-rimmed eyes and yellow teeth, crawling down one side of the passageway on all fours, using the skirting board as a guide to find her way back to her room.

Catherine went back to bed for a while until she believed her own promise to herself that there were only three people inside the building.

When she'd mustered the courage to return to the bedroom door, she opened it more noisily than she would have wished and stared into darkness. Poking her head further out, she peered to the right, down to where the passage opened onto the L-shaped landing and stairwell beneath.

There was some light down there. The kind of luminance that glows from a distant open door, but one out of sight, as if a door in the next passage that contained Edith's bedroom, were open.

The elderly slept little at night. Maybe Edith had summoned Maude who had knocked at her door. Yes, she had heard Maude on the stairs and then Edith being carried downstairs, as opposed to being transported in the clanking lift. Not a pleasant thought, but it was all she had to go on.

So what had been outside her door? A cat, a dog, a rat, an animal of some kind had come in through a window. Those meadows were uncultivated. The garden was overgrown. This was deep country. Anything could find a way in.

Against the distant halo of light that defined the silhouette of the corridor's far mouth, and what must have been a vague banister rail beyond, came a sudden movement. But her eyes must have deceived her, because it looked as if a figure might have stood up and passed out of the corridor. An ill-defined shape. About the size of a large dog rising and fleeing. It must have been an animal because it was on all fours. Or was it? She couldn't tell, it had moved so quickly.

The face at the window, on her first day. Could there be a child here? One concealed from her. Had it been on the floor outside her room, crawling? Neither idea reduced her confusion and unease. Ridiculous. An animal. It must have been an animal that had crawled inside the house.

Catherine hastily swiped on the overhead light in her room to augment the weak offering from the bedside lamp. The new light was mostly stifled by the sombre wooden panels and dark-red drapes, but some of it fell into the corridor outside. Into which she ventured, shivering from the cold.

In the passage she had another idea, one worse than the first two. Had she just witnessed, or at least half seen, some kind of impromptu nocturnal marionette show operated by Maude, using something from the nursery. *Don't Never Come Back.* Was the mannish drudge trying to frighten her away from the only home she knew, that Catherine had come to destroy?

From the more frantic wings of her imagination she saw Edith proclaiming, 'My uncle and mother often took the troupe out at night to amuse me. How many ten-year-old girls have been so lucky?'

In her state, at this hour, she genuinely doubted the Red House would ever run out of traditions, rituals and habits passed down from the deranged to the demented, just to horrify a guest. Leonard had warned her of tricks, and now anger began to warm and eclipse her fear. But she didn't want to jump. Anything moving suddenly in the dark would make her scream. She hated being surprised. Her youth had been plagued by wretched practical jokes and she despised those that played pranks.

Catherine walked to the stairwell and winced at the intermittent creaks of the floorboards. She passed closed doors she remembered and fumbled for light switches she couldn't remember and door handles she could not see. She found two handles but the doors were locked.

On the landing she identified the source of the dim whitish glow. As she suspected the light originated from the passage that held Edith's bedroom.

She leant over the banister and the lightless hole of the stairwell, and felt she was listening with her entire body. Nothing but her indistinct feet was visible. If a voice was to rise out of the darkness beneath her toes it would stop her heart. None came, but she did receive an unwelcome sense of movement below, and probably from the ground floor.

Catherine thought she could hear the subtle shift of what sounded like limbs within clothing. But circling down there in the darkness. Round and round beyond her feeble vision. Maybe a ring of silent infants, looking upwards with plaster faces. She pulled her head back and repressed the careless byway of her imagination.

Animals, rats, something that crept indoors and roamed at night inside old houses.

She padded across the landing, but kept close to the inner wall, until she was able to peer into the adjacent passage. The doorway emitting the pale light was some way down the corridor. The door was only ajar. Edith's bedroom was near the stairwell and the door was closed. The room next to Edith's was the nursery and it was from here that the light issued.

Catherine turned and fumbled away, stifling her frantic breath as best she could. As she bumped against the walls and swatted her hands through the darkness like a blind woman, she heard a scattering of motion in different directions, two floors down and out of sight. And it was then she remembered Edith's final words that evening. 'It would be better to go to your room. And to stay there.'

TWENTY-NINE

'That smell . . .' The odour she detected on her first visit, and had been aware of intermittently since, had been seeping out of this room, Mason's workshop.

'I'm so used to it. I barely notice unless I come in here.' Edith smiled. 'Would you believe it brings me comfort?'

The odour hit Catherine like heat outside an air-conditioned building, and the miasma stung her eyes. She cleared her throat. 'Chemicals?'

'Perhaps it is the soap. Shredded soap and chalk in white arsenic. It could be the formalin. Or perhaps a residue of my uncle's formulas.'

The stench was more than a residue. To linger decades after the space was used suggested it was highly toxic.

'To this day my uncle's pickling and tanning processes have remained highly guarded secrets. There were some who would have paid dearly to understand how he achieved such remarkable results. And this is where my uncle spent much of his life. We have left it as he left it. I so wanted to show you.'

The workshop was as perfectly preserved as the creatures he'd restored. Catherine once read how a taxidermist at the Museum of Natural History had been baffled by how the tension in the whiskers and mouth had been achieved in a surviving Mason piece. 'May I?' Catherine held up her camera. She hoped to fill the memory card in her camera today, too, to make the best use of her time during daylight hours. Because she was not spending another night here, though she hadn't told Edith that yet. Her experience during the previous night was not one she was eager to repeat. During breakfast in the dining room, she'd tried to engage Edith's interest about what she'd heard and seen, or thought she'd seen. Edith had mocked her tentative queries, and made her feel like a foolish, jittery child. Maude, apparently, was a light sleeper. And 'often roamed'. As was Edith. Catherine's insistence that she must have heard an animal was met with a snort of derision and the conversation was over.

Edith looked at her camera with distaste, but nodded.

Catherine took pictures of the tiled floor and the iron drain-grate in the middle of the room. 'Was this once a scullery?'

'It was adapted. The mangle and range our old house-keeper used are still in the laundry. A much smaller room.'

The shallow Belfast sink dated from the 1800s, and the glazed ceramic was one of the few items in the house that showed signs of wear. The rest of the room was free of dust, so Maude must have cleaned it ahead of her visit. A hot-water copper and cold-water hand pump stood beside the sink. When she neared it, a small window above the copper looked and smelled to have been recently washed with vinegar. Branches from a bush pressed against the glass.

'This house went on forever. Or so I thought as a child. To me it never ended.' Edith peered up at the iron drying racks that hung over the long workbench. 'My uncle needed the space in here for messy work. And he put it to good use, as you have seen.' The woman's smile looked like an indication of delight at her guest's discomfort.

Catherine forced a smile of her own until her mouth ached. She focussed her camera on the long and bewildering rows of ceramic and glass jars shelved above the work-bench. Photographs would provide good illustrative material for the auction catalogue, though final print copy would require the work of a professional. These pictures she took for Leonard. She doubted another example of an early-twentieth-century taxidermist's workshop existed. A great many historians would kill to see the room. Perhaps English Heritage would want to reassemble and display it.

'Be careful not to touch anything. Sodium arsenite is a poison. Quite deadly. My uncle also used borax, but preferred arsenic.'

Catherine photographed acetic acid beside alizine beside alum and asbestos. She zoomed in and shot pictures of beeswax, boric acid, carbolic, chloroform and cornmeal. Mason had been meticulous with his labelling, with alphabetizing his ingredients.

'He killed some of the animals with chloroform. You can see it right in front of you.'

'How . . . where did they come from? The animals?'

'Our neighbours. The farmer's dogs caught the rats, along with my uncle's rat catchers. And there was a time when only one kitten from a litter was kept. But all of our dear neighbours knew where to bring a litter so he could take his pick. The squirrels were trapped and shot. The foxes, badgers, weasels and stoats too.'

Catherine turned her face away from Edith to conceal her

distaste. The thought of small animals destroyed on an industrial scale, twinned with the appalling stench, made her light-headed. Nausea wasn't far away. So she would have to be quick, but wanted more pictures.

She photographed the jars of ether, formaldehyde and glycerine, and unsuccessfully tried to ignore Edith's enthusiastic narration. When she focussed on the sulphuric acid, Edith said, 'He made his pickling solution from that. He often allowed me to watch him work and always warned me about that jar. "You must never touch this, Edie. It could burn you!" Beside it you will see the tow. He used tow on every single rat in his tableau. For winding. For their necks and tails. Their legs are very short. Always the hardest part to get right. My uncle—'

'I feel a bit funny. Sorry.' If she wasn't mistaken, she could detect an underlying odour of micturition, of decay. Catherine wondered if she'd also inhaled something poisonous.

Once again, Edith demonstrated her uncanny ability to follow her thoughts. 'If you can only imagine how many skins were fleshed and degreased in here, Catherine. And some of the carcasses were not fresh when they were brought here as gifts. My uncle was no stranger to the smell of death. Nor was I.'

Catherine coughed to clear her throat. 'His tools.'

'You will not find a finer collection in the county.'

Or even the world, and they were probably made to order. Each handle was inlaid with rosewood. The metal components were oiled and glinted. She couldn't see a speck of rust upon a single item. As she raised her camera with weak arms and photographed what resembled implements of torture, she knew she had no stomach for learning their true function.

'My uncle measured everything first, and made plaster casts before the animals were skinned. The callipers were used to take the most minute measurements for the artificial bodies. The distance between the outside of the eyes was very important, in order to create the desired expression.'

Catherine repressed a reaction from the smoked kipper she had felt obliged to swallow at the breakfast table. 'Fascinating.'

'Isn't it!' Edith had never been so excited. 'Above you. Look there. There! To the right. You will see the carving tools. Look. Look up, dear! He first made the heads from balsa and plaster moulds. But found the natural skulls were far better. He would clean the flesh away. Boil it off. You can see the brain spoons. Not there, dear. There! He refashioned the muscles of the head with tow and cotton. A master sculptor could not have bettered the facial expressions of my uncle's pieces.'

The room seemed to grow darker as the terrible smell overwhelmed Catherine's sinuses, and then the entire space of her skull. She looked at the window with longing. Wanted to cast it open so she could gulp at the air. The flies were back. As heavy as ripe blackberries they circled the window and occasionally propelled themselves against the panes of glass. There were at least a dozen. Two landed and investigated the frame for access. She intuited a will, a desire to get inside. 'I don't feel—'

'That knife was his favourite. It was always in his hand. The long blade disjointed the larger bones.'

Catherine held her breath for a while, but felt heavy and

exhausted and almost began to pant. 'The garden. May I? Which way?'

'But you haven't seen the awls and curriers' knives. His diagonal cutters were made for him specially, in Birmingham. They were adapted for the smallest bones. How else do you think he managed so many rats?'

Edith's thin, pale face was alive with an excitement that might also have been rage, or even ecstasy. It was hard to tell in Catherine's swimming vision. Her scalp chilled and her vision speckled with tiny flashes. She tried to get around the wheelchair, but it filled and blocked the doorway. A shadow passed across the small window, as if someone had leant down to peer inside. Either that, or she was about to faint. The stench had poisoned her. 'Another time.'

Edith's voice seemed to come to her from a great distance, and then it reappeared inside her ears as if through headphones. 'Look, look. The ear openers. They may look like a jeweller's pliers, but they open the other way. He used them on every set of rat ears. Can you imagine the patience that required, dear? You haven't even seen the needles. Don't you want pictures? Three-cornered for the hides. Surgeons' needles for the thicker pelts. Those are the curved ones. You are not looking, dear.'

'I'm . . . sick. Please.' Catherine fell as much as stumbled to the large galvanized metal tub and seized the side with both hands to prevent herself from toppling over.

'Be careful. Don't lean on that.'

The blocked window, the cruel locks and chains looping like serpents from the drying racks, Edith's discoloured teeth inside the lipless mouth, the brain spoons, all floated through her liquid vision. She leant her head over the side of the tub.

'It's had gallons of ethanol inside it, dear. It's poisonous. It's where my uncle pickled—'

She didn't hear the rest. Only the noise of her own gullet emptying itself of Maude's oatmeal and kippers onto thin sheet metal.

Outside of her blindness and choking, her panic and misery, Edith's handbell began a terrible racket close to her head. She wished and she wished that it would stop.

THIRTY

Blue-black, the heavens pressed at the earth with an angry weight, as though night was too close to a summer sky and breaking through. A storm, anticipated by the warm motionless air. Occasional gaps in the funnelling hedgerow allowed Catherine glimpses of the sky, the fields. Above the pink and yellow flowers and the golden waves of the meadow, the air shimmered in a thick heat.

But the further she walked from the Red House the more her senses and her head, and so much more, began to clear. The bone-deep weariness and pallor that overwhelmed her in Mason's workshop dissipated. She tugged the fragrant air into her lungs, and after running from the house without looking for the kitchen she longed for a bottle of water.

Her red Mini was like the sight of a familiar face after days amongst hostile strangers. Through the car windows the sight of her AA map, sunglasses, chewing gum in the coin holder, even the steering lock, hit her with a sudden awareness of modernity. An impulse to clamber into the car, drive away and return to a world that made sense, was wrestled down with reluctance.

She caught a whiff of the terrible chemical stink that hid traces of decay. It was in her hair, or on her skin, or caught within her clothing. Even outdoors she reeked of the Red

House and its artful mutilations. She panicked at the idea of being tainted.

She desperately wanted a breeze to air her clothes of the stink. But the air did not move at all here, it never did during her visits. Was always still and heavy, weighted by expectation, or exhausted and snatching a reprieve after some mighty exertion that was soon to resume.

The more she looked at the great indigo sky and the waist-high meadow grasses, the more she felt too visible, but also insignificant, alien even, and defenceless, tense. Being physically free of the house only made her think of being inside it. Where she was manipulated. *Prepared.* Introduced to terrible things that weren't right. Unnatural things that had no place or context beyond that huddle of spiny roofs and between those murder-red walls.

The horrid old women were trying to asphyxiate her with terror and nauseate her with disgust. She'd begun to hate them. Yes, they were horrifying her. Deliberately. All of what she had experienced had been staged. She was sure of it. They were hamming it up, even Edith was wearing costumes. Tricksters. How could they be bothered at their age? She'd thought as much while being sick into the horrid tin bath, with the plump bodies of flies crawling around the window. She was being tormented, unwound and rewound back to times and feelings she'd long tried to forget. But why? It felt horribly personal, and prescribed, if not inevitable. Either the world was unpleasant or she evoked its harms. She was never sure.

Or perhaps her hosts had lost the ability to behave in any other way, while her paranoia and anxiety had been kick-started by it. It was hard to tell. Here, the mad led the mad.

Edith had not wanted her to go outside for a walk. Had asked that she would remain inside and 'accompany' her to the stifling drawing room, to sit amidst the clutter of dead animals and their antics amongst the busy ornaments. Edith wanted her sealed inside like another doll added to her collection. 'But we must do the fitting, dear. There is no time for strolls.' *The fitting*. What was that? She hadn't paused to ask.

'And the pageant is nearly upon us. You must be correctly outfitted. It comes but once a year.'

In her haste to get into fresh air she'd also lacked the presence of mind to ask about this pageant. The will of Edith and the will of the house were terrible, tangible. A constriction against her thoughts. She'd been rejected by the present, was confined by the past. Totally enclosed. Her journey had taken a detour she had no control over. She felt as if she was being pulled back rapidly towards something she could not define, and wanted to see coming before she was lost.

Stop it. Stop it. Stop it.

Catherine stopped and held her head until her thoughts slowed down. She was too sensitive to such things. To everything.

She was paranoid. She had to remember that. She needed to reactivate the ritual of cognitive behavioural therapy exercises. To identify the seeds that grew to these elaborate conspiracies that she wove around her mind until she couldn't move or function. Mike's betrayal had paralysed her. He'd even brought her trances out of remission. That was the root of this.

But for God's sake, don't let your job contribute too. If you lose that you've got nothing.

Her bag and laptop were still inside the house, and she'd

left her camera in the workshop too. The exhibits, the furniture, the grand interior, the catalogue, press release, the unsigned contract, the news story, the immediate elevation of her firm's profile, Leonard, who had done so much for her, who had been so kind . . . all of these things twisted. They built into something like heartburn.

It was not possible to leave yet. She'd run from the unpleasant for so long she might never stop if she ran now. And where could she go if she left today? Back to her flat, and to work in house-clearances containing a few silver items, incomplete dinner sets, the occasional oil painting of a racehorse? After being exposed to the treasures of the Red House, it would be hard to get excited about a Napoleonic sword ever again.

An old house with a strange history, and occupants who were unstable refugees from another time. Elegant rags on half-forgotten bones. Little could prepare a person for them. But she should have been prepared. She had seen the mouse-infested warrens of two separate shut-in millionaires, one in Ludlow and one in Monmouth, who had not just died, but become desiccated upon the beds on which they expired, in rooms with sealed windows. Spaces so cluttered with rubbish they'd probably not been refreshed by natural light for decades.

And she was familiar with the apocryphal tales of her trade, the Turners, Constables and Bacons found in the attics of the deceased. Weirdness went with the territory. And this was her find, her moment. An opportunity. Not a trial she could run away from like London and university and school and her hometown, and everyone that she ever encountered in any of those places.

She needed to settle down. Survive today, maybe another day after that. But she would definitely drive home this evening, before they made another dreadful attempt at formal dining. She would go back and apologize for throwing up in M. H. Mason's ethanol bath, and then return tomorrow morning with Leonard at her side, and actually begin the inventory. What she was here for, not a fitting or a pageant. And Edith would be made to understand that. Leonard would have to be firm with her. And she would return for as many other mornings as it took to complete the inventory and evaluation, but only with her boss.

In the village she would buy water. There had to be a shop. And she'd have a nice lunch with a glass of white wine in a pub to settle her nerves. A sit down, respite from the tension, the creeping about in the awful silence broken by what she could not see at night, and the stink of chemical formulas and death.

The village wasn't far along the lane. Barely more than two miles. She'd walk in the fresh air. That would revive her.

THIRTY-ONE

There would be no lunch or wine. Not even a sip of water. The village was deserted. Under closer inspection Magbar Wood was not much more than two streets with tired, perhaps empty, terraced houses slouched on either side of the narrow footpaths.

She'd driven through the main street at least four times, but never taken much notice of the place in her car. The solitary cul-de-sac that led to a small church had not even registered with her before today. Fixated on not getting lost while being aware of the expanse of rare meadowland, or watching her phone screen for a signal, was all she'd had the mental capacity for when driving through.

Now, not a single sound issued from the buildings as she walked its length. Beyond the main street, at either end, were more uncultivated fields and meadows, defined by hedgerows and broken by distant hills tufted with copses of black trees. She imagined she was trapped inside a painting of a dead grey town in an idyllic landscape.

Enough.

She turned around and walked back between the flat-fronted tenement cottages made from a muddy-red brick. The slate roofs were weathered, the gutterings comprised of iron and rust. All of the street-facing windows were dark and begrimed with an accumulation of dust. Either that or the shadowing sky thinned the light and overcast the colours.

The first shopfront she looked at had once been a clothes shop. Yellow cellophane was still taped inside the window panes to protect the displays of 'High Street Fashion for Men, Women, Boys and Girls'. The plastic made the shopfront look like the lenses of cheap sunglasses sold to children on holiday. She pressed her hand and face to the glass, but stepped away quickly. Beyond the crinkled protective screen stood a row of dressed figures.

She waited for them to move. Then sighed with relief and felt foolish. Mannequins. She returned to the window and peered inside. Old mannequins with nylon toupees and painted plastic faces. The man wore what looked like khaki shorts and a khaki shirt, matching socks were pulled up to his knees. The female figure was naked. It was too dim inside to see what the boy and girl wore, and they had tilted or been leant against empty shelves inside the door. Their arrangement suggested the children were holding hands. Behind the dummies, the shop floor was concealed in darkness.

Further along the main lane she found a second store. A small convenience store, also closed. It didn't look to have been open or restocked for years. Fake plastic grass lined white trays in the window display. The trays had once stored meat. Half-a-dozen bluebottle flies crawling inside the foot of the window explored old habits.

A faded decal on the main window promised FRESH BREAD EVERY DAY. There were stickers for local newspapers she'd never heard of, stuck to the inside of the door, as well as a sun-bleached Walls ice-cream poster she remembered as a child: a boy and girl sat back to back against a vanilla background. The room beyond the window was unlit, but she could see a carousel of postcards, a fridge cabinet and one wall lined with tinned goods.

As she turned away, she stopped, and crouched down. Behind the lower half of the front door, as if peering through the stickers, was the solitary effigy of a small boy wearing shorts. Callipers were attached to each of his plastic legs. He held a money box with a slot in the top. The weather he was now protected against had worn most of his face away, as well as the name of the charity for whom he once collected. Beside one foot in a large brown boot, a rain-smoothed spaniel pup beseeched with too large eyes.

She'd not seen one of these effigies since childhood. After not thinking of these little figures for years, she'd been made to consider them twice in as many weeks. The coincidence made her sad, but uneasy.

The existence of the plastic charity boy and the derelict shops suggested there had been no life in the village since the early eighties, if not longer, which could not be right at all. The distant sound of a car would have provided immediate reassurance, which made her realize she was desperate for any sign of life.

Outside one of the cottages, she leant over and looked through the solitary casement window set beside a grubby front door. The net curtains were yellowing like icing on an old Christmas cake. A tear in the nets above the window sill allowed her to press her nose against the glass and squint into the gloom.

The room resembled a vintage photograph taken in poor

light. There was evidence of the space being cramped with heavy furniture. The walls were bare, the ceiling light without a shade. When she failed to detect a door in the plain walls she suffered an irrational fear that a person could become trapped inside the room. The feeling was even worse than the unwelcome idea that the room was not, as she had suspected, unoccupied. And that whoever was hidden in there amongst the clutter was now staring back at her.

Catherine continued along the sloping footpath, the curb steep as if the village was accustomed to heavy rains and gouts of floodwater. A flicker of motion drew her eyes across the road.

She thought, but wasn't sure, that a yellowy net curtain had just moved behind a ground-floor window.

She then looked up quickly, directly above herself, and had to clutch at the wall to keep her balance. She may have been mistaken again, but from the corner of her eye she was sure she'd seen the dark outline of a head rear backwards, away from the window into what must have been the darkness of a bedroom.

Afraid she had misjudged the village, and had been nosing through the windows of occupied buildings, she briskly turned the corner and entered the cul-de-sac.

And now it was as if her very presence had disturbed the place into some semblance of furtive activity. Because she was certain she had just seen another face, this time a pale smudge withdrawing from a downstairs window of the house no more than a few feet before her. She didn't suffer the impression the face had been watching her, but that the person inside the house had been waiting for her approach. Which felt worse than being watched.

Cocking her head to one side, she made the pretence of rummaging inside her handbag outside of the building in which she had seen movement, number 3, while sneaking glances at the window. There were no nets here. The houses in the cul-de-sac were even shabbier and more neglected than those on the main lane.

And yes, there was someone inside a front room that opened onto the street. A figure, close to the window, but with their back turned away from the street. A small woman, she thought, wearing something long, maybe a dark dress. Their posture implied a wall was being studied, or perhaps the woman simply stared into the murky fireplace that Catherine could barely make out.

The pale head was thickly haired, but looked tatty. It was hard to see much more, and if she lingered any longer her scrutiny would become intrusive. But what did stand out in the light entering the dirty window, was the hand upon the back of a chair placed against the window sill. The hand was so pale the person must have been wearing gloves. Catherine moved on, quickly.

Before she reached the street, concluding at the church grounds, she found one other storefront and crossed the road to look inside it.

The store was empty. There was no security shutter or grille across the broad window front. What the shop once sold eluded her. The wooden awning had been painted over with a thick brown emulsion the colour of creosote. Bizarrely, the sign on the door indicated OPEN. But the lights were off and nothing was for sale. In one corner of a broad wooden tray inside the window, a large moth fluttered its last. Against one wall she could see an ancient sewing machine and some bolts of cloth.

Deeper inside the empty shop was a counter, an open serving hatch, and a broad pane of clear glass fitted behind the counter, as if to invite customers to see a hive of reassuring activity behind it. Now, there were only shadows and indistinct items of office furniture back there. But as she turned away from the dirty window, movement became apparent.

The motion was beyond the second pane of glass, and continued while she squinted into the murk. Someone was standing up, but incredibly slowly. They were not fully upright, or could not get upright. And the vague silhouette, deep within the dusty gloom of the shop's interior, remained hunched over, the head bowed and crowned with unhealthily thin hair. But what were they doing? Staring at the floor, or at her?

The nape of her neck prickled as if she stood in a draught. She peered around herself in the street, took in as many of the other windows as she could, looking for faces.

Nothing. Just more of the sombre house fronts with old net curtains, most without.

She looked back into the empty store. Whoever she had disturbed was no longer visible, but her reluctance to see them again hurried her up to the church.

A small Anglo-Saxon building, and the place where Mason had once preached, proved to be another disappointment. It was no bigger than a cottage and had water-stained wooden boards in place of stained-glass windows. The cemetery and grounds were waist-deep with weeds and grass. The main doors were padlocked and the noticeboard in the porch was empty. Like the town, the church's congregation had faded away. She wondered if the village lost its faith when M. H. Mason did.

Beside the church, occupying the last plot of land before the low stone wall of the cemetery, stood the only other evidence that communal gatherings had ever occurred in Magbar Wood. A long wooden bungalow with a rust-red roof, the doors padlocked with chains. Flaking signage above the double doors read: SE SC UTS.

Inside the cabinet mounted on a post before the little gate, a yellowing piece of paper hung to a corroded pin behind a pane of grubby glass. It advertised events within the building, but gave no dates, or even any indication of what year they had occurred. It looked like a programme of performances. There were no explanatory details, or footnotes.

THE BLIND BEGGARS OF BETHNAL GREEN
THE CHILDREN OF THE WOOD
FAUSTUS
THE BIRTH OF HARLEQUIN
THE BOTTLE IMP

When the first cold drop of rain struck her forehead Catherine began her journey back to the Red House. But never made it past number 3 in the cul-de-sac. She saw the house's front door open at the same time she heard a voice come out of it. An old voice, reduced by its years, but still thick with the local dialect said, 'You sin 'er? Eh? Eh? 'Scuse me. Scuse-meeeee. You sin 'er?'

Catherine stopped walking, though she wanted to carry on because the voice didn't promise the kind of interaction she wanted, or even craved by this time. For a moment, still flustered and coming down from the brief fright the voice had caused, she was sure the person was asking her if she was a 'sinner'. Then realized the speaker, whom she could not see, was asking if she'd *seen* someone. This 'er' being referred to was a *her*.

She approached the door, now ajar but ready to close. 'Sorry? Were you talking to me?'

'Yous'll wake them up, you go knockin' them up. It's too early.'

'Pardon?'

Through the lightless gap between the door and its frame, she heard a muffled retreat, followed by scrapes on the inside of the wooden door, as if the figure had pulled itself behind the door to hide in fear of her. Though the little squeal she heard also made her suspect the unseen person was excited, which was worse than them being afraid.

She didn't get too close. 'Are . . . do you need help?' she was going to say 'ma'am', but wasn't certain of the speaker's gender. It must be the elderly person wearing the white gloves she had seen through the living-room window. A woman then?

An odour of damp, musty fabric drifted from the building and across the narrow footpath. The house was wet inside and virtually lightless. How could anyone see in there?

'You been up the house? You seen her, who went up the house?'

'Who? Sorry, I'm not sure what you're asking me.'

'Fings must turn a bit more, you fink? Not time yet for our lady.'

In the same spirit of her tour of the dismal village, communication with the only inhabitant she'd found was futile. But there was a surety and earnestness in the voice that made her linger. Catherine sensed this person believed that she was entirely aware of a set of facts upon which the speaker wanted a conversation to be based. Only she wasn't aware of these facts, but to walk away would be rude. 'Sorry. I don't understand. I don't think I can help.'

'Here, here. Yous'll want this. Run down that shop and get us half a pound of it.' A thin arm came around the edge of the door. Some way above the limb, what looked like artificial greyish hair indicated the position of the mostly hidden head. But the person must have been small as the tuft of hair was no higher than her own shoulders and the threshold of the house was raised one step off street level.

Catherine recoiled from the arm, tightly clad in dusty black cloth that ended in a small and bloodless hand. There was no glove. The skin was papery and almost transparent, the nails yellow and uncut. The woman must have been elderly, perhaps mentally ill, terribly neglected, and had mistaken her for some fragment from her failing memory. If offering money had been the aim, the proffered fingers were empty.

'The shop is closed. I thought the village was empty.'

'Half a pound, and some of them biscuits he does.'

She wondered if there were neighbours or relatives she could call for the woman. 'Sorry. I said it's closed. The shop. Everything. Here. It's all closed. Can I help you? Get someone?'

'Ain't seen her since she went up that house, is all. Going all black over them roofs now, dunnit eh? Still some turning to go. Turning, arr, afore the sliding in and the sliding out.'

Catherine walked away without another word.

The door never closed on the disappointed silence that seemed to swell behind her. In the empty store across the road, she was half aware of someone waving to her from deep inside the building behind the dirty glass. The arm appeared too thin, but that effect must have been caused by the angle at which she moved to ignore the motion, combined with the dim light.

She kept on walking, but more quickly now.

THIRTY-TWO

Even when in sight of the Red House's chimneys, the dreary and abandoned spirit of the village still discoloured her thoughts. Turned them into an old photograph, dour and brown with age, corrupted by blemishes.

Maybe this great house, this mausoleum that honoured loss and madness, had drawn all the colour, light and life out of the village. Bled its vitality up the lane years ago, to this dreadful edifice. Itself erected on ground verdant with meadows, briars, thorns, and tough grasses, as if the land was also returned to some former time that no hedgerow or wall could restrain. All around the Red House was forgotten, untended, and left to grow wild, while the building remained perfectly preserved.

Catherine patted down her damp and clinging dress. The cloudburst had been short, but ferocious enough to soak her to her underwear. She hurried through the hawthorn tunnel and returned to sunlight to continue drying out.

The front door was open as she had left it, the house silent, the grounds wet and sparkling as they dried. She checked her watch. Edith would be sleeping. Maude in her scullery, washing the dishes from the luncheon she'd missed.

But before she went inside, she wanted to inspect the

garden to discover what it was the bee-keeper had been doing beneath her window. She desperately wanted something to start making sense around here, and had a savage impulse to smack her own face until reason returned and stayed put.

Guests still had rights and she was done with being kept in the dark, and distracted, manipulated. Mike, Tara, Edith, Maude, they were all taking and taking and taking something from her. Even if they were not present, their bullying influences were. Here, at best, she was being humoured, but also deceived. She'd tried to loosen the noose, but the village thwarted her.

It was irrational to think this.

Why did she allow people to affect her so much?

Beside the porch she found vestiges of a path made from greening flagstones that hugged the foundations of the building. Catherine followed the path, often untangling the hem of her skirt from the prickly things with rhubarb-red stalks that intruded upon the narrow space between the house's walls and the garden's overrun borders.

Her progress along the side of the house was enclosed by shadow, and slow, and impeded by great rose stems that adhered to the bricks like tropical vines. She grazed her bare legs, cut the back of one hand. The abrasions stung and her skin itched.

When she rounded the rear corner of the house she was presented with a view of the snarled orchard and lawns grown to the top of her thighs. The flies were also waiting, fat and lazy, corpulent with easy nourishment. But noisy and angry in their defence of some boundary she had unwittingly crossed. They circled, bumped her arms and face. She flailed her hands and thought of going in search of the back door. But the idea of Maude's scorn kept her outside.

Discomfort combined with a fear of being observed from the back of the house, which reared behind her like a dark mountain of dull windows, a hideous thing that watched her with an amused contempt.

Not shod or dressed for the trespass, she made an ungainly zigzag through the garden. As if wading through seawater, she raised her feet high to stride through the grasses entwined with bright weeds. By the time she rounded the rotted arbour and reached the lichen-encrusted fruit trees, her dress was begrimed beyond salvation. Through the trees there was more of the deep grass, and so slippery close to the earth she could not see.

Two stone statues, suffocated by a concealing strata of dead brambles and living ivy, presented themselves like unrelieved guardians. One of the stone pieces had been entirely overwhelmed by the garden. The second statue showed part of a faun's grimacing face. What had they once protected? Most likely the abandoned greenhouse. Beyond the cloudy sea-green panes of glass, that made the structure resemble a neglected aquarium, shadowy growths like ungroomed heads were supported by overburdened necks. Between the heads spiteful fingers at the end of skeletal limbs were poised to claw. Much of the roof was smashed and vegetation tufted out of the gaps, yearning for the sky.

Beside the derelict greenhouse four dilapidated wooden cabinets hummed with energy. The hives. They had once been painted white but were now mostly green and at a tilt.

Beyond the row of hives was an iron gate in the ivy-smothered walls. It led to the meadow. And from the gate to the hives was a worn path that continued past the hives to the far side of the garden.

Catherine paused to scratch at her stinging legs. Maybe Edith had not been lying and some local still dutifully attended to the ruined hives. Maybe Maude had a secret friendship, because she could not imagine Maude having anything else. Perhaps Edith, in her spite and arbitrary use of authority, had forbidden the trysts. It would account for the hostility between mistress and housekeeper. DON'T NEVER COME BACK: a warning about Edith's cruelty?

Her presence close to the hives had been detected and instigated a boisterous activity. The hum inside became an angry buzz. Catherine panicked and lunged to where the grass was worn into the makeshift path. If the threatened bees were riled she would make faster progress back to the house along that route.

But she stopped and coughed when she found herself enshrouded by an awful stench of decomposition. Then recoiled at the suggestion that a carcass lay hidden in the long grass. Something had come here to die.

Fast as she could, over unseen impediments and through slapping weeds, she stumbled past the hives, holding her breath. Level with the cabinet at the end of the row, she realized the stench originated not from the grass, but from the hives. The same hives that were active not with bees, but flies.

Busy like atoms once they were airborne, the flies emerged from the rear of the mouldering cabinets, rose into the air and moved in the direction of the house.

Catherine raced along the path of trodden grass, rounded the orchard and hurried up to the house. She could see a plain wooden door, the back door, beside the small window of Mason's workshop. The door must open onto the utility corridor.

When the terrible smell of micturition subsided, so did her shock. The hives must be filled with kitchen waste. She must have smelled pheasant carcasses and meaty scraps incubating within old beehives. Out here, there wouldn't be a waste collection and they had no means of visiting a tip.

But with so many flies breeding and hatching within the fetid confines of the rotten hives, why was such a practice continued so close to where they lived? And who was the man in white? What would he want with the old hives? She thought of the dark interiors alive with oily maggots and her stomach tried to turn itself inside out. Witnessing violence would not have sickened her more. The flies, the decay, the Red House was an assault against decency. She should leave now. She must leave now. Get her things quickly and go.

The decision to leave quelled her anxiety, as if a valve had suddenly opened to release a huge pressure, and its venting was close to bliss. All here was unhealthy, toxic. Was damaged and infectious. It was a bad place. Some places just were. She'd long suspected it. Here was confirmation. The Red House had corrupted then killed the village. The house and village had expired and should be buried, but clung on. And they'd seeped into her like a poison.

Around her mind her thoughts buzzed incessantly and altered direction as quickly as the flies that pursued her through the wretched garden. Until an awareness of a scrutiny hit her. She looked up as if someone had just barked her name.

Stood rigid, she caught sight of a small white face. At a window amongst so many dark panes within arches like eyebrows raised in disapproval.

Edith in a black wig? No, it had looked like a child.

The face retreated quickly, or was yanked away, but had lingered long enough to give the impression of being masked, or made of cloth. Soft and pressed into the glass, the features had appeared flat, the mouth black and open in surprise. Thick dark curls of hair spilling from a lacy hat made the figure look like a child, a girl. So it had been a doll? The face had been behind a second-storey window, next to the big bay window at the conclusion of the second-floor corridor. So the face had been at the window of her room. Someone had held a doll against the window of her room.

Maude? But why?

Maude had seen her trespassing in the garden. And knew she had seen the flies, and where and how they dispensed with organic kitchen waste. Maybe.

The fright left her exhausted, and she was shivering. They were trying to frighten and disorient her and drive her mad. As mad as they both were. They were unreasonable, they were unhinged, they were sinister people. Leonard had warned her, but not seriously enough.

The back door was unlocked. She slipped off her sodden trainers and passed into the passageway, its floor coated with a plain cloth. At the passage's far end she saw the ruby glow of the hallway. Between there and the back door the corridor remained in shadow.

The first doorway on the right-hand side led into Mason's workshop. Her camera might still be inside the room. She would retrieve it, then her bags and laptop from her room and leave without saying goodbye. And she would go home to her flat, her sanctuary.

Around her the chemical stink cloyed. In her mind the flies buzzed, and she could still taste the taint of the hives. In her imagination, dim straggle-haired figures stood up, over and over again, behind dirty windows at the back of damp rooms.

No more.

The door to Mason's workshop was open, perhaps airing after she'd been ill. She could see the jars of chemicals and formulas, the cruel hooks and tools, the workbench and horrible galvanized tub. And there was her camera where she had left it. All was as she remembered that morning save one thing. This other *thing* had not been present earlier.

She approached and walked around the object. Using what of her available mind was not taken over with anxiety, she tried to work out what it was.

The shape was adult-sized and carved from a block of wood. Balsa wood turned by hand into the torso of a female figure. It had a crude bust and narrowed at the waist. At mid-thigh level, the form had been levelled off and mounted on a black iron stand that descended to a three-toed base. Cloth arms connected to a metal and canvas harness were attached to the shoulders of the carving. At the end of the arms, heavy ceramic hands with chipped fingers hung inert. She thought of them clapping, and shuddered.

Had it been positioned here to confront her, for some unfathomable reason? Another unpleasant barrier to inhibit her? Catherine moved away from the ugly effigy and picked up her camera.

A tiny scream of wheels moved through the corridor outside the workshop. It gave her a start. She turned to confront the doorway into which Edith was wheeled.

The elderly woman's skinny hands were gloved and clutched the handrests either in rage, or with a determination not to be spilled from the chair. She looked awful, drained and haggard. A waterproof cape was draped over a heavy tweed skirt dwarfing her frail body. What was visible of the outfit reminded Catherine of what female motorists wore before the war, the first war.

The ghastly white face was again overburdened by the terrible cottage-loaf wig. And Maude's face seemed peculiarly ape-like as it glared beneath the mannish haircut, out of the darkness behind Edith.

Edith studied Catherine with her cloudy, disapproving eyes. 'Did you see all you wanted to see?'

'I came back for my camera.'

'What were you thinking? We've been out there. We couldn't find you.'

'There was no need. I just wanted some air.' The idea of the two horrid figures, one pushing the other through the rain, searching for her, made her want to scream.

'One should never leave this house so unprepared. Maude will draw you a bath. And then we will proceed with the fitting. Your clothes are ruined and it is about time you wore something suitable. The pageant is the highlight of our local calendar, and no guest of the Red House will be tolerated looking like that. Follow me.'

The information or order, or whatever it was, came quickly. The will behind the voice was indomitable, but brittle and close to rage. She was trapped again, coerced by muscular social currents she was unable to evade and was unequal to. Edith's horrid white face and voice filled her head. It did not seem possible to resist the woman or deny her anything.

'If it's all the same—'

'Maude will bathe you on the second floor.'

'I need to get back.'

'Back! Back where?'

Catherine swallowed the constriction that always occupied her throat before those glaring red-rimmed eyes. 'I need . . . I'd like to go home now.'

Edith grinned with what looked like a bored delight at her resistance. 'You'll catch your death. You're shivering.'

'I'm all right. I'll—'

'Out of the question. We don't have much time to get you ready. I'm far too old to go through this again, and I do not have the time for your stubbornness. Everyone will be so disappointed with your lack of enthusiasm.'

'Everyone? I've been to the village. It's empty.'

'Empty?' Edith turned her frowning face to Maude. 'What does she mean?'

Maude stared at Catherine in disapproval tinged with pity.

'Our local traditions take a great deal of time to prepare. And you are expected. It would be selfish, heartless, to disappoint us all. Don't you think?'

'Ma'am, please. I've been here two days and I still haven't begun the valuation. There are other things I—'

'There will be time enough to admire our things. After the pageant. Now come along, dear. I am not accustomed to repeating myself.'

THIRTY-THREE

'Why do you need to measure my head?'

Catherine yawned, again. Sleep pulled at her edges and softening corners. Maude's hard hands prompted her body to stay upright with short tugs and prods whenever she felt herself start to lean. She was sick of apologizing. 'Sorry' when she swayed. 'Sorry' as she blinked herself back awake. 'Sorry' as she moved an arm to stifle a yawn.

Country air and the four miles she'd walked to and from the village had left her dead on her feet. The deep hot water of the bath she had taken in Edith's own bathroom had been preceeded by a bowl of mutton broth she'd wolfed down with a portion of home-made bread in the dining room. The medicine Maude spooned into her mouth for her chill had been bitter but instantly warming. And now she'd stopped moving, her head and body felt heavy and she desperately wanted to sleep. In her dimming thoughts, she was concerned at how tired, at how unfit she was, but a confrontation about skipping dinner and retiring early had to be risked. 'I'm sorry, but . . . I'm so tired. And I need to—'

'Not long now, dear.' Edith turned her face to Maude, who fussed behind Catherine, and she urged the housekeeper to hurry with no more than a frown. 'And then we shall get you to bed. You need to rest after this morning's foolish escapade.' Edith's voice softened, was almost soothing, as if Edith Mason was calmed by the sight of Catherine stood before the long oval mirror, dressed in white like a daughter who was to be a bride.

And Catherine nearly thanked her host for granting her sleep. She would go to bed, have a nap, then resume . . . no, begin the valuation . . . No . . . she would leave later, tonight. Her thoughts swam and sank without trace.

She had been escorted from the dining room to Edith's own bathroom on the second floor, then collected again and returned to the utility floor. She'd felt like a patient in an old hospital. So many stairs, doors to be unlocked, aprons and long skirts swishing, wheels turning.

And the one-piece dress she now wore had been waiting upon the wooden bust in Violet Mason's 'sewing room'. A place sealed behind a locked door close to M. H. Mason's workshop.

Wicker baskets overflowing with costumes lined one wall of the room, beneath shelves cluttered with paints and craft materials. Carpentry had not been beyond Violet Mason either. Unusual for a woman of her time, but the vintage tools, and the bench still littered with twine and timber, buttons and cloth, revealed evidence that great labours had been undertaken in the room to support her brother's vision.

Catherine's own vision swam. So she focussed on the dress, bowing her head to see the embroidered cotton. From the 1920s, she thought, with the elbow-length sleeves and no waist. Edith had said, 'Nothing else will fit you. My mother was petite. She carried me at the time she wore this.'

She had been too sleepy to be offended, though the insult helped to revive her enough to become aware of the dress's scent. From the ancient gown wafted a fragrance of stale perfume trapped in fine cloth, and of the wooden furniture that had stored the garment for decades. The fabric was unmarked, but had sallowed to an ivory tinge along the seams and at the edge of the lace hems.

She disliked the transforming effect of the dress in the dark mirror. Bare-legged, her hair tousled where it had dried without styling, under dim coppery light from an overhead bulb, the dress faded her sense of herself. But also distinguished her anew with a fresh identity, as though she existed in a photograph taken from an old cardboard box after a funeral, from a collection where the bronze images of mustachioed men in uniform, and little girls in ribbons and white dresses, suddenly confronted the onlooker with a sense of origin, and an insignificance they had not considered before.

Behind her image in the mirror, Edith's bleached face hovered, disembodied from the avian form so tightly wrapped in a high-necked gown of black silk. Maude must have changed her mistress while Catherine bathed in the cast-iron tub, filled with steaming green water and fragrant with salts she could not identify, that was waiting for her and most welcome after her meal. She wished she was still inside the perfumed water now, soaking, dozing.

Her eyes closed. She tried to remember the bathroom to stay awake. It had a bath made no later than the 1880s. A tub mounted on ball feet. A unit with an old steel needle and spray shower fixed around the enormous taps. She'd never seen one before. Carved mahogany cabinets on the walls. Tiles hand-painted with wildflowers. Like taking a bath in someone's study.

Maude jerked her awake.

'Sorry.'

Aches had crept into her spine and her skin was sensitive. The sun's warmth had reached her too late and she had a chill. She'd never been good in the rain. The white noise of anxiety and the exhaustion of London had permanently impaired her immune system. Maybe the terrible stench of the workshop and the hives had stayed inside her, too, poisoned her. But she had no temperature. Her stomach was fine. She had difficulty swallowing, though. Her throat was hot and dry.

She needed to go home. Needed to be in her own bed, dosed with paracetamol. She wanted to call her mother.

Was she well enough to drive? Once she was in bed, after a few hours' rest, maybe she could leave a note and slip away. And go home.

Before it was too late.

Where had that thought come from? She mustn't let herself think like that. She'd been told. She knew what to do when she had thoughts like that.

The dress was removed, slipped over her head. She was quickly covered in a quilted dressing gown.

Maude helped her back to her room as if *she* was the old woman who needed care. And once Catherine was settled in bed, she noticed Maude's eyes were wet with tears. It was the last thing she saw before her eyes closed of their own accord, and her mind turned over and slid backwards into a bottomless and irresistible unconsciousness.

THIRTY-FOUR

'You's comin' up the big house wiv us, Caff?'

Catherine stood up in the wet den and started to cry.

Up on the hill of the special school, the boy with the painted wooden face held the hand of her best friend, Alice, who had been missing for three months. One lens of Alice's glasses shone in the grey light of late afternoon.

Catherine was forbidden to come here. She'd returned to remember Alice.

The last time she visited the den, that distant, bright time with sunlight bathing the ecstasy of finishing a school year, Alice went through the hole Catherine made in the green fence. In July. It was September now, and only four months until Christmas.

Alice started down the grassy slope towards the new fence the council had built. 'They's callin', Caff. Hear it?'

And that was exactly what Alice said to her as Catherine poured invisible tea into greening plastic teacups at the beginning of the summer on the very day Alice vanished. And precisely what Catherine had told her parents when she arrived home, wet through and crying. It was also what she had told Alice's mother and the police ladies and her nan.

Catherine had heard the call back then too, just like she heard it now. 'Greensleeves' from a distant ice-cream van.

Coming out of those red-brick buildings with plywood over the windows.

That first time, Alice said, 'I's going, Caff. Comin'?' but nothing else. Splashing through the stream and scrabbling up the riverbank to the hole in the fence before Catherine could stop her; up the grassy bank the little figure had climbed on her hands and knees, as Catherine stood motionless with fright behind the wire fence. She'd whispered for Alice to come back. 'Don't, Alice. Don't. We're not supposed to. You're not allowed to.'

But Alice had continued up the grass bank to the school where the air was going all wavy up there, over the black roofs, because the special schoolchildren were also moving up the far side of the hill to the buildings. Alice hadn't seen the ragged shapes intent on meeting her at the summit. And Alice never turned around once, or even seemed to hear Catherine, who stayed behind and gripped the links of the fence.

When Alice disappeared from view amongst the buildings that the other children had reached first and hid within, Catherine wet herself in fright. It was the last time she saw Alice.

Catherine had run and fallen, run and fallen, all the way home. Then shut herself inside her room and stayed there until Alice's mum came round.

But today Alice was back. And coming closer to the green fence, while the boy with the painted wooden face stayed up on the hill and watched from the distance. And it really was Alice, with the same tangled hair, the pale bespectacled face. Only Alice was happy now.

'There's nice kids up there, Caff. There's Margaret and

Annie and all them others. Nice kids. Like us. Come away, come away wiv us, Caff. They's got nice fings to eat. Ladies in dresses, and flowers. They's got mices fightin' battles. Cats is princesses. Foxes wear hats. Them puppet shows from olden times. Everyfing. Always sunny there, Caff. There's a rabbit that talks and a monkey in a dress. Better than down 'ere.'

Catherine came awake and gasped for air. And some of the dream came out with her, then dissolved and left her thinking of being taken for tests, seeing specialists, being diagnosed as a slow learner. A Mongol, a retard, a thicky.

The bullying at the second school was worse than the first, mainly because the tormenting skills of infants hadn't sufficiently developed in junior school. She remembered feeling so sick with nerves each morning for the best part of two years that she could barely eat and spent most of her playtimes and dinner breaks hidden in various parts of the small school.

As a child she prayed and wished and prayed, until she gave herself headaches, that the children of the special school would come back and take her away like they did Alice. She'd had her chance when Alice came back for her that afternoon in September, and she'd just relived it in her sleep as clearly as the day it happened. She'd even remembered all of the words.

Had she been asleep or was it another trance? Consciousness had withdrawn so far inside her, the external world was still blurred.

These weren't memories, she urgently reminded herself. These were childhood fantasies constructed to explain the abduction of Alice. Her friend had never said anything about the Red House on the day she imagined the little girl had come back for her. Or had she? She didn't know.

The time the boy with the wooden face came into the playground to save her, and the reason why all the children suddenly stopped bullying her, as well as the belief that the teachers were frightened of her, was not real either. None of it.

She felt nauseous in the darkness of the room, as if her brain had just slipped sideways. The slide had been accompanied by a fear of falling, and had jolted her back to the world. Her chin was wet with what she guessed was blood. Thick vestiges of the trance were unclear, but stayed trapped behind her eyes.

Moving into a sitting position hurt her back, her neck, and she suffered a sense of overbalancing. Either that or the room tilted and the bed moved along the floor. She could not see her hands, arms, or the bed in the darkness.

Her skin shivered inside the long gown provided at her bedside. Accepting the nightdress had felt like dependence, or even sublimation. Another item she had been too tired to resist. The ancient garment was ruffled into wet creases along her spine.

The bed she'd awoken in was also dampened by sweat gone cold. Her eyes had been open for some time, too, but she had not been awake. A sense of her jaw being active lingered around her mouth. She must have been talking or crying in her trance.

The bitter, chalky residue left by Maude's tonic for her chill grew stronger on her tongue. She swallowed and her throat burned. The room stank of wet wood and unclean air.

She groped about the bedside table for the lamp, for the water Maude provided. Her fingertips found the glass and she guzzled the stale liquid, but she could not fit her other hand under the lampshade to find the switch and couldn't see what she was doing. Her fumbling bumped her phone, which fell off the bedside table and thumped the rug below. As the handset bounced the small screen lit up, casting a pale-green glow over the bed.

Faint underwater light bathed a dense black shape at the foot of her bed, upright, but poised as if to lean over. Either that or it had just retracted from reaching for her.

Her phone settled on its front and smothered the frail light of the screen, leaving her inside a greater darkness than before. Catherine dropped the glass onto the bedspread.

She couldn't breathe for fright. Her limbs had seized. Beside the thump of a heart that felt too big for her chest, she could think of nothing but the presence at the foot of her bed, one that must have stood inches from her feet as she slept.

Kicking at the sheets she twisted onto her knees, upsetting the glass, which fell and rolled off the mattress to the rug, and onto the wooden floorboards. Around her skull the sound of the rolling glass circled, as if it were inside her head grinding through her panic.

Her useless fingers could not find the neck of the lamp. She was certain the trespasser was swiftly bustling around the outside of the bed, was moments from touching her in the lightless void of the bedroom. When her desperate fingers found the lamp switch, the act of turning the light on took what was left of her strength. Dizzy with terror, she thought she might faint.

Ox-blood walls reappeared around the bed. On the brink of a scream Catherine turned to face the intruder. Her vision swam and settled. The figure was still there, immobile, faceless, waiting.

The dressmaker's dummy. And hung upon shoulders that were positioned as if the missing head was proudly raised, was the dress Edith had picked out for her to wear to the pageant.

The crashing of relief left her panting like a tired dog. A dull concussive ache returned to the place behind her eyes, as did the burning sensation in her throat. She was nauseous too, as if whatever was in her system was wearing off and leaving side effects.

What had they given her to drink? Were the ingredients of the medicinal concoction so old they'd become toxic? Laudanum? A tincture of opium, wasn't that bitter tasting? The very idea they took opiates here wasn't implausible. She imagined old, frail, untrained hands pouring a white powder into the liquid she had struggled to get down. But she was soporific long before she swallowed the 'tonic'. Something in her food then? Hadn't Edith said as much about Maude?

The mute housekeeper must have carried the dress and dummy inside the room as she slept. And Catherine had been talking to the dummy, mistaken the vague presence of a dressed bust as company, jabbered to it in her delirium. If she wasn't so shaken she would have felt foolish.

She fingered her face. Her forehead and cheeks were cold, she had no temperature and wasn't feverish. Her state was akin to waking up drunk. But wakefulness did not dispel unease. She had heard no one enter the room, nor did she have any recollection of a light being turned on by whoever had come in. How was that possible? And why was it necessary to bring the horrid maternity dress, that Edith's mother had worn nearly a century before, in here while she slept?

She felt too woozy and too weak to decide whether this was another strange arrangement, some protocol of the Red House, or whether it ranked as another sinister tactic to unsettle her.

Catherine sank into the pillows, shifted her position to the portion of the bed not moist and creased. She pulled her knees up and into her belly, cradled her head with her hands and tried to figure out what to do. With the harsh grit of Maude's medicine tainting her gums and tongue, she passed into, and back out of, and then into a semblance of sleep.

Catherine roused again with a sense of her own voice loud within the room. Her eyes were already wide open when she came to.

She rose from the bedclothes gasping from another delirious episode that felt uncomfortably similar to a trance. From deep sleep into a trance again? Never happened before. They only occurred when she was absent-minded, but awake.

The second unbearably vivid dream receded. Though not quickly enough. A group of small figures had been stood in a row at the foot of her bed. Or they were children wearing masks. Faces she recalled in unpleasant flashes.

She flopped against the headboard with her face clutched in her hands to stop the swaying of her vision and the motion sickness it caused.

Two of the figures had been smiling and holding the ceramic hands of the dressmaker's dummy. A girl in a tatty bonnet, and a figure with the stature of a boy and the bearing of a doll. Real hair had been threaded into his colourless porcelain scalp. An old-fashioned tailored suit had made a tight fit on his small limbs, like the boy had outgrown the suit or been given a younger child's clothes. The girl's face within the bonnet was too withdrawn to offer anything but the glimmer of a bony chin and one row of discoloured wooden teeth.

But in the nightmare, the dummy's shoulders had carried a head. A white face. With moist black eyes, partly obscured by a veil attached to a wide-brimmed hat. The hat had been decorated with dark flowers like an ancient wedding cake.

Among the other childish figures, there had been a wrinkled and leathery black face, the eyes white and horribly eager. A small mouth in the tar-black face had been open, gleefully revealing yellow peg teeth. The ape from the film that made off with Strader's head?

Another of the small shapes looked to have suffered an accident, or been misused. Its pottery face was discoloured, cracked, and there were small punctures or scars. The Master of the Revels?

Elsewhere amongst the crowd, she retained a suggestion of uneven whiskers sprouting from a threadbare head of a large hare. It must have been a mask concealing something much worse underneath. The face hidden by the hare's pelt had painted wooden eyes, adrift from the sockets of the outer skin.

Behind the figures she'd received the impression of tails swishing with impatience, and then whipping with excitement for the entire time she spoke to them. They'd riposted with nonsense and rhyme she couldn't remember in any detail, but their jaunty words had made her want to get up and skip around the room like a child.

Catherine trembled for a while, her eyes searching every inch of the visible room, until the impact of the dream lessened and she was certain she was alone.

She had dreamed of the dolls in Edith's bedroom, and in her state amalgamated the dolls with the murky features of Mason's puppets from the BBC film. *Please let it be that.* If she could rely on one thing in her life, it would be her imagination turning against her in the worst circumstances.

Her body now felt as desiccated as one of Mason's preserved creations. The medicine she had been given – *but for what?* – maintained the mineral rime around her tongue and lips. It was all she could taste, and she was desperate to swill it away with water. Her glass lay empty upon the floor.

Each step she took towards the enormous washstand fired a jolt of pain through her skull. She touched her arms and face, which registered in her mind as being hot and tender, but were actually cold and clammy. Her nightie and underwear were wet. She picked up and clutched the dressing gown around her shivering body.

There was no water in the basin of the washstand, or in the jug beneath the bowl. No taps, it wasn't plumbed. She thought she might cry. She needed painkillers for the incessant judders in her head, not some ancient sickening tonic concocted from stale ingredients.

Nausea took her back to her bed, where she sat and peered at the door. She would have to go and find the nearest bathroom and source of water, a medicine cabinet. What was the time? Her phone claimed it was 2:30 a.m. *Is that all?* Now she thought about it, her writhing and gibbering seemed to have stretched into days. Catherine closed her eyes. If they had poisoned her she should try and be sick.

They had drugged her to take her out of her life, out of the world. The dress on the dummy was a new skin, a new identity. They were refashioning her, to become one of them.

Stop it!

She had a chill, a virus. New places, new bacteria.

That's all.

Stress has made it worse. That's all.

That's all it is.

Outside her room she again failed to find the light switches on the walls between the doors in the long passage. There was a switch at the mouth of the corridor by the landing and stairwell. She was sure of this, but by day had previously been guided by the window overlooking the garden at the passage's end. The window was no help now, so only the glow of her bedroom door and phone screen guided her through the heavy darkness that pressed inwards and swallowed the Red House. The lightlessness had crept inside and filled the old spaces, clothing timbers and bricks. But with the dark came a shift in character. One she remembered noticing before.

The house was colder than it had been during the previous night, as if the building was now open to the elements. She could smell damp in fabric and wood, the pungency of black spores on water-softened plaster, as if the garden's decay had seeped inside the building. Even the unseen floor felt rough beneath her bare soles. So vivid was the change in character, within the pathetic halo of greenish light cast by her phone screen, she had to make sure the Red House was as she remembered it to be, by pushing her face an inch from the wall to see the wallpaper's pattern.

When she found it, the air of the closest bathroom was icy. As though her life depended upon the tooth-aching water, she bent to gulp at the ropes of freezing liquid that thundered from the tap above the sink. She needed to dilute the disorientation, the inebriation of illness and sleepiness.

Behind the wall, pipes juddered, clanged.

Too ill to care about the noise, she left the bathroom, but made sure the door stayed open, same with her bedroom door, so at least some of the grubby light fell into the passageway from two lit rooms. It would allow her to do more than stumble through the hideous absence.

How could they stand it here? Perhaps darkness was more of a natural state than daylight. Weren't stars just pieces of glittering debris slowly winking out on their journey to entropy? So what came after?

Stop it!

No light pollution here. This is how it is in the country.

By the time she reached the landing about the stairwell, a door below clicked open, and then closed. Briefly, a dim but comforting glow appeared downstairs. Catherine paused to listen. A second door opened more slowly, deeper inside the vast building.

Maude.

She wanted to be reassured by the idea of the housekeeper being up and about at this hour, but wasn't. Would the scowling drudge be of any assistance with anything but another home-made remedy, or poison?

But these women were old, their joints must ache, Maude limped, Edith was in a wheelchair, so there had to be modern pain relief somewhere inside the house. And she must take enough of it to drive home. In strange dark houses you needed a goal, and she made this her purpose as she descended the first flight of stairs. If need be, she'd search every one of their bathrooms and kitchen cupboards.

On the way down to the first floor, she gripped the banister rail. The mere effect of moving this far left her breathless and dizzy.

Peeking over the railing, some thin light was reflected off the polished wood of the hall floor. Light originating from the adjoining utility corridor that contained the tableau, workshops, perhaps the kitchen, and Maude's room.

The first floor was dark. But a few feet of sight was afforded by her phone screen, so at least she could see each step ahead of her.

She moved across the first-floor landing to the next set of stairs, her eyes imploring the oblivion that encroached upon the feeble glow of her phone, which returned nothing to her eyes besides the glimmers of brass door-handles. She was at the top of the next staircase when the movement below began.

She peered over the banister and caught sight of a small shadow fall across the faint light on the hall floor. A scuffle of cloth accompanied the motion. Instinct told her that announcing her position was a bad idea.

And there it was again, what she understood to be a scampering, close to the floor, in pursuit, she intuited, of the first figure. Neither noise resembled Maude's distinctive side-to-side shuffle. The noise suggested a small group or pack of animals.

Cats?

Rats.

Catherine stifled a scream. The Red House could be teeming with rats at night. Had she not heard them last night too? A fitting revenge for M. H. Mason's extermination of the species, but not a vengeance that offered Catherine a shred of comfort while on the stairs.

The screen of her phone winked off. As it periodically did to save the battery if she didn't keep the pitiful glow activated. And just before the screen light came back on, there was no question in her mind that footsteps had just announced themselves on the staircase behind her.

She turned quickly, lost balance and thumped down four steps, flailing at the banister with her free hand. Before unintentionally casting her phone away, the handset lit up the silhouette of a small head. And what might have been hands covered its face.

The fact the figure behind her had been so close was worse than what she thought she had actually seen. Whimpering on her hands and knees she cast about to retrieve the phone. She snatched it up and held it before her face fearfully, as if expecting a blow from out of the darkness above her.

The pallid phosphorescence of the screen cast its meagre range onto empty wooden steps and the banister rail. There was nothing there and could not have been. She raised the phone higher and her own shadow stretched up the empty staircase wall.

A mind made strange with inebriation in oppressive darkness could see anything it wanted. Despite telling herself this, she struggled to rid her imagination of the notion that a small head, further up inside the darkness, was now turned in her direction and watching her.

Silence returned to the stairwell. She chose to suppress, rather than dwell on, the scent of cold outdoor air brought in on someone's clothes that gathered around her. Catherine peered over the banister rail, but saw and heard nothing more from down there. Rodents were scared of humans, *weren't they?* Clutching her phone as if it was a flame and her only hope of rescue and survival, she continued down.

Stood in the middle of the hall, she looked up and into the stairwell. The darkness was total. A swirl of vertigo, and a panic that she could be hoisted up and into the space by something above, seized her. When the fear passed another replaced it. Whatever she thought had been following her down the stairs might drop upon her, from up there.

At the walls of the hall, she pawed the wooden panels looking for light switches. Something that was becoming an unpleasant habit for her in this house. There were at least three switches down here. She had noticed them – *hadn't she?* – between the framed photographs. One of which her phone screen illumined. A black-and-white picture taken of the Masons in their garden.

In the photograph they appeared older and thinner than she'd seen them before, but were dressed as formally as ever. Sunlight reflected off their bespectacled eyes. Violet Mason wore a white hat to match her dress and carried a parasol. M. H. Mason wore a black suit. Behind the Masons' straight forms, some of the trees were hazy as if moving in a breeze. What was visible of the puppet theatre between the Masons' heads was blurred, as if active with motion too rapid for the shutter speed of the camera. Either a child, or a figure on the backdrop, seemed to be running sideways. There was a small black arm and a distorted head emerging from the unclear portion of the photograph.

She'd not looked at many of the pictures closely during her tour with Edith, but wished she had done so. If she had, she might not be on her own in the darkness looking at one right now.

Towards the dimly glowing mouth of the passage leading to the service area, she moved with her arms stretched out.

At the end of the corridor, on the left-hand side, was a slot of rectangular light, as if a small lamp were switched on in a large room with the door mostly closed. From here, the thin light on the hall floor that she had seen from upstairs originated.

A cold draught swept her hands and face in a steady stream. She suspected the door to the garden, at the far end of the corridor, had also been opened upon the cold night. The current of chilly air was too concentrated to be coming from a room indoors.

The draught built into a breeze and she stifled the idea that it wasn't a door or window open at the end of the passage, but a much bigger portal ahead of her in the darkness.

The moving air was either entirely without sound, or her own hoarse breath was so loud about her face she was drowning out the sound of the wind.

Stumbling through what now smelled like an unlit tunnel, her situation began to feel like she'd passed out of the Red House and was now journeying beneath its walls. The idea of being beneath the house seemed far worse than the frightful apprehension of being inside it. Only the approaching luminance of the partially open door assured her she was still inside the building.

'Maude. Maude,' she called, in a voice just above a whisper. But didn't know if she was announcing herself or calling for help. She felt an urge to scream, and a competing urge to sit down in petrified silence and to wait for whatever came next from out of the darkness. Why was she even down here? She should have stayed in bed.

With her phone screen creating a small, weak sphere about her face, she almost broke into a run to reach the partially open door. Because someone must be awake. It was her only motivation for putting one foot in front of the other, and so quickly now.

Mere feet from the door, the intensification of the chemical pungency hit her full and stinging in the face and brought her to a stop. The stench came from the entrance to what she knew, but didn't want to acknowledge, was Mason's workshop. *Why was it open at this hour?* The light bleeding thinly from the space beyond the door now resembled light issued from ashes glowing in a gate, or a small desk lamp with a crimson shade.

With one hand clasped across her mouth and nose, she peered through the gap.

And looked away. She heard herself whimper and say, 'God.'

She glanced back into the dim ruby air and again saw the vertebrae of an impossibly curved spine, and so pronounced beneath the dead white skin, the bone joints seemed in danger of breaking through the bloodless flesh of the small figure hunched over inside the galvanized metal tub. Mason's ethanol bath. In which, what must have been Edith sat facing forward.

Without the cottage-loaf wig of rags and false hair, the back of a mostly hairless skull confronted Catherine. The shoulders were so narrow and pinched and the scapula so defined, she was not sure anything so wizened could still be living. But it was the mere glimpse of the scar, from a long dorsal incision, reaching from the nape of the scrawny neck to the black water's lap-lap-lapping edge, for which her shock and revulsion were mostly saved.

A second figure she could not see, but heard sobbing, was also inside the room.

Maude?

Catherine fell as much as fled back through the oblivion of the utility corridor to the front door of the house. In the surreal confusion of her partial sight, the image of that emaciated form shivering within the black water hounded her. And she knew she would rather risk freezing to death outside than spend any more of this night under the same roof as these grim creatures that conducted such ghastly rituals in the early hours of the morning, in a house alive with rats.

For the first time in her friendship with Leonard, she felt hot knots of anger towards him.

The two great front doors of the Red House were locked. And whoever had locked the doors had taken the keys.

THIRTY-FIVE

When she awoke, the bedroom was still lit by the small lamp.

Catherine sat up slowly and held her head in both hands until the swoops settled. The concussive ache in her head had lifted, as had the shivering and sensitivity of her skin. Maybe the hot constriction in her throat had awoken her, because the need to gulp at cold water was urgent again.

A great distance of time and space separated her from the memory of running through the house to her bed. Her recollections of the previous night were murky. While more conscious than she had been in some time, she still struggled to distinguish between what had been a nightmare or delirium, and what had been real. Poor bald, scarred Edith, that had been real. *Or had it?* The children in the costumes a dream? And the mannequin with the head? *Impossible.* Just part of a nightmare.

Illness, being drugged with what the old fools thought of as medicine, must have opened a distant region of her mind. The part she used for dreaming had accelerated its activity when she was half awake. Her trances verified she was susceptible to this. And God only knew she'd had a few of those. Until she could get out of the building and get home, she could not afford to consider her experience to be anything else. Her sanity was dependent upon it.

She opened the heavy drapes and looked out at an indigo sky from which the light dissolved. Catherine quickly checked the time on her phone. 8 p.m. *Not possible.*

Surely it was 8 a.m. and the last vestiges of night were surrendering to the dawn. She had dropped the phone on the stairs the night before, her fingers had been clumsy about the handset's controls, she might have accidentally reset the clock.

Weak and unsteady on her feet, she opened and fired up her laptop on the writing table. Like the phone the computer showed a red battery level. But she had been recharging them. She remembered doing it.

She reattached both chargers to the wall sockets. Even though there had never been a signal here, the idea of the phone and laptop being lifeless suddenly seemed too terrible to consider when surrounded by such ponderous antiquity.

Once the laptop screen loaded, she was confronted by the horrible shock of having slept all day following the troubled night.

8 p.m.

Her stomach was cavernous and burned with hunger. It's why she was so clumsy, so weak, why her thoughts were struggling to coordinate beyond bursts of clarity in a fog of bewilderment. She'd been out of it for twenty-four hours with little water and without food.

The door to her room was locked from the inside. At the thought of being here again after dark, she twisted the key then yanked the door open. And stared down at an antique silver tray, filled with cutlery, plates, two silver tureens. An envelope rested between the teapot and butter dish. Beside it, a red hatbox, with a folded cream garment laid upon its lid, and a pair of narrow white slippers.

Carefully, Catherine brought the tray inside and placed it on the writing table. The tureens were cold. But she'd eat the old hat before she touched another morsel of Maude's food. Where did they even buy it from? The presence of food in the house was incongruous. Nothing, nothing at all, was making sense. Three days to be upset by a horrid film, frightened repeatedly, chased through the grounds by flies, to suffer the kind of delusions she attributed to the insane . . . Edith in that metal tub. The smells. The stairs. 'Stop it. Stop it. Stop it.'

She had come here as a valuer of antiques, but that role now seemed so distant as to be irrelevant. She hadn't valued a single item. Because they were still testing her, assessing her. Maybe no stranger from the outside world could just saunter in here and make off with the kind of haul that would make international news. Or was all of this preparation?

But for what?

Her hunch about Edith's dementia extended into fears of a dreadful complicity, as if she had made an agreement with something poorly explained to her, or deliberately concealed.

Catherine could smell the delicate floral perfume wafting from the ancient lace of the gown upon the wooden dummy. It tried to insinuate its presence inside her head. She fingered the yellowing cotton of the hat; the silk flowers piled about its brim were brittle with age. The embroidered shawl was probably a hundred years old and even touching it made her shudder. So small and stiff were the handmade shoes she

231

could tell at a glance she wouldn't get three toes inside them.

She tore open the envelope and drew out the stiff paper, watermarked with Mason's initials. The same stationery posted to the office and hand-delivered to her home.

She struggled through the contents of the note, written in Edith's unsteady hand. When she finished she slumped on the bed and stared at the dark window.

My Dear Catherine

We did not wish to disturb your rest, but have been called away to supervise tonight's events. Maude has left you supper. Refreshments will be provided after the performance of The Martyrs of Rod and String. A more modern drama from the Caroline period. We do trust you are now well enough to join us. Our theatre is a spectacular local tradition, with origins pre-dating the first Roman footstep on British soil. Though exactly when they started I cannot tell you. My uncle thought he knew and told me, but I forget.

Your dress has been altered. A hat and shawl have been provided. Do take care of my mother's things, they will not be easy to replace. We begin when the first stars unveil.

With kind regards, your fond friend
Edith Mason.

P.S. There was a gentleman caller, a Michael, here this afternoon. A very agitated and persistent individual, who seemed keen to speak with you. We told him you were unwell and resting. And he brought a girl with him who had far too much to say for herself. I did not catch her name, though that hardly matters. We sent them away to the pageant to wait for you. In future will you please inform us when we are to receive visits from strangers! I thought I had made myself perfectly clear about our desire for privacy.

Was he truly here? Had Mike come for her? The very idea of him being close made her feel sicker. No, he had not come to save her, because he had come with a girl. *Her*. Mike had brought *her*, Tara, with him. Such an act of feckless cruelty suddenly suggested to her that she had never really known him, and may only have been prey to her own wishful thinking for the entire duration of their relationship. How could she have been so wrong? On what level, and in what way, were his actions even remotely acceptable?

And why was he here? How did he find it? Leonard! Leonard may have confronted him and let it slip out. Or even told him she needed help, reassurance, a friendly face, something like that, after she'd made the emotional phone call to her boss at the end of her first day. The very idea of Leonard interfering made her furious. It would mean Leonard had ignored her wishes, and thought he knew what was best for her. If he still wanted to sell M. H. Mason's shit, after what she had been through, she'd wheel him here and he could do the valuation himself. Time for her boss to step up because she was stepping down.

Tara was now within the orbit of the Red House, and its considerable treasures. So maybe this had nothing to do with Leonard, because Mike may have already told Tara about what Catherine was valuing here, the Mason originals, and Tara had insisted they come here. *Bitch*. Tara would have smelled the house's immaculate antiquities from the porch.

233

Tara had taken her boyfriend, but that was not enough. She'd be pitching for a television documentary by tomorrow morning. While she'd been reduced to delirium and a half-crazed paranoia, Tara had come to spoil her and Leonard Osberne's exclusivity.

She suddenly felt so deeply persecuted she thought herself condemned. Her past, her trances and her enemies all seemed to have gathered here, in some dreadful critical mass, specifically for the purpose of destroying what was left of her mind. She sensed a powerful controlling force, behind her life, tactically planning her downfall. Maybe it had always been there, as she had often suspected, and she was a hapless marionette in a cruelty play that began the day she'd been born and given away by her natural mother.

'Oh Christ. Oh Jesus Christ.'

She felt unstable. Dangerously volatile, like she could hurt herself out of sheer frustration.

Clothes, bag, camera, laptop, phone. *Get your shit together, girl, and just go.*

No, wait. To flee in her car would mean passing through the hideous village and the pageant. But there was no other way out. The Red House was a trap at the end of the lane. The village a gatehouse.

They all wanted her at the pageant. The festival needed a fool. A star attraction to be mocked, betrayed, and deceived.

But who could possibly be down there? The idea of a pageant in that place was patently ridiculous. Another delusion of two twisted old women who'd either drugged her, or made her condition worse to keep her here. What she'd seen, or thought she'd seen, of the village's residents weren't fit to participate in anything but their own funerals.

She hurriedly packed her things away, then turned to the chest of drawers to retrieve her clothes.

The drawer was empty. Her clothes were gone. Had been taken. Her dirty laundry had been inside a tote bag, and there had been one day of fresh clothing. Catherine looked at the hideous white gown upon the manikin's torso and swallowed a sob. Slumped on the bed beside her belongings, she drew her fingers down her pale face.

She had to stay strong, not make bad decisions. *When you are ill, and on your own, you can't afford to.* Hadn't she learned this the hard way before? And was she now alone within the Red House?

THIRTY-SIX

Tonight she was transformed into a woman in white. Had become a flitting spirit from another era, barefoot like an urchin, playing a part in a performance foisted upon her because the house seemed intent on turning everything into a drama.

She was wanted at the pageant, where the rest of the cast and audience had gathered, but she would not go. She would speed through the village in her car and leave them all behind without a word, leave everything behind if necessary, even Leonard, who had introduced her to this mess and may have brought serpents back into her life. She could even go missing. Had often fantasized about disappearing, as if such an act of desperation presented great life-changing opportunities, not tragedy. It was time to improvise, to tear up the script.

But she would not leave before she explored this terrible old house and understood it, demystified it. Edith may have scattered the truth like crumbs but an opportunity to better know the Red House, and the instability of its occupants, had presented itself. For the sake of her own long-term sanity, she could not risk her mind's entrapment beneath this spiky roof.

And nor could she deny that she was still captivated by the mystery, by the sheer impossibility that such a place could exist in the modern world. She *needed* to know how this house was possible. *Here*, the house was still *here*. Like this. With Edith and Maude inside it. Who felt like a facade for something else, behind the scenes.

But what?

If any of these doors were unlocked, she would go through them.

Catherine walked through the Red House and switched on every light she passed. She told herself she would not be frightened. She would be as alert and as focussed as her enemies were. Time to turn back the tide of fear and bafflement, a tide scouring her shores since she'd arrived, and for a lifetime before that too.

The dull pressure of the receding headache still made her squint, her balance had not returned to normal, and her skin was coated with a sheen of cooling sweat, but on through the passages she went. In her wake, light burnished and lacquered the timber panels and floors of the second storey with a bloody sheen.

In the second passage that led to the stairwell she found three unlocked bedrooms; all empty of life and filled with treasures unused since the death of M. H. Mason. Spaces that waited in faint light for guests who never arrived.

Without fear of rebuke, she entered Edith's bedroom. A room also left unlocked. Perhaps it was permanently unsecure, so Maude could make swift passage to her ailing mistress.

Catherine photographed the wall of doll faces. Open-eyed, impassive, lifeless expressions in wood and cloth and ceramics, who had watched over Edith Mason since she had been a little girl.

Once open, the two great wardrobes and the chest of

drawers confirmed her preposterous suspicion that Edith only possessed clothes predating the Second World War. Edith had mimicked her mother and uncle in their prime, long after they had died. But had she also worn her mother's clothes while her mother was alive? Had Edith truly existed for so long inside one place, with no curiosity of what stretched into infinity outside of the grounds? It seemed so.

Catherine photographed the dresses and the contents of the drawers. She would have photographs and prove to herself and others that she was not mad. This was all *here*, really here.

Once the overhead light had been switched on, the next room she surveyed from the doorway shook her so profoundly, it took most of her will not to scream as she steadied herself against the doorframe. The nursery was a place she could not bring herself to enter.

Ten small beds aligned in two rows, beneath walls hand-painted with scenes of animals dressed as people. Animals that took tea, sailed little boats, flew kites, and ran in eager groups with wild white eyes and clawed feet as they chased rats.

The only significant difference to the room on this visit was that each of the little white beds was now empty. And all of the bedclothes were neatly made, to suggest the beds had been unoccupied for a while. The vintage leather passenger trunk was also absent, as were the small leather boots and silken slippers that had been at the foot of each bed.

The absence of Mason's morbid creations was reassuring, but only superficially. Catherine recalled her notion that small forms had followed her down the staircase the night before, and inhabited the lightless spaces below.

No!

The marionettes had been removed by people, to be used in some vile performance at the pageant. She told herself this as she stood frozen in the doorway of the room. And then she told herself the same thing again. The second time her lips moved.

After taking one photograph, she closed the nursery door and walked to the far end of the passage, where an alcove was visible beside the arched window overlooking the garden. Inside the alcove four narrow steps ascended to a rosewood door. There was an iron handle in the shape of a ring. It would lead to the attic under the pointed roofs with the thin arched window casements that she had seen from outside. The door was locked. She stood against it and listened.

Did she hear a *tap tap tap* from the other side? In the distance. Maybe. Yes, a faint far-off knocking. Wood on wood. Up there. A rhythmic motion. Something stirred by the wind. Or a mechanism. Could be anything. She pulled away from the door when she thought of the chipped wooden hands of the Master of Revels clapping.

On the first floor, Catherine made hesitant progress. She avoided Edith's drawing room due to an irrational fear that the preserved animals would tell their owner she had been inside the room without permission.

Next to the drawing room, she peered into a games room. There was a long-unused billiard table and an iron fireplace. The part of herself that used to evaluate houses and their contents felt peculiarly distant, but tried to revive itself when she looked inside the library.

The Eastlake bookcases that housed Mason's books, she

was sure would fetch between five hundred and a thousand pounds each. The first editions lining the shelves she could not even begin to evaluate. There were at least a thousand volumes.

She traced her finger along the spines closest to the door: *Preparation of Scientific Specimens of Mammals in the Field*, 1931, Museum of Zoology, University of Michigan; *Directions for Preserving Specimens of Large Mammals*, 1911, Museum of Vertebrate Zoology, Berkeley.

The door beside the library opened onto light produced from twin desk lamps, as if the room was in use. This was the study. The place of M. H. Mason's death.

Catherine half expected to see someone rise from the chair before the desk, or to turn away from the bookcases that were packed tight with more leathery book spines and bundles of paper tied with twine. Before the one window, a draughtsman's drawing board was angled to catch what light fell through the glass.

She sniffed at the air. A trace of stale pipe tobacco. Leonard coated the office with a similar odour. But how had this room still retained a vestige of M. H. Mason's own pipe smoke?

She sensed a lingering presence, that of a man driven and uncompromising, who would tolerate no intrusion or interference with work that had been encyclopaedic, and curious, with unfathomable goals. Work that had eventually killed him.

Whatever he had achieved inside this house, she was seeing mere residues. An old, damaged, grotesque film, poorly lit photographs in dim corridors, a room populated with preserved mammals, beehives crawling with bluebottle

flies, a nursery of marionettes with an ancestry Edith pre-
posterously claimed stretched back centuries. But his vision
was greater. She could sense this, but not define it. M. H.
Mason's endgame eluded her. His niece spoke only to
obscure and tantalize and mislead. And half of what she said
was fantasy. But Mason's ultimate goal seemed intent on
suggesting itself to her in terms that could not be understood
logically.

Her irrational instincts suggested that her recent dreams
offered a more suitable path to enlightenment. Could she be
stuck inside a giant doll's house? They had even got her to
dress the part. Or maybe the Red House was a continuous
puppet show in a vast theatre, in which the cast performed
nonsensical and abstract scenes from dramas composed by a
once-fine mind, long-since damaged and haunted into the
grim-surreal.

She cut off the suggestions from her imagination when she
realized this was how the mad must consider the world.

Edith declared the rooms of the house had remained
completely unaltered since her uncle's death. If it were true,
the pipe and open earthenware tobacco jar, and the neat
arrangement of pencils beside the open notebooks upon the
huge desk, had stayed in the same position for fifty years. As
had the crystal tumbler, and what had evaporated to leave a
brownish stain at the bottom of the glass. Perhaps only
Maude's duster had made contact with anything within this
capsule, frozen from the moment its master expired by his
own hand.

'You crazy bitches.' Catherine confirmed her gravest fear
when she spotted the ancient black stain spread across the
leather desktop. Mason must have opened his throat over

the desk. And Edith's mother had left the blood to dry. Catherine took one photograph and looked away.

But Edith's curatorial integrity had been compromised by one thing. The straight razor was missing. It should have been upon the desktop, or beside the chair where it fell from cold white fingers. Perhaps the sight of that was too much, even for Violet Mason. And for Edith too.

The household, his own family, had fostered Mason's delusions and morbid insanity. When he had gone, they'd preserved it. Why? The dying village honoured him with a pageant. Why? It was incredible, and incredibly sick. What was the attraction? If the devotion to his legacy was not inspired by any kind of charismatic allure that she could determine, or sustained by any attempt by the creator to conceal what was evidently misguided and unhealthy, and if loyalty was not rewarded with material wealth, then what kind of a hold did a deranged former army chaplain still command over the entire area and his only surviving relative?

Gingerly, Catherine approached the first wooden cabinet in the study. The thought of actually touching anything in M. H. Mason's study made her giddy, excited like a child. The cabinet was similar to the kind of furniture that held index cards in old university libraries. The drawers were unlabelled, but the top drawer contained hundreds of letters. As did the three drawers beneath. She walked her fingers across the top of the ancient paper. At random she pulled out envelopes.

A great many had been sent to him by a Hessen, Felix. The name meant nothing to her. Coldwell, Eliot, also appeared in abundance in the top drawer. She had never heard that name before either. Many of the Coldwell letters seemed more recent. He had been writing to Mason as late as the early sixties. The index cards were alphabetized and Coldwell and Hessen consumed most of the top two drawers. There were also a great many letters from someone called Mathers, Samuel, catalogued with S.R.I.A beside his name. Mason had once conducted lengthy correspondences with a small number of people, but she had no idea who any of these men were.

The adjacent cabinet was filled to capacity with ageing photographs protected within dividers made from brown card. She raised a folio at random and leafed through the pictures. They featured the construction of the puppet theatre upon the rear lawn when it had known better days. Mason must have been behind the camera. Whenever she was featured, Violet Mason was dressed like a man in dark overalls and worked without looking at the camera. The construction appeared to be highly organized, if not systematic, with the building materials laid out beside large paper plans.

Another bundle of brittle photographic paper revealed dramas in progress upon the stage of the theatre. Mason and his sister were absent from the murky pictures and must have been behind the scenes operating the marionettes. The shots were all taken directly before the front of the stage, perhaps on a timer. Little detail of the activity on stage was revealed. The motion was always blurred, as if the antics of the puppets were too quick for the shutter speed.

There were a great many pictures on browning paper of the derelict church she had seen at the head of the village. And even more of the perimeter walls, the oldest headstones and their indecipherable inscriptions. Much attention had been paid to one dingy and poorly lit corner of the cemetery.

In another folder, there were hundreds of photographs of

243

some kind of excavation, or earthworks, on the side of a small hill surrounded by open ground, though she had no idea of the location, which wasn't marked in anything but some sort of code that resembled ancient Greek interspersed with Roman numerals. But it looked as though something was in the process of being dug up. What appeared to be small bones and fragments of cloth were set beside a measuring tape.

The next drawer down repeated the obsessional character of the collection, though these pictures featured small paths and lanes, captured from all angles, upon open countryside. From a hill, the tracks had been traced onto some photographs with ink, like grooves in the earth.

Desperate for embellishment, for an explanation, she moved down to the next drawer, at the bottom of the cabinet. The final drawer was comprised entirely of folders containing pictures of the night sky and moon in its various stages, as if Mason had picked up astronomy as one of his compulsions during an enigmatic journey that included marionette theatre and the extermination of thousands of small mammals. His approach to whatever interested him was always fastidious, even scientific, but his goals still utterly bemused her. This was no good to her, to what she wanted to know. She kicked the final drawer shut.

Catherine moved her attention to the second cabinet. Its contents were more in keeping with what she expected from Mason, but soon regressed into a creative degeneracy that made her feel so sick, she wondered if she would ever recover from what she saw.

The dissection, emptying of internal organs and then meticulous fleshing of hides, of what were undoubtedly small animals, filled the entirety of the top drawer. She looked at no more than seven of the pictures – four rats, a squirrel and what resembled a peeled badger upon a slab – before she had to look away and press her knuckles to her lips. But it was the final picture that most affected her.

At first, she was convinced Mason had been preserving a dark-skinned child. A closer, less horrified scrutiny, revealed it to be an ape that Mason had photographed after making a long dorsal incision in its back. At that point in the procedure, the monkey's arms draped long black rags of hairy skin that had been rolled down from its hands. The empty strips of flesh looked like Opera-length gloves.

On the reverse side, Mason had written 'Felix Hessen's Hoolock Gibbon from Regent Park Zoo'. So perhaps it had been a private commission to preserve an ape. The shock of believing, for just a moment, that Mason had been skinning a child forced Catherine to slam this drawer shut.

The collection in the next section of the cabinet was equally disturbing. Carefully indexed photographs featured the still-articulated bones from animal remains, augmented with line drawings of wooden limbs replicating the true movement of joints. Several large albums' worth of individual doll parts had also been photographed against black cloth. Body parts removed from what had once belonged to a set of expensive and lifelike J.D. Kestner and Simon and Halbig dolls. Jointed limbs, mohair wigs, rotatable hands, the bisque socket heads of female dolls, and torsos moulded out of porcelain to resemble children's bodies abounded. The classic blue glass eyes and open mouths lined with little moulded teeth were the giveaway that they were German. After opening thousands of animals, Mason seemed to have progressed to disarticulating the more sophisticated varieties of doll.

The files of photographs that followed the doll parts forced Catherine to utter, 'Dear God' into the air of the now stifling room, so fragrant with stale tobacco, brittle paper and polished wood.

A vast collection of amputee photographs from the Boer war, Great War and even the American Civil War awaited, as did line drawings and photographs of tin and wooden limbs, alongside their laced leather harnesses and the complicated hydraulic systems that replicated human joints. One-hundred-year-old catalogues, featuring the most sophisticated prosthetic limb designs, from Gustav Hermann and Giuliano Vanghetti, had been slipped amongst the antique medical photographs.

Mason may have mastered taxidermy to a level unmatched in his lifetime, or since, but it had surely functioned as a precursor to the next step: an obsession with real surgery, and with the fitting of prosthetic limbs to stumps, and with suturing torn human flesh.

Randomly, Catherine flicked through half a dozen of the medical photographs, and saw all of the dead skin, patch-worked with stitches, that she ever cared to see. She closed the drawer using what little strength remained in her arms.

Incapacity. Disability. Deformity. Amputees. The horrors of the front. His own facial disfigurement. Callipers, crutches and wheelchairs. It all swirled like a horrible carousel through her mind, and made her nausea worse. The man had been traumatized by his experience of war and his great personal loss to such an extent that he must have been insane the entire time he lived in this house after coming home from the front. He'd incubated here, cultivating his regressive, though artful, vision. He had evolved here. But into what?

The contents of the penultimate drawer seemed to attest to her theory, and revealed evidence of experiments of a far more intimate nature that so shocked Catherine she knew that when she left the house tonight she would never return.

Amongst a sizeable private collection of Victorian Momento Mori photographs, featuring doleful families in their Sunday best, sat around the smartly dressed and waxen-faced cadavers of their recently deceased infants, Mason's curious obsession had turned to his sister.

In the 1940s, according to the dates on the rear of the pictures, printed in Roman numerals alongside more of the Greek code, he had photographed his own sister in a variety of foundation wear and crippling S-Bend corsets against a black backdrop. Despite the severe countenance of his sister's thin masculine face, the pictures issued an uncomfortably erotic charge. Though the composition and style of the photographs still suggested an artistic purpose was behind their creation.

Violet Mason's flesh was never naked. From the throat down, she had been stitched into some kind of patchwork second skin, made from the type of brown cloth once used to manufacture the stuffed bodies of dolls, at a time when only the heads and hands of dolls were constructed from china or porcelain. Over the tight sackcloth skin, layered petticoats were then arranged, layer by layer, to eventually produce a complete constriction, a muffling of the flesh. In addition, Violet's middle was always bound tightly to shape her torso.

Her legs were gripped by iron callipers and thick leather

boots, as if she suffered some crippling disability. The arrangement also resembled a form of punishment. Perhaps it was. Edith must have been an illegitimate child. So was this Mason's reaction to his sister taking a lover?

On two pictures, prior to the layers of boned foundation wear and underwear being built over her thin body, Violet's loins were revealed. Stitched with an alarming suggestion of permanence, her abdomen had been fitted into what resembled brown leather shorts.

Applied over a layer of the cloth-like skin, the leather breeches were sown up her inner thighs, in the same way Mason had stitched closed the skin of an animal over an artificial wooden body, or a plaster mould in other pictures. It looked like a primitive chastity device.

After each binding session, Violet Mason must have been cut out of the shorts and cloth suit, or the stitches would have been unpicked. At least, Catherine hoped so.

What was being done to Violet Mason's head was equally strange and sinister. Perpetually built up to grotesque levels, her hair was intricately piled in the cottage-loaf style that Edith had replicated. Catherine knew from other pictures that Mason's sister had thin black hair, so the seemingly endless array of profiles of his sister's head proved that the elaborate styles that dwarfed her bony face had been constructed from donor hair and rags.

As the studies of the head section of the pictorial archive progressed, the face of Violet was consistently overlaid with a series of veils from the broad brims of Watteau hats. Behind the sheer face veils, the Masons had begun experimenting with a crude form of masking combined with theatrical make-up. Violet's face was often so tightly bound with gauze, her features were restricted into a narrow pout, with her mouth forming a small dollish O.

Increasingly, her eyes were painted on too, over closed eyelids, with huge black lashes strikingly visible through the layers of netting. She had also worn porcelain masks that had either been decorated with cosmetics, or were actual life-sized doll faces, but always further obscured through a layering of veils.

It was as if M. H. Mason was fetishizing his sister as a doll, or perfecting something upon a living model that Catherine did not want to consider.

Before opening the final drawer, she questioned whether she could tolerate any more. What had begun as a frenzy of rummaging had tailed off into an appalled gaping.

She steeled herself, knelt down, and opened the last compartment, silently praying for a collection of seamstress dress patterns.

Catherine held onto the cabinet to prevent herself from sitting down and allowing the shaking to take over.

Her recognition of the buildings, photographed in black and white and collected at the front of the first drawer, had been immediate. The Magnis Burrow School of Special Education. The home. The special school for special children in Ellyll Fields.

An earlier incarnation of the institution than the one she had known, this version had lawns cut and trimmed within paths, long black windows, and old cars parked out front. But what had Mason been doing messing around with that school, and a place within a few hundred yards of her home? She scrabbled through the pictures looking for dates. 1951,

1952, 1957 in Roman numerals. Long before her time. It offered some relief, though not much.

Inside another file she saw a face she had known since childhood, a face of an innocent, smiling girl with sightless eyes that had always filled her with dread: little Angela Prescott. The blind girl of her nan's stories, who had been snatched from Magnis Burrow before Catherine was born. This was the iconic face of Ellyll Fields that most of its inhabitants had tried to forget.

The photograph of Angela had been cut out of a newspaper. As had the likenesses of Margaret Reid and Helen Teme, her companions in tragedy, that were also stored in the same file. The cuttings were inside a transparent envelope, the type stamp collectors used. The same images from newspaper clippings that her nan once kept in a biscuit tin.

The connection of Mason to the abducted girls filled her mind with a static of confusion that was underpinned with a dread so cold it made her shiver. The shock settled into a feeling of nausea, and a fear for her own safety that made the hair follicles of her scalp prickle. She closed her eyes and took deep breaths to settle herself.

Mason was an old man when the girls went missing. And at the time he was also a man not long for the world. He'd killed himself in the early sixties. Cut his throat. So was this why? Because of what he had done to little girls? From animals to puppets to children . . .

She thought of the pretty little kittens in dresses. And the demented, but grotesquely beautiful world of preserved animals and dolls he had created inside his own home. His connection to the missing girls suddenly seemed plausible. Back in the fifties would anyone even have thought twice about an elderly man, with a priestly bearing, taking photographs of a school?

Or was he just an archivist, or a historian of the locale's stranger byways and most curious events? *Please let him be.*

There was nothing else in the two Magnis Burrow files to condemn him as a kidnapper and murderer. Just the clippings and scores of photographs of the school and its grounds.

She shouldn't even be in the room, she was trespassing, but she suddenly wanted to confront Edith with the pictures.

Her horror dwindled into confusion when she perused the next file. The photographs were mounted in embossed paper frames and all featured another child, but one she did not recognize. Judging by the quality of the paper and the tones in the photographs, she guessed they were developed in the forties. Dates on the rear confirmed her hunch.

The first picture showed a little boy sat in a wheelchair outside a stone cottage. His legs were withered. The same boy appeared in two other pictures taken on the perfect lawn of a large orderly garden. In the first garden picture he was alone, smiling at the camera. In the second picture he sat watching the blurred activity upon the stage of Mason's theatre. So the latter two pictures must have been taken in the rear garden of the Red House. There had been a disabled child at the Red House around the time of the Second World War.

Catherine screwed up her eyes and scrutinized the blurred frenzy of activity on the stage of the puppet theatre. But the only details she could determine were suggestions of an old bonnet around an indistinct face, and what appeared to be two thin arms thrust into the wavy air above the bonneted figure's head. She looked away, dizzy from a powerful jolt of déjà vu.

Questions darted through her mind but would not settle into coherent answers. Maybe this was Edith's son? She might have followed her mother's example and had a child out of wedlock. There was no evidence of Edith's father in the house. And she had been too polite to ask about Edith's dad.

If Edith was his mother, the boy could have been carrying the same congenital deformity that beset Edith. But Edith had lived to her nineties, so where was the child now?

In another picture the disabled boy sat between Violet and what Catherine assumed was a young Edith Mason. Violet wore a long black dress that concealed her feet at one end and pinched her throat at the other extremity. Edith was dressed in a near-identical fashion. The severe expression on Edith's face matched her mother's. Only the boy was smiling, and he held Edith's pale hand.

Catherine's trembling fingers, that she could not still, loosened another photograph from out of the paper folder. The picture featured the boy in the wheelchair and M. H. Mason, the patriarch, sat in a garden chair. Mason wore a white linen suit and hat, but had failed to fully conceal the devastated side of his face, even with his head angled away.

Behind the boy's chair, Edith, draped in her widow's weeds, stood ramrod-straight without the aid of a wheelchair. So she had not been disabled when younger. Her face was as bloodless and long with misery as it seemed to have remained into her ninth decade. Catherine wondered if Violet had been the photographer.

Her fascination soon turned to panic.

In a separate envelope, the disabled boy reappeared as the subject of two further photographs. This time none of the Mason family were in shot, though the little boy was not alone. Because it appeared that one of Mason's troupe of marionettes had joined him for a photographic opportunity.

'No.' Catherine wanted to unsee the figure perched upon the disabled boy's lap in the manner of an ancient ventriloquist's dummy.

The puppet was almost the same size as the boy, its callipered legs at least as long and thin. But what was most striking about the puppet in the little tight suit was its wooden face and long black hair.

She'd seen this odd and scruffy thing before, in her own childhood trances, at her school that one time in the playground, and outside of her den on the other side of the green fence that Alice had climbed through . . . Which would mean her trances were memories? Albeit repressed, but true recollections?

Catherine hung her head between her shoulders and took long deep breaths to try and stop the shaking that had come to her limbs.

But Mason was long dead when she was a child, had been gone twenty years. Violet would have been dead by then too, or extremely aged. So had Edith, Maude, or their collaborators, brought this troupe to the derelict Magnis Burrow School, and into her life when she was a six-year-old child?

And if the figure with the wooden face and callipered legs, that Catherine had seen when she was a child, was no hallucination – *it* couldn't have been – the figure could not have been a puppet either, because when she had seen *it*, there had been no puppeteer.

The thing with the wooden face must have been an actual child then, wearing a mask and dressed as one of Mason's puppets.

But if a costumed child had been at the Red House in the 1940s, to be photographed with the disabled boy in the wheelchair, then who had worn the same outfit in the early eighties, when she had seen the figure with her own immature, six-year-old eyes?

Had she caught a glimpse of a similar figure, right here, in the nursery, too? There had been a mostly concealed head with that kind of wig. She had seen its messy black curls, but no face. She wondered if it had featured in the BBC film of Henry Strader's execution; she couldn't be sure, as the puppets had been in period costume, and she'd kept covering her eyes.

'You sick, sick fucks.' A terrible suggestion arrested her mind, which still felt like it was swimming with drugs and aching from trying to process so much unpleasant imagery and information. But had the Mason family snatched all of the little disabled children from the Magnis Burrow School in Ellyll Fields in the fifties and sixties? Had the Masons been befriending lonely and disabled children in that school with a patsy: a costumed, masked go-between? Perhaps using other children dressed as Mason's beloved troupe of marionettes to function as mimics, as saviours to the defenceless and vulnerable? The disabled boy in the wheelchair might have been just such an abductee, maybe one of the first in the forties.

In her trances, Catherine had seen what she'd thought of as strange children within the buildings of Magnis Burrow, as Alice had climbed the grassy bank leading up to the school. She hadn't imagined it. She wasn't crazy. Here was proof. And her trances may have been submerged traumas. Her contact, or her reunion, with the Red House must have brought the memories back with force. There was a connection.

If two generations of Masons had been haunting that school for decades, they would have taken Alice. And would have wanted Catherine too.

But then who were the children disguised in the marionette costumes? Other abducted children? Vulnerable children groomed, recruited, and then made to star in the sick plays of the Mason family, upon their lawn, for years? And to lure others to the party at the Red House? Alice too?

Alice . . .

If her suspicions were true, no wonder the Masons were still hiding from the world. Which begged another question she wanted the answer to: was Edith really broke and looking to sell up, or was she confessing to Catherine? Or doing something much worse? Now that Catherine was a woman, who had once been the child that got away, because she hadn't followed Alice through the fence, was Edith Mason hoping to resolve unfinished business? It was possible.

'Oh God, oh God.' Had they come back for her, these two horrid old women, to finish the child-snatching work that M. H. Mason had started decades before she'd even been born?

Had she not seen a child in the Red House too, at the window, on her first visit? Or was that a doll? Someone had pressed a doll's face against the window when she was returning from the hives too. Maybe that wasn't a doll and there was actually a child or children here.

The locked attic! A cellar! What had really been in those nursery beds? The movements at night. A small figure standing up at the end of a dark corridor . . . What she had thought was a trick, or an animal.

Catherine clutched her face with her hands. She felt weak, woozy, wanted to throw up all over Mason's hideous study. It was preposterous. She didn't know what to think. Maybe it was her that was truly mad, eaten alive by paranoia, and she was only rationalizing her presence within this building, as well as its very connection to what had always been dismissed as her childhood hallucinations. The worst thing about being mad was not realizing that you were mad.

Evidence, she needed more evidence.

Those few scrolls of parchment she still had the stomach to take down from the honeycomb of boxes in the study, and to untie, were all written in what she thought was ancient Greek. As were the bound volumes of Mason's black notebooks that filled a small bookcase. Same again with the four upon the desk he had filled with writing right up until his death. The neat but incomprehensible text was only ever relieved by chemical compositions, and what looked like trigonometry.

The M. H. Mason legacy didn't need a valuer or an auction, it needed a psychiatrist, and a secure archive within a private hospital, where the monomania that his niece had mistaken for genius could be studied at length by those accustomed to the sophisticated expressions of the incurably damaged.

Catherine ran back to her room and grabbed her bags. Then made her way down to the ground floor with her car keys clenched between her teeth.

THIRTY-SEVEN

Before Catherine moved any further from her car, she tried to identify the source of the dim, coppery illumination at street level in the village of Magbar Wood. The light appeared to originate from within the houses, which barely qualified as silhouettes, bordering the two streets that formed the entire village. The faint glow seemed to emit from weak bulbs, screened behind the net curtains and grubby windows she'd seen during her last visit.

The light barely touched those gathered for the pageant, and only occasionally made the jerky suggestions of a crowd visible. But a bustle was evident down there, a milling of shapes, though there were no raised or excited voices.

She guessed that around a score of people were scattered along the visible portion of the two lanes, moving between the flat facades of the stone cottages. Buildings she was certain were near deserted during her last trip.

From where the crowd had gathered was a mystery. It seemed impossible those assembled were indigenous to this place due to its state of dereliction. If they had travelled from neighbouring locales to celebrate the memory of M. H. Mason, then she could only assume they were privy to a secret tradition, and also mad.

A candy-striped pole of metal blocked the narrow road

that led into the village. Hidden within the hedgerow on either side of the lane, her desperate hands had just passed over two stone bollards upon which the pole was chained in place. She would get no further by car.

It was as if her movements had been anticipated.

Maude had even stolen her shoes, because Edith wouldn't let her leave. Beneath the soles of her bare feet, the stones dug deep and made her shift her position. And now that her unprotected feet were moving across the ground, she knew there was little chance of her reaching the nearest A road. She could barely even see her feet, let alone road signs.

Above her, the great canopy of black sky featured an array of stars unobscured by cloud. And for a moment she stared upwards at the heavens and felt she could have been on a mountain summit, surrounded by thin air.

The black eternity resembled a night sky she had once seen in Northern Spain, one immediately unfamiliar and too vast. A sky that frightened her with the sense of belittlement that comes swiftly downwards in a sudden awareness that one stood insignificant, nullified by an infinite surrounding void.

As she had done in her room during her first night, Catherine looked away from the sky before the realization became too complete.

She dithered beside her car, nervously watching the village from a distance. Just getting out of the car had taken all of her willpower.

Currents of cold air pressed through the thin white dress that had been laid out for her. She shivered while her thoughts scratched about for an escape route. Because that was what she had been reduced to, *escape*. The nightmare she had stumbled into at Green Willow, when she stood amongst the dolls in the room of a scruffy guest house, would not end.

Without an alternative, Catherine climbed over the pole and entered the village.

The first heads she saw were crowned with large hats. Little more of the figures was visible. The people would veer close to the lit windows, then shuffle away.

She wanted to believe the crowd moved about refreshments and concessions on the narrow pavements. But the motion of the throng also suggested some kind of dance was being performed, as the movement of the half-lit shapes seemed to replicate itself in a pattern.

The poor light, combined with her fragile senses, may have warped her perspective too, because the people seemed too small to be adults. *Children?* The harder she stared, the energy of the assembly also struck her as similar to that of excitable toddlers released from houses to play outdoors.

She wished she were not wearing white. A desire that grew with every step deeper inside the village. And where would Edith, Maude, Mike and Tara be, the only guests she could count upon as being familiar? The sole buildings representing any kind of communal area were the Sea Scout hall and the church.

A desire to sneak to the far side of the village, and then keep on creeping for as long as her bare feet lasted, felt urgent enough to be desperate. But she had to find Mike. If her suspicions about the Masons' legacy of abduction were true, then Mike needed to be warned. Tara could go to hell.

Would she get past pain and rage if she saw Mike? She

would have to, because Mike had come here in a car; Tara's car, because Mike couldn't drive. To get out she had to find Mike and the bitch he had come here with. Tara's car must be parked on the road that ran into Magbar Wood from the other end of the village high street.

She told herself, then reminded herself, that Edith and Maude were hardly threatening, physically, as long as she didn't swallow anything they gave her. But were the two elderly women working alone? This is what she needed to know. She thought of the thin bee-keeper beckoning to her from the garden as she stood at the window. And were they still using a child?

But what happened to the children of the Red House when they grew up?

She needed to get far enough away to pick up a phone signal to call the police. Her story would be preposterous, but then so was the household she was trying to flee. Whatever had happened at the Red House in the past, it was up to the authorities now to fathom out.

The sparse crowd withdrew at her passage inside the village. She offered a nervous smile to the vague covered heads of what she was now sure were elderly adults. She had encountered at least one here before. Children wouldn't be out so late, unaccompanied by adults. All of the people were small because they must be wizened by age. Though the two capering figures that passed a lit window to her left, as if keeping pace with her, made her anxious. Their antics, even in darkness, suggested something unsupervised and out of control. Her attempt at a friendly smile ached like the rictus of an insincere grin maintained before a bad joke.

At the intersection of the two lanes she looked to the

church and scout hall, but could see no further than the last residential buildings in the second lane. When she looked at the houses, only glimmers of flat dirty stone and coppery light behind calcified nets was visible. Inside the open doorways there was darkness.

Two women tottered past her and were either veiled, masked, or had painted their obscured faces. Because faces could not be so pale without embellishment.

The efforts at masking failed to conjure any sense of romance, or the illicit behaviour associated with masquerades. What the women's outfits did inspire was a deep uneasiness about the intent and purpose of the tradition being celebrated within the miserable village. Thoughts of Violet Mason's bony face, half concealed behind netting, were inevitable but unwelcome.

Unless you are one of them you cannot know them.

But what could these frail old things do to her even if they wished her harm?

Moving past the intersection and towards the far side of the main lane, her vision jumped and flitted as she searched for Mike. But if she wasn't mistaken, her progress was now being thwarted by changes in direction from the stooped-over figures moving closer to the house fronts.

The people who slowed her progress appeared to hobble across her path, as if wearing shoes that were too tight on their hidden feet. An observation she soon heard, and occasionally saw, augmented by the rapid patter of the metal tips of canes across tarmac and cement.

For one horrible moment she thought of herself as an animal being run to ground, incrementally worn out by the patient circling of a pack. Or were they just as equally fascinated by her, as she was by them?

There was nothing she could see to account for such agitation in the crowd either. Or was it excitement? No concessions, as she hoped, offered food or souvenirs on either side of the lane, so where were they all headed?

Under closer scrutiny, the energy of the crowd now struck her as being akin to the jostling she associated with festival crowds in the darkness of night, before a star attraction came on stage, suggesting all here were waiting for something that had not yet happened.

A woman whose footsteps Catherine tried to follow stepped into a brief wash of light to reveal a three-quarter-length cape and high Medici collar tied about her neck. The woman's tiny head was concealed by a Pompadour dome of what must have been, at one time, someone else's hair. It was now puffed out on an invisible wire frame and held in place by tortoiseshell combs, and what looked like long iron pins. Propped upon the elaborate wig was a little Juliet cap constructed from pearl beads.

On a sudden whim to ask who was authorized to remove the barrier pole so she could drive through the village, Catherine reached for the woman's elbow.

The little woman altered her course and crossed the street. But not before Catherine had seen half of a deeply lined face beneath several layers of black netting. In the brassy light, the skin of the woman's face was as white as a clown's in full make-up.

Catherine turned round. Because the three figures whom she confronted with her shocked silence, also stopped moving at the same time as she did. She was sure they had been whispering.

The figures dispersed around her, as if terribly eager not to miss something up ahead in the street. As they fled, Catherine received an impression of yoke collars and floor-length pleated skirts. She saw the back of an Eton jacket with swallow tails and a short knitted cape. Clothes that hadn't been fashionable in a century.

They were all covered from chin to toe. And again, all she had made out through their patterned veils were smudges of white. Their faces must have been coated in stage make-up, or were clad in colourless masks.

Their wake was a thick scent cloud of lavender. An odour failing to mask the competing ones of camphor and the mustiness of clothes left in damp conditions.

'What . . . Hello, wait! I'm looking for . . .'

Her plea was ignored. There was a snigger at her outburst from another direction. Which was shushed. The cackler desisted, but whoever had scolded the giggler now laughed, too, before darting away.

If they're laughing at me they should see themselves.

At the end of the street she discovered another iron candy-striped pole blocking access to the village. She wanted to scream.

Beyond the barrier was a darkness unrelieved by a tree-line, hedgerow or moon-silvered fields. Her imagination suggested the world reached its edge at the horizontal pole. And it was too dark beyond the barrier to see any evidence of the car that must have brought Mike and Tara to Magbar Wood.

Huddled together beside the beery light of the last window of the street, a small gathering of silent, rapt shapes distracted her.

An elderly figure in the centre of the group performed a

curious skipping upon the narrow pavement. She caught glimpses of its prancing between the vast hats of the onlookers. The dance had long passed from fashion, or perhaps never extended beyond the borders of the village, and what she could see of the dancer's head was mostly engulfed by a black wig. Where the tresses parted, the revealed features were covered in white greasepaint. The cheeks were rouged and the eyes decorated with long lashes like an aged cross-dresser. Around his throat the dancer wore a Mr Toby ruffle. His painted eyes were closed in concentration. His grin was pure music-hall farce. *Clackclack clack clack* went his tap shoes upon the paving.

Having seen more than she cared to, Catherine turned about to head back to her car. She'd sit in it and sound the horn. Mike would hear it. If whatever functioned as official-dom at the pageant also heard the horn, she would demand the maypoles that blocked the road be removed. And inside a locked car she would feel safer.

Her decision was thwarted by the sudden electric crackle and hiss from the adjoining lane. The interference was followed by a brassy groan like the iron hull of a ship grinding against stone.

Catherine clutched her ears. A burst of music followed, that suggested it had been made at the dawn of recorded sound and was being played at the wrong speed through ancient speakers. A discordant, metallic fanfare. Loud music played tunelessly, but still recognizable as 'Greensleeves' as if blasted from out of an ice-cream van decades before.

The crowd about Catherine paused, in what she took to be awe, before they all turned towards the junction of the two lanes.

The shock of the reappearance of 'Greensleeves' in her life made her want to sit down in the street and sob. And the music was clearly a summons to those gathered for the pageant, who now tapped and rustled through the darkness, between the stone gulley formed by the houses, towards the intersection.

'Can you tell me what's happening?' she called, on the verge of tears, to a figure that hurried past her with the aid of two walking sticks. She thought the old woman smiled behind the netting that dropped from the wide brim of her hat, but she did not answer.

Two small men bent double with age tottered on frail legs to move around her. 'Please. Sir. Can you . . .' Their narrow faces were hints of white beneath the brims of ill-fitting Homburg hats, that failed to contain unkempt hair that trailed over their collars.

She reached out and seized one of the men by the upper arm. And quickly released the limb. Not only because it was as thin as a wooden flute beneath its drapery of black cloth, but because the man let out a shriek and fell.

'Oh, I'm sorry. I never meant . . . Here. Let me help . . .'

He was soon back on his feet, helped up by a man in a three-button frock coat and someone of indeterminable gender swallowed by a tweed cape. With their gloved hands they snatched at the elderly figure who had virtually disappeared against the unlit road surface.

'I'm really sorry,' Catherine said to the back of their hats.

She joined the crowd's momentum, if it could be called that, with the intention of returning to her car at the opposite end of the lane. Which wasn't far, though the determined crowd either blocked what little light issued from the windows of the houses, or the lights had dimmed in some co-ordinated fashion, which was impossible and must have been her imagination.

Perhaps a residual effect of Maude's tonic still ran strong in her blood, because she endured a few terrifying moments in which she thought she hung within a moving nothingness. There was no edge or border to the night, no horizon, and she wanted to crouch and place her hands on the earth, until the rustling of old limbs in vintage cloth had ceased in their surges about her.

Only as the vestiges of the motley horde thinned, and the most infirm of their number tottered and guided each other around the obstacle of her body, did some of the whisky-tinted light cast enough of a glow for her to move again, and without the sensation of falling backwards.

Once more, the world around her had become insubstantial and unreal. Maude's tonic must have combined with the cold and darkness, and with her being ill, and her meddling with old dolls, antiques and taxidermy. All this had integrated to contribute to her disorientation. She also wondered when she would stop seeing things not as they were, but transformed.

She needed to calm down and stay upright and clear of the small shadows that hobbled about her. And she must remove herself from Magbar Wood, because hysteria wasn't far away.

When she reached the place where the two lanes merged, she could see that the doors of the derelict church were now open. A full blare of the hurdy-gurdy fairground melody clanged against the stone walls of the chapel and bulged outwards. A dim red light was emitted.

Before the covered gate of the churchyard, the glow was joined by a ruddy luminance from the doors of the neighbouring scout hall, as if this was now the heart of the pageant. Catherine continued towards her car.

A hand gripped her elbow. 'You won't find this in the *Guardian Guide*.'

She shrieked.

Mike.

'What are you fucking doing here?' It was out of her mouth before she knew it, when she only wanted to fall against him and sob.

He released her arm and stepped away. The smile receded from his mouth and vanished from his eyes. Mike looked away, then at his feet. 'Leonard called me. Said you would be here, he said you needed help. He told me to come and bring you home.'

'Leonard?'

'I'm sorry. I'm sorry, Cath. You don't know how much. About . . . Look, forget that. We need to get out of here. Tara's car is . . . Your nose is bleeding.'

The strange night sounds and sights retreated, and her focus on Mike's pale and miserable face surprised her, as if she had awoken from a trance she'd endured for so long it had begun to feel normal, only to rediscover her will once the soporific spell had broken. Her chin and lips were indeed wet.

'How could you? How could you, with *her*.'

'I'm sorry. Sorry.'

'Fuck you!'

'Look, when you told me about the girl that you hurt, in London, I only answered her messages because . . . I wanted to hear from her. About what happened. Before we got any deeper. Her side of it.'

'And then you met her!'

'I wish I never had. You were right. She's poison. She's been using me. I can see that now. And I'm a bloody idiot. I don't know what I was thinking.'

'I bloody well do!'

'Things weren't great between us, Cath. Not since . . . you know. I didn't know what to do . . . shit!' He swallowed at the bolus of pain that constricted his throat. But was he swallowing his anguish at being betrayed by Tara, or remorse at what he had done to Catherine?

'You slept with that horse-faced bitch.'

'I . . . Look . . .'

And for the second time in her life she struck someone's face. This time there was no closed fist, but an open hand.

Catherine turned towards the church as if it offered some hope of sanctuary. Through her blurred vision, trembling from the emotion that shook her body, she was sure the aged and diminutive members of the tatty assembly had all gathered at the top of the lane and were turned in her direction, to watch the confrontation of two strangers on the border of their village.

'Cath, something's not right here. I mean it.'

Catherine turned away from the church to find Mike so close they both flinched. 'No shit! You don't even know the half of it. '

'You can hate me for ever. I don't expect you to forgive me, or to even talk to me again. But come home with me, yeah? Tonight. Please.'

'Where's that bitch's car?'

'In the lane. On the other side of that pole. But I can't find her. She's gone.'

'Gone? What are you saying?'

'We got split up. We went up to that church. She went inside. I didn't . . . I didn't want to. Didn't like it. But she hasn't come back out. I can't find her. She's got the car keys. We all need to get out of here.'

'She's still in there?'

'I don't know. Yes, maybe. I saw . . . I don't know. Up there, I saw something really weird. Horrible. What the fuck is this place? Leonard had to show me on a map.'

'But you still brought her here. You betrayed me with that bitch, and then you brought her here too. Were you thinking of her career? Because I know she was!'

'What could I do? I shouldn't have said anything about the house. I know. Damn it, I know. But I did, before I knew what she was doing to us. Then it was too late. And she wanted to see it, the antiques and stuff. This guy, Mason. His animals. She knew about him.'

'You stupid bastard.'

Mike held her arm. 'She would have come out here anyway. She's already been looking for that house since I told her about the animals. But she couldn't find the village. I still have no clue how we found it today. By accident, I think. But I needed her to drive me. When Leonard said you were in trouble, I had no choice. I don't have the money for that kind of cab fare from Worcester. I told her I wanted to find you, told her it's you I really care about.'

'Liar!'

'This is all so messed up.'

'You messed it up.'

'Tara didn't care. She just wanted to get here to see the house. She's so driven, she's mad. Even after what she's done to us, she didn't care about a confrontation with you, as long as she could get to see the house.' Mike clenched his fists as if he were going to punch himself. 'Shit. Shit. Shit.'

Catherine looked at the church. The strained and rapid rotations of 'Greensleeves' swirled about her and grew louder. Even the stars moved in a circle above her tormented mind, or so she imagined.

'That bitch is up there?' Her chest felt like it had been pierced by something cold and made her breath shuddery. This night was the endgame to what started in the torture chambers of tarmacked junior school playgrounds. *Of course!* But at last she could see the end. Fuck therapy. What could a counsellor or doctor do to prevent destiny? She had been right all along. She knew it. Beneath all of the reassurances, she had always known that other forces guided her down the tragic spiral of life like magnetic fields sucking water through a grate, a circular but inevitable descent. You either endured it and suffered, or you did the unthinkable to your enemies and at least went down with a sense of justice being served.

Mike's voice brought her out of her miserable absorption. 'There was some kind of service in there. Singing. Around this glass coffin, or something. Pretty damn sinister. I split, but Tara waited to see if she could find that crazy old woman we met up at the house, the one in the wheelchair. To see about looking at the stuff in the house.'

'Edith.'

'Yeah, Edith. Tara wanted to talk to her about a film. Edith said she would be here, with you. But we couldn't find

Edith, and Tara hasn't come back out of that church. This is all wrong. Jesus, this place. We should just go, now.'

'Keys. The car keys! We've got to find your bitch.'

'Hey, I told you. I messed up. I was wrong.'

'Bit late for that, don't you think?'

'Don't go up there. I'm not. Not again. It's . . . I think it was a funeral, or something. I can't look at that woman again, in the coffin.'

'What woman? What are you talking about?'

'I don't know. She was in this case. It was all lit with these red lights. I was watching from the door. Then the lights went out. The doors shut. But Tara was still inside. What the fuck are they doing in the dark?'

'Jesus Christ.' Catherine began walking to the church. She would get the keys, but she wouldn't look at the woman in the case. Almost certainly more of Mason's handiwork. She'd seen enough of that for a lifetime.

'Don't go.'

'What about the car keys, you moron!'

Mike bit the inside of his mouth. She'd never seen his eyes so wild-looking before, never seen him this frightened.

'Fuck the keys. Let's walk out of here. But I'm not going back in there. I'm taking off.'

'I don't have any shoes! How can I walk?'

'Shit! Look, if we get split up, I'm going to wait for you. By the car, yeah? It's parked in that lane, by the pole. I'm not leaving you out here. This place is all wrong. I'll be waiting, yeah? Cath! Cath!'

'My hero!'

'I don't care what you think of me. But I won't leave you here. If you two go back to that house, I'm coming up there to get you, yeah?'

She was right. Tara had come here. No doubt with the sense of the antiques documentary story of the decade filling her nostrils, as well as a perfectly laid-out vengeance narrowing her reptile eyes with anticipation. Take Mike and break off their relationship. Show up at the Red House and inveigle herself into Edith's confidence, as only Tara could do, to spoil the valuation and auction with promises of a lucrative television contract, augmented with lies about what Catherine had done at Handle With Care. Edith would be thrilled by the subterfuge and scandal. Her lonely, mad existence would be lit up with even more of Catherine's misery, and with new talk of the greater riches available through Tara's influence.

'I'll kill . . .' Catherine's attempt to speak broke into a sob of rage that felt like it could damage her.

But then she smiled, and she felt as if a terrible constriction had been released from around her heart.

Let her have it. Let her waste her time.

Even if Edith had been in possession of the Rothman treasures, lost when the *Titanic* went down, Catherine knew she'd rather die than value the Mason estate. Tara was welcome to the Red House. And she was welcome to Edith. It would all be evidence soon, in a police investigation. There would be yellow tape strung across that porch not long after she found a phone signal and directed the authorities up that lane.

'Cath! Cath! Cath!' she could hear Mike's voice behind her.

Catherine pinched her nose to stop whatever was running out of it, and even more strongly now, and carried on to the church. As she moved she located the wet wipes in her bag and tore one free to wipe at her face.

Once she was level with the gaping red doorway of the shabby scout hall, a needle was scraped out of a groove inside the church. The awful metallic rendition of 'Greensleeves' stopped abruptly.

In the sudden silence, behind her and further down the street, a door slammed shut.

She turned her head to see if her craven ex-boyfriend had followed her up the street.

The blood-light from the church and scout hall dwindled into shadows as it bled down the narrow lane. But Mike was no longer standing where she'd left him only moments before. In fact, there was no one behind her, or even present in the lane.

But all considerations of her ex-boyfriend were erased at the sight of the vessel, as well as its murky occupant, that lumbered through the light of the church vestry. An object preceded by a bustling crowd in vintage costume.

The casket was lowered to skim beneath the arch, but then rose, shaking, as if those who transported it had suddenly stood up straight.

Catherine took the long box for an antique coffin, made out of long glass panes held together by iron brackets. Some kind of sarcophagus as Mike had suggested.

What she could see of the occupant of the rectangular casket looked like a mannequin. A small female dummy dressed in a lavish black gown and sat upon a high-backed chair; tiny and immobile, save for the wobbles as it was clumsily manoeuvred down the church path. Nothing of the face, beside a small whitish oval, could be seen behind its black veil.

She began to fear she might be in the presence of an

embalmed body of local significance. Thoughts of Edith's mother came to her again and were as unwelcome as before. Had Violet Mason been preserved as a saint and locked inside the wretched church? But if she'd died after her brother, then who had preserved Violet?

But then, it couldn't be Violet; the body was too small.

Since her first visit to the Red House she wondered if anything seen thus far had filled her with as much revulsion as the strange glass canister and its shrunken occupant. She tried desperately to convince herself that the effigy had been constructed from papier-mâché and dressed in funereal black clothing. Unless a child had been employed to represent a female character pertinent to the tradition of the village.

A float draped in black silk followed from the church to join with and to bear the horrible cargo.

The crowd chattered excitedly in voices too low to hear. They merged into one messy column in the shadows before the front of the scout hall.

Catherine looked back down the lane. Mike had gone. But this is what he had seen. Something that really upset him. She understood why.

Catherine took two steps away from the scout hall. But while she'd been staring with a horrified fascination at the relic, the crowd and their effigy had produced a ring around the front of the hall and church, blocking the entire width of the lane. They moved the wobbling sarcophagus right at her.

Again, with what felt like a horrible inevitability, she was trapped. She retreated up the little path and ducked inside the hall. There was nowhere else to go. And nothing could have tempted her to stand her ground and be made to peer inside the upright glass cabinet. If she hadn't moved so swiftly she would have been forced to see the occupant of the sarcophagus in much greater detail. She would have been face to face with it.

Inside the hall she came upon multiple rows of collapsible wooden chairs older than the narrow building that encased the furniture. The only light was frail and filtered through the dirty glass of three small stage lights, fixed above the curtained podium at the far end of the hall.

Catherine moved along the back row of seats and sat in a tiny uncomfortable chair at a distance from the aisle, and as far away as she could get from a small wooden stage draped in velvet curtains.

She bit her bottom lip, and dabbed a wet wipe at the fresh blood gathering under her nose. She must look a fright. Barefoot in the white dress with blood running over her mouth. Somehow her ghastly appearance seemed fitting.

Tara must still be close. She must have been inside the church to watch whatever pageant service had recently been conducted. Tara hadn't come out of the church but may have been at the end of the procession. Maybe she was with Edith. If Tara entered the scout hall with the crowd, Catherine would have to get the car keys off her, find the car and leave. But how would she get the keys?

When she realized her hands were shaking, she clasped them together in her lap. Maybe it was the thought of seeing *her* again that contributed to her palsy, or perhaps she had entirely, finally, lost her wits.

All she had seen this night might appear eccentric but unthreatening to a mind less disturbed than her own. It was possible that her sanity had unravelled and she was now stuck in a continuous loop of grotesque fantasy erupting from her subconscious mind. In fact, within near total darkness in unfamiliar surroundings, she must remember that anything could seem to be just that: *possible*.

She prayed she was delusional, ill, drugged, anything but fully lucid. Because if she were mad, at least what she was experiencing was imagined and not real.

And into the hall they came. They hobbled and they scuttled. They shuffled and they crept. But moved in haste to find seats.

Some of the little figures crowded the floor before the stage like children before a Punch and Judy show, until the hall was filled with the groans and squeaks of small bodies shifting upon the wooden chairs. And they all looked forward, at the stage.

Catherine suspected they were aware of her, but deliberately ignoring her.

The members of the audience were so shrunken in their capes she doubted a single one was younger than ninety. But how had some of them moved so swiftly outside?

In the vague burgundy light she also stared at enough vintage millinery and evening dress to fill a small museum. Watteau hats and great headdresses drooped with leaves and half-roses, forming misshapen rows of black humps up to the stage.

The closest veils in her row were black, some spotted, some patterned, and all covered hints of bleached faces. Gauzy and spangled fans quickly spread. All of the men needed a haircut. She felt like she was stuck in some vast and surreal Memento Mori photograph.

Hair and nails continue to grow after death.

She stopped the train of thought, because it led to assumptions that would be unbearable while trapped in the dark among these 'people'.

There was still no sign of Tara, or Edith or Maude for that matter.

From the seats before her, the fragrance of musty fabric began to drift and settle about her, as if the garments had only been recently released from confinement in damp, airless spaces. In unheated rooms in old houses. She knew the odour from the house clearances she had attended. Old bottled scents similar to Edith's perfumery had been lavishly applied to cover the smells of age, and to conceal something else: a trace of the chemical pungency of the Red House. It made her sick in Mason's workshop and began to turn her stomach again now.

She rummaged in her bag for more scented wet wipes so she could hold a handful against her nose and mouth. It was too late to stand up and make her way out. She would draw attention to herself as she climbed over the little laps in the dark.

She would be forced to sit in the stench. The hall was airless, the windows blacked out; if the door closed she might faint.

Where was Tara if she had not come in with the congregation? And Mike? He was there, behind her in the street, and then . . . Could he have moved out of the lane so quickly? And had Tara left the church and found Mike? Would they leave without her? She swallowed a sob.

Directly beside her, though the small woman had covered her face with a fan, her neighbour's exposed lower legs distracted Catherine. Wool gaiters were side-buttoned over the woman's high-cut shoes. Above the covered ankles, two pale legs were visible.

As if aware of her scrutiny, the legs withdrew beneath the seat of the chair. But not soon enough to prevent Catherine's glimpse of what resembled carved ivory limbs within iron callipers; legs that curved out of a hint of leather straps about the knees.

Catherine made to stand up and get out. But the doors were now closed.

The glass sarcophagus stood upright before the sealed entrance, as if the figure inside was present to watch a performance. The wooden throne inside the glass case was festooned with briars and flowers were entwined around the legs of the chair. The tiny figure upon the throne remained still, the veiled face obscured. Before the lights dimmed even further, Catherine noticed a tiny hand upon the armrest. It was as white as bone.

She stifled a scream.

The whispers, shuffles and creaks around her settled to silence and anticipation inside the black hall. Only the stage was now visible.

Her sense of the walls and ceiling and floor slipped away with the going of the light. All was removed from the world and the invisible audience hung in darkness before the stage. Where she was in space and even time, she feared she was now losing her grasp of.

The curtains shrieked across their rails and revealed the stage.

THIRTY-EIGHT

In the tense darkness the din of applause subsided.

Catherine was sure the audience had been stamping the heels of their feet against the floorboards. But the noise of applause, the sound of wood knocking against wood, was too high up and she felt no vibrations through the soles of her shoes. So they must have been banging their chairs with hard objects and not clapping with wooden hands. An idea her paranoia was only too happy to revive.

Now the performance had ended, the stage lights slowly glowed red, but illumined little beyond the head of the hall. When as much light returned as the tired bulbs were able to emit, she was relieved to see that the curtains around the stage were closed. The performance had drained her. She would be unsteady on her feet if she tried to stand.

Now the tired old world had re-formed around her, its dusty ruins could not compete with the vitality of the drama. The duration of the play was intentionally short, because no one could have withstood any more of it.

What she had seen through her fingers in snatches was all she had been able to bear in the reeking darkness of the blacked-out hall. The recording of what must have been the voices of M. H. Mason and his sister, Violet, she had plugged her ears against with torn wet wipes.

What the script had been based upon she did not want to guess. What she'd heard of the narration accompanying the activity of the marionettes had been as original and insane as what Mason had left in his study.

The hanging of the Martyr, Barnaby Pettigrew, and the burning of the Martyr, Wesley Spettyl, had nearly made her sick. The audience had wept and groaned as if at a funeral.

During the execution scenes, most of the marionettes had posed as children. Ragged, terrified children who watched their masters' ghastly public demises carried out by court order and mob respectively; executed for witchcraft and necromancy, or so the crackling voice of the narrator had droned from somewhere behind the stage. Something only Jacobean playwrights would have dreamed of depicting in such detail.

Before each scene, the plaster-faced Master of Revels had walked centre stage upon its canine hind legs, grinning despite missing a nose, to deliver soliloquies in what Catherine guessed was a mostly indecipherable English in the Tudor idiom.

She'd once heard a fragment of Tennyson, recorded on a few surviving wax cylinders, reciting his poetry, and the narration to the M. H. Mason play had been about as clear. She hated the idea her imagination mooted that the script was far older than Mason, and had been transmitted to him from the past. No wonder the BBC had packed up and run in the fifties.

At its heart the drama was some kind of morality play. In her glimpses of it, the hare-headed puppet and the bonneted girl with the long chestnut hair had presided over the sentencing of Pettigrew and Spettyl, in some distant court or municipal authority. The same roles they had played in the smashing of Henry Strader upon the wheel in the BBC film.

But in return for the sentences they'd handed down to the puppet masters accused of sorcery, the marionette cast had visited the judges in their beds at night and hauled them away in their nightwear, to wooded scenes depicted by a backdrop, where a grisly revenge was taken and fates were decided.

What had been most disturbing in the haphazard fragments of the drama she had seen, were the episodes that featured the judges yanked off the stage and upwards into darkness. The judges had kicked their legs as they went. At the same time the recording had unleashed the sound of animal screams. To which the crowd had twitched and hissed with excitement.

If their diminishing though continuing cries could be trusted, the violent ascents of the judges into the air didn't so much indicate the end of their lives, but the beginning of less merciful torments. All this in return for what they had done to the Martyrs.

The procession of the performers at the play's conclusion depicted the cast as ragged urchins and stumbling invalids who disappeared, one by one, through a hole in the cloth wings of the stage. An aperture they drifted towards on strings Catherine had been unable to make out at any time during the performance.

She'd also scanned the cast to catch sight of the figure of the wooden-faced boy from Mason's photographs, from her childhood trances, and from her own memory. All of the marionettes were in various costumes in each scene, but there had been crowd scenes in which she had seen something with girlish curls bouncing upon its small head. From where she was seated at the back, in what little she could bear to watch, that character had also seemed disinclined to show its face to the audience. She was now paranoid enough to believe the figure had known she was seated in the hall and was deliberately concealing itself from her.

When the performance finally ended she'd found herself breathing hard into her hands, which covered her face. The doors to the hall were open and the effigy sealed within glass had been taken away. What was left of the crowd had jostled from the hall with a weary determination. Most members of the audience had already found their way outside in total darkness while she still waited in petrified silence, praying there would be no encore.

At least the terrible movements of so many small limbs in rustling fabric, all about her in the darkness, was over. What the village had dressed and gathered for had finished, perhaps for another year.

But why keep it alive?

Beside her on an empty chair her bag gaped open. During the performance, it had been somewhere by her feet. But now the bag was upon the seat next to her.

The bag was empty, ransacked. A white piece of aged paper was all that had been left behind by the thief. Had it been the elderly woman in the vintage dress?

Catherine took out the notepaper, opened it. And tried not to cry.

YOU LOK SO PRITY SO STITCH UP YOR CUNT ELSE HE'LL PUT HIS PIZLE IN THAR AND BRAKE YOR HART APART.

Catherine dropped the piece of paper and moved quickly to the doors of the empty hall. As she ran she knocked aside the little chairs on both sides of the row. It was like running through a large Wendy house.

Amidst the clatter of her rout, she looked to the distant curtains of the stage, terrified they might open again. The only goal to her purposeful scrabble was the dark lane that led out of Magbar Wood, and the car that must be waiting there for her. Mike would not let Tara leave without her. And despite all Mike was guilty of, she now wanted to cling to him like he was driftwood in a freezing black ocean.

As part of the incongruous irrelevancy that can accompany the exhaustion of fear, she wondered if she should post Violet Mason's antique maternity dress back to Edith. Which made her wonder whether the Red House was even visited by the postal service. It must be, because Edith had said they received enquiries about her uncle. They also had food, so Maude's fare had to be procured and delivered from somewhere. These little shreds of evidence that Magbar Wood and the Red House were real, while the horrid suggestions of the things she had half seen in them were not real, were all she clung to as she walked, as quickly as it was possible to walk without breaking into a run, out of the hall and down the lane from the church. Which now looked to be deserted again. The lights were out, the doors were closed.

But the small theatre crowd had not dispelled. It milled in the distance, in the adjoining street she would have to cross to reach the barrier pole and the lane that led away from the village. The people had gathered about their icon; the glass in their midst was catching the thin light.

As she neared, the crowd appeared less animate but more organized. The attitude of the mob suggested it was waiting for her, like the girls at school had once waited outside the main gates. She recognized the feigned indifference of small bodies about to circle. Her scalp iced with panic.

She told herself she couldn't be in any danger. They were elderly people. Cut off in a rural backwater and just going through the routine of a tradition. One revived by the mad old Masons who had the local population under their influence. She had been ill, Maude had drugged her, and they had put someone up to stealing from her and inserting the obscene message inside her bag.

The ghastly nonsense of the Red House and of M. H. Mason had postured for long enough as some form of alternate reality. She had to fight its influence with every ounce of strength in her mind and her body.

But the horrible notion that she was part of a scripted performance, that had yet to reach its final scene, persisted.

Catherine broke into a run.

She was having a breakdown. She thought she had become better when she moved home to Worcester. *But you are only better as long as nothing goes wrong.* Mike had gone wrong. Tara had come back. She had been lured to the Red House. She was being dragged back to the condition of her childhood. The will and fates of the world had reasserted themselves into her life.

At several times in her thirty-eight years, she'd come to believe the world was a wholly insidious place. Tonight confirmed it. And now she just had to get out and away, and keep running as far as her unshod feet could take her. Maybe until she reached the sea, where she could crawl around the coastline and find a tiny spot where she would be left alone.

Where the two streets met, three small figures stepped through a doorway to vanish inside a house. From her angle of observation, they appeared to step upwards and disappear into a fold of nothingness rather than merely enter an unlit doorway.

To cleanse her eyes of any more hallucinations she looked up. But the sky seemed closer than it should have been to any part of the earth. She returned her gaze to the ground only to see the faces of the remaining crowd all turned in her direction.

A shuffle of small shapes came towards her. She avoided looking directly at them in case acknowledgement allowed them access to her. They didn't need permission.

By the time she was hurrying past the encroaching group, she overheard things she was sure were intended for her, but indirectly as if the speakers feigned fragments of conversation she happened to overhear in the street.

'There'll be some raw-meating soon, my love.'

'Aye, let porcelain mingle with flesh. One be smooth, one be wet.'

'There's them . . . hobble on wooden stumps.'

'. . . little boots . . . '

'Stitchin' eh, stitchin' to be sure.'

'Needles need work.'

'Brace us neck and pop in cold eyes.'

'Salt the hide, keep out grubs. Stuffin's sawdusty dry.'

'They's come in all right, they's don't get out, does her.'

'Stop it!' she screamed before she reached the end of the miserable collection of buildings and ran at the darkness, towards the memory of where she had seen the candy-striped pole at the border of Magbar Wood.

'Hearken her,' someone said, and cackled.

*

On the other side of the barrier, Catherine groped with out-stretched arms, her fingers spread wide in the dark.

Her hands met nothing but empty air.

It was as if existence and matter had ceased to be. When she looked down she failed to see her own feet where they slapped about the uneven road surface.

She wondered if she was now somewhere else, lost and blind beneath the stars of a different night.

Where was Tara's car, and where was the hedgerow? The lane seemed much wider than it could possibly be.

She had walked a few hundred metres into a cold absence and found nothing. She couldn't see anything, let alone a parked car, and would never know for certain whether she had stumbled past it.

Maybe the car wasn't there any more. She would have seen headlights or an interior light if it was occupied. Had they already fled and left her behind?

Her imagination stood in for logic. Cars were not welcome and were removed, and there were never any other cars here because the village had remained unchanged for a century, perhaps longer. Mason had somehow preserved the place and its occupants like he'd preserved the rats of his dioramas. The people had not been wearing costume, but their actual clothes. The entire area was a cruelty play that repeated its trickery like a vast clockwork toy, year after year.

A surge of panic overwhelmed what little of her reason had just driven her into the lane. 'Oh God, oh God, oh God,' came as a mantra through her startled breaths. 'Why are you doing this to me?'

She tried not to cry. Useless shrieks issued from an inner room in her mind. Her body felt weightless like all of the blood had suddenly evaporated through her skin.

It would take her all night to walk a few miles in such a lightless void. Beneath the soft soles of her feet, sharp stones on the rural lane were already making her hop and wince. Even the dim amber glow of the village buildings appeared reassuring compared to the pitch-black lane.

She gripped both sides of her face to slow everything down inside her head. *Mike.* Mike had said he would go back to the house to find her if she didn't return to the car. Mike wouldn't leave her out here alone.

He might have already gone on ahead while she was trapped in the scout hall. She had been foolish and wilful and should have stayed with him when she had the chance. If Mike was up at the house, they could find a way out together. A flicker of comfort, little more, but it gave her a tenuous purpose.

But whether he was there or not, she would have to return to the Red House. She would freeze out here. The village was hostile. The Red House was, at least, familiar. It had lights, or a more reasonable excuse for light than Magbar Wood, where she could not bear to remain.

Catherine turned about and began fumbling her way back towards the village.

On the other side of the village, in the lane that would return her to the Red House, only when she had grasped the unruly intrusions of the hedgerows did she stop hobbling.

She knew at once that her own car was no longer where she had left it.

They had stolen it with the same spiteful intent with which they'd emptied her bag. But when did they steal it, and how, let alone why? She'd not heard a car engine anywhere near the village. And surely the population was too old for car theft.

Had they taken Tara's car too?

None of them were allowed to leave.

Stop it!

Catherine glanced back at Magbar Wood. She'd just run through it, huddled into herself, too afraid to look up and about. But she'd known the night's celebrations were far from over.

As she'd run through the village, she'd hoped the effigy in the glass cabinet would have been returned to the church and that the pageant crowd would have begun dispersing. But the crowd appeared to be regrouping. Perhaps for the next stage of the pageant. A notion reinforced by the formation of one purposeful mass in the main lane, and what now appeared to be a lit procession about the relic that had been mounted onto the float.

Horrified, she stood and watched the glass casket glitter amidst a haphazard concentration of candles at the intersection of the two lanes, no more than twenty metres away from where she stood shaking.

She was sure the veiled face inside the transparent case was now watching her.

Catherine turned and ran.

Every step further away from Magbar Wood became one step closer to what she guessed was the destination of the ghastly parade: the Red House.

Behind her, the discordant rendition of 'Greensleeves' fog-horned and twisted its horrible ditty into the air.

THIRTY-NINE

The newspaper cuttings beneath the plastic coverings in the album were either yellowing or fragmenting. Grease from his fingers and crumbs from his desk had further tainted the paper whenever it was brought out for his delectation.

Leonard raised the metal shade of the desk lamp further from the album. With expertise in the preservation of old precious things he wondered at his carelessness in the matter of this newsprint, but also remembered that had the police investigations ever neared him, he may have been required to dispose of his interest in certain local matters.

Maybe the original stories from the newspapers had been archived somewhere. Or had been, what did Catherine call it, 'digitized'? Or was it 'digitalized'? He couldn't remember, but it wasn't entirely out of the question that he might replace his copies one day. Though inquiries might still carry a risk.

Leonard briefly looked to the drawn blinds. Outside the office the street had fallen silent. He had not heard a car for over twenty minutes.

Even though he could recite the best part of each article from memory, he bent to his reading. And started at the beginning of the album featuring the first of the ridiculous

Pied Piper stories and the initial rumours of 'the green van'. The stories began in 1959 and lasted until 1965.

Leonard wiped a tear from his face when he saw the photographs of Margaret Reid and Angela Prescott smiling back at him. The portraits were taken at the children's home the two girls resided in, until their leaving of it in 1959 and 1962 respectively. A long time ago their pictures were displayed in every national newspaper.

Margaret had Spina Bifida, Myelomeningocele. Poor Angela was born blind. They'd both been abandoned young. The Magnis Burrow School of Special Education was the closest thing to an actual home they'd ever known. A place where they made the kind of friendships that lasted for ever. And the place in which they found the path to salvation.

No arrests were ever made after the disappearance of Margaret Reid. But two male care-home workers, who were lovers, were interviewed after the abduction of Angela Prescott, and later released. At the time of Angela's disappearance the green vehicle was described as a tradesman's Morris Minor van with no signage, then briefly the vehicle even became an ice-cream van in some news reports.

Leonard moved on and read the front-page story from a long extinct newspaper about the Magnis Burrow School of Special Education's closure in 1965. Then he progressed through the album to find the news stories of Helen Teme, a Down Syndrome girl local to Ellyll Fields, who vanished from the reopened and refurbished Magnis Burrow School of Special Education in 1973.

In the Helen Teme pages, Leonard paused to treasure each photograph of the holiday snaps of the hapless Kenneth White, beloved of those distant Sunday tabloids. In each picture, strands of White's comb-over rose in the breeze that came off the water of a choppy sea in Rhyl. The same three bleached pictures supplemented every story of the sex offender's arrest for the suspected abduction and murder of little Helen Teme. There were pages about his release, re-arrest, re-release, and subsequent suicide by asphyxiation in his white Austin Princess outside his council flat in 1975. Case closed.

Kenneth White had been a volunteer with disabled children, from whom he'd once taken his pick. And Ken was prolific with Down Syndrome girls, which led to him being investigated when Helen Teme disappeared. But Magnis Burrow was an institution that White had never worked at, nor had any contact with, and probably never laid eyes upon when he was active in Leominster during the sixties and early seventies. He had form.

One paper even tried to resurrect the Pied Piper story of the sixties around White. Leonard marvelled at the ignorance of the press. The Pied Piper led able-bodied children away and left the lame behind. But surely this story was the complete opposite.

The Magnis Burrow abduction cases weren't consistently picked up by anyone but the American journalist, Irvine Levine, who wrote a series of stories for the *News of the World*, while working in England at the time Helen Teme's abduction made headlines. Levine was a tenacious man and the first hack to champion the link between Helen Teme and the two earlier cases of missing children, the all but forgotten Margaret Reid and Angela Prescott. Three abductions from the same home across its two incarnations.

Leonard remembered that summer being one of great personal unrest. But it seemed the press at the time hadn't much stamina for the story of a handicapped girl's abduction. After making his brief link Levine became busy with a bestselling book about something else entirely. Case forgotten.

As with Margaret Reid and Angela Prescott, Helen Teme was never found. The school that all three girls had been taken from was closed for a second time in 1975.

When Alice Galloway was said to have been abducted from out of the disused Magnis Burrow School's grounds in 1981, after climbing through a hole in the perimeter fence, the story made the nationals for a week, and the locals every day for three months. ALICE ISN'T IN WONDERLAND.

Plenty of people were interviewed by the police that time, though none were arrested. Leonard read of the hopes and then the dashing of these hopes with renewed relish. Alice Galloway's parents campaigned for the police to do more in their search for the missing girl.

The next time the Magnis Burrow School made the head-lines in Leonard's clippings, but only at local level, came with the decision to demolish the derelict school buildings, in 1988, along with most of the surrounding residential area of social housing in Ellyll Fields.

The last part of the album dealt with the human remains found by labourers after earthworks were conducted to level the Magnis Burrow School to build a dual carriageway in 1989. Briefly, the smiling faces of Margaret Reid, Angela Prescott, Helen Teme and Alice Galloway reappeared for a week, as did the Pied Piper name once given to the child snatcher who had never been caught. But this time, the green van, and ice-cream van, weren't mentioned.

Once the human remains were found to be those of

children intered over a century before the disappearances of Margaret Reid and Angela Prescott, the story died. With certainty, it was decided by archaeologists and the police, the discovered remains were those of infants laid in unmarked graves by the orphanage staff on the same site. No one dug any deeper.

Leonard found the sensation of reading all of the articles together, now they were much improved and enhanced by time, akin to being drunk after a funeral.

Finally he removed the pictures he always saved for last. On top of this prized collection was the only photograph he possessed of himself as a boy, a picture that was now faded to a brown smear. But he didn't need to see much to remember himself in the picture as a thin pale lad in an old wheelchair; his withered legs slack, small black boots at rest upon the footplate. It was taken outside a little stone house in Magbar Wood, the place of his birth.

He remembered other pictures being taken of him at that age too, on a grass lawn so sweet and bright with sunlight that he was sure he had been in heaven when he first saw the garden, up at the great house of the Last Martyr. But those other pictures of him were kept in a place no one would ever see, unless invited.

The last four pictures in his portfolio featured another child. Three of these pictures were in colour. A pale sun-bleached picture of a little freckled girl in school uniform, whose pretty green eyes were telescoped behind the cumbersome spectacles she was once made to wear.

There was a picture of her as a baby, too, sat in her little pram covered in Union Jack flags on the blessed ground. A third picture featured her wearing a pink pinafore dress. She was looking at the camera, smiling. In her hand she held an ice-lolly shaped like a coloured rocket.

The final photograph of the girl in this part of the collection was in black and white, when she was much younger. And it featured the young mother of the girl in a room so dark and small and dismal, it could have been a room for another poor woman giving birth at home, a hundred years before. The woman held her new baby against her chest for those few precious minutes before the little girl was taken away.

Leonard shuddered from the emotion that came into his heart like an electric current. And he wept silently for a while, then wiped at his face. 'You were given away.'

He blinked back tears. 'You were despised because you were gifted. But you were not forgotten by those who cherished you.' Leonard kissed the photograph of the little girl holding the ice lolly. 'Time to come home, Kitten.'

Leonard turned in his chair and spoke out loud to the window, and the world beyond it, as if in accusation. His voice was broken by emotion, but carried by anger. 'One must never forget the enchantment and the terror of childhood. For some it will always be acute. Their path is much closer to ours. What you discard, we will cherish.'

Leonard placed the pictures back inside the album. He closed his eyes and gathered himself, then shut the album and looked across to the open safe.

From the top drawer of his desk he removed a pair of white cotton gloves and slipped his thin fingers inside them. Then removed a blank cassette tape from the drawer. He pushed his wheelchair back from his desk to the wall and applied the brakes. Then placed his hands upon the armrests of the wheelchair and stood up. Stretched his back and raised his white hands to the ceiling. His stiff knees cracked.

Unsteady on his feet, he walked across to the little stereo system he kept in the office to listen to the weather reports after Catherine had left the office. She'd once tried to play a CD on it but found the CD player to be broken. She didn't have any tapes.

Leonard opened the cassette deck and fitted the unmarked cassette inside the door. Closed the lid. A tremor passed along his index finger. He pressed PLAY.

From out of the static and wear on the tape the great voice of the Last Martyr, Mason, rose to begin the recitation.

Keep one kitten, destroy the rest . . .

Leonard half closed his eyes for a moment to savour the sound of the Martyr's voice before moving to the corner of the large rug between the two desks. On his hands and knees he rolled the rug back to the far wall, until the faded white circle of the Ring o' Roses was completely uncovered.

Drowning is the preferred method . . . up by the hind legs, a quick blow to the back of the head . . .

Upon the bare wooden floorboards he slipped off his shoes. Unbuckled his trousers, let them drop. Removed his pullover, tie, shirt, socks, and underwear. Folded his clothes and placed them upon his desk.

Once he was naked, he carefully removed his hairpiece. Against his scalp the adhesive tape issued a ripping sensation, but caused him no discomfort. He placed the mop of grey hair upon his clothes. Then removed his eyebrows with two sharp tugs and returned to the circle.

Relax a dried skin to reintroduce suppleness. Bathe with warm water, ammonia, sulphonated neatsfoot oil. Place the

*specimen in a moist box for one night, then scrape the skin
. . . wash the skin . . .*

In nothing more than the illumination from his desk lamp, Leonard moved his arms through the air and studied his scars. Stroked the furrows where great rents had been made in his flanks. Caressed the long ventral incision down to his hairless pelvis and shivered, rolled his eyes up. Gently pressing the thin, pale flesh of his abdomen, he closed his eyes to delight at the parcel of sawdust packed inside the cavity.

Once salted, fresh skins of large mammals can be washed with Ivory soap, rinsed three times, then degreased with petroleum . . .

Such was his excitement a little warm urine trickled down his inner thigh from the pink hole in his smooth groin.

Plug their openings with cotton, apply corn starch and wash the blood away . . .

The man some people called Leonard sucked in his breath. His legs trembled. Those parts of his hairless arms that were still capable of sensation were blessed with shivery bumps that had nothing to do with being naked.

He took his mind from the recording for a moment and focussed his eyes on the safe. It was too easy to go to the ground and give in to the golden rushing of things through himself.

Clean a skull with soap and water mixed with ammonia and sodium sulphate . . .

From the cavity in the wall he withdrew the wooden chest bequeathed to his care by the Last Martyr. He tried not to remember the time of his succession in detail because it still caused him great pain. A time so grey in his mind when his master could no longer bear the burden of the Great Art and what his troupe demanded of him. Mason, the man who had found him as a boy and shown him miracles. The man who had appointed him successor and servant of the great tradition.

Leonard carried the box across to Catherine's desk, the altar she had sat behind for twelve months, bathed in his adoration. Leonard opened the chest.

The wax mould of the face should be applied to the mannequin at this stage . . . boomed the voice of the Last Martyr. And such was Leonard's ecstasy at this point, he heard no more from the recording.

As Leonard raised the small golden effigy of a hand from its velvet compartment inside the wooden chest, tears burned his eyes and blurred his vision.

The blessed Hand of Henry Strader, the first of the known Martyrs; the hard polished fingers of the relic were relaxed above the palm as if the hand were acknowledging a crowd from atop a raised arm.

Leonard's own gloved hands shook around the smooth, gleaming container, and his fingers became as insubstantial as feathers. He wept.

'Saintly mentor,' he said through his sobs, 'extend thy reach through this vessel.'

He wanted to shriek out his prayer, but kept his voice down in case the accountant next door was working late, or someone should pass in the street outside. 'Open this pathway to sublime knowledge that we may carry the true cross.'

Leonard sniffed and blinked away his hot tears.

So little was salvaged after the routing of Henry Strader's broken remains by beggars, in that filthy street on the morning of 6 June 1649. The power of the revelation, that never dimmed with time, struck him hard: he actually held, in his own humble hands, one of the few surviving parts of the first of the known Martyrs. One of the actual fingers no less, returned to Strader's birthplace after his murder. The very idea never failed to paralyse Leonard with astonishment.

'Grant that such heavenly treasures will bless your keeper's pilgrimage.' Leonard kissed the side of the golden hand. 'And that other wretches will be saved as I was saved.'

From the wrist portion of the reliquary of the Hand of Strader, Leonard unscrewed the golden cap and gently removed a small parcel from the hollow canister.

Carefully, he unfolded a fragment of protective material. The fabric was stiff and brown; a glorious shred from the shirt of the king who lost his head. From within the wrappings, Leonard removed the wizened third finger from Strader's right hand. The relic was as black as liquorice and almost weightless.

When he cupped the finger in his palm his entire body convulsed, and he longed to slot something sharp beneath his meagre flesh.

Before he fainted from the touching and the blessing, he slipped the soiled linen upon the girl's altar and placed the finger of the Martyr upon the cloth.

Leonard regained his breath and wiped the sweat off his forehead and nose with the back of one gloved hand. Gently, holding the aged chin of the leather face with his fingers, he then raised the *Mandylion of The Smooth Field* from the wooden chest. And with the Mandylion came the perfume of stale incense and old sweat.

Long curls of raven hair fell from the relic and tickled his knees. He could barely stand upright at the sight of the mottled ivory of Henry Strader's skull fragment stitched within the discoloured fabric of the scalp. So glorious was the sensation of holding the head of the Martyr he became terrified he might urinate again.

Holding his breath, the lean tendons in his legs quivering like catgut strings, he placed the *Mandylion of the Smooth Field* upon his old hairless head. When the skull fragment rested upon his flesh, he collapsed to his hands and knees and began to whisper from behind the blank mask of leather, pressed so close and hot to his face.

'Live through me, Lord. So that I may do thy bidding. Let thy will be resurrection. As thou did raise them, we too are saved.'

FORTY

'His religion didn't understand it. His science couldn't explain it. But my uncle found something. And it passed across a distance you cannot imagine. Unless guided. As you have been, my child.'

As soon as Catherine's feet skittered across the polished floor of the hall, Edith's sharp voice had come down at her from the vaulted airiness above, to cut short her breathless cries of 'Mike! Mike!'

The mistress of the house had spoken from where she waited behind the first-floor balusters, sat in her chair, a carriage that appeared to have absorbed the frail body inside it. A body that now appeared as little more than a collection of bones wrapped in an evening gown of black silk. Edith's small face was but a pale smudge, high up in the air, at the furthest reach of the red lights of the hall walls.

Mike had not been outside the Red House, that great spiky monolith with roofs and chimneys and finials she could no longer see, all rearing into a night that itself lacked definition and borders. Catherine had been calling, and then crying his name in the lane that tapered cold and lightless to the black front gate. There had been no answer.

The front entrance to the house was open in expectation and emitting the unwelcome red glow of the interior. Tonight, each of the arched front doors had been swept back to the reception walls, as if to provide access to a group of guests.

From the distance the amplified blare of 'Greensleeves' still drifted, as if broadcast from a nightmarish ice-cream van that collected children after midnight. The encroaching sound had finally propelled Catherine through the front entrance.

But was Mike even here? If he was, the idea now troubled Catherine more than she wanted to admit. And what was Edith talking about? The sudden sound of her voice from above had nearly stopped her heart. But as ever, the old woman's meaning was obscure and disingenuous. 'What do you mean?' she cried out to the small figure above her. 'What are you saying? I don't want to be guided!'

Edith pretended not to hear her. The distant head of the woman was angled upwards at the skylight. 'My uncle found the places where they rested. Buried with the remains of their murdered masters. In unmarked places they hid themselves, and waited. Eager to perform. You know of Henry Strader's fate. And you now know of the fates of the other known Martyrs. Blessed Spettyl, blessed Pettigrew. They too heard the calling from hallowed ground.'

'I don't want anything to do with this! Where is my bloody car! You've no right!'

Edith ignored her pleas and continued to speak as if to an audience peering through the skylight. 'My uncle spent years looking for what remained of them, for what had returned itself to our soil after the Last Martyr fell. But maybe my uncle was found. Chosen. Perhaps the other known Martyrs were too, in their own times. Who can really say in these matters?'

'I do not want to know any more, or see any more. Nothing of what you are trying to show me.'

'But what called out to the Martyrs was a life most precious and sacred. Not life many would recognize, or believe in, unless they were young. But this life came back to certain things when called upon, my dear, in the right places. Small things were repaired. There was resurrection, blessed resurrection, for them and for those who revered them.'

'Enough of this! Mike. My friend, Mike. Is he here? My car has gone! My bag—'

'Do be quiet! You are hysterical. I will not conduct a conversation about a stairwell. It is undignified.'

Edith's chair rolled backwards out of the winey light. But how she had been moved, or by whom, Catherine didn't understand. The regular squeak of wheels rotated along the first-floor landing in the direction of the drawing room. The wheelchair moved as it had done so during her first visit, a time that now seemed like an old and weird dream. And one she wished she had once taken better heed of.

Either she had gone mad here, or nothing but a total relocation back to a recognizable world would create a discontinuation of the house's manipulation of her mind, her memory, her dreams and imagination. The very structure and its trapped chemical air were like a powerful psychotropic drug, one whose effects prevented the organization of clear thoughts.

Catherine climbed the stairs. Perspiration from her race back to the Red House cooled beneath the thin dress and made her shiver. Both of her feet bled.

Perhaps she'd never been this ill before, *mentally ill*. But if she had to seize Edith by that scrawny neck she would have answers. Edith had not invited her to the pageant so much as sent her there. Edith had not been present because Catherine would have seen her enter the wretched hall. But who had operated the marionettes? Maude?

Please let it have been Maude.

When Catherine stood in the doorway of the drawing room, a hundred glass eyes glittered in the dim light around Edith, who grinned behind a gauzy veil. Like an old exhibit returned to its place in a public display, her wheelchair was back in position beside the fireplace, with Horatio curled around the iron footplates.

'I just want my car back and my things . . . and then I will go.'

'Go? Where, dear? Back to where you came from? Preposterous. Why would anyone want to go back over there? It's been quite the ordeal, I can assure you, just tolerating the place again for a short while.'

Catherine approached the old woman. 'I have a life—'

'A life? Why, really.'

'A family—'

'Not your real family, dear.'

Catherine reached out her hand and steadied herself against the back of a chair. Her thoughts scrabbled. She was at the heart of a cruel conspiracy. She was asleep and this was a nightmare in which she was endlessly persecuted. 'What do you know about me?'

Edith smiled and softened her voice to a tone of patient understanding when speaking to a confused child. 'You were given away, dear. And picked up again. That was very kind. But you didn't get far because you were born in Magbar Wood. The last child, no less, practically within the shadow of the First Known Martyr's tomb. So you could hardly fit in anywhere else, could you? Our people never did. You may never have amounted to much, but nonetheless there are those for whom you were always special.

'And since my uncle returned enchantment to our little corner of the world, there are some opportunities that are granted to so few. We mustn't spurn opportunity, dear. Don't you agree? Your little friend, Alice, has known marvels since she joined us on your behalf.'

Catherine sank to her knees. She needed to be close to the floor before she collapsed. She was so tired now her breath shook its way out and her legs trembled. Once she'd got her wind back, she would set off again, with or without Mike, through the garden gate and across the fields. Eventually she would reach a road. On a road there would be cars with people inside them. People that belonged to the world she knew. She found herself staring at the hem of Edith's long, antique dress.

'Try and understand, dear. All my uncle ever tried to do was startle us awake. Into wonderment at what lay beyond us. After us. We all became party to what chose us to see such sights. Things that had not performed in this part of the world for many years.'

'Please, I don't want to hear this. You are mad! Your uncle was insane—'

'Perhaps he lost his way at the end. And he lost his nerve, dear. He was old and tired. But he was once a man of God, let's not forget. It was perfectly natural for his old faith to return when it was too late. You must understand, as we have all had to accept, that what was fetched out from those hills, and from the church, my dear, was not so easy to put back – it was too late for that.'

'What are you saying? I don't understand. My car. My friend, Mike—'

Edith gazed into the middle distance. 'When my uncle opened his throat, he only seemed to tighten his relationship with *it*. You could say he even strengthened the whole family's association. He was the first to be saved. My mother was next. I can't even remember when. And then it was my turn.' Edith smiled her yellow smile. 'And we've all made a great effort to welcome you, too. But we're tired now. It's very demanding on us to be here, even for a while.'

'Please, what is happening?'

'How many little girls were ever offered such a gift? That is what you should consider.'

Catherine gripped the wheelchair, as if a closer proximity to the old woman would add weight to her pleading. 'Gift? I'm not well. Please. I need help now. Edith, please.'

'It would have been better if you had come across with your friend, Alice. We saved that little stowaway because you weren't ready. You still wanted to fit in somewhere, out there, in a world that despised you, rejected you. But all of this unpleasantness could have been avoided if you weren't so stubborn! Their arms are always open for the lame, and the forsaken. Of course, you may find it strange at first. We all do. It's much easier for the little ones.'

Beyond Catherine's hot tears, Edith's shape blurred to a shimmer, itself vanishing into the dark mantel and fireplace. The wheels of Edith's chair squeaked. Something clicked above her head. She briefly thought of knitting needles as small fingers, cold as porcelain, combed through her tangled hair and touched her scalp.

'I want to leave. Where is Mike?'

'Hush.' Edith's voice dropped to a whisper. 'I tried to leave once. When I was twelve I ran away. I didn't get far. About as far as my poor father did before me, though I never met him. When my mother caught up with me, she remarked at how I had followed my father's footsteps, into the meadow you'll never find the end of. Then she put me in a room with Grizell Killigrew for a day, and I never ran again. I can tell you.'

Catherine raised her head, frowning so hard it hurt the muscles around her eyes. She pushed herself to her feet, swallowing the constriction in her throat that seemed determined to render her mute. 'What are you doing . . . what . . . to me?'

'Enough of my old tales. Your young man, your beau, is waiting for you.'

'Mike?'

'He came with that girl who had too much to say for herself. Maude was the same once. Compared to your friend, I'd like to say poor old Maude got off lightly, but then I doubt Maude would agree with me on that matter.' Edith tittered.

Catherine's voice was more intention than sound. 'Mike's here? Tara?'

'Strangers have never been welcome. How could they understand us, Catherine?' She said *us* and looked at Catherine in such a way as to include her. 'We have made a rare effort for you and your needs.'

'Needs? I don't—'

'All must learn there are consequences for what they desire.'

Catherine wrung her hands together until her fingers hurt. She stepped away from the mad old thing in the chair. 'Stop

306

this! Stop it now! I don't want to hear any more of your crazy shit!'

'When you were mooching in my uncle's room, did you not come to a better understanding of our history? We hoped you would. It's why we let you go in there. So you could see how my uncle was tutored in the Great Art.'

'The girls. Those girls from Ellyll Fields, what did he do to them?'

Edith continued reminiscing, as if Catherine had not even spoken. Nothing had changed between them, even now. 'To my uncle, I think they returned changed. Much changed. They were not so gentle then. No, dear. You see, in their beginnings, the troupe hid while the savagery of this world was unveiled. Oh, they saw injustice and tragedy unfold upon those they loved, and those who loved them. Tragedy that you can't imagine. It's why they made the cruelty plays to remember those who were murdered. But my uncle found the troupe damaged. As children are disturbed. As we are all changed by adversity when we are tender and innocent. By terror. By cruelty. Such things change us, dear. Shape us.'

Edith spread her spidery white fingers. They were back inside the tight silk gloves, for which Catherine was glad, as they had been so cold upon her scalp. She wasn't sure who Edith even spoke to any more, but the woman kept on talking. The brittle voice filled her head. She briefly imagined being trapped inside the Red House, listening to the woman's words, for ever. She wanted to scream.

'They recognized my uncle's suffering. It was akin to their own. And he put a troupe of those wretched shadows back together, as others had done before him. Through him they continued the tradition. And they are very much looking forward to picking up with you too, from where they left things. A long time ago. But not so long for them, dear. Or Alice.'

'Stop it, stop it, stop it! You don't know me. Who I am. You know nothing about me. You are frightening me. Please. I just want to go home.' She looked at the window as the discord of 'Greensleeves' neared the Red House. 'You're sick. Your uncle was sick. This house is sick. You took those girls. Alice.'

'Sick! You little fool. Is not the world that persecuted them sick? The world that burned and broke and hanged their fathers sick? They only want to save you. Save you as they saved the other poor wretches that were discarded. They have only ever offered sanctuary to those who are as broken as they were broken.'

Edith seemed to lose interest in her after the outburst, and looked fondly at the kittens in their glass cabinet. Wide of eye, curtseying, their tiny furred faces seemed scandalized behind the spread fans.

Catherine had come up to this room in desperation. And she had run back to the Red House because there was nowhere else for her to go. *Don't even think that!* But on reflection, she wished she'd just hobbled into the darkness on the road leading away from the village, or clambered across a ditch and fled into an unlit open field. Even if those old things, those *people* from the village, had come after her, and moved around her, whispering in the void, it would have been better than this.

Catherine backed towards the door. She fought hard to suppress all of the instincts that tried to make her accept something impossible. She fought against thoughts that wanted to become as insane as the Masons and the house they had filled with so much confusion and horror.

In the doorway, she weighed up her options, which still didn't add up to much more than an escape through the meadows at the back of the property, in complete darkness, alone.

'My parents will be looking for me. You understand that don't you? My colleague Leonard will tell them.'

'Are you sure?'

'Yes! The police will come here!'

'I hope not. They'll waste a great deal of their time, because they won't find us. This is one of those houses where an invitation is necessary.'

'Stop it! Mike. Where is Mike? You said he came here. He wasn't invited—'

'Are you sure of that? And they will not let go of those they love. Not again. Not ever. We are the exhibits to small tyrants. You were never our guest, but theirs. No one is ever anything else here.'

'Tell me where he is. Tell me!'

'And they will remake their guardians in their own image as angels have always done.'

'Shut up you horrible bitch!'

The fact that the face Edith turned upon Catherine was veiled, she considered a mercy. 'The salacious ape that followed your scent? Is that all you can think of at a time like this, when you witness miracles? Your hosts will be so disappointed in you, Catherine.'

'Where is he?'

'Your beau was *invited* inside to wait for you, and wait he does. You will find him in my uncle's workshop. With his lover. Those who wrong you will always be taken care of by those who love you. Your mother certainly was, after she gave you away.'

'My mother . . .'

'Has known such torments for what she did. *They* saw how you suffered. *They* shared the pain in your dear little heart. Now you are here her suffering can end.'

'What are you saying?'

Edith grinned. 'Here you are wanted. Here you are loved.'

'I don't want to be loved by anything here!'

'But you do. It's what you've always wanted. Your heart bled in the right place at the right time. They came to you, like they came to my uncle. They came to bring you home. Where wonders never cease. Where you will be loved.'

For several seconds the suggestions behind Edith's words did not register. Catherine's entire mind was one morbid but half-conscious blank in which she could hear the rushing of her blood mixing with the cacophony of the pageant outside the front of the house.

She slipped into one of those rare episodes when the separation of her consciousness into three divisible minds occurred. One was frantic with fear and panic about a terrible outcome. Beneath that maelstrom she was aware of a strange feeling of acceptance that almost cried out for calm. Deeper still, was the edge of an awareness that partially understood the impossible, and had always done so, but never converted comprehension into a lasting belief or wisdom she could call upon.

She decided she must be stuck in someone else's nightmare, as if she were trapped in the residue of M. H. Mason's consciousness, or Edith's, and whatever it was that consumed this house. The sense of this idea retracted as soon as it had begun and was submerged again. Only fear and despair were left behind.

She'd been driven to what she sensed was the end of her mind. The situation even stopped feeling peculiar. And for barely a moment she came near to a precipice of understanding something much bigger than anything she had ever known. She was brushing against something so monumental her reaction to it would be pure terror. But she must get beyond the terror and find peace or she would break.

She found the strength to run, out of the drawing room and into the dimly lit passage beyond. It was there, as she fled for the stairs to the ground floor, that she heard Edith's final words. 'They are the ones who offer justice now, my dear. And their justice can be terrible . . . what they did to your poor mother.'

By the time she made the ground floor and stood within the hall, another voice spoke. *To her?* She couldn't be sure. But it groaned and circled down the stairwell as if from beyond the roof of the Red House, like some great unseen mouth now covered the place where the skylight of red glass was normally positioned.

It was a voice she recognized. A man's voice. The one narrating the play in the village. And one just as unclear and obscured by static, as if broadcast through poor reception across a great distance of time. Another old recording, because no voice spoken in the present day was capable of such solemn and dour intonation, with a timbre degraded so horribly by age.

Keep one kitten, destroy the rest . . .

Much of the speech she didn't catch, words slipped into

white noise and became garbled. What she did hear she wanted to block her ears against.

Drowning is the preferred method . . . up by the hind legs, a quick blow to the back of the head . . .

Catherine moved across the hall.

Bind the tow with cotton threads . . . Push the wires through the false body . . . Pack soft stuffing around the wires . . .

She looked at the gaping front doors. The music in the lane had stopped. She could see nothing but the tips of blood-lit weeds beyond the porch and a long line of candle flames.

Treat larger mammals in the field . . . depends upon the circumstances . . . the trap . . . placement, temperature . . . before you carry it indoors . . . never cut the throat . . .

'Mike!' Catherine screamed and ran into the unlit passage that led to the back of the house. At the far end of the utility area of the building one door was open and its murky light served as a beacon. 'Mike!'

The voice from above came down and filled the spaces of the Red House, to both push and chase her through the corridor.

A ventral incision through the belly, or a dorsal entry through the back . . . Breastbone to tailbone . . . undress from the incision . . . scissors to disjoint the arms and legs. Pull down the skin to the toes . . . cut across the foot . . .

Without light, because her slapping hands failed to find the switches, she was at once ungainly and glanced off a wall. The blow forced her to slow down. To all but stop moving.

She could not see what was around her feet any more.

Had something moved near her feet? Was that a quick series of bumps close by, footsteps? *Maude.* Was Maude a child killer? Catherine imagined the woman's mute head, mopped in white hair, close by. Waiting with one of Mason's fleshing blades in her angry old hand. It must be a trap. Edith had lied about Mike to get her down here. They'd stolen her car and bag and phone. Cut her off and were tormenting her. Was that how it went down here?

How did they know she was adopted? Had they killed her natural mother? Isn't that what Edith had said? For giving her away? No, Edith had said that her mother's suffering would end now she was here, which implied her mother was alive. But where was she?

Lies. Half-truths and manipulation; all she had ever been offered in this house. But Alice? They knew about Alice.

Go through, Alice. Go through, Alice. Go first. Go first. It's all right . . . Don't! Alice, Alice, come back. It's not safe. Alice. Please, Alice. We're not allowed. Come back.

She cupped her hands over her ears to drive out the sound of her own memories and the drone of the man's voice, which made her nerve endings shriek. The static-corroded voice was inside her head. Such was her disorientation she thought she might fall in the dark and not be able to get up again. She swatted her hands about her body to ward off what she thought was Maude.

Trim close to the skull. Around the eye orbit detach the lids. Remove the eyes. The lids must be arranged under a magnifying visor as microbes are moved beneath a microscope. The smallest adjustments give the effects of panic and terror.

'Stop! Stop it!'

313

She ran to the open door of the workshop, to the dim, dirty light. There was no other light here. It was a place where you squinted and crept and tottered and brushed against things in the darkness you could not identify.

Trim the ear to the base, separate the skin from the cartilage . . . then turn the ear inside out . . . unglove the head with sharp tugs.

'Mike. Mike. Mike,' she cried at the open door of Mason's workshop.

Flesh the meat from off the skin . . . Degrease the skin. Rinse in plain water.

She looked inside the workshop for a moment that seemed much longer than a moment. Then sat down just inside the room with her back against the wall. The wall held the weight of her body that her legs could no longer support.

A degreased skin can pickle for months and incur no damage . . .

FORTY-ONE

The flesh of the lovers was pale. Only what looked like a long sideways mouth, which ran down Mike's entire back, offered any variation to the dull gleam of his skin.

Before him sat a woman whose face Catherine did not need to see to know her identity. She knew it was a woman because one of her heavy breasts, as white as a fish's belly with a nipple like a bruise, was visible between Mike's elbow and ribs.

Their dark, wet heads rested together, forehead to forehead, as if they shared a whispered secret like a boyfriend and girlfriend in a scented bath. A dark fluid filled the tin tub to their upper arms.

Unmoving, Catherine looked at them for a while, nonsensically feeling her presence was an intrusion upon a moment of deep intimacy. She also felt the cold shock of carnal betrayal. A disgust at death. And grasped the horribly simple fact that someone could be alive, but go to the wrong place and then not be alive.

Some time passed before she realized the unfamiliar sound in the room came from the pit of her own stomach, rhythmic, like hard breaths. The sound of a stranger in a dark room.

*

Catherine left the lovers and walked to the back door of the house. The sound was still coming out of her mouth like she was giving birth. It was strangely reassuring because it made her aware she was still alive and real, *for a bit longer*.

The back door was locked. *Of course it is locked.* She peered through the little panes of glass in the top half of the door and saw stars. She looked down upon stars too, or was that a strange effect of light upon the glass? *What light?* But the very thought that there was nothing outside any more, no earth or trees or sky, didn't surprise her. She didn't really know what this place was, could only be certain of one thing: she was tired of running. It didn't seem to be getting her anywhere. She felt like she had swum the English Channel in her clothes. So if there was no more running in her, or point to it, there was only here. And her walking through this place and not thinking much for a while, like she'd reached the end of something important. Herself.

In her right fist she held tight the rosewood handle of a scalpel she had taken from the workshop. She wondered if she would be capable of using it on anyone who came near her in the dark corridor, or who tried to prevent her from leaving the house. Or maybe she could use it on herself to frighten them. That would be easier. She used to stamp on her glasses at school and slap her own head until a teacher came. One of the quiet girls with white socks pulled up to the knee, who would never be her friend, would always run for a teacher when she went crazy. Crazy, she learned when very young, was as good a defence as any if you wanted to be left alone. The Red House, she mused, had played the same card.

From up above, came the crackle-static-fizz of the old

recording. The great M. H. Mason she had come here for, continued to speak across time in a place he'd curated into an elegant hell, one that smelled of that which disguised death. For posterity he'd recorded his apocryphal madness to inspire others.

They are illusion and deception.

She caught snatches of the dreary announcements within the interference, and only half heard them when the voice passed into clearer bursts.

They are conjured. Their history is obscure and . . .

Along the length of the utility corridor she met no interference. She tried all of the doors because the rooms beyond had windows big enough to smash and they faced the outside. If there was nothing beyond the panes of glass then maybe nothing was still better than this.

Every door was locked. The passage was a funnel, it had led her to the workshop and demanded she come back out again.

The front door was also shut against whatever was out there, too, or had been out there. There was no more music, no more 'Greensleeves', the things with the candles had not followed her inside.

Were they ever there?

From the inside, the doors had been secured and the keys removed from the brass-framed keyholes in the locks. So someone was inside the house with her, securing doors behind her? They could see in the dark and they had something special planned for her. *Maude. You mute bitch.* Catherine turned and headed for the stairs.

I find the presence of immobile rats far more confirming and comforting than I find the company of my own species.

She had to stay within the fraying boundary rope of reason. Even though her thoughts and half-thoughts and assumptions were being blown about by currents of fear and confusion, there was an explanation, a rational explanation for this situation.

Edith was no killer. She was too infirm. Maude? Maybe. M. H. Mason and Violet Mason had once been real, mad but real. Yet Maude and Edith were behind this. They were continuing whatever M. H. Mason and Violet Mason had started.

Think. Think. Think.

Edith and Maude must have taken Alice all those years ago. With help. There must have been a team effort behind the abductions of Alice and all of those helpless children who went missing from Magnis Burrow, the ones her nan had told her about. M. H. Mason and Violet had begun something here, others had continued the tradition. Wasn't that what Edith was getting at?

And in the Red House M. H. Mason's descendants had continued to play out their fantasies, their psychopathic delusions about some nonsensical but hideous legacy of marionette theatre, and upon her, too, whom they had long coveted because she got away in 1981.

Edith was now trying to make her accept the surreal rites of her family, trying to insert them into her thoughts as some kind of alternative reality, some bending out of shape of natural law.

It was preposterous, and she wasn't entirely convinced by her theory, but it was all she had to go on.

But were they going to kill her? Was she right now being batted about like a mouse in sharp claws before the coup de grâce?

Making herself acknowledge that *this* was all for real, gave her a cruel sense of comfort. Because above all else, she must refuse to accept the impossible things the Red House and its constituency were suggesting to her. Otherwise she was lost.

Catherine stood in the middle of all the small, finely dressed animals. As she stared at an empty wheelchair Horatio watched her with an eternally wet eye. M. H. Mason's niece, his loyal priestess, was missing from the drawing room.

The absence of Edith mingled with recent memories she no longer wanted, of the old figures prancing about the pageant and of something jabbering from behind a door down there. Her coma of numbness, her brief spell of reason broke. She shook. She sucked at, more than breathed, the air. To fight the swoops of nausea that circled her cold scalp, she sat upon the rug.

A small avalanche of dust in the fireplace made her shriek. She sat back on her heels and stared into the great centre-piece of the room. Another trickle fell into the clean black grate. This time she just flinched. She could hear nothing but the droning of the recording. Which seemed to come out of the fireplace, too, now.

In the corridor outside the drawing room, and about the stairwell, Catherine went and patted her hands along the wood panels for the light switches that blended with the walls. Those she found she slapped on to commit more of the dim ruby glow to the staircase. *They have electricity, they must pay bills, people know they live here.*

The two adjoining corridors of the first floor remained in darkness. Going inside the lightless mouth of either to find a switch was more than she could endure. They wanted her to go up.

The children must dance for someone . . .

Maybe she should start the cutting up there.

FORTY-TWO

Though they were both in no condition to do anything but loll like mannequins upon their seats, if either of the occupants of the attic were to move, she believed she would pass out.

Catherine imagined she was in the attic room of a doll's house, equipped with two dolls, and filled with the amplified noise of a badly tuned radio. Under the roof the noise of static and the metallic voice was so loud, she looked up to make sure she had not walked beneath an enormous asthmatic mouth with a microphone pressed to its lips.

Thrust out before her, level with her shoulders, the scalpel trembled because she held the handle so tightly. Her other hand was clamped across her mouth to smother the kind of whimpers most people never hear themselves utter in an entire lifetime.

The walls of the space she had entered were cluttered and obscured by old wooden tea chests, a set of dining chairs under dust sheets, and a painted rocking horse as big as a pony. Her vision flashed across all of these things and more that didn't even register, as she searched for movement amongst the furniture. None was forthcoming.

As the terrible voice buzzed, she detected the whir of a clockwork toy. Mechanical parts in what looked like a

Frenophone in perfect condition. She'd once seen one in a museum, but it had not been as polished and shiny as the one sat upon the little collapsible table. The device looked like a gramophone but it didn't play records. It was designed to pick up faint radio signals. And it was operated manually. Hanging from the side of the wooden box was a black handle.

But who had turned it?

She returned her attention to the two bodies in the attic. Surely the withered figure slumped upon the chair behind the table had been incapable of operating the Frenophone. Dressed from head to toe in a white suit and apron, the hands concealed in buff-coloured protective gloves, was the fly-keeper she had seen in the overgrown garden.

Scalpel leading the way, she approached the table at which the figure may have once sat upright, and stood as close as she dared in case it twitched. Through the gauzy front of the mask an indistinct head was just visible.

Catherine tugged off the mask and stared at what remained of a yellowing face, as dry as parchment like that of a pharaoh on display in a museum. Some of the face was missing, burrowed back above one eye socket. The lipless mouth was open and as dry as a bone inside. The gleam and lustre of the open and static eyes assured her they were made of glass. The dried sinews of the throat were neatly sown together by a line of stitches. It was M. H. Mason.

The protective clothing seemed to have settled around the thin and collapsed shape inside. But it could move, she had seen it move. *How?* At the sudden recollection of *its* movements between the trees at the foot of the garden, Catherine withdrew from the table.

She promised herself that what she had seen in the garden, that vestige of humanity in white clothing, was not some old toy, wound up to stagger feebly through an old routine, as if set off by a mischievous child trying to get her attention. There were no scarecrows of poorly preserved human remains temporarily occupied by what other life existed here, or behind here, or was close to here, that Edith had alluded to. A force she thought she had sensed, but could not see. Because thinking like that, and believing such things, was just what Edith wanted her to do, and she must not accept Edith's lies.

So there was another occupant of the Red House who had worn this outfit in the garden on that first day. A third inhabitant. There was Maude, Edith, and one other who had waved to her from the foot of the garden. And she had seen faces at windows, disguised faces. So maybe this *other* she had yet to meet was the killer of Mike and Tara, and little Alice. Perhaps he was the disabled child from the old photos in Mason's study. The one she guessed might be Edith's son. He would be very old by now, past seventy.

Under his mother's tutelage, Edith's son may even have preserved his grandmother and great uncle. The house was so insane anything now seemed possible. And it could also have been this *other* she'd heard creeping around the house at night. Crawling outside of her room.

Catherine turned to the second occupant of the attic, who sat and grinned inside the casket like a satanic version of the Madonna. It was the relic she had seen at the pageant. Housed within glass, she made an educated guess that this was almost certainly Edith's mother, Violet Mason. A woman now revered as a saint by the local vestiges of life, if you could even consider them as the living.

323

Under closer inspection, the facial skin of Violet Mason's remains was as pale as an unearthed grub and as wrinkled as a wet cotton sheet. So shrunken was the form, the crumpled features under the great black hat and behind the patterned veil would have been at home upon the head of a child. The eyes were open and bright and almost certainly made of glass. German. The dress was made of finely embroidered black silk and covered the figure's limbs. Only the hands were visible. They were as colourless as putty, with fingers as thin as pencils, but looked alarmingly soft. The garlands inside the casket were fresh, as if plucked that very day from the meadows.

Someone had preserved Violet and stored her and her brother's remains up here. It was ghastly, but Catherine knew she must stay on the side of reason or she was lost, completely gone. These were embalmed corpses, they were not living.

But how was Violet's corpse transported up here? The corpse had been in the village, then in the lane. *How? How? How?*

When she was in shock, in the workshop, Edith's emissaries must have carried the glass casket up here. Maybe while Maude took Edith from her chair in the drawing room and carried her away, somewhere. This all could still make sense. *Only just, but stay with it.*

The glass coffin had been placed before an antique telescope made from brass and mounted on a wooden tripod. The lens faced an arched window. Catherine had seen the window from outside the building when down in the lane. She remembered the star charts and photographs of the night sky in M. H. Mason's study; the obsessiveness of a talented amateur that was barely scientific. This is where Mason had looked to further reaches, and implored the sky for a meaning that he had found an absence of in his own world.

As he went mad.

Catherine turned her attention to the monogrammed leather trunk, but made sure to cast her eyes into the shadows between the hummocks of sheeted storage, though she wasn't sure what she suspected could move within these darker places. But this was definitely the same leather trunk she had seen in the unoccupied hotel room in Green Willow after Edith first made contact. She had seen it again in the nursery.

The brass clasps were turned upwards, the trunk was unlocked.

Catherine took her hand from her mouth and steadied her fingers enough to hold the clasps. She stifled her breath, then tugged the lid of the trunk upwards with all of her might. The lid flipped backwards with a squeak and slapped against the rear panel.

She stepped away, sunk to a crouch, the scalpel held out front.

The top of the case was fully open. It was lined with what looked like oilcloth. Nothing rose from the musty confines.

She leant forward and peered inside.

When the noise from the Frenophone abruptly stopped, the sudden silence of the attic was obliterated by her own scream.

Catherine couldn't stop her body shaking. It took a while to realize she was also stepping from one foot to another, as if wet and trying to dry off and keep warm. Using what remained of her wits, she guessed she was going into shock.

Because Edith's lifeless form lay inside the trunk. Collapsed like a doll with its mouth open. Entirely white eyes were turned upwards inside the small skull. And Catherine knew from a glance there wasn't a single breath of life inside the woman. It appeared the figure had just been dropped inside. Perhaps once some unspeakable function was over.

Uncovered by the disordered hem of the gown she wore, Edith Mason's little feet were sealed inside ankle boots that buttoned up the side. Fixed to the heels of her footwear were ugly iron callipers, which disappeared inside the multitude of petticoats and skirts beneath the black dress.

Catherine didn't know where to go next, but she moved to the staircase she had climbed to enter the attic. She was only able to focus on getting out of the foul room at the summit of the house, one step at a time.

On her way down the flight of stairs, she became aware she was descending into bright red light. The second-floor passageway that contained the attic entrance was now better lit than she thought it was possible for the corridor to be.

Down each side of the wood-panelled walls the glass shades of the lamps now burned brightly and the light issued was no longer murky like sunlight trapped inside syrup. Instead the wall lights possessed an incandescence that stimulated an emotion within her that was so unfamiliar, it took her a few moments to identify her reaction to the new visibility: reassurance.

This new light must be another trick of the Red House, of Maude, the killer, or both.

Or whatever else inhabited the building that could not be seen.

Stop it!

She steadied herself against a wall before moving on. She was being directed to something she could not second-guess.

Play along and identify it.

Sudden jolts of recollection made her whimper. Edith's collapsed and lifeless body. The separation of flesh on Mike's back, that black slit. A cold, bloodless breast above the murky surface of the fluid in the bath. The crinkled face of Edith's mother, those supple but limp hands. Catherine tried to douse the sparks of recent memory before they lit her up with panic.

The preposterous and sickening nature of what she had been made to confront in both the workshop and the attic she didn't so much refuse to examine, but was now unable to consider. If she even tried to, she knew she would fall to pieces and not be able to put herself back together again.

She raised her face to sniff at the air that now blossomed with a floral aroma. The corridor was infused with a scent of roses. And the air was warm enough for the blood to return to her skin.

Perhaps it was another trick, or a late welcome from a building she must resist. But she could not suppress her gratitude for the return of her sight, and for a smell beyond the caustic burn of the chemicals, and for something to touch her skin that wasn't cold.

The Red House was silent.

She moved on with the scalpel held out front. As she passed the closed doors in the passage, she watched them closely and felt her neck tense once they were behind her. She was as wary of the building as she would be of a violent bully that occasionally smiled at her.

At the stairwell she looked over her shoulder. The corridor remained empty and well lit.

The fragrance of flowers was even more potent by the stairs, as if the aroma filled the great stairwell to the roof. The wooden floors and walls of the adjoining passage were also lit with a hearty crimson radiance from wall lights that had previously emitted a murky glow.

She peered over the banister rail. The hall floor looked as if it had been recently polished and buffed. She went to the arched window of the landing, opposite the corridor that held Edith's room and the nursery. Drew the heavy curtains to be confronted with a wooden shutter. She opened the shutters and peered through.

Saw nothing but her own pale and haggard face in the reflection. The glass was so clean and the world beyond the window so black, the pane functioned as a mirror. Over her shoulders, she saw the second floor of the Red House tunnel away into the distance.

A casement window. She put the scalpel down upon the little padded bench before the pane of glass and gripped the latch. Turned it and gingerly pushed the window open onto cold air and a night so still, lightless and silent, she could have been looking into a void. The windows of the ground floor must have been concealed behind drapes and shutters too, because not a streak of light escaped from below to illumine the absence.

Where had the people with the candles gone? *Were they like Edith and Mason, the fly-keeper? Did they come alive and then fall down like dolls?* She killed the train of thought because it made her hands tremble.

Catherine sat down upon the window seat and pulled her

ankles together, placed her hands between her knees and began to rock backwards and forwards. She did it out of habit in moments of great anxiety, and God knew there had been a few of those.

What to do?

The doors to the rooms downstairs were locked and their windows were unavailable to her for an escape. She would never be able to bring herself to jump from a first-floor window, unless the place was on fire.

Had the world truly been removed from outside these solid walls?

Stop it! Stop it! Stop it!

Where was Maude? She must have turned up the lights and locked the front and back doors. Catherine stood up. Her vision blurred with hot tears. 'Maude! Maude!'

No one answered.

She clenched her jaws and looked at the scalpel to usher a spurt of lunatic courage, then ran back at the corridor housing Edith's bedroom and the nursery. She turned the door handle of the nursery. Locked. Ran to the door across the corridor and tried that. Locked. Worked her way back down to the end of the passage and yanked at the handle of every door. Locked, locked, locked, locked.

She wanted to scream again, but doing something, anything, kept her mind off matters her chaotic mind must be prevented from dwelling upon.

Catherine arrived back to where she'd started her search and stood outside Edith's bedroom. Without much vigour left in her limp arm, she pushed the handle. The door clicked open.

She went through and shut the door behind her, then

locked it. This room she was allowed inside. She was allowed to see the attic and she was allowed to see the workshop. Something without speech, perhaps even without a tongue, was telling her a story. It was like walking through the cells of a horrible comic book with red pages that smelled of flowers. And on this page she was allowed inside Edith's bedchamber.

Scores of dolls watched her with their perfect and placid faces. Their tiny glass eyes caught the scarlet light. The bedside lamps, the standing lamp and the ceiling light all burned brightly. The curtains were drawn against the absence beyond the windows.

Catherine raised the skirts of the heavy eiderdown and looked under the bed, but refused to contemplate what she was looking for. She saw nothing down there besides a ceramic chamber pot.

She opened each of the great wardrobes and then pulled the hung clothes back and forth with one hand. In the other hand, the scalpel was ready to jab. She opened drawers and raised the lacy tablecloths on the small tables. She peered behind the great mirror of the dressing table. She filled the grate of the fireplace with spare bedlinen and packed it in tight, before concealing the aperture with the black iron cover.

She sat in the middle of the bed and watched the door. She rested the hand that grasped the scalpel beside her thigh, and waited.

FORTY-THREE

When Catherine awoke with a gasp, she was still propped up in the middle of the bed, inside Edith's room, with a row of plump cushions supporting her back.

The back of her eyes felt bruised and she was nauseous. All of the muscles in her legs ached, her feet were terribly sore. She was ill, exhausted, fatigued by going in and out of shock, still drugged, but she had only passed out from sheer exhaustion. And for no more than a few seconds before some inner alarm jolted her awake.

About the room, the lights still burned and the house remained perfumed with the sweet scent of roses. Though the room had taken on a new aspect. All of its dimensions and accoutrements were as she remembered before she nodded off, but the air had changed. Had become delicate.

The alteration might have been imperceptible were her situation not so desperate, but she identified a lessening of the density and pressure of the room's atmosphere. It was also no longer warm and airless. The space she occupied felt softer and flimsier, cooler. Perhaps it was her imagination, and despite her physical discomforts, she no longer felt so heavy, but was marginally more buoyant, or even insubstantial, upon the bedding.

Catherine climbed off the bed and approached the door.

She glanced up at the dolls and refused to engage with a sense that they appeared happier. Beneath the bottom of the door a hint of white light had appeared on the floorboards.

Making as little noise as possible she turned the key in the well-crafted lock. The key turned and issued the merest click. Catherine inched the door open. And blinked in sunlight.

On the landing, and at the end of the corridor, the curtains and shutters had been opened and the corridor was flooded with strong unseasonal sunlight. Down below, she received an impression that the heavy front doors had been cast aside as she slept, and that each and every arched window on the ground floor had been thrown wide to welcome the light, as well as the crisp warm air and its scents: a bouquet of freshly cut grass and crowded flower beds sweet with pollen.

From above, the scarlet glower of the stained glass had been replaced by a pinkish hue that tinted the air in a way she thought enchanting. She couldn't have been asleep for more than a few seconds, of that she was almost certain, but somehow she had woken in daylight.

The great perfumed house seemed joyous at her waking, keen to show itself as a place of luxury and discernment, as she had once hoped it would be; a peaceful magnificence that guarded the beauty and craftsmanship of an age she had studied and admired her whole adult life. It was no longer a place of small shadows and a murderer's light. The stench of death had left its rooms. It was making a new declaration of intent: *This is a house you would not wish to leave, and you could only dream of a return to a house on the borderland of wonders.*

She visualized the dusty lane that she must run down to

get away. Restraining her desire to rush madly for the front doors, she descended the stairs slowly, her eyes everywhere, especially up the stairwell to spot small faces that might peer down. There were none. Then her scrutiny turned to the ground floor where a lumpen figure, with a thatch of white hair, might be ready to welcome her with a fleshing tool, or worse. But Maude was nowhere to be seen either.

Catherine paused in the hall as her nerves cried for her to delay no longer, and to rush at the front doors before they were closed and locked upon her as they had been the night before.

The light outside the Red House was near blinding. Here was the first sunlit and cloudless day of summer, but one that burned stronger than any she had known.

The arched doorframe resembled a planetary eclipse, as if some great star moved through the firmament. The light that entered the building infused her, began to open a receptivity to a sense of beauty and hope she had received but glimmers of before. It was irresistible. Childlike excitement fizzed awake and tingled in every cell of her body. A broad comprehension of something significant that remained indefinable, tried to spread through her with the warmth and light. True meaning was within her grasp and an anticipation of the revelation shortened her breath. A sense of something her conscious mind resisted by trying to confront and understand.

When she looked into the light her mind had never been so clear, so awake, so vital. Every sense and nerve ending stretched to its euphoric pinnacle.

She shielded her eyes as she took a few steps closer to the entrance. Through the glare she could see a cultivated front garden, and beyond the garden wall a great ocean of meadowland stretching to the shore of distant, pleasingly rounded hills that shimmered in a nourishing heat.

You could walk forever in that direction, but you would return here.

She paused on the threshold. This world outside was lit by a great white sun, one that complemented the vista as if her own eyes were covered with a camera's soft filters. It was like she was in the same building as yesterday, but somewhere else too. If she were to walk down the lane she would arrive at the village and the church. Any further in that direction and all would be unrecognizable. She sensed this, but didn't know how.

She turned and looked behind her. Beyond the hall and at the far end of the utility corridor, the distant back door of the Red House was now open. The doorway was a rectangle that issued an even more intense light into the building. Light that flooded the previously unlit passage.

The dazzling rear doorway briefly flickered as someone moved across it. From the aperture she heard the distant clink of cutlery upon china. Above the fragrance of the flowers wafted the aroma of warm cakes and fresh bread. She smelled hot sweet tea and the refreshing zest of chilled summer wines. Her mouth watered. She drank deep of the breeze that refreshed her face like a plunge into transparent seawater on a stifling day.

Her face was wet with tears.

She crossed the hall and walked towards the back door. Out there were her answers. The lump in her throat was the most tangible and solid part of her weightless body and its effortless drift towards that square of light.

She covered the distance quickly, between rose-tinted

walls. Proud doors were shut on wonders that would surely overwhelm her if she entered any room. She approached the light of the garden without fear and near burst through the portal that beckoned her with such urgency.

So verdant was the garden, the sun's reflection on the lawn made her shield her eyes. She'd never seen land so fertile. Intensely green foliage and grass, sprayed with orange, buttercup and purple flowers rendered her breathless at the beauty she surveyed.

Behind the glinting panes of the greenhouse came the suggestions of great waxy tropical plants. The garden furniture was as white as a cricket pavilion in a dream. The wood of the theatre gleamed between velvet wings and below a watercolour backdrop Monet might have painted. Beyond the trees that bordered the garden's far boundary she caught glimpses of a vast English meadow that shimmered in the heat.

The bee-keeper raised his gloved hand and waved from behind a trellis, from which roses both entwined and burst red, white and pink. Behind the mesh of his hood she could see no face, she was too far away. But the gentle grandfatherly ease with which he moved amongst the indistinct hives faded her memory of the unpleasant thing she had so recently seen in the same outfit.

Seated at the wrought-iron table, its paint so brilliant a white it made her squint, the two women, dressed from throat to foot in black gowns, sat within the shade of a tree. Veils had been unfurled from wide-brimmed hats, and obscured the blanched faces they had turned towards her. Their pale hands matched the china of their raised teacups. A third chair was drawn back from the table.

There was no surprise or tension in the posture of the three people in the garden. They were casually waiting for her to join them.

Catherine turned to face the presence she sensed behind her, deep within the Red House. And started at the sight of the three figures stood where the utility corridor met the hall.

There was no mistaking the thick limbs and stocky torso of Maude. Even from a distance, the mannish face beneath the thick hair, cut so crudely and unstyled, expressed such a longstanding dissatisfaction with a housekeeper's lot that her patient resignation seemed to have passed into weariness. How was that possible on such a day as this?

Catherine's interest moved to the housekeeper's two small companions. They stood on either side of Maude and each of the children had one hand enclosed within the housekeeper's thick fingers.

The disabled boy with the wooden face and thick black wig was dressed in the same dated suit he had worn the last time Catherine had seen him so vividly, when she was a child, and his thin legs were still encased by a scaffold of calliper. He raised his free hand into the air, as he had done when Catherine was only a child who peered through a wire fence at the derelict and vandalized school for special children. The little raised hand and its fingers were either closed, moulded or carven. The face on the tiny wooden head that confronted her across the distance between them was painted on. It smiled sadly under the encroach of the unruly hair.

On the other side of Maude, light glinted off the thick lenses in the plastic frames of the little girl's glasses. One eye looked unusual at a distance, and Catherine guessed the eye socket was filled with gauze and the lens of her glasses was still covered in sticking plaster, as it had been when Alice was six, the last time Catherine had seen her childhood friend. The only other feature that struck her, and with a suddenness that made her scalp chill, was Alice's teeth. And she hoped their exposure formed part of a friendly smile.

FORTY-FOUR

Catherine awoke, propped upright in the middle of the bed inside Edith's room. Behind her the cushions had slid about as she'd moved in her sleep.

Without having been conscious of them being open, her eyes stung. Her chin was wet and her mouth dry from where it had gaped for . . . *how long*? The white light of day under the door had vanished. She was returned to night.

The door to the room was still locked. The scalpel lay on the bedclothes where she'd dropped it.

She had been in a trance like no other. She clutched her face and almost cried at the thought of having departed the profound vision only to find herself still trapped.

But what she had just seen was surely too vivid to have been a trance. There had been such strong smells and temperatures. She'd come out of it with a clear, but diminishing notion of being intensely happy.

Not since her childhood had she been rendered so incapable and woken so fatigued by an 'episode'. Their early potency and the narratives in her mind she had been unable to adequately hold in her memory. But she knew hours had passed during the more arresting episodes when she had been a girl. Her mother used to call them 'one of your naps', but they both knew they weren't naps. What she had

338

just experienced exceeded even her most intense childhood trance.

She had been inside the Red House too. Alice had been present, and the boy from her childhood trances. And it was as if whatever was in the building, or perhaps the Red House itself, was trying to reveal its connection to her childhood, an unseen bond that had always been in place. Her instincts suggested this. But the idea didn't frighten her as much as it had done before. Because of Alice and the strange boy with the wooden face. The same boy she'd imagined as a child and once thought real, even a saviour. It was like the return of the boy's presence had added a different atmosphere to the Red House.

In the intense vision, it had also been morning and the sun was bright, the day beautiful. A light of salvation. The light of her childhood trances. All over again she'd felt the joy of being taken out of herself; removed from a world that tormented her.

She was no longer being hunted in the dream, no longer frightened. In the dream she had been *welcome*. She knew that much. The Masons had also been present, but alive and all too real within the beautiful garden, a place she had only ever known as a repository for weeds, flies and decay. And she'd awoken feeling the dream had provided some much needed hope of liberation.

As recovery from a trance often encouraged her to do, she tried to re-engage with the physical world, and the one she'd grown up to accept was the only world. A world she'd slipped away from too easily since her arrival here. Catherine clambered off the bed and stumbled for the door. Then found she didn't have the courage to open it. She hesitated, fretted, tried to hold back tears.

Logic attempted a brutish and clumsy reappearance. Why would Maude, and possibly a second presence she had yet to see, kill Edith and throw her remains in the attic trunk, as well as start the Frenophone to frighten her?

She held her face and muttered to herself, trying to force an explanation that would deliver her from a confusion so awful she thought she might have a seizure. Maybe the body of Edith in the trunk had been an effigy and Edith was still playing an elaborate trick on her. She came from a family of performers. Or had Edith been playing dead? And maybe the lights were on dimmer mechanisms. Had to be, because they weren't so bright now. The interior was returned to its usual obscurity and horrible dim light verging on no light.

The scent? The scent of roses could have been created by some kind of infusion.

Mike and Tara? She tried desperately to think of how they fitted. The household and the village suggested they were some kind of clan protecting awful secrets. She felt this instinctively. And if Edith had become aware of Catherine's return to Worcester, tracked her down and invited her here, then Mike and Tara may have inadvertently become embroiled in some protracted ritual. One that only made sense to a couple of isolated and deranged elderly women, and those in their service.

She didn't know. She didn't know anything. She wanted to know, and she wanted a natural explanation; she would have given anything for this to make sense logically, no matter how repellent the truth.

Her desperate explanations still felt insubstantial, as though she was repeating wishful thinking to believe something she knew to be false.

Edith had been making preposterous claims that she and her biological mother were from the village. She knew nothing of her natural parents, only that her mother had been poor and unable to cope.

Could she and her mother really have been from Magbar Wood? The village would have been under the awful influence of the Masons then. Judging by the age and state of the closed stores, she imagined her birth would have occurred around the time the village stopped functioning. Maybe her mother had tried to save her from what was happening by giving her up for adoption?

If there were a grain of truth in any of her suppositions, then all that had happened to her since she first drove to Green Willow felt inevitable, some kind of destiny; even a part of something mystical that M. H. Mason had started, that wanted to reclaim her. Wasn't this what Edith wanted her to believe?

No. She could not allow herself to accept what was being suggested to her by Edith, about what Mason had excavated and brought inside this hideous house. Something from the past. Something that had transformed the Masons, if not taken over their lives, and those nearby. She would not accept Edith's madness. Because it was patently impossible. Absurd and irrational. Nonsensical superstition.

But what did they, Edith, Maude, and whoever else was here, really want from her, of her? And what did they want her to think right now? That the Red House was alive? That existence could stop beyond the windows too, as if the building was some kind of doll's house that changed and played out its stratagems with living occupants? Edith had said something about a great effort being made to remain here. What had she meant by that?

She thought harder on what she knew. Mason had spent a lifetime meddling with pieces of things that predated the Romans. The house and the land it was built upon had been significant to him in some way. And she seemed to have been infected by the place as he had. So maybe the taint that poisoned M. H. Mason had endured. One that let you see through to other things, other sides. It took Alice . . .

Stop it!

Maude had drugged her. She was now susceptible to anything. She could be full of LSD; she had no idea what she had been given to drink. But people had died here. Had been murdered here. Or had they?

She had to get out.

Catherine unlocked the door of the bedroom. But waited, with her ear pressed to the wood, the scalpel gripped so hard the handle hurt her hand. She heard nothing outside the room. Tensing her body, she turned the handle and stepped backwards as she pulled the door open.

And stared across the unlit passage at the glimmer of the closed door opposite. She moved into the doorway. Tried to direct her hearing further into the corridor she couldn't see, to detect a creak of a floorboard, a footstep, a breath.

Nothing.

She peered to the right. Nothing visible beyond a few feet of near total darkness, partially relieved by whatever thin light fell out of her room. To the left, a glance informed her the stairwell was lit, but only just. All was as it had been before she came down from the attic to lock herself in Edith's room and fell into a dream-filled coma. So this, the house in this physical state, was real.

She shivered. Was dressed in only the thin white pageant

gown while stood in a draught. One that grew stronger as if there was a window open nearby. But not in her room. No, the current of cold air blew from elsewhere, *outside*.

Yes, a window must be open in one of these locked rooms because the air smelled of . . . wet leaves, slippery brown leaves, layer upon layer of rotten leaves and rotten wood. Black soil. Long wet grass. Cold air on a cloudy day with a hint of bonfire smoke. Impossible, but her senses told her she could now be outside on a winter's day.

The fragrant draught blew through the passage from the window at the end. If it were open, she could climb out onto the roof outside, find a way down and run.

Catherine moved through the darkness, the scalpel leading, towards the source of the breeze like it was an escape route detected in an ancient tomb. She swiped the blade in arcs before her. If anyone stood in her way, the surgical steel would find them before she did.

And if she wasn't mistaken there was also an aura of greyish light visible around the curtains as she approached the casement window. It must be open. Perhaps it had been all along. Or was she meant to find it open?

Dawn could be breaking. Blessed morning might have arrived.

She drew aside the curtains and pulled back the half-open shutters to see what looked more like dusk. She might have been in a trance for so long she'd gone through the day and woken late again. *But in winter?*

And she must still be in a trance because how else could she explain what stood upright, down there amongst the high grasses of the overgrown garden?

She put the scalpel against her forearm and pulled it back

in one quick slice to make sure she was awake. The pain made her jump and in the grey light she saw a dark, wet line appear on her skin.

Catherine whimpered. She must be hallucinating, but didn't feel drugged any more, not even vaguely soporific. The trance was over. It might have left her mentally drained and physically tired, but she wasn't dreaming this.

There are other places.

She closed her eyes and shivered before the open window. Blood trickled down her left forearm and tickled her wrist. She opened her eyes. They were still there.

A line of ragged children with odd-shaped heads stood in the thin light. They looked up at her in silence, just as they had watched her so many years before.

The tatty silhouettes of their heads she better understood now to be mostly comprised of animal ears and poorly fitted wigs. The tallest child was a girl and wore a bonnet. Closest to the house, the boy with the painted wooden face and unkempt black hair raised one arm as if to wave. His other hand was enclosed by the small fingers of a little girl. One lens of her glasses was covered in sticking plaster.

Somehow Catherine found the strength to turn on her leaden feet and to flee back to Edith's bedroom with her hands clutched across her eyes.

None of this was real. She must still be stuck in a trance. A powerful one she had become conscious inside and remained conscious within. Or she had been drugged. Powerful chemicals were making her see things.

In her mind she could see Edith's lipless mouth and thin yellow teeth. *One of my uncle's formulas.*

Or had she just seen children wearing masks? She had

heard children here, seen their faces at windows. Hadn't the Masons once dressed children up here? But Alice . . . Alice was impossible. If Alice was even alive she would be the same age as Catherine was.

Catherine fell upon the bed and began to scream to wake herself up. But the sound of her hysteria only seemed to alert the inhabitants of the house, because now there was a commotion downstairs, and then in the stairwell, and then in the corridor outside. And she could clearly hear the sound of feet running to the door of the room. Little feet. A crowd of little feet.

FORTY-FIVE

She came awake with her fingers clutching cold metal on either side of her hips. Old steel bedsprings protested with enough groans and squeaks she barely heard herself whimper, 'God.'

Sunlight slotted through chinks in wooden boards nailed across the window frame. A draught scented with earth and dew brushed her face.

She remembered she had been stood before a window looking at the children in the garden. Then she had come back to Edith's bedroom and fallen upon the bed, where she must have passed out . . . but she hadn't passed out on this bed.

What came after her return to the room was vague, or receded to fragments, and no matter how hard she swiped at the pieces of memory they mostly sought oblivion. Perhaps mercifully. Because there had been a commotion. A rushing of small feet towards the room. And then inside the room there had been a bustling. The activity had been all about her face, accompanied by the smell of old clothes, of neglect, and fresh earth, winter air. She remembered the sounds and the smells . . . had a wooden face pressed itself close? And then . . .

Nothing.

Bits of another bad dream between other bad dreams.

She must have dreamt that she had seen children in the garden, wearing masks, but looking up at the window she peered through. Before that there had been another dream of the Red House filled with sunlight, the perfume of flowers. People had waited for her in the garden.

All of this must have been part of a trance. Imagined. *She'd had two trances then. Or three?* Or one so powerful it had felt like several. She didn't know because the passage from one place to another, and now to here, was less like waking from a deep sleep filled with vivid, urgent dreams and more like waking into a new day, with the actual memories of the last time she was conscious quickly fading.

It was not possible for such hallucinations to feel like actual memories. Her visions were delusions. That was one thing she must not kid herself about.

In the reeking darkness of the strange room, she was too stiff with fright to move. So she remained motionless, no less inert than a doll, but one filled with horror. Until the terror subsided and she thought she had been emptied of the capacity to feel anything.

Her skin was cold as if she'd been exposed to the elements all night, or even longer. But though she was cold the sensation wasn't one of physical discomfort.

Shock also rendered her unable to speak, or even cry out. Thick-headed, she could have been mistaken for thinking she hadn't slept in weeks, or maybe she'd slept for weeks and only half awoken.

She pinched her wrist. As she performed the simple manoeuvre her arms were numb, heavy, cold, her fingers thick, half paralysed. But she was awake. This was real.

A thin cut on her forearm poked beneath her sleeve, and had recently begun to scab over.

She could not see the scalpel or any bedclothes. And what was she lying on? Bare springs, because there was no mattress.

In the vague light that passed through the boarded-up window she could also see that she had been changed into a garment that looked and felt like a dress. Even her throat was covered by something tight, a stiff collar. The gown reached her ankles and she could feel its constriction about her hips. The garment was old. What she could see of it was grubby, once white.

The light was dim, but she was also certain there were no dolls on the far wall, or furniture in the room. Where they ended their journey, the shards of white daylight struck unclean walls.

So had she been drugged, which had made her imagine everything? She couldn't accept that, her recollections of the house and all that had happened were too sharp, too vital.

While she was unconscious her clothes must have been changed, and someone had left her sitting on bare metal springs, slumped against a metal headboard. But inside a new place, another building, or maybe in a part of the Red House she had never seen before. Or the physical world had been transformed again, and in a manner more radical than ever before.

The idea that she was still inside the Red House, and still in Edith Mason's bedroom, and lying upon her actual bed, grew through her bewilderment and close to a horrible acceptance of the impossible. And if she needed prompt confirmation, beside the bed was a great black wheelchair, tipped on its side upon the bare wooden floor.

Gradually, her eyes adjusted to the darkness. Mould blackened the walls she could see lit up by bands of watery daylight. And that's what she could smell. She recalled noticing the same odours before, in the darkness of her room, in the corridor outside her room, and inside the dining room.

Most of the remaining wallpaper was mottled into neglect. Leaves and loose bricks lay upon the floorboards. Part of the ceiling had fallen in too, because slats of wood were visible. The wiring had been stripped from the walls. A decomposing mattress was slumped against where she remembered a mirror to be. Continents of black stains had joined up on the mattress. Parts of the fabric and stuffing formed wet lumps on the floor.

She clutched her face with hands so cold and heavy they felt like they belonged to someone else, or were, at the very least, near paralysed. Her features were slippery with some kind of cream or ointment. She looked at the sleeve of the ancient white nightgown from which an unfamiliar perfume drifted. Gingerly, she touched her head. Her hair was pinned up inside a cap across which her numb fingers scraped.

On the floor beside the bed were shards of mirrored glass, smashed out of a frame many years before and now glimmering among the detritus. With a slow and ungainly arm, she reached down and picked up the closest piece, breaking it free from a rime of dust and a glimmer of silvery insect trails. She rubbed the section of dull speckled glass with a thumb. Turned it to her face. And stared at the sight of something so pale it was almost blue. Whitened skin, her skin.

From outside came a sound she never thought she would hear again. The rumble of a car engine and the ripple-pop of tyres across a rough surface. Beyond the sound of the car birds issued terse cries into the cool air.

Stepping off the bed took all of her strength. For a moment she'd thought she was fastened to it. But once she was up and on her ungainly feet, moving was much easier than the act of pinching her flesh, or picking up the broken piece of mirror. Now she was upright she even felt agile, nimble.

Through the unlit room her legs carried her swiftly across the dross and wet bricks to the blocked window. Frantically, she moved her face behind the rough, damp-darkened boards until she found a suitable gap to peer through.

A vehicle came into view. A green van, an old model, even vintage, that was driven carefully. It stopped moving at the end of the overgrown front garden. An area now protected by a metal chainlink fence she had never seen before. Most of the brick wall she remembered was missing.

The sight of the man who stepped out of the car made her dizzy, and then relieved, and then close to paralysis.

Without the aid of his wheelchair, Leonard Osberne stood beside the open driver's-side door. He then walked stiffly around the bonnet of this vehicle she had never seen before, and stood before the fence.

He held something in his hands, something black and hairy that he placed with great care upon the roof of the van. He turned to face the house. He removed his jacket slowly, his trousers from his thin legs, his shirt. And all with deliberate care as if his actions were rehearsed or a prelude to a special act. By the time he was looping his underwear over one unshod foot, Catherine had closed her eyes upon the sight of his pallid and wizened torso, separated into a patchwork of thick lines faded purple and white. Scars.

When she reopened her eyes, she dug her fingers between two of the wooden boards nailed across the casement frame and clung on to them to stay on her feet, because Leonard Osberne's face was no longer visible.

Leonard's head was titled upwards, towards the front of the house, and was covered in a dark leather mask. The mask was featureless. And that, she considered, was the only mercy in what she was being forced to endure.

Cascading about the outside of the mask, and down past his bony shoulders, were luxuriant black curls of hair. The horribly feminine tresses reached his protruding ribs.

The rest of the man's body that she could see was naked, save for a soiled bandage around one thigh, visible when he unlocked the metal gate built into the security fence. Carrying a grey sack, he walked up the path, under the porch roof and out of her view.

She became aware that she was now panting against the rough wooden planks, but her breath was weak, soundless, and must have been muted against the wood.

Blind with panic, as much as going blind among the black spaces between the thin shards of white light in the room, she fumbled around the wet crumbling walls and used her hands to feel her way to the door. Little impeded her stagger. There was a hole where a handle once turned.

She stepped through the doorway and into a vista of ruin. Behind her, the door drifted shut.

The Red House was derelict. The air inside was cold and lightened enough to suggest the great skylight of crimson glass was no more.

No rugs, no carpets, no pictures, no light fittings either.

A great pungency of damp wood and urine assaulted her senses.

The stairwell was missing most of its banisters. The ends of the two corridors were lost to darkness. Floorboards were warped and even absent above what looked like deep black cavities about her feet. Leaves had blown in from somewhere and settled into mounds of mulch against the walls, joined by fallen chunks of plaster.

But down below there was movement. And a sound she had heard before. A sound she was too transfixed with fear to investigate as it shambled through the neglect and half-light, two storeys down, out of sight. Footsteps. The distinctive side-to-side shuffle of a heavy-set woman with a limp. Maude. From deep within the bowels of the building the housekeeper now moved into the hall directly beneath the stairwell, as she had once walked to collect Catherine so long ago.

A chain slid through a metal loop. Down there. Metal was rattled and wood groaned out its resistance at being moved. The great front doors were unlocked and the light increased in the stairwell as the doors were opened. And then they were closed and locked again with the same slow procedure. The light downstairs dimmed.

Two sets of feet scuffled and creaked across what was left of the hall floor. But there were no voices, no greetings between the housekeeper and her visitor, which was even worse than the sound of their feet beginning a noisy ascent of the stairs.

Carefully, upon the broken and uneven floor, Catherine slipped backwards and into the mouth of the corridor she had come out of. Once back within the shadows of the passage, she crouched down and tensed. With her cheek pressed into the moist, crumbling plaster of the wall, she peeked out at the stairwell.

In a grotesque and nonchalant parade, Leonard came into view with Maude following. The naked and scarred body of the old man she had come to love and trust moved with a casual ease up the stairs, his spine too straight for a man of his age, his head and upper body covered by the horrid locks that swayed as he walked. His face was blanked out by the old leather mask that offered no suggestion of eyes, mouth, or nose in the dank and dim space the shaggy head rose through.

Behind Leonard, with her face cast into the usual dour indifference, Maude dragged her bandaged foot upwards, one step at a time.

Catherine did not want that black leathery face turning in her direction so she slipped backwards without a sound, deeper into the corridor, as her captors made the second-floor landing. Her mind scrabbled for a solution of where to flee if they came for her.

Fear turned to relief when she heard their footsteps crunch, bump and scuffle into the adjoining corridor that housed the bedroom she had stayed in.

Behind her, and next to Edith's disused bedroom, she could see the vague outline of the nursery doorway. It was open.

She eased herself to the empty doorframe and peered inside. In a haze of light emitted around the hardwood board, that had come loose in both top corners over the far window, she could see that the shadowy space was empty. The walls were as softened by moisture and mould as the walls in the rest of this building that she had awoken within, so confused and frightened.

She fled back to the landing and listened. In the distance, from out of the adjoining passageway, she heard the muffled sounds of something being dragged around a floor and knocked about a distant room.

Catherine fled across the landing and began a descent of the stairs, her only relief being her skill at moving so quietly and swiftly down to the floor below.

On the first floor, the wooden walls had been smashed through or were black and buckled with damp. A quick look into the gap that had once been the entrance to Edith's drawing room revealed it to be an empty shell that stank of urine and worse. Somehow the curtain rail above the boarded-over window had survived. She made haste to the ground floor.

Some of the floorboards of the hall were missing to reveal rubbish-filled spaces and crumbling cement between crossbeams. Great rusted nails reared like small serpents in the thin light, and she delicately moved her feet around them to prevent spearing the sole of a bare foot.

The front doors had been shut behind the visitor. A dull glimmer of iron chain looped about the handles suggested they were secure.

Catherine turned and fled into the dark utility corridor, keen on reaching the back door while Maude and Leonard were upstairs.

They must have come out of the corridor on the second floor because she heard their feet creak and bang about the upper storeys. They must be looking for her and were going to search Edith's room. The thought made her need to escape greater.

There would be time enough to fathom what had happened here, how she had been kept prisoner and mesmerized or drugged. Or whatever they had done to make her experience a derelict building in its former glory, an illusion generated by her own imagination.

Mason's magic worked.

Bewitched.

Impossible.

Stop it!

There will be time, there will be time.

There would be time, and for the rest of her life, but for now she begged herself just to get outside.

It was dark in the utility corridor and she could not always see where her pale feet stepped. But through some of the gaping doorways smidgens of daylight fell around the boards nailed across all of the windows.

She quickly peered inside the rooms she passed, and there were no longer any great tableaux beneath glass. Each room was empty. One squalid room had the remnants of a wet sleeping bag bunched up amongst plastic bottles, piled at the foot of a stained wall.

There was some evidence of an old kitchen, with a few cardboard boxes and plastic bags scattered across the wooden counters that had not yet been torn from the patchy walls. The grocery bags and the messy assortment of discarded tins and glass jars were modern and new. A loaf of bread spilled white slices onto a murky bench surface. So someone had been feeding themselves and using that space to prepare basic food. Maude? *Oh Jesus Christ.* So what had she really been eating here? It didn't appear to have been pheasant.

Catherine slowed down as she approached the workshop, not just because of what she remembered having seen in that terrible space, but because it was the only room in the corridor with the door in place. Not an old door either, but a temporary one, the kind she had seen in chipboard walls around scaffolding on building sites. The door was closed, padlocked.

As was the back door she had run to. And the door was not only closed, but also sealed with a padlock and chain and fresh hardwood panels that had been added to the frame at some point recently. The acrid smell of new wet timber was still detectable about the surface she ran her hands across.

In desperation, Catherine began to cry and whisper and whimper as her pawing became clawing and scraping and a hopeless shoving at the wood of the back door. Until she disturbed whatever, or whoever, it was that began to fumble about inside the sealed workshop. And whatever was inside the workshop soon scratched at the other side of the makeshift door. The pattern of footsteps and the incoherent grunts suggested an animal, or someone helplessly drunk had been imprisoned within the room.

Catherine backed away, up the corridor towards the doorway of the stinking kitchen area.

The figure contained within the workshop began to moan and then bark like a dog with something stuck in its throat. The scratching of the fingers evolved into an angry hammering. She realized she wasn't so much afraid of who was on the other side of the door as much as she was afraid of why they were being kept inside the room.

Because they kept captives here, drugged captives, and killed them. Leonard was in on it. He was the Masons' accomplice. He had set her up. The valuation, her entire job, was a sham, a prelude to this. Maude was his ally. It must have been going on for years. Since before she had been a child in dismal Ellyll Fields. She thought again of Alice clambering up the riverbank to the hole in the green wire fence, of the black and white faces of the disabled girls in Mason's study. Margaret Reid, Angela Prescott, Helen Teme. They must have all been brought here.

How had they snatched the first three girls? Using children, like those she had seen in the special school, dressed as Mason's marionettes? On M. H. Mason's orders? With the intention of drugging and killing disabled and vulnerable girls here? Were they still doing it?

Leonard and his confederates must have waited for Catherine all these years too, for decades. Because she was a witness to Alice?

Preposterous, because Alice was still a child here, or had that been a hallucination? And where, or what, was Edith Mason?

The house . . . the house could not have altered so radically. There was no drug in existence that could make her see it as it had been, that gloomy, oppressive, but perfectly preserved, revival house. It was not possible.

Her situation was impossible, like the story in a horror film, and her explanations didn't work. But here she was, right now, in a place as real and as vivid as any she had known in her life.

From the other end of the corridor the sound of two sets of feet descending the stairs to the hallway compelled Catherine to duck inside the kitchen and to press her back against the far wet wall.

Briefly, she inspected the kitchen windows to see if one of the boards could be levered off. The bottom panel had been kicked in at some point and clumsily reattached. The wood looked like wet cardboard. She tried to peel the sheet of chipboard away from the nails as quietly as possible. In the distance of the house she heard a chain slide through door handles.

They were going then? Leaving?

She crept to the doorway of the kitchen and noticed a small camp bed pushed against the wall, on the side of the room opposite the window. A mottled pillow without a case, indented by the impression of a head, lay at the top of a single tartan blanket. So who slept here? Maude?

When they had a victim to torture and kill.

Catherine stuffed her fingers inside her mouth to still her whimpers and to hold her jaw that was now quivering uncontrollably from shock and fear.

She peered out into the utility corridor.

In the distant gloom, Maude dragged M. H. Mason's leather trunk through the hall and into the little reception corridor before the open front doors. Leonard carried bedding folded over his arms. Was that what she been sleeping on? If so, were they taking evidence of her visit out of the ruined building to dispose of? Perhaps that's why they had been in her room, to remove traces of her now the time had come to kill her and finish this deranged ritual they had started when she was sent to value antiques.

Oh God Oh God Oh God.

Who were these people? Was Edith still inside that trunk they must have fetched from the attic? And if so, was Edith Mason alone inside it?

She was going mad from the impossibility of it all, from the continuing maelstrom of confusion and terror the house would give her no respite from.

Footsteps approached. Someone was walking through the utility corridor. Catherine cast about the kitchen, found a breadknife in a tub of margarine crawling with ants. Pulled the knife free and backed against the wall beside the window, out of sight of the corridor, and waited. She stayed silent, trembling as the two sets of feet shuffled and bumped outside in the utility corridor.

No one came into the kitchen, but she could not believe they were unaware of her.

She heard Leonard and Maude unlock the workshop door.

What they pulled out of the room did not put up a struggle. It came out groaning and coughing and seemed to be willingly led by its silent captors through the utility corridor towards the hall.

Crouching in the stinking darkness against the wall, Catherine waited and listened until she was sure there were three sets of footsteps moving away from her position and back towards the front of the house. When she was certain they were returning to the hall, she peered around the kitchen's doorframe and saw a clump of slowly moving figures blocking the light that seeped into the passage.

Once the group had struggled out of the utility corridor and into the hall, they were lit up by the light falling through the broken skylight and by what shone through the open front doors. And what she saw fused her enduring terror with a greater incomprehension, so quickly, she thought she might faint.

Between the skinny, naked figure of Leonard and the squat, lumpen Maude, was the silhouette of a woman in what appeared to be a long grey dress and white apron; the same outfit Maude wore. A bag, or a garment like a hood, was pulled over the figure's head.

The woman was unsteady on her feet and occasionally issued a grunt or piteous cry as she was shoved about the hallway. When Leonard and Maude released her arms, the captive spread pale hands as if she were suddenly finding her feet upon an icy pavement.

Catherine clutched her ears to try and stop the spinning inside her skull that demanded she just run down there, screaming, and get it over with. Just have them put an end to her, and this tortuous theatre of cruelty she was still stumbling around as an unwitting player.

She had been on centre stage. It had been all about her. But since she had woken in the derelict building she seemed to have been marginalized. This notion should have brought comfort, but instead, the greater and more sinister mystery the day had introduced was taking her to a point where death might even be something of a blessing. She thought she had been here before, at school as a child; in London; when Mike left her; even inside this house. But none of that had even been preparation for this morning.

As she continued to gape at the grotesque spectacle within the dilapidated hall, Catherine became attuned to a scrutiny that made her shiver from head to toe. Taking her horrified stare from the tall upright figure with the hooded head, that grunted and swiped at the air about its concealed face, Catherine looked at Leonard and was quite sure the emaciated naked figure had now turned its indistinct leather face in her direction.

She ducked back inside the kitchen and was sure if she heard a single footstep approach her position her heart would simply stop.

The next thing she heard, from the front of the house, was the doors being closed and chained shut from outside the building.

Catherine peered out again. And saw the thin hooded figure in the housekeeper's uniform, alone and stood within a broad shaft of dusty sunlight falling from above. The slow, painful and wretched fumbling of the thing commenced, and the draped head groaned as if in pain while reaching for what it couldn't see.

Leonard and Maude were no longer inside the great hall. They had gone, left the building. The doors of the Red House were closed and sealed again. *Why?* Why had they left the hooded captive inside the hall, as if for her to find?

Catherine left the kitchen.

Hesitantly, she walked towards the ghastly hooded occupant of the hall. The woman was tall and thin. And as she drew closer, she was reminded of someone who had just stumbled away from a traffic accident. The woman was in shock after what had been done to her, which might also account for the sounds she made.

Catherine glanced around the hall and up the staircase to the next floor. Empty. Maude and Leonard had really departed and left her alive and alone with this bizarre spectacle of helplessness dressed in a vintage housekeeper's uniform.

Upon the head of the tall woman was a sack, not a hood. A dirty old sack that fell to the woman's collarbones.

Inside the hall Catherine cleared her throat. 'Don't be frightened.'

The woman let forth a surprised grunt. Her hands rose and batted at the air as if she was trying to fend Catherine away, or reach whoever had just spoken and broken the silence.

'Don't move. The floor isn't safe. Have they gone? Can you hear me, have they gone?'

The woman oriented her frail body to where Catherine's voice had risen. As she turned she nearly fell.

Catherine moved to her and held her elbow. With her other hand she tugged the sack off the woman's head.

Transformed by the dress and apron, making sounds unrecognizable as even human, and the fact that the woman had been harrowed by torments that had seen her blinded, still could not disguise Tara. Not even the glass eyes fitted into the red eye sockets, or the fact that no tongue moved within her wide open mouth, could protect the appalling creature's identity.

The sound of Catherine's whispers in the airy hall unbalanced Tara. She broke from Catherine's hold and fell against the grubby wall, where she crouched near the broken skirting boards with her dead glass eyes open wide and her bloodless hands clasped to her cheeks. Her mouth gaped, but nothing save a rasp seeped out as if the disfigured creature was losing the last of its air. And probably dearly wished that it was.

'Oh God,' Catherine heard herself say. 'What have they done to you?'

When she was struck by the notion that what had been done to Tara had been done on her behalf, Catherine then felt as if everything had stopped moving inside her body. *For her.* She remembered Edith's words and began to shake. *They are the ones who offer justice now, my dear. And their justice can be terrible.*

This was for her. But it wasn't possible. Tara had been killed with Mike. They had been slaughtered and drained. She had seen the livid sutures upon his back in the metal tub, the tub in which the balding Edith had also once shivered like a wet foal, unleashed from some hideous womb. But if Tara was still alive, then what about Mike? Where was Mike? And what had they done to him?

Keep one kitten, destroy the rest.

Catherine thought of the rotten hives hectic with corpulent flies and whimpered.

She had been sure that Tara was also lifeless in that ethanol tub. Had she been alive but unconscious? But how could she have survived the awful wounds inflicted upon her head?

Catherine looked to the stairs. She thought again of Edith so lifeless inside the trunk that she had just seen removed from the building, and she thought of Edith's mother and uncle sat like motionless mannequins inside the attic. Whatever hope drained from her body during this moment of reflection, she knew would not be returning anytime soon. 'No. No. Please, God, no. Oh God . . .'

She ran across the broken floor to the staircase. And seemingly without breathing, leapt as much as she ran, with her foul skirt hitched up to her thighs, to the first floor and across its landing, and up the next staircase and onto the next landing, and down the first corridor to the room she had so recently awoken inside. Edith's bedroom. The room of dolls.

She never made it far inside the room.

'Who are you? Who are you?' she screamed at the figure sat upright upon the bedframe surrounded by so much rot and decay. 'Who the fuck are you?' She settled upon her knees. 'Please. Please. Tell me. Tell me, please. Please.'

The skein of light that had originally roused her now fell upon the figure sat upright upon the bed. A woman with a face Catherine recognized as her own. The very same pallid face that Catherine had seen, only partially reflected, in the shard of mirrored glass.

'You're not real. You're not the real one. You're not. You're not. You're fucking not!'

As she drew closer to the bed she saw that the seated figure's mouth was open, and about the mouth the flesh was purple, as if there had been a struggle to push something past a resisting jaw. The front teeth were broken.

From the dark lump of the body, left so lifeless and without rigidity, the arms had flopped hopelessly. After some vigorous commotion had occurred upon the rusty metal of the old iron bedframe, the hands had fallen open upon the unclothed springs, wrists upturned, one featuring a small vertical cut from a scalpel.

A magnetism came with an abruptness that seemed to pull Catherine from where she stood at the foot of the bed, and jolted her head forward. She thought she might faint within the eager force that sucked her towards the ghastly figure of herself propped up on the bed. Until some new and unwelcome instinct suspected that if she were to lie upon the bed, she would join in some unnatural union with the lifeless figure, only to have to break apart from it again.

Flashes of things sparked across her mind: a bee-keeper raising a hidden face within an overgrown garden, a figure standing up behind the counter of an abandoned village store, the scurrying aged of the pageant.

Catherine stumbled away from the bed and sat down hard upon the floor. She recalled the rushing of small feet through the house to the door of her room, and the sense of a frenzied activity around her face . . . before she had awoken here, in the ruined house. *The real version.*

So where had she been all that time when it had looked so different? Did it also exist . . . in another place? *Places?* And if that was her body upon the bed, then . . .

Into her thoughts came a memory of Edith's lipless mouth, spouting its madness. *Small things were repaired, my dear. And there was resurrection, blessed resurrection, for them and those who revered them* . . . She had said something about their guardians being remade 'in their own image', like angels had done. They tutored Mason in the *Great Art* . . .

Dear God, what did you bring into this house?

No. The thing on the bed was not real, was not her. This was still a dream, she was still imprisoned within a trance. Her entire consciousness was now a trance.

On the floor she was jerked into an awareness of the car engine being turned over in the lane outside.

Catherine crawled to the window and pulled herself up the wall. Slammed her hands against the wood. She was real, not dead, not a ghost; the thing on the bed was an effigy. She could hear the sound of her hands against the wood. Yes, she could. They had only made an effigy of her. They must have done because she could think and feel and move. Edith had been able to move and talk too. And Catherine could still move ever so swiftly . . . she had virtually glided up and down those stairs . . . over broken floorboards and rusted nails without incurring a scratch. The cold was not unpleasant . . .

She snatched out her hair and screamed. 'Stop! Stop! Stop!'

But down there, between the security fence and the brick walls of the Red House, Maude stood in profile and did not even turn towards Catherine's cries. Maude had raised her chin, but betrayed no emotion beside the usual stern disapproval on a long-suffering face. She had also raised her arms, as if it were her turn to be measured for a fitting.

Naked but masked, Leonard stood before Maude. An open straight razor filled one of Leonard's bony hands, his other hand gripped Maude's throat like she was livestock.

The blade glinted silvery in the mackerel light of this terrible dawn. His leather face was angled towards Catherine, to where she peeked from between the planks of wood, and the eyes behind the featureless mask, she knew, were fixed upon her window. Because he wanted her to watch. Had waited for her to look out and to witness this.

With a quick jerk of a bony arm, the taut bicep so bumpy with scar tissue, Leonard sliced the razor against Maude's rotund belly, then punched his whole hand inside her. And deep within the unresisting lump of the woman's dense body, his hand went to work.

He tugged the razor upwards like he was trying to free a stuck zipper on the compliant servant's clothes. With quick, hard jerks, and sometimes a sawing motion, he worked his hand up until the razor was buried between Maude's heavy bosom. Through the gaps in the wooden boards Catherine heard the ripping of linen and worse.

And in shocked stupefaction, she watched Leonard hold the housekeeper upright by the throat, while his other hand unspooled the housekeeper into the overgrown grass.

Catherine's muffled grunts that came around the fingers she'd stuffed inside her mouth failed to obliterate the sound of Maude's spilled innards dropping heavily into the weeds.

The squat figure seemed to sag and deflate forward, onto her executioner, like a sack of emptying meal slit down the side. Ungraciously, Leonard tugged and pulled the collection of rags and string and tow and sawdust and hard brown lumps from out of the loosening skin of the housekeeper, which soon flopped about his shoulder, the head still heavy and bobbing like a waterlogged football.

His coup de grâce was to yank the white wig off Maude's scalp, which was revealed to be stitched like a moccasin. And the neck supporting the pale head never recovered its posture. The heap of clothing and thick lifeless limbs that once was Maude was stuffed untidily into a grey mail sack that lay waiting in the wet grass.

Catherine watched Leonard drag the full sack out of the gate and toss it into the back of the green van.

So complete was her horror Catherine remained still and silent. Empty and numb. Until the final part of the truth appeared to her in the form of a memory; a recollection of the insane words that had croaked from Edith Mason's horrid mouth. About her mother. Her real mother. Who had suffered. Who had known torments for giving her away. Who would be released . . .

Those who wrong you will always be taken care of by those who love you. Your mother certainly was, after she gave you away . . .

Maude.

DON'T NEVER COME BACK.

The housekeeper's eyes wet with tears when she put Catherine to bed when she was ill.

The sound of her sobbing in a dark room while Edith bathed . . .

Because *she* knew what was happening. Something she could not stop. A terrible sequence of events she was commanded to take part in. She had been neither alive nor dead. Here, they had done away with such distinctions.

Maude.

Mother.

After the door was slammed, this old man of great and inhuman strength that she knew nothing of, stood alone beside the van in the lane, and angled his leather face up to the Red House as if in awe of it. He raised his two thin scarred arms to the air in salute, or as if he was making a command that she did not hear, nor would understand if she had. And just for a few seconds, she thought, but was not sure, the air around his black wigged head shimmered like summer heat above a meadow.

FORTY-SIX

When the green van was long gone, Catherine rose from where she had been slumped upon the floor. She walked past her body upon the bed and drifted down the stairs of the Red House.

In the hall Tara still leant against the wall, but had found her feet again and gingerly prodded one dirty bare foot about. Within the housekeeper's dress her body trembled. If Catherine were to undress her old nemesis, and check her flesh, she knew she would find a long scar.

The new housekeeper's hands were raised, but performed no meaningful function. At least she had fallen silent. Not from acceptance, but perhaps from what preceded acceptance.

Tara flinched when she became aware of Catherine's silent presence moving down the stairs.

When she reached the hallway, Catherine had no curiosity left about what would happen next, but inexplicably in her shock, knew the worst was over. But she did wonder again, in a vague and emotionless way, about what would happen if she were to lie down upon the bed with her old self. She knew it wasn't allowed yet, and that it would be a struggle for her to get off that bed again. But when she did, at least there was a wheelchair and someone in the house to push it.

There was work to be done upon the specimen upstairs. When she looked at Tara, and when she thought of Maude and Edith and the old keeper of flies that was M. H. Mason, and Violet Mason in her case, and the population of Magbar Wood, she understood this. And she knew bitterly that the things she had seen in the attic, and the one slumped upon that bed upstairs, had been left as a form of explanation that no words could ever suffice to explain.

And Catherine wasn't to remain here for long. Not in the building as it was here, but as it was in another place. In other places and in other forms that she had already seen. Now she had stopped screaming and sobbing and banging her hands against the damp wooden planks, the knowledge came to her as naturally as anything she could ever remember. Because the old house was telling her things now and she needed to listen. And when the awareness had dawned and broken through shock and resistance and fear and regret, and the daze that all of those things had reduced her to, she had risen and come down the stairs.

Perhaps Tara was to for ever remain as a hobbled ruin in the great house, as her mother had existed here, in whatever state the great house chose to show itself. Maybe Tara was here now to serve a new mistress, until the time came when the housekeeper would also be opened and emptied into the grass outside, and put inside the sack by the man in the mask. As Tara's predecessor had been, as Catherine's natural mother had just been, right before her eyes. One day perhaps this housekeeper would have her suffering relieved too. It seemed to be the way of things. She didn't know, but she knew something would tell her soon.

The sound of the back door opening, and the sudden

warmth and brightness of the light that spilled through, made Catherine and her unseeing companion turn towards the rear of the house. One woman turned towards the sound, the other turned to see the light that reached through and reddened the timbers and burnished the polished floors.

And outside, from the beautiful garden, came the sound of voices. The voices of many children, high and chaotic with the joy of play, circling like a flock of excited birds.

This place of decay began to fall away in the swift tide of transforming light, that rushed through to alter every brick within the brightness of a world older than the one she was about to leave, for ever.

Against the silhouette of the distant doorframe, as if a new sun of a new world was beaming onto the rear of the Red House, other figures moved and threw their small shadows onto the increasingly visible walls inside the building. Bright-blooded walls that soon reached the hall as it too was filled with a glorious light. A light she remembered from childhood, a light of comfort and confirmation and of safety and love that vanished whenever she'd awoken from a trance.

The visitors all seemed eager to get past Alice, and the three little girls beside her, who walked so slowly and in such an ungainly fashion. Because those others that entered the Red House behind the lame girls were keen to greet the mistress they had chosen and the servant they had provided.

And so together, the troupe of little tatty figures came inside from the divine garden to be with her. And to stay with her for some time to come.

Catherine knelt on the floor and opened her arms.

ACKNOWLEDGEMENTS

Decorating and furnishing The Red House was aided by *The Victorian House Explained* by Trevor Yorke, and The *Victorian House Style Handbook* by Linda Osband (ed. Paul Atterbury). The function and history of its owner, M. H. Mason, was abetted by *Still Life: Adventures in Taxidermy* by Melissa Milgrom; *Walter Potter and his Museum of Curious Taxidermy* by P. A. Morris; *An Annotated Bibliography on Preparation, Taxidermy, and Collection Management of Vertebrates with Emphasis on Birds* by Rogers, Schmidt and Gütebier; *Taxidermy Step by Step* by Waddy F. McFall; *A Chaplain at Gallipoli: The Great War Diaries of Kenneth Best*, ed. Gavin Roynon.

Filling the house with its occupants was enriched by *Puppets Through the Ages: An Illustrative History* by Günter Böhmer; *The History of the English Puppet Theatre* by George Speight; *The Complete Book of Puppetry* by George Latshaw; *The Handbook of English Costume in the 20th Century* by Alan Mansfield and Phillis Cunnington; *The Ultimate Doll Book* by Caroline Goodfellow; *Treasures of Heaven: Saints, Relics and Devotion in Medieval Europe* (ed. Bagnoli, Klein, Mann, Robinson). And in the first place, were I not such an admirer of the work of Thomas Ligotti, I may never have written this book. The short story by Reggie Oliver, 'The Children of Monte Rosa', introduced me to the existence of preserved animals in tableaux, and also inspired me to write about them.

At the risk of absurdity, I must acknowledge the effects of the old ATV television puppet shows, *The Pipkins* (and its star Hartley Hare) and *The Adventures of Rupert Bear*. In addition one third of *A Trilogy of Terror* (1975), and *Doctor Who: The Talons of Weng-Chiang*, may have been the two most frightening things I watched on television in the first half of my life. A long time ago they all captivated and terrified me in a manner unique to puppets. It was only a matter of time before these influences clambered out of their dusty trunks to perform for me once again.

Many thanks to my readers, Hugh Simmons, Clive Nevill, Anne Parry, and the late James Marriott, my editors Bella Pagan and Julie Crisp, Louise Buckley, Sophie Portas in publicity, and my agent John Jarrold.

It would be ungrateful and inappropriate to not thank the writers, critics, publications and websites who have supported me and my books with some of the kindest words a writer could ever wish to read. So my bony hands rise in salute to Gary McMahon, Eleanor Wixon, Simon Bestwick, Ramsey Campbell, Mark Morris, Tim Lebbon, Stephen Volk, Johnny Mains, Sarah Pinborough, Reggie Oliver, Joseph Delacey, Mathew Riley, Bill Hussey, Stephen Deas, Peter Mark May, Shaun Hamilton, Michael Wilson and This is Horror, Simon Marshall Jones, Ginger Nuts of Horror, Black Abyss, Jonathan Oliver, Professor Danel Olson, *Rue Morgue*, *SFX*, *Wormwood*, *Black Static*, Eric Brown and the *Guardian*, Forbidden Planet London and Birmingham, Alt Fiction, and The British Fantasy Society. Much thanks also to Facebook, for providing a medium for writers to meet their readers, their peers across the seas, and all those enthusiastic about horror. Never has the world been so accessible without having to move.

Above all, to my readers, I thank you for your time and your patronage.